DEAD AIM

Raising the pistol, Cain thumbed a pressure switch at the rear of the handle. A diode on the trigger guard beamed a thread of red-orange light along the target acquisition line.

Laser sighting system.

Trish could almost feel the pinpoint of low intensity light on her forehead. The bullet would enter just above the bridge of her nose.

Cain nodded as if reading her mind. "You got it, Trish. Do anything dumb, and I'll put a jacketed hollow point right between those pretty blue eyes."

Trish felt herself shaking. Couldn't help it.

"I won't try anything," she whispered.

And waited for what was coming next.

Cain was a killer who liked to kill cops. But Trish was more than just a cop. She was a lovely, slender young woman, and with that kind of captive, Cain liked to do more before the savage climax. . . .

MORTAL PURSUIT

MORTAL PURSUIT

BRIAN HARPER

A SIGNET BOOK

SIGNET
Published by the Penguin Group
Penguin Putnam Inc., 375 Hudson Street,
New York, New York 10014, U.S.A.
Penguin Books Ltd, 27 Wrights Lane,
London W8 5TZ, England
Penguin Books Australia Ltd, Ringwood,
Victoria, Australia
Penguin Books Canada Ltd, 10 Alcorn Avenue
Toronto, Ontario, Canada M4V 3B2
Penguin Books (N.Z.) Ltd, 182–190 Wairau Road
Auckland 10, New Zealand

Penguin Books Ltd, Registered Offices:
Harmondsworth, Middlesex, England

First published by Signet, an imprint of Dutton Signet,
a member of Penguin Putnam Inc.

First Printing, December, 1997
10 9 8 7 6 5 4 3 2

PUBLISHER'S NOTE
This is a work of fiction. Names, characters, places, and incidents either are
the product of the author's imagination or are used fictitiously, and any
resemblance to actual persons, living or dead, events, or locales is entirely
coincidental.

ACKNOWLEDGMENTS

Sincere thanks to everyone who helped me with this book, and especially to:

Joseph Pittman, senior editor at Dutton Signet, who guided the story from initial proposal to final draft with his usual blend of sensitivity and enthusiasm.

Jane Dystel, my agent for more than a decade, who signed me up when I had only a few magazine articles in my résumé and has stuck with me through thick and thin.

Michaela Hamilton, associate publisher at Dutton Signet, and Elaine Koster, publisher, both of whom have shown me continuing and deeply appreciated support.

All the marketing and sales personnel at Signet, who do an outstanding job of getting the books into the stores.

My good friend Spencer Marks, who reviewed the whole manuscript for accuracy in the depiction of police procedure, firearms, and security systems. Whatever verisimilitude the story achieves in these areas is largely to his credit. Any remaining mistakes are entirely my own.

—BRIAN HARPER

1

Cain pulled on the black ski mask and checked the pistol's clip.

Seventeen rounds. He nodded, satisfied.

"Rack 'em back."

Five clicks as the slides were cycled on five Glock 17s, his own and four others, each feeding a 9mm Black Talon round into the chamber.

"Let's move."

He slung a black duffel bag over his shoulder and headed out of the clearing, pursued by a low tramp of boots.

Moisture fogged the air, a breath of mist carried from the lake. The buzz-hum of every cicada, the rustle of every leaf, was sharp in the stillness. There was no other sound, even on a Saturday night in August—no traffic noise, no car alarms or boom boxes, not even the distant barking of a dog.

Cain thought of the places he had lived when he hadn't been in prison, the one-room holes in urban war zones where the thump and howl of ghetto music chased a man even in his dreams.

Nothing like that here. This was a peaceful place.

But not for long.

At the edge of the road he looked back, squinting into the last sparks of twilight.

The dark green GMC Safari van, parked in the clearing, was screened from sight by a stand of ponderosa pines. The four figures treading in single file behind him were nearly invisible also.

Like him, they were outfitted in black. Black Magnum Hi-Tech SWAT boots, high-cut. Black nylon sweat pants with elasticized drawstring waists. Black leather gun belts, the stainless steel buckles covered in electrician's tape to cut glare.

Clipped to each belt, a ProCom M54 handheld transceiver, brushing lightly against the sheath of a Cold Steel Tanto combat knife.

On the opposite hip, the holstered Glock, its sound-suppressor tube poking through a hole in the swivel holster's base. Adjacent to the holster, a cartridge case holding two spare magazines.

Black nylon jackets, Velcro-fastened, the manufacturer's decals taped over. On each left wrist, an Indiglo digital watch, the steel band replaced with black leather, a red filter taped over the LED display to preserve night vision.

Black Isotoner gloves. Black ski masks—no mouth cutouts. Black camouflage paint around the eyes, striping any visible portions of skin.

All four toted knapsacks and backpacks. The backpacks contained miscellaneous equipment—rope, padlocks, a length of chain, extra flashlights, other things.

The knapsacks were empty. Soon enough they would be filled with treasure, the haul of a lifetime in a single night.

Yet only a minor bonus, a fringe benefit when compared with the ultimate payoff.

Mindful of that payoff, Cain had spared no effort or expense in mounting tonight's operation. Clothes, radios, guns, silencers—all of the highest quality.

Every detail had been reviewed, every tactic rehearsed. Nothing could go wrong. Failure was not merely unacceptable. It was unthinkable.

He would succeed or die. There was no other option.

Drawing slow breaths through his mask, Cain looked down the road. A mountain road, rutted and winding, lightless, empty of traffic.

It dead-ended fifty yards beyond the gated entrance to the Kent estate, directly across the way.

2

Late and running scared.

Trish Robinson shrugged off her pullover as she crossed the ladies' locker room. The room was empty, the silence ominous.

She opened her locker, then sat on the bench, quickly shed her clothes, and began to change.

Normally she was never late—certainly not for work during her first week on the job. But this was a case of circumstances beyond her control.

At seven p.m., just as she was leaving, her toilet had overflowed . . . again. The landlord had ignored her repeated pleas to fix it, and her jury-rigged repair job hadn't lasted.

By the time she found the shutoff valve, the bathroom was flooded. It took ten minutes to mop up the mess.

Then naturally her car wouldn't start. She spent an additional ten minutes cranking the ignition key before the engine finally turned over. The '79 Honda badly needed a tune-up—or something—but after her recent moving expenses, she didn't have the means to pay for it.

Bad apartment, bad car, no money. She supposed life was meant to be like this when you were twenty-four.

Roll call was at 7:45. She checked the clock on the locker-room wall. 7:42.

Pull on trousers, then a short-sleeve shirt. Button down. Tuck in. Hurry.

Trousers belt. Shoes.

7:44.

The leather gun belt hung from the inside of the locker door. She snugged it over her hips, hooking it in place.

Rapid check of her gear. All there. The Smith .38 heavy in its high-ride swivel holster.

Her badge was already pinned to her shirt. She slipped her I.D. holder in the back pocket of her pants.

Anything else? Her hair.

She wore it shoulder length when off duty, but was required to keep it above her collar while in uniform.

From a shelf in the locker she grabbed a barrette, wound her blonde hair in a chignon, clipped it in place.

Done. Go.

The locker slammed. Padlock clicked.

7:46.

She sprinted out the door, through a puzzle of windowless corridors lit with fluorescent panels.

Rounding a corner, she nearly collided with two plainclothes officers. One of them put a fatherly hand on her shoulder.

"Whoa, darling. No running in the halls."

He and his partner laughed.

Jerks.

She continued, walking at a brisk clip, red heat on her face.

The roll-call assembly room lay at the end of the corridor. She eased open the door.

Sergeant Edinger paused in his remarks as she stepped into the room.

He made no comment, didn't even look at her, but in the momentary interruption of his monologue, he communicated an unmistakable reproof.

She sat in a chair in the last row. Pete Wald, her training officer, cast a glance in her direction, then turned coolly away.

Edinger resumed speaking. "Four eighty-eight at Chet Kesler's Mobil station late last night. Maybe fifty, sixty bucks in quarters ripped off from the Coke machine. Same M.O. as the Thrifty-Wash theft last weekend. You find any juveniles carrying sharpened screwdrivers, I want to have a word with them."

Trish struggled to catch her breath as she glanced self-consciously around the room. Aside from Wald and herself, only two other cops were in the audience, each cruising solo. A total of three units—standard for the mid-P.M. watch on a late-summer Saturday night. The watch ran until 4:00 A.M., overlapping the tail end of the night watch and the first hours of the graveyard shift.

"Another bicycle theft at Crestwood Apartments. They took somebody's Schwinn off a bike rack in the carport. If you're in the vicinity, swing through the parking lot and check it out."

The steel rims of Edinger's glasses flashed, his eyes screened by ovals of glare. He had the most completely hairless head Trish had ever seen.

"Oh, and one more item. You'll be glad to know we successfully supervised another duck crossing at Lake and Third. There were no casualties."

A scatter of ironic applause. Trish managed a smile.

Duck crossings, she had learned, were a common police call in town. Traffic would be stopped while a sluggish procession of waterfowl marched from curb to curb.

"That's about it. Any questions?" There were none. The meeting started to break up when the sergeant added, "Robinson. See you a minute?"

The others, filing out, avoided looking at her as she made her way down the aisle.

This was bad. This was a demerit noted in her phase-board review.

Edinger stood with head lowered, making check marks on his legal pad, for a good deal longer than he probably had to, while Trish waited stiffly.

Finally he looked up. "Bored, Officer?"

She didn't understand. "Sir?"

"Bored with your job? Disappointed, maybe? Work not living up to your expectations?"

"No, sir—"

"I guess you're finding it hard to take your duties seriously. Vending-machine rip-offs. Stolen bikes. Duck crossings. Not what you drilled for, is it?"

She knew no answer was required.

"Drama, excitement. That's why you joined up, right? You wanted to be Starsky and Hutch. Didn't you?"

"No, sir." She didn't even know who Starsky and Hutch were.

"This is, what, your sixth night on patrol? What's the most exciting call you've been on?"

"Uh . . . shots fired at Graham Park."

"And it turned out to be . . . ?"

"Kids setting off firecrackers."

"That's fairly typical of a busy night here. You know, the last homicide we had in this part of Santa Barbara County was back in 1984. You would have been how old then? Ten?"

"Eleven. Sir."

"Long time ago. Now, down in L.A. it's a different story. L.A.'s got two thousand homicides a year. That's where all the crazies are. You want excitement, go to L.A. You read me?"

"Yes, sir."

"Don't be late again."

He turned away, and she realized she had been dismissed.

Her stomach rolled and her shoulders shook as she retraced her steps toward the door where Wald waited.

Excitement, Edinger had said. What a joke.

She'd already had more than enough excitement for one night.

3

Alone, Cain crouched by the wrought-iron gate and unzipped the duffel bag.

Outside the gate stood an intercom mounted on a post. Below the speaker was a second, smaller panel featuring a digital keypad and an alphanumeric display—an alarm-system controller.

The system covered only the front and rear gates and the twelve-foot fence. Magnetic contacts on the gate latches would trigger an alert if separated while the system was armed. Motion detectors aimed at the fence made climbing into the yard impractical.

To disarm the system, Cain needed to enter the four-digit access code.

From the duffel he withdrew a digital decrypter.

Last Saturday night, exactly a week ago, he had opened the controller and wired the decrypter to leads running from the keypad to the central control panel inside the house.

With his tampering concealed, he had waited until the Kents returned from a night out and disarmed the system at the front gate. The decrypter's I.C. chip had recorded and stored the access code when it was keyed into the pad.

Later he had removed the decrypter to prevent its discovery. Now he had to reinstall it.

His black leather gloves, skin-tight, compromised his dexterity not at all as he pried open the bottom of the controller console with the blade of his knife. Quickly he again wired the decrypter to the leads.

Then he downloaded the stored data, sending the access code to the controller in a burst of electronic information.

He looked at the keypad's one-line liquid crystal display.

SYSTEM DISARMED.

The words remained in view for ten seconds, then blinked off, the screen going blank.

The gate's latch was easy to defeat. He didn't even require his locksmithing tools. The knife was enough.

He motioned to the others. They came fast across the road, brushing past him as they slipped through the open gate.

Before following, Cain downloaded the access code a second time.

A low buzz sounded, a pre-alarm warning, as the alphanumeric display flashed a new message.

SYSTEM REARMS IN 30.

The two digits ticked down, counting seconds.

29. 28. 27.

The grace period was designed to allow the home-owners to reset the alarm before entering. Very convenient.

He had no time to disconnect the decrypter, but that was all right. He was happy to let the police find it. The equipment, purchased on the black market, could not be traced.

He closed the bottom panel, sealing it with a strip of duct tape from his duffel. From the street no sabotage could be detected.

11. 10. 9.

Better move.

Toting his duffel, Cain stepped through the gate, then let the latch click shut behind him.

The buzzer fell silent.

It was doubtful anyone inside the house would check the system in the next five minutes, but taking this precaution cost him nothing. And he wasn't being entirely paranoid. One of the interior keypads was visible from the dining area, and there was at least a small chance someone would look in that direction.

Turning, he surveyed the grounds of the Kent estate, spacious, dense with shadows.

The front yard was empty. Already his crew had fanned out to the side and rear of the house, taking up their positions. They would stay clear of the fence to avoid being picked up by the motion detectors.

He checked his watch. 8:00. Right on schedule.

Despite the high stakes, the operation ought to be simple enough. Cain's sole concern was the two Sharkey boys—last-minute replacements for Hector Avalon.

Avalon had been a seasoned ex-con, cool and professional, ideal for this job as long as he was clean, and he'd sworn he was. Then two nights ago Cain had found him dead in the front seat of his rusted-out Palomino, white powder frosting his nose. Cardiac arrest or some goddamned thing.

And suddenly Cain's crew was short-handed, with the deadline closing in.

That was when Cain, not an introspective man, discovered something about himself. He was getting old. Old for this line of work, anyway.

He had no network of contacts. The men he'd known well enough to trust were mostly dead or in prison or burned out on booze and smack.

In desperation he'd remembered somebody Hector had mentioned in casual conversation, a kid in San Diego named Blair Sharkey. Cain wasn't sure exactly what business the two had transacted, but Hector had put the kid down as a comer, and Blair's number was jotted in Hector's address book.

Six hours later, Blair had arrived at Cain's trailer in the Mojave, bringing with him an unwelcome surprise—his baby brother, Gage, all of sixteen. Cain didn't want any damn kindergartner in his crew, but the Sharkey boys had been adamant. It was a two-for-one deal.

There had not been enough time to train them properly or to learn if they were reliable under stress.

But probably they would work out okay. Hell, they had to.

Nothing could go wrong tonight. This was it, his big score, the climax of his career, and it would go off without a hitch.

Of course it would.

Sweating, Cain moved forward into the dark.

4

The blue-and-white Chevy Caprice was parked at the rear of the police station under a bank of sodium-vapor lamps. Trish slid in on the passenger side, and Pete Wald climbed behind the wheel.

Trish was silent, her heart still pumping hard. With peculiar vividness she recalled a visit to the principal's office when she was in the first grade. The specific offense that had occasioned the reprimand was long forgotten, but the awful mixture of embarrassment and guilt still clung to her memory, tenacious as a barnacle.

Had the principal used the same tone of voice she'd heard from Edinger? Probably.

Wald cranked the ignition key and steered the cruiser onto Adams Avenue, the town's main thorough-fare. Though it was only eight o'clock on a Saturday night, the street was empty of traffic, void of activity. Cardboard signs reading *Closed* were propped in shop windows. No cars lined the curbs.

The police scanner under the dashboard cycled between the two main frequencies used by the department. Both were quiet. Slow night. As usual.

"Ed gave it to you pretty good," Wald said over the engine's drone.

Trish wasn't sure if Ed was really Sergeant Edinger's first name or only a nickname. Somehow she hadn't had the nerve to ask.

She frowned. "I was late."

"You didn't miss anything. No serial killers or terrorists in the area, at least as far as we know. Incidentally, Officer, your shirttail needs a little work."

"Oh, God." She groped behind her and felt a flap of fabric overhanging her waistband like a panting tongue. Hastily she tucked it in. "You mean I was running around the station like that?" She wanted to die.

"I'm sure nobody noticed."

Trish thought she saw a grin tucked away at the corner of Wald's mouth. She couldn't be certain, but the odds favored it. Pete Wald seemed characteristically amused by her.

Perhaps it was his prerogative to feel that way, a privilege of age and experience. He was a veteran officer, a twenty-year man, two decades her senior— big and gray-headed and molasses-voiced like some frontier patriarch.

She remembered his exaggerated astonishment upon learning that Reagan was the first president she distinctly recalled. "I watched Kennedy debate Nixon," he'd said, chuckling. "I saw a kinescope of that on PBS," Trish had offered, but the comment merely had elicited another, heartier laugh.

Smiles and laughter and lightly stressed superiority—that was Pete Wald. Trish almost preferred the screaming insults of her drill instructor at the academy.

The car cruised north on Sullivan. The lighted marquee of a movie theater glided past. Double feature, both films six months old, one of them already available on video.

A week ago, feeling restless and lonely on her first night in town, Trish had gone by herself to the movies. The screen sagged, and the picture had been projected out of focus. Fewer than a dozen patrons had occupied the wheezing straightback chairs. She had left before the start of the second feature.

She watched the marquee shrink in the sideview mirror, a rectangle of light diminishing to a postage stamp, gone, and then there was only darkness again.

"He read you the L.A. speech," Wald said, "didn't he?"

"Speech?"

She saw his cheek dimple as the threatened grin was realized. "Every boot on his watch gets to hear it. Ed waits for the first mistake, then launches into his routine."

Trish felt a little better.

"Of course," Wald added, "he could be right."

She flushed, her momentary relief fading. "About me?"

"About L.A.—and here. A lot more happens in the city, you know."

"I realize that."

"Out here you're a hundred miles from the nearest riot zone. Even Santa Barbara doesn't have all that much going on, and when you get this far inland— well, it's rural America. Strictly small-town."

"I knew that when I signed up. But ..." Trish

looked away into the dark. "Sometimes bad things happen—even in small towns."

For a moment she forgot the humiliation of roll call, the flush of shame, her beating heart. She was wrapped in old memories, memories that melted into half-remembered fragments of dreams.

Then she realized Wald was studying her, eyes narrowed and thoughtful.

She shrugged, as if the thought had been safely philosophical. "Or so I've been told."

5

The dinner party was going smoothly, really wonderfully well, until Barbara Kent saw the prowler in the backyard.

At least she thought it was a prowler. She got only a glimpse of what appeared to be a dark figure moving furtively through the olive trees near the gazebo.

Then shadows swallowed the man—if it was a man—if it had been anything at all.

She flipped a wall switch. White glare spilled over the patio and the hedge-lined flagstone path to the gazebo, but the gazebo itself, pale and stark, was barely touched by the glow.

Though she leaned closer to the kitchen window, her nose brushing the screen, she saw nothing more.

Imagination? She wasn't prone to seeing things that weren't there. Her father had called her a level-headed pragmatist while she was still in elementary school; she remembered looking up *pragmatist* in Webster's and being pleased by the definition.

Daddy had been right too. She was a realist and a skeptic, and if she thought she'd seen someone in the yard, then surely she had.

She was turning toward the phone on the wall when

Charles and Ally entered the kitchen, carrying the last of the dinner dishes.

"Sink or dishwasher?" Ally asked.

Barbara put on a false smile. No need to alarm her daughter. "Sink."

Ally deposited the dishes in the soapy water, and Charles did the same. Impatiently Barbara waited for them to go.

Her gaze ticked from the countertop Quasar television with built-in VCR to the Krups espresso machine on the central island, currently brewing four demitasses, then to the hand-rubbed pine cart laden with stainless steel Ottoni cookware, then to the matching hutch, its shelves lined with Waterford crystal.

Expensive things. She thought of what she was wearing—sterling silver earrings from Neiman-Marcus; a herringbone choker, eighteen karat, from Tiffany's; a gold bangle on her left wrist from Eximious of London. There was more, much more, in her jewelry box and in the wall safe in the den.

"Great dinner, Mom." Ally's voice pulled her back to the moment.

"You helped."

"I didn't cook anything."

"You helped by being here. And by lighting up the room."

Ally blushed, and Barbara felt a blind surge of love for her, mingled with relief that Charles's misgivings—and her own—had proved groundless.

At fifteen, Alison Kent was going through a rebellious phase. Of course, it was probably hard not to be rebellious when your parents argued all the time, when your home life was a succession of angry fights and ominous silences.

Still, there had been embarrassing incidents—that messy business at the Carltons' cocktail party last Christmas, for one.

Fearing a similar disaster, Charles had argued for sending Ally to a friend's home tonight. Barbara had stood her ground on that. Their daughter was good enough for the Danforths and for any other guests who might be hosted in this house.

But privately she'd fretted—and for no cause. Ally had behaved beautifully. Wearing a sleeveless white cotton dress and her best manners, she had charmed the adults, making not a single misstep. Perhaps her parents' good behavior had brought out her own.

Then in a wrenching shift of perspective, Barbara saw her daughter the way a desperate man might see her, a man who lurked in shadows and violated people's homes. Her smile faltered.

The clock was ticking. She had to get on the phone.

"You're the life of the party." Barbara patted Ally's arm. "Now get back in there and keep Philip and Judy entertained."

"I think those five whiskey sours are keeping Philip plenty entertained as it is."

"Naughty. Now scat."

Ally left, giggling—she was still not too old for that—and Barbara turned instantly toward the cordless phone. She lifted the handset.

Charles, pouring espresso, arched an eyebrow. "Who are you calling?"

"The police."

6

Crouching low, Cain approached the bay window of the living room.

From twenty yards away he could hear the faint murmur of conversation and the clink of tableware, broken abruptly by a woman's high-pitched laughter, brief and stabbing like a scream.

Sound carried easily here, in the mountain stillness. He hoped the others had the sound suppressors tightly screwed to the gun barrels, hoped they remembered his admonition to economize on gunfire. Even the best silencer was only partially effective, and then for no more than three or four shots.

The Kent house was the only residence within miles. Still, he was taking no chances.

Though he had never been on the property before, he knew the estate intimately, could visualize every detail of its layout. The house, five thousand square feet on a fenced acre, was a Mediterranean ranch, facing south, with a detached garage to the west.

A paved path between the garage and the house led through the spacious, parklike backyard to a rear gate, then down to a lakeside dock a quarter-mile below. The path and gate were wide enough to accommodate a car, should the Kents wish to tow one of their sport boats into town for service.

Rich people. The wife was, anyway. She'd inherited her money, and hubby had married it.

Now they had all this, while Cain had spent half his life in one prison or another, busted for conning or stealing only a fraction of what the Kents had obtained with no effort at all.

Life was a bitch.

But tonight, for once, Cain meant to make that bitch put out for him.

The front yard was landscaped in rosebushes and jacaranda trees. Cain crept past tangled drifts of roses, avoiding the clutches of their thorns.

As he neared the windows, he seal-walked on his elbows, dragging his lower body. He remembered crawling this way in an alley in San Bernardino to surprise a careless man lying in ambush for him, a man who had died in a gurgle of froth.

It was a hard world, kill or be killed, and Cain had learned hardness and made hardness part of him, and he had survived.

Five yards from the front of the house, he ditched the duffel bag behind a bush, then withdrew a folded pair of Tasco binoculars from his side pocket and lifted his head.

The front windows, open to admit the night air, looked in on the spacious living room and attached dining area. Only three people sat at the dining table: the daughter and two dinner guests. Charles and Barbara Kent were out of the room, perhaps busying themselves with coffee and dessert.

Cain wondered what dinner had been like. Better

than prison food, he guessed. And the beds in this house—more comfortable than the bunks in a twelve-by-twelve cell.

He took out his ProCom transceiver and activated channel three.

"Mr. and Mrs. Kent are off the scope. Who's acquired them?"

There was no risk in using names over the air. Under ideal conditions the transceiver's maximum range was only four miles. Though the Kents' nearest neighbors and the occasional passing car would be within reach of the signal, the odds of anyone other than Cain and his associates monitoring this particular frequency were infinitesimally small.

"I've got them." That was Gage. "They're in the kitchen."

Cain tipped the binoculars again. At the rear of the dining area he could see the kitchen doorway, but the kitchen itself, in the back of the house, was cut off from view.

"Keep watching," he said. "Let me know when the room is clear."

"Right . . . There's one more thing."

Cain waited, knowing from Gage's tentativeness that the news wasn't good.

"I, uh, I might've been spotted."

Cain held his voice steady. "How?"

"Kitchen window. I think the wife got a look at me. She turned on a light."

"God *damn* it."

Never should have let the kid tag along. A goddamned sixteen-year-old, zits on his face, a whining baby—

Calm. Stay calm.

"Can she see you now?" Cain breathed.

"I'm hunkered down behind the gazebo."

"Stay there." Under the mask, a single droplet of sweat, like a cold fingertip, traced a meandering course from Cain's hairline to his chin. "And pray you didn't fuck this up."

7

An arc of espresso splashed on the kitchen island. "The *police*?" Charles said in a stage whisper.

"I saw someone in the yard." Barbara switched on the phone.

He grasped the handset. "Wait a minute."

From the dining area Judy Danforth's laugh rose in response to one of Philip's witticisms.

The thought flickered in Barbara's mind that the Danforths had been married fourteen years, nearly as long as she and Charles.

When was the last time Charles had made her laugh?

She pushed the question away. "Someone's out there. I'm calling for a patrol car."

"Nobody's in our yard, for God's sake."

His hands were shaking slightly. He had been tense all day. The party, long-planned, was important to him, as he'd never tired of pointing out. Philip Danforth was rumored to be looking for partners in a new investment scheme likely to prove as profitable as his previous ventures. Charles wanted desperately to be in on it.

Now he must be worried about how it would look if

a squad car showed up at the front gate just as the Danforths were finishing dessert.

Admittedly, it would put a rather unpleasant spin on an otherwise faultless evening. Later, the visit by the police would be what Philip Danforth remembered, not the filet mignon brushed with creamy Bearnaise, not the baby carrots in sweet butter, not Ally in her white dress with her white smile.

Barbara understood all that, but still, facts were facts, and she was her daddy's level-headed child.

"I saw something," she said evenly.

Charles seized on the last word like a terrier snatching a bone. "Some*one*, you said a moment ago. Now it's some*thing*. What did you see, exactly?"

"I think it was a prowler."

"You *think*."

"I can't be sure, but there was movement by the gazebo."

"Movement."

"Yes, movement, damn it." He was pushing her buttons, as he did so well.

Charles released a little snort of disbelief, a haughty aristocratic sound typical of him. He glanced out the window at the floodlit yard. "Well, no boogeyman's out there now."

"He's hiding."

"Or maybe he never existed."

"I saw him."

"The system's armed. Nobody can penetrate the perimeter."

She hated it when he talked that way, in pseudo-military jargon, as if he were a CIA intelligence officer

31

fresh from the Peruvian jungle and not an overpaid defense attorney, his manicured nails innocent of dirt.

Still, she hesitated, wondering if he had a point.

"I thought," she said slowly, "you turned off the system to open the gate when the Danforths arrived."

"I did. But I reset it afterward. Look."

He gestured toward the kitchen doorway. Barbara peeked out, looking past the dining area, across the spacious living, to the foyer. A wall of shelves hid the front door from her view, but the alarm-system keypad was visible, mounted alongside the intercom box and the remote front-gate control.

The foyer was dimly lit, and in the shadows a red diode glowed faintly beside the controller's alphanumeric display.

"Satisfied?" Charles added with his smirking smile.

A reply was unnecessary. In triumph he darkened the yard light and left the kitchen, toting a tray of demitasses.

Barbara wondered how she ever could have found that smile attractive, even manly. It was his good looks that had done it, she supposed—the high, patrician forehead and sculpted jaw. At twenty-six she had been young enough to assume that the outer man must reflect the man within.

Well, she was forty-three now.

Alone, she thought about the alarm system. It secured only the fence and the front and rear gates— the perimeter, as Charles liked to call it. She had rejected the idea of additional zones covering the house itself. Living in a fortress was not her style. She liked open windows and doors, moving currents of air, the fresh breeze off the lake.

Now she wondered if a fortress wouldn't have been a better idea.

True, the boundaries of the property were protected. But if an intruder somehow had gotten onto the grounds, he would face no further obstacles except the locks on the doors and the latches on the window screens.

In the dining area Charles started telling his story about the tennis tournament in Ojai. He thought the Danforths hadn't heard it, but in fact he'd recounted the anecdote to them just last month at the country club.

Maybe he was wrong about this too.

Her mind made up, Barbara lifted the cordless handset and touched 9-1-1.

8

Crawling again, dragging the duffel bag, Cain approached the front door.

Through the bay window he could see Charles Kent, having returned to the dining area, serving coffee to his guests. A well-dressed man, Mr. Kent, tanned and urbane.

Nearly time to strike. By now the others must be ready.

Tyler and Lilith were at the northwest corner of the house, where a side door opened onto an east-west hallway. The hall led past the cellar door and the laundry nook, into the kitchen.

Blair was on the patio. Via the back door he would enter a rear hallway which fed into the dining area. Gage would join him when it was time to go in.

That left only Cain himself. He would use the front door at the house's southwest corner. It opened on a small foyer that would permit him to enter without being seen.

Kitchen, rear hall, foyer—the only exits from the living room and dining area.

Each escape route soon would be cut off.

His radio buzzed. It was Gage. "She's on the phone."

Cain needed a moment to register the information.

She. Barbara Kent, of course. On the phone. There was a phone in the kitchen.

Calling the police. Hell, was she calling the *police*?

The telephone line always had been a weak link in the operation. Cutting it would have been a sound tactical move. But if the phone service was interrupted for any reason, an alarm automatically would be triggered at the security system's central monitoring station.

"What do we do now?" Gage asked.

Cain didn't hesitate. "We're committed. No going back."

"If she got a look at Gage"—the demurring voice was Blair's—"she might've called for a squad car."

A gnat whined close to Cain's ear. He caught it in a gloved hand, snuffed it between thumb and forefinger.

"We can handle a squad car," he said coolly.

No one disagreed.

9

"All units." The dispatcher's voice crackled over the radio.

"We'll take it," Pete Wald said.

Leaning forward, Trish unclipped the microphone and keyed the mike. "Four-Adam-eight-one. What've you got, Lou?"

Lou was Louise, one of two night-watch dispatchers. The other was Thelma. They'd both caught their share of grief about that.

"Caller reports a possible ten-seventy," Lou said in her cigarette-froggy rasp. "Twenty-five hundred Skylark Drive."

Wald gunned the engine, the Caprice speeding up. Trish's heart accelerated with it.

A 10-70 was a prowler call.

"Get the details," Wald said.

Lou didn't need to be asked. "Nine-eleven operator says the caller was sort of vague. Might've seen an intruder in her backyard in some bushes or trees. Just a glimpse—dark clothes, no other description. Funny thing is, they've got a security fence, and the alarm didn't ring. You want backup?"

Trish looked at Wald, his face lit from below by the

spectrum of colors from the dashboard. He shook his head.

"Negative," Trish said into the microphone. "We'll handle it."

"I'll have another unit in the area just in case."

"Copy that. We're en route, code two high. Ten-four."

In answer Lou read off the time military-style. "Twenty-oh-five." It was the one formality she consistently observed.

Wald shot onto a side street at sixty but left the light bar and siren unactivated. Only a code three call permitted their continuous use.

"The Ashcroft place." He frowned to himself.

Trish replaced the microphone and waited for him to elaborate. When he didn't, she asked the obvious question. "Is that where we're going?"

Wald nodded. "Actually I'm the only one who still calls it by that name. It's been the Kent place ever since Charles Kent became man of the house. Maybe sixteen, seventeen years ago."

"Where is it?"

"Way up in the mountains."

As if to punctuate the thought, Wald veered onto a branching road that came out of nowhere, a two-lane rural route twisting northwest into the foothills.

"Lake there," he added. "Most of the area around it is woods. State park and a picnic area. Mr. and Mrs. Kent's house is the only residence. Only one for miles."

"Isolated."

"Very. Twenty-five hundred Skylark is the end of the world."

Half hidden in stands of pine, trailers and mobile

homes swept past. The Chevy's high beams carved twin funnels out of the dark, illuminating a double yellow line to the left, a smear of guardrail to the right. Ruts bounced the sedan on its shocks.

"Why'd Lou think we needed backup?" Trish asked.

"On a prowler call it's not a bad idea to have more than one unit on hand."

"So why'd we turn it down?"

"Because the alarm wasn't tripped. Caller just saw a dark shape. Could be anything. Out in the boonies, like where we're headed now, nine times out of ten it's a raccoon. They grow pretty damn big out there, and they prowl at night."

"I see." Her voice caught on the second word.

Wald gave her another, sharper look. "Nervous?"

She wanted to deny it, but after all, he was her training officer, and she had to be honest with him.

Even so, she hedged a little in her answer. "Sort of."

"You should be."

"I thought it was probably a raccoon."

"Nine times out of ten, I said. But there's always that tenth time. That's when you need to be fully alert."

"I'm real alert right now."

"Good."

The Chevy barreled higher into the mountains. Through the open windows the warm night rushed in. It was the final weekend in August, but in southern California summer lingered to the end of October. The worst heat was still to come.

Trish watched the last homes melt away, and then there was only a dark blur of trees.

"How much farther?" she asked.

"Three, four miles."

At this speed, no time at all.

The wire mesh partition behind her rattled loosely. On a switchback curve her shoulder harness locked, exerting brief, painful pressure on her right breast until the strap disengaged.

She swallowed, wishing her mouth weren't so dry.

Nervous? Sure. Frightened, even.

But below her fear she was conscious of a not-unpleasant thrill of adrenaline.

This was what she'd wanted, after all. This was why she'd sweated and trained, why she'd endured long days and sore muscles and relentless hectoring—to wear a blue uniform, to charge into danger in response to a distress call in the night.

She only hoped . . .

Hoped she wouldn't . . .

"You get over it." Wald's voice startled her.

"What?"

"Opening night jitters. You get over it."

She tried a smile of her own. "I thought it was good to be scared."

"There are two kinds of fear. Fear of what might happen—and fear of how you might screw up. You get over the second kind."

How you might screw up. That was it, all right. That was the real fear coiling in her stomach and stopping her breath.

Trish wondered how Wald had known about that, how he'd been able to get inside her head and dissect her feelings.

Then she realized he must have trained a dozen probationers just like her, as raw and green as she was.

And once, long ago, Wald had been a rookie cop himself, answering his first priority call. Funny how she hadn't ever thought of him that way.

"It's just . . ." She hesitated. But remember: honesty. "It's just that I've never really been tested."

"You'll hold up fine, Officer Robinson."

Trish sat tensely in her seat, fingering her holster strap, and hoped Pete Wald was right.

10

Barbara rejoined the others in the dining area, serving tiramisu. Her entrance inadvertently disrupted the humorous climax of Charles's Ojai tennis story. She saw him suppress a frown.

The Danforths made the usual appreciative comments as she dished out dessert from the sideboard. Philip was a former college athlete, his paunch spreading in middle age, his florid face further inflamed by those five whiskey sours Ally had mentioned. His wife was attractive but desperately thin, her arms like tanned bones, her face revealing too much of the skull beneath. She spent hours at a fitness club and never ate anything.

As if to prove the point, Judy Danforth risked only a birdlike nibble of tiramisu. "Barbara, this is delicious." She had said the same about the filet mignon, although she'd consumed less than half of the six-ounce cut.

Barbara nodded her thanks, a false smile fixed on her lips, while she seated herself across from Charles.

The 911 operator had said a patrol unit would respond as soon as possible, but what did that mean? Five minutes? An hour?

Discreetly she checked her watch. 8:10. Realistically she couldn't expect a response time of less than ten minutes. The house was secluded, after all.

Secluded—bad word to think of right now.

"Barbara?"

Her head tilted up, and she saw Philip regarding her with a quizzical smile. Vaguely she was aware that he had said something she'd missed.

She blinked. "Excuse me?"

"Just wondered if I could have the recipe. I do a bit of cooking around the house—"

"*All* the cooking," Judy amended with a smile that stretched her skin drumhead-taut.

"She's got me well trained."

"Now don't start that."

"Certainly," Barbara said, breaking into their banter because the brisk, bright voices were giving her a headache. "Charles has a copier in his study. I'll Xerox the recipe before you go."

"Mom's a terrific cook," Ally said with a radiant smile.

Barbara wished she could take pleasure in the compliment, but it was difficult to concentrate. Her gaze kept straying to the windows as she hunted for a glimpse of movement in the front yard.

Ridiculous, of course. The man she'd seen had been out back.

But how could she be sure there was only one?

Professional burglars worked in teams, didn't they?

Teams. Just listen to her. Crazy talk.

She wished the police would come.

11

Through the windows five people were now visible at the table. All present and accounted for.

Cain pocketed his binoculars. Lugging the duffel bag, he crept along the flagstone path and up the steps to the front door.

From one of the bag's zipped pockets he removed an L-shaped tension wrench and a homemade lock pick fashioned of medium-gauge piano wire.

Silently he slipped the tension wrench into the keyway, applying light pressure to the plug, then slid the pick alongside it and probed for the first of the pin tumblers.

When the pick jostled the pin to the shear line, the plug turned a fraction of a degree.

He advanced the pick to the next pin, then the next. With each success the plug rotated a bit more, its infinitesimal slippage apparent only to his sensitive touch.

When the sixth pin was raised, the plug turned fully and the door was unlocked.

There was a dead bolt, but it was not secured. Cain eased the door ajar, knowing he was screened from the view of the Kents and their guests by the foyer wall.

He could enter at any time.

Dialing the radio's volume low, he thumbed the transmit button. "Tyler," he whispered, "report."

Softly: "We're in."

"Blair?"

"Us too."

Tyler and Blair had no proficiency in locksmithing. They had used Lockaid pick guns, customized with sound baffles, to open the side and rear doors.

Cain glanced at his watch.

8:10.

All he had to do was give the order, and the drill they'd practiced so many times would be carried out for real. In exactly sixty seconds, the Kents' dinner party would suffer the rudest of interruptions.

He hesitated.

It was still not too late to turn back, abort the mission, try again another time.

Gage had been seen. The police quite possibly had been called.

Roughly he bulldozed his apprehensiveness aside. Cops didn't scare him. He had killed two in his lifetime.

The first was a random hit, done on a dare when he was seventeen. He remembered the startled terror in the patrolman's eyes as the bullet punched into his skull.

Then just last year, a CHP car had pulled him over on a lonely stretch of Highway 62, east of Twenty-nine Palms. Writing a ticket, the cop had glanced into the back of the van, where a sawed-off Mossberg lay on the floor.

Carrying a firearm was a violation of parole. And

the shotgun's barrel had been trimmed illegally short. The two convictions would send Cain back to prison for a long time.

He had spent half his life incarcerated. Never again.

The cop had just noticed the Mossberg when Cain pulled an airweight .22 from the glove compartment and shot him between the eyes.

For a day or two afterward he'd worried that the man might have run a DMV check on his tags before getting out of the car: standard procedure. But news stories reported that the DMV computer had been down that afternoon, so no trace had been run.

Cops weren't anything special. Wearing uniforms didn't make them superheroes. He could kill two more if he had to.

Besides, tonight was his night. He could feel it. Every nerve ending, every corpuscle of blood, sang to him of the future's bright promise.

He would never have this chance again.

8:11 precisely.

His decision was reached.

Cain lifted the radio and breathed one word.

"*Go.*"

12

Ally touched her mother's arm. "Aren't you going to try any?"

Barbara realized she had yet to sample dessert. "Of course." Mechanically she lifted her fork to her mouth, then swallowed without noticing the taste.

Charles was trying to recover the thread of the Ojai story, still oblivious to the fact that the Danforths had heard it already.

Barbara tuned him out and listened to the house.

Faintly, a whisper of wind chimes.

She heard the faraway notes and shifted in her seat.

The chimes hung in a mobile on the patio. Ordinarily they couldn't be heard from inside, certainly not from the dining room—unless the back door had been opened.

Absurd.

The sound was carrying on the breeze, that was all. Carrying through the kitchen window.

"So instead of *two* tickets," Charles said as the Danforths smiled dutifully, "we had *four* . . ."

In the kitchen, the creak of a floorboard.

The noise was low. Barbara couldn't be certain she'd heard it.

Anyway, houses did that. They settled.

Of course they did.

The candleflame bulbs in the chandelier seemed suddenly too bight, their sparkle painful. She blinked as if in a blaze of light.

"—trying to scalp the damn things, and the match has already started . . ."

Charles went on talking, the others smiling and eating, and Barbara felt a twitch of rage at them for being oblivious and happy.

She caught Ally looking at her, puzzled apprehension in her serious brown eyes. For her daughter's sake Barbara swallowed another forkful of tiramisu.

Acid trickled into her belly. She didn't dare taste the espresso. The strong, hot coffee was sure to make her sick.

Another creak, this one from the rear hallway.

She thought of the wind chimes again, the rear door that would let someone into that hall.

The back of her neck, cold, prickled with tiny hairs.

Someone was here, inside the house. More than one of them.

She knew it.

With irrational certainty she *knew* it.

"Did you hear that?"

The voice surprised her because it was her own. She hadn't realized she was speaking.

Charles glanced at her, irritated at having the Ojai anecdote spoiled twice. "Hear what?"

"A noise." She wanted to smile, but her mouth wouldn't work. "I thought . . . in the hall . . ."

Philip pushed back his chair with alcoholic bravado

and immediately started to rise. Charles waved him back down.

"Don't trouble yourself, Phil. Barb's got sort of an overactive fantasy life."

Barbara stiffened. "Fantasy life?"

"Of course, it may be merely a twisted plea for attention."

"Not from you."

Ally was looking down at her plate, intoning in a small voice, "Please don't. Don't fight."

Only Barbara heard, but the soft, plaintive words cut like glass.

"What kind of noise?" Judy leaned forward, worry hunching her bony shoulders. "Someone in the house? Is that what you mean?"

Barbara hesitated. Suddenly her fears seemed embarrassingly insubstantial.

Maybe Charles was right. Maybe she was imagining all of it.

Certainly she'd proved her father wrong. She hadn't behaved at all like a level-headed pragmatist.

"I guess I did get a bit carried away," she said without conviction.

Charles nodded vehemently. "Carried away. Exactly. That's what I've been telling you."

He lifted his fork with wounded dignity.

"So if we all could just settle down and finish our dessert . . ."

The first masked figure came up fast out of the foyer, and Barbara had time to wonder what he was doing there when she'd heard sounds from the back of the house, and then two more intruders burst in from the rear hall and another pair from the kitchen, all of them armed, black pistols gleaming in gloved hands.

A napkin drifted to the floor in a flutter of white. Judy Danforth was out of her seat, screaming. The nearest intruder hit her, hard. Crack of knuckles against her jaw, her cry silenced as she fell into her chair, Philip rising belligerently, shouting a righteous objection. A second gunman delivered a palm heel strike to the side of Philip's neck—a hard, fleshy *whap*, the sound of pounded meat in a butcher shop, a welt blooming on Philip's neck, soon to be a purple bruise, and Philip sat down, stunned and blinking and looking as if he were about to vomit.

Irrelevantly it occurred to Barbara that none of the intruders had yet spoken a word.

The table was surrounded with impossible speed, like a jump cut in a movie. The chandelier bulbs cast orange glints on the pistols, tiger-striping the jet black frames and silencer tubes.

Ally gripped the fringe of the tablecloth, the damask stretched taut. Barbara reached out, patted Ally's hand.

The terror she felt was less for herself than for her daughter. Her own life was over. Well, she could accept that. She was forty-three, hardly old, but she'd had time anyway, she'd had years.

But Ally, only fifteen—why, fifteen was nothing, it wasn't even a start.

She gazed blankly at the men ringing the table, big men, muscular under their clothes . . . except for one who was shorter, almost lithe.

With a distant, anachronistic sense of shock, Barbara made out twin hills of breasts half concealed in folds of crinkled nylon. A woman.

But women don't *do* this, she thought, scandalized, while a remote part of herself mocked her own naiveté.

All five of them wore identical costumes, black jumpsuits or sweatsuits, something like that, sleek and nonreflective and Orwellian. Mouthless ski masks hooded them, leaving only their eyes visible, shiny in the dark surround.

Charles stared straight ahead, his gaze fixed on nothing.

Ally began to whimper, a dismal mewling noise.

Judy hiccuped a moan, the prelude to another scream and perhaps more violence.

And the man from the foyer lifted his pistol and fired one shot into the beamed ceiling.

Despite the silencer, the gun's discharge made an audible crack. Wood chips from the rafters pattered on the floral centerpiece. A cartridge casing, ejected by the slide's recoil, rolled across the tablecloth and came to rest at the edge of Ally's plate.

The room froze.

For some timeless interval there was no movement, no sound save Charles's ragged breathing and Ally's low sobs.

Almost casually the man checked his watch. "Eight-twelve."

His voice, slightly muffled by the mask, was harsh and gravelly. In his curt nod of satisfaction he conveyed an air of command.

Barbara thought these people might be terrorists. Terrorists in her house.

And terrorists were zealots, fanatics—no bargaining

with people like that. They killed for vengeance and salvation, killed women, children. Ally . . .

Tramp of boots.

The man who'd fired the shot was rounding the table, each heavy footfall imprinting deep tread marks in the carpet's thick pile.

Directly before Barbara he stopped. The gray eyes in the ski mask's slits fastened on her.

Her heart twisted.

"Who did you call?" he asked.

On the margin of her vision she saw Charles go pale.

She didn't answer. She sat rigid, her spine and shoulder blades pressing deep into the spindles of the chair.

He stepped closer, and though she couldn't see his mouth, she could sense his feral smile.

The gun lifted. "Who did you call, Mrs. Kent?"

He knew her name. She wondered why she feared him more because of that.

Her chest rose, fell. She stared down the black hole of the silencer tube, and it stared back, a lidless eye.

"No one," she whispered. "A friend."

"Bullshit."

"Just a friend, I had a question about a recipe—"

"Who did you call?"

Barbara shut her eyes and gave up all hope of life.

"The police," she answered almost calmly.

"Oh, Jesus Christ . . ."

It wasn't the gunman who'd spoken. It was Charles and, incredibly, he sounded angry.

She looked past the gun and saw her husband glaring at her, his eyes unnaturally large, his cheeks unnaturally white.

He always had hated to lose an argument.

"Damn it, Barbara." Charles swallowed, nearly choking on speech. "I thought we agreed—"

"That no one could penetrate the perimeter?" This was funny. She coughed out a broken laugh. "Well, I hate to be obvious about this, dear . . . but it looks as if somebody did."

13

Headlights splashed on a wrought-iron gate.

"Some spread, huh?" Wald smiled. "And no noisy neighbors."

Trish didn't answer. She peered into the darkness beyond the gate, her pulse ticking in her ears.

Leaning out, Wald pressed a button. Brief silence, then the crackle of a man's voice. "Yes?"

"Police."

"Oh. Yes." A cultivated voice, mildly flustered. "One moment, please."

Trish peered past Wald and saw a security system control panel below the intercom. The display flashed a message: SYSTEM DISARMED.

A moment later the gate eased open automatically, operated from inside the house.

Wald drove through, guiding the Chevy down the long driveway. Trish scanned the yard, big and full of shadows. Fear caressed her with cold fingers.

"Funny," she said evenly. "Porch light isn't on. Or any floodlights, either. You'd think . . ."

"If they saw a prowler, they'd light up the yard? Yeah. Like you said—funny."

The house was a sprawling ranch with the red tile

roof emblematic of southern California. The side walls were whitewashed stucco, the façade a seamless sheet of quarried granite.

Distantly Trish wondered how much the place was worth. Her mind stalled at two million dollars, but the likely figure was far higher.

"I read a profile of Charles Kent in the *News-Press*." Wald's words cut into her thoughts. "He's a lawyer, practices in Santa Barbara."

"Lawyer," she echoed. It was the only word she'd picked up.

"Criminal defense. His clients are high rollers. TV stars, athletes, corporate types. They get busted for DUI or a gram of coke, and Charlie gets them off. Usually with a minimum of publicity."

"Nice work if you can get it." The statement was meaningless, a reflexive response to whatever he'd just told her.

"Yeah, Mr. Kent does all right. He's not paying the mortgage, though. Well, actually there is no mortgage. This property has been in the Ashcroft family since the nineteen hundreds. House itself isn't that old, of course; the original was torn down and replaced in the seventies. Anyway, all Charles had to do was marry Barbara."

"Barbara Ashcroft." The name registered in Trish's memory. "She was featured in the gossip columns when I was a kid."

"You mean yesterday?"

"I mean fifteen, sixteen years ago," she snapped, tired of Wald's jibes.

Then she realized this smiling banter was simply an attempt to lighten the mood, relieve her tension.

"Sorry," she added in a chastened voice.

Wald nodded. "You'll hold up fine," he said, the remark out of context but fully understood.

The blue-and-white eased to a stop behind a black Porsche parked near the detached garage. The Kents' car? Or did they have guests?

Wald killed the engine. The sudden stillness seemed explosively loud.

"Let's do it." He threw open the driver's-side door. "And Robinson . . . watch your back."

He was out before Trish could read his expression and gauge his seriousness. She wondered if he was just being cautious, or if he felt what she felt—an indefinable foreboding.

Opening the door, she glimpsed herself in the side-view mirror. Her eyes were wider than usual. Cobalt eyes, startling and intense.

In the academy dormitory there had been jokes that she wanted to be a cop only because the uniform would go so well with her eyes. Right now it seemed as good a reason as any.

She swung out of her seat. Stood.

The warm night enfolded her like a blanket. Crickets sang, and somewhere a toad croaked in counterpoint. The sky was clear, the wide scatter of stars undimmed: no moon tonight and no city lights here.

Wald came around the car, and Trish saw that his holster flap was unfastened. She unhooked hers also while following him along the flagstone path toward the front door.

Time ran slowly, a sluggish current. Her senses were heightened, small details vivid to her: the click of her shoes on the stones, the low sputter of the radio clipped to her gun belt, a thread of blonde hair escaping from the barrette and beating gently against her left ear.

She was conscious of the tension in her abdomen, the strain in her shoulders. Dull aches, like the pleasurable soreness after a full workout in the gym.

Ordinarily she felt an unspoken confidence in her lithe body, her low resting pulse rate, her stamina and endurance. Her arms were toned daily by biceps curls and triceps extensions, legs strengthened by calf raises, squats, and lifts. Shoulder presses and rowing exercises firmed her back. Abdominal crunches and bent-knee sit-ups kept her belly tight.

Tonight she was aware of how little any of that meant, how ridiculously vulnerable she was.

It would take one bullet to stop her heart. Just one.

She wished she were wearing a vest, Kevlar or something like it, heavy and solid. Beneath her summer uniform—open-collared short-sleeve shirt and lightweight pants—there was nothing but cotton underwear, damp with sweat. She might as well be walking naked up the path, a target painted on her chest.

The door opened as Wald reached it. Limned in the light of a foyer was a man of perhaps forty-five in a double-breasted navy blazer and a silk shirt.

She knew who he had to be even before he told them.

" 'Evening, officers. I'm Charles Kent."

Walk handled the interview. "Mr. Kent, you called nine-one-one?"

"That was my wife. She imagined she saw someone in the yard."

"Imagined?"

"Yes, well, the security system wasn't triggered."

He stood in the doorway, making no move to let them in, displaying none of the automatic courtesy to be expected of someone in his social class. Trish thought he seemed nervous, but maybe she was projecting her own anxiety onto him.

"No system is foolproof," Wald said mildly. "I'm surprised you didn't turn on the yard lights as a precaution."

"Well, I did, of course. But not seeing anything, I turned them off."

"Under the circumstances, didn't your wife object?"

"Not at all. She realizes she was mistaken."

"Perhaps we could speak with her."

"She's somewhat embarrassed about the whole thing."

"There's no need for embarrassment. May we see her?"

"The fact is, we have guests, and it could be awkward. I mean, for her to explain matters in front of them. You know."

A bead of sweat glistened on his forehead. He *was* nervous. Trish didn't doubt it now. Of course, many people were nervous around cops, but this man was a trial attorney.

"I'm not sure I understand." Wald spoke with the poised professionalism that had deserted Charles Kent. "Your wife *did* telephone nine-one-one?"

"Well, yes."

"Then she must have believed she saw something. I'm sure she isn't the type to make prank calls. Is she?"

"No . . . certainly not . . ." He was trapped. "Oh, all right. Come in."

Before entering, Wald cast a sharp sidelong glance at Trish, wariness in his eyes.

She didn't need the silent warning. Quite obviously Mr. Kent was hiding something.

Maybe his wife had been drunk when she'd phoned, and he was fearful of gossip.

Maybe.

Trish took a last look at the yard, then drew a breath of courage and followed Wald inside.

14

So this was how the other half lived.

The words, foolishly predictable, flitted through Trish's thoughts as she stepped across the threshold into the first mansion she had ever entered.

The foyer floor was stained parquet. The walls were black slate. A potted rhododendron, ten feet tall, its twelve-inch leaves an impossibly deep green, loomed on one side of the doorway, opposite a pair of oak sliding doors that must open on a coat closet.

Where the left wall ended, there was a rack of tubular shelves displaying vases of crystal and earthenware, each piece individually lighted by small hidden bulbs, the total effect as artful as a museum exhibit.

Don't be intimidated, she told herself. They're rich and you're poor, but that doesn't make them better than you.

Even so, she caught herself glancing down as the floor tiles ended and deep pile carpet began, guiltily afraid she was tracking dirt into the house.

The foyer opened onto an elegant living room, preposterously large. Any of its corners could have contained the entire studio apartment she was renting for four hundred dollars a month.

In the adjacent dining area three people sat at a long table under a brilliant chandelier. There was something peculiar in the way they were seated. An image jumped into her mind: posed mannequins on display.

Now where had *that* come from?

She and Wald accompanied Charles Kent to the table. Charles made introductions.

"My wife, Barbara ... our dinner guests, Judy and Philip Danforth."

Smiles and nods from around the table. Philip picked up a demitasse spoon and stirred a cup of espresso, the spoon clinking musically against the porcelain.

Trish focused on Barbara, detecting no hint of inebriation or even embarrassment. She sat stiffly in her chair, hands folded near her plate. The hands could have been modeling for a still life, so motionless were they, so attractively toned and textured in the warm overhead light.

Barbara Kent was perhaps forty, slightly younger than her husband. Superimposed on her face was Trish's memory of young Barbara Ashcroft of the society pages twenty years ago, heroine of debutante balls.

Though older now, she was no less striking. The familiar arched eyebrows and high cheekbones were unchanged, and the threads of gray in her elegantly coiffed hair only reinforced her mysterious allure.

"There are five place settings," Wald said.

Trish, preoccupied with her study of Barbara,

hadn't noticed that detail. A rookie error: she should have been looking at hands and laps, not faces.

"Yes." It was Barbara who answered, her speech refined but free of artificiality. "Our daughter, Ally. She went to bed early. Upset stomach." Thin fluttery smile. "I guess her mother's cooking was too much for her."

"You saw the prowler, ma'am?" Wald, Trish observed, was casually scoping out the room as he spoke.

"Yes, well, I really must apologize to you, Officer Wald. And to you, Officer Robinson." She'd read their nameplates—sharp. "I'm afraid that with all the excitement of the night's festivities, I got a trifle overwrought."

Overwrought. An ice sculpture could not have been more coolly self-possessed.

"You mean," Wald said mildly, "you hallucinated a prowler in the backyard?"

Barbara's silvery laughter struck a jarring false note. "Hallucinated—next you'll want to test me for LSD, I suppose. It wasn't any hallucination, just the shadow of a tree. Charles pointed it out to me, and I do feel like such a fool."

Trish was looking at the empty place setting, the one used by the Kents' daughter. A slice of dessert cake, half-eaten.

She scanned the other plates, saw the same dessert on each. Barbara's was barely touched. The remaining three had been half-finished—like Ally's.

The girl must have left the table only a couple of minutes earlier. Just when Wald buzzed the intercom.

"Oh, you shouldn't blame yourself," Judy was

telling Barbara with a brittle smile. "Anybody can make a mistake."

"I called the police once." Philip went on stirring his espresso, the spoon jerking in his hand. "Reported a suspicious person in the bushes near our property."

"Turned out to be our next-door neighbor," Judy said. "His dachshund had gone into the shrubbery in pursuit of a rabbit, and he was coaxing her out."

"Damn dog wouldn't budge, and finally one of the police officers had to crawl in and get her." Philip laughed, but his face was all wrong, a caricature of mirth.

"Well," Barbara said, "it's good to know I'm not the only one who's paranoid."

Judy and Philip and Charles smiled at this, smiled too much. It was as if they were all playing a game, but Trish didn't know the rules.

Then Philip's smile faded. "The way things are, these days"—he looked hard at Wald—"it's difficult not to be paranoid."

Barbara cut in hastily, as if unnerved by the remark. "Oh, I don't know. This is a safe area. Nothing ever happens here."

"It's a very safe area," Charles agreed, nodding vigorously. "Lowest crime rates of any California county this far south."

"Is that true?" Judy asked Wald.

"I believe Ventura County may be slightly lower overall, ma'am." Wald clearly was perturbed, uncertain how to react to the strange show these people were putting on. "Violent crime rates are about the same. Property crime—"

"Well, *violent* crime is what we're really concerned about," Philip said with another focused stare.

"Isn't everybody?" Barbara laughed gaily, but there was no gaiety in her eyes or in the hectic flush of her cheeks. "Fortunately, we needn't worry about it tonight. The only crime here is the crime of wasting these two officers' valuable time. Is that a felony, Officer Wald? Or only a misdemeanor?"

Wald shot Trish another glance. He sensed it too—the giddy unreality of the scene. The dialogue was almost right, but the performances were badly off center.

Trish thought of a college word: *subtext*. There was a subtext here, but she was missing it.

"If you don't mind," Wald said to the Kents, "maybe we'd better look around out back, just to be sure."

Barbara wore her frozen smile like a mask. "It's quite unnecessary."

Trish's gaze drifted back to Ally's place at the table. Something small and cylindrical and metallic lay under the lip of her plate, nearly hidden from view.

The empty casing of a 9mm round.

Her heart stuttered. The breath went out of her, and her fingers tingled, suddenly cold.

A gun had been fired in this room. Fired into the ceiling—wood splinters littered the floral centerpiece.

And Ally didn't have an upset stomach. She was a hostage. She was the off-stage presence who'd prompted these bad actors to deliver their unconvincing lines.

Abruptly Trish focused on the tapping of Philip's spoon, a strangely rhythmic sound.

Three soft clinks. Pause. Again. Pause. Again.

SOS.

He had been signalling the whole time. Brave of him . . . or foolish.

With effort she held her face expressionless. As surreptitiously as possible, she brushed Wald's elbow.

Her partner's eyes cut sideways, and she nodded almost imperceptibly toward the table.

He dropped his gaze. A muscle twitched in his cheek.

It was a small reaction, but enough. Instantly everyone at the table was looking at the cartridge case on the white damask tablecloth.

Philip stopped tapping. Conversation ceased. There was no sound but the soft intermittent crackle of Trish's portable radio, scanning between the two frequencies used by the dispatchers, and somewhere a whisper of wind chimes.

She met Philip's eyes and slowly inclined her head.

The silence was stretching taut. Wald covered it with a safely meaningless remark. "You say, Mrs. Kent, that it was the shadow of a tree?"

Barbara swallowed. "Yes. That's right."

"You're sure of that?"

"Quite sure. Charles showed me. Didn't you, Charles?"

"An olive tree near the gazebo." He went on staring blankly at the cartridge case, his lips barely moving as he spoke. "Hard to explain, but it threw a shadow that looked just like a crouching human figure. Anyone could have made the mistake."

"I'm sure that's true," Wald said.

Trish wasn't listening. To Philip she mouthed: How many?

He laid his left hand on the table in a fist. One at a time he extended his fingers.

Index. Middle. Ring. Pinky.

Four of them, Trish thought numbly, and then Philip's thumb curled into view also.

Five.

A chill skipped lightly over her shoulders.

Five intruders. If one was armed, it was safe to assume they all were. Surely one or more of them were watching the table right now.

From where? The windows? Or one of the three doorways around the dining area and living room?

The pounding racket in her skull was the steady beat of blood.

"So you're certain you didn't see anything," Wald was saying.

Barbara managed an unconcerned shrug. "That's what I've been telling you."

"Okay, then. Guess there's no need for us to hang around. Though I've got to admit, that dessert looks damn good."

Laughter from Judy Danforth, high and airy and too shrill.

Wald stepped away from the table, Trish following. Irrationally she felt a stab of shame at leaving. But two cops alone couldn't handle five armed criminals or rescue a concealed hostage. Their best move, their only move, was to return to the squad car, then radio for backup and the sheriff's SWAT team.

"We'll call it in as a wild goose chase," Wald said

without inflection. "Mrs. Kent, no offense, but try to be more careful next time."

"I will, and again, I'm so very sorry."

"No harm done," Trish heard herself say. The words, the first she'd spoken since leaving the car, seemed to come from nowhere.

Her whole attention was focused on the space around her and the desperate need to act natural. God, please don't let her screw up now, because it wasn't just her life on the line or Wald's; it was the Kent girl who would die if this wasn't handled right.

How young was she? As young as Marta had been?

Doubtful. A cup of espresso rested by her plate. A teenager, probably.

Don't think of Marta. Don't think of anything but getting out of this house alive.

Now she and Wald were in the living room, passing the sofa with Oxford stripe slipcovers, the silverado chest that served as a coffee table, the sea grass rug under the rattan magazine basket.

Trish scanned the room, alert for likely hiding places. To her left a door stood slightly ajar, darkness behind it. Most likely it opened on a den or study.

The doorway offered a clear view of both the foyer and the dining area. At least one of the intruders must be watching from that position.

Her hand brushed her holster. She couldn't draw her gun without precipitating an attack.

Charles shadowed them, smiling anxiously. "Really a shame you had to come all the way out here."

Wald nodded. "That's all right. Hope your little girl feels better in the morning."

"Oh, it's nothing. Nothing we can't take care of, I mean. Yes. We'll take care of it."

He was babbling, his voice uncomfortably loud. Trish wished he would shut up.

"Just a headache, after all," Charles added. "It'll pass."

Damn. He'd just made a mistake. Barbara said Ally had an upset stomach, not a headache.

Had their hidden observers noticed? Suspicions aroused, were they preparing to strike?

She and Wald reached the foyer. Front door ahead, standing open.

The thought flashed in her mind that the foyer was the perfect place for an ambush. Tight space, little room to maneuver.

Carpet gave way to tile. She followed Wald toward the door, her back to the den. A marksman would aim midway between her shoulder blades. A clean hit would cut her down before she heard the gun's report.

Five feet to go. Three.

Wald, nearly on the threshold, glanced back. " 'Night, Mr. Kent."

Charles lingered in the living room. He seemed unable to answer, merely raised a hand in a shaky wave.

And still nothing had happened.

Trish allowed herself to hope they were going to make it, and then she remembered the coat closet opposite the potted plant.

Instantly she knew.

Too late.

The closet door blurred open, two ski-masked figures bursting out.

Panic burst like fireworks in her mind. For a heart-beat she stood paralyzed.

Wald reacted faster. With a backward lunge he threw himself clear of the closet, perhaps trying to shield her, perhaps simply putting distance between himself and the assailants.

His hand scrabbled at his service revolver, and Trish heard a single percussive beat, like the muffled pop of a champagne cork.

She didn't realize a shot had been fired until spray misted her hair, and then she saw Wald's face was gone, erased in a cloud of blood.

He toppled, dead weight, his gun belt clanking on the tile floor as he thudded down, and now there was nothing between her and two lifted pistols targeting her heart.

Her revolver was only halfway out of the holster. Useless.

Trish froze, knowing with total clarity that this was the final moment of her life.

From the den, a man's voice.

"Wait."

15

Silence, stillness, her racing heart.

Wait, someone had said, and she was still alive, still in the world.

The two killers glanced toward the den. She followed their gaze and saw a man in the doorway, masked like the others, watching her.

"Hands up," he said without emphasis or inflection.

Shakily she complied. Her pulse throbbed in her neck. The pungent odor crowding her nostrils was the reek of her own sweat.

"Hook her."

The thugs shoved her sideways, her face flush against the wall, rhododendron leaves in her hair. Pain flared in her shoulders as her arms were wrenched behind her back. From her gun belt, handcuffs were appropriated, the steel rings locking on her wrists.

Manacled, she was helpless, at the mercy of Wald's murderers.

She fought to suppress the nausea coiling in her belly as the service revolver was removed from her holster, her trouser legs methodically patted down in a fruitless search for an ankle gun.

They'd blown Wald away without hesitation. Was she next? Or would they keep her alive now that she posed no threat? They had no reason to kill her, but were they likely to be reasonable?

She was panting but couldn't get any air.

Never should've become a cop. Must have been insane.

Gloved hands closed over her shoulders. One of the thugs hustled her out of the foyer while his partner held a gun to her face. The suppressor tube nuzzled her cheek with cold affection.

Leaving, she threw a backward glance at Wald, his head a blasted ruin, one eye staring. A stain discolored his crotch; at the moment of death his bladder had released.

He was the first cop killed in the line of duty in the department's history. She could be the second. Strangers would leave flowers at her grave.

Stop it.

The living room and dining area seemed immense after the foyer's claustrophobic narrowness. She blinked at light and space.

Charles Kent leaned on the mantel, his tan drained by shock. Blood speckled his navy blazer. He'd been standing close enough to be peppered by Wald's arterial spray.

Trish glanced down at her shirt, and her stomach flipped as she saw dark blemishes on the blue fabric, wet and irregular like spattered pasta sauce.

The three people at the table were still seated in their frozen poses, now overtly guarded by a fourth gunman. They hadn't heard the silenced shot, hadn't seen Wald go down, and only when Trish was hauled in, blood soaking the front of her uniform, did they fully understand what had happened.

Judy Danforth started murmuring quietly, one hand on a silver bauble dangling from her neck. The bauble might have been a crucifix, and the murmurs might have been prayers. Philip's mouth worked but produced no sound.

From a rear hallway a fifth killer appeared, training a gun on a high school girl, her eyes red from crying.

Ally, of course. Barbara Kent made a small, shuddering noise of relief when she saw her daughter alive.

The girl was pushed roughly into her chair. Her escort, Trish noted, was shorter and slighter than the others. A woman? Yes.

Had Wald been here, he might have made some crack about an underdeveloped maternal instinct, flashing his wry grin.

Forget Wald. Wald was gone. She was on her own. She had to handle things.

What was she trained to do?

Observe. Remember. So later she could make a report.

If there was a later. If this wasn't the end.

She memorized details of the killers' attire and equipment. The guns looked like Glocks. A 9mm Glock was a combat handgun, as efficient and deadly as any firearm available.

"Bring her here."

The man from the den.

He sat on the arm of a sofa as the two killers hustled Trish across the room, each gripping one elbow, steering her with painful twists of her arms.

She stopped a yard from him. He studied her with a cold appraising gaze, his eyes gray and shrewd and empty of compassion, and she stared back, trying not to flinch, wishing she could shut out the beating furor in her head.

"You're a kid," he said finally, the words punctuated by a derisive snort.

She lifted her chin. "I'm a patrol officer."

The thug to her left giggled.

"A patrol officer," the man echoed with patronizing politeness. "Well, of course you are. Been on the street long, Officer Robinson?"

"Little while." Her lips were very dry. She found it difficult to form words.

"Couple years?"

"About."

"Couple weeks is more like it. I can smell a rookie. A boot, they call 'em. You a boot, Officer Robinson?"

She knew her silence said yes.

"How old are you? Wait, let me guess. Seventeen?"

Anger throbbed in her, side by side with fear. She said nothing.

The female killer moved closer to the sofa, watching her with feral fascination, a predatory animal absorbed in scrutiny of its next kill.

"Are you seventeen, Officer Robinson?" the man pressed. "Or haven't you made it that far?"

Baited, she answered. "I'm twenty-four."

"That old?" Feigned surprise. "You don't look it. I'll bet you still get carded. What's your first name?"

She wouldn't speak again.

A flip of his wrist, and instantly the thugs who flanked her were emptying her pockets.

She stood motionless as they turned out the linings. Past the sofa she could see the people in the dining area, watching ashen-faced. Waiting for her to die as Wald had died, not wanting to see it when it happened, yet unable to turn away.

Every feature of her surroundings stood out with sharp clarity. Oversized book on a glass end table. Small discoloration in the sofa's upholstery. Lost penny glinting on the carpet near a wicker wastebasket.

Her mother always said that any day you found a penny was your lucky day. Was this her lucky day? She didn't think so.

Her I.D. holder was tossed to the man in charge. He passed it unopened to the woman, who examined the police identification card inside.

"Patricia A. Robinson," she reported, speaking the name slowly, savoring it as a spider savors the leisurely ingestion of a fly. A lisp slurred the sibilant sounds.

The gray eyes narrowed. "Pleased to make your acquaintance, Patricia A. Robinson. What does the *A* stand for? Amateur?"

Laughter from the thugs flanking her.

"Annette," Trish whispered.

"Annette? Very nice. Very wholesome. Wasn't there a Mouseketeer by that name?"

She swallowed slowly.

"Were you a Mouseketeer, Officer Robinson?"

"No."

"Or a Girl Scout? That seems more your style. I'll bet you were a Girl Scout. Sold a lot of cookies. Am I right?"

The hell of it was that she had indeed been a Girl Scout. But she would never admit it to this man.

"Way off base," she breathed.

"I don't think so. You're the all-American girl, Officer Robinson. What do your friends call you, anyway? Pat? Patty? Patsy, maybe? You look like a Patsy to me."

New giggles from her left. The thug on her right clucked his tongue behind his mask.

"Trish," she said without expression.

"Trish. Even better. Well, that's what I'll call you, because I'm your friend, too. We're all your friends. You know that, don't you, Trish?"

She used the only threat she could think of. "This was a priority call. Other units are in the vicinity. They'll be here—"

"Unless you get on your radio"—the man interrupted so smoothly as to suggest an unbroken line of thought—"and say everything's okay."

So that was why he hadn't let them shoot her.

"Of course," he continued in the same conversational tone, "it's always possible you'd be tempted to try something stupid. Like trying to warn the dispatcher."

Raising his pistol, he thumbed a pressure switch at the rear of the handle. A diode on the trigger guard beamed a thread of red-orange light along the target acquisition line.

Laser sighting system.

She could almost feel the pinpoint of low intensity light on her forehead. The bullet would enter just above the bridge of her nose.

He nodded as if reading her mind. "You got it,

Trish. Do anything dumb, and I'll put a jacketed hollow-point right between those pretty blue eyes."

She felt herself shaking. Couldn't help it.

"Now, I don't think you're foolish enough to throw away your young life. But I could be wrong. Maybe I'm dealing with some kind of hero." The gray eyes glittered with dark mirth. "So here's my hole card."

He nodded toward the dining area, and the killer guarding the table put his gun to Ally's neck.

Reflexively the girl stiffened in her chair. Barbara groaned, and Judy went on stroking her crucifix.

"Any bravery on your part," the man said, "and the young lady dies too."

Trish stared across the room into Ally's wide brown eyes and saw another, younger girl.

"I won't try anything," she whispered.

Slowly the man inclined his head. "All right, then. Get on the horn and say you found no problems here. Your unit's leaving the scene, and you're requesting a code seven."

Code seven: out of service. It wasn't entirely a lie. Wald was code seven, all right—permanently code seven—and she soon might follow.

"Okay," she said, her voice husky and low.

"Do it."

The thug to her left unclipped the radio from her belt and pushed it close to her face.

"Which channel?" the gray-eyed man asked her.

"One."

The thug activated channel one, taking the transceiver off the scan mode, then pressed the transmit button.

"Four-Adam-eight-one." Somehow Trish kept her voice even.

Crackle of static, then Lou's response: "Go ahead, eight-one."

"We're clear of the detail. No sign of a prowler."

"Guess Pete was right. You didn't need backup."

"Ten-four."

"Hey, is that the Kent place?"

Oh, God. Slow night, and Lou wanted to chat.

"Ten-four," Trish said again, hoping her stiff formality would preclude further conversation.

It didn't. "Thought I recognized the address. I was there on a house tour once. Nice digs."

Suddenly Trish saw a way to drop a hint, a very subtle hint but perhaps one Lou would pick up. Pete Wald had said Sergeant Edinger gave the same lecture to every rookie. Lou, who'd worked at the station for twenty years, surely would be familiar with the routine.

"Yeah, it's nice." Trish tried to sound normal, but it was hard to do with those deadly gray eyes watching her intently. "A lot like some places I've seen in L.A."

"L.A.?" Dubious.

"You know, Bel-Air, Beverly Hills. Ed and I were just talking about that." Come on, Lou, read my mind. "About how things are in L.A."

"Funny. Never knew Ed to pay any attention to architecture. And I don't know when was the last time he was down in the city."

Clearly the message hadn't gotten through. Worse, Trish had aroused the suspicions of her captors. Restless stirring around her. A pent-up explosion in the air.

The gray-eyed man made an angry cutting motion: Wrap it up.

"Anyway," Trish said, her heart beating faster, "we'd like to go code seven now."

"Hey, your watch just started. What gives? Pete taking a nap?"

"You know it." A long nap, Trish thought, wondering if it was about to be nap time for her, too.

"Request granted." Lou signed off. "Twenty twenty-eight."

The radio was withdrawn. Trish waited, afraid she had pressed her luck too far. She hoped Ally wouldn't pay the price. Please, not her.

"What was that all about, Trish?" the gray-eyed man said with cold amiability.

"Nothing. Lou wanted to talk, that's all."

"L.A. Someone named Ed. Where'd that come from?"

"I was just, you know, making conversation. Ed's a guy who works at the station. He used to live in L.A., still talks about it a lot. It didn't mean anything."

"I don't believe you."

"It's the truth."

"I don't trust you, Trish."

"I did what you wanted."

"You tried to mess with me."

"No."

He turned to the woman at his side. "How about it? Can you sound like her?"

"Easy." She lisped the word.

Then her breathy voice altered its pitch, climbing an octave higher, and the lisp was magically gone, her delivery clear and sharp.

77

"Four-Adam-eight-one. We're clear of the detail. We'll be going code seven."

The mimicry was more than adequate.

Her boss nodded, then looked at Trish again. "My associate can pass for you. I'll feed her the codes and phrases."

The implication wasn't subtle. Trish's wrists twisted uselessly behind her back.

"Won't work," she whispered. "Lou knows me. We talk all the time."

"If we keep the transmission short, we can pull it off. These rover radios are crap anyway. All the voices sound pretty much alike." He said it then, said what everyone was thinking. "I don't need you, Patricia Annette Robinson."

No more words. Rigid, she waited for the bullet.

The man watched her a moment longer. Then his gaze shifted, focusing on the killer to her right.

Some silent message passed between them, instantaneous as a spark, and the butt of a pistol clipped her hard behind the ear.

Coldcocked.

Trish had time to think it was better than getting shot. Then pain washed over her in a stinging wave, its undertow dragging her away.

Her last thought was a question: Will I ever wake up?

Then no questions, no fear, only a humming void and a wordless sense of peace.

16

Cain watched Trish Robinson drop to the carpet in a graceless sprawl. A spasm ran briefly through her body, and she made a low retching noise, coughing up spittle, then lay still.

"You should have iced her." Agitation brought back Lilith's lisp, making her sound like a petulant child. "I wanted to see that."

"Bad idea." Cain kept his voice low.

"I don't see why."

Ordinarily she didn't need things spelled out, but blood made her slow-witted. It was like catnip to her.

He nodded toward the dining area. "I'd rather not get our friends any more worked up than they already are. We pop the rookie right in front of everybody, and things could get out of control."

"So what do we do with her?" Tyler wiped blood off the handle of his gun. "Lock her up?"

"No."

Cain hated cops, all cops, even pretty little lady cops who'd barely gotten their feet wet in the field. Cops were bugs, meant to be squashed.

"She disappears," he said softly, his gaze fixed on Tyler. "Her and the other one and the car they came in. No muss, no fuss. You know that old Bobby Darin number? Splish splash, Trish was takin' a bath. . . ." His hand made a downward sliding motion. "You and Blair make it happen."

Tyler's heavy-lidded eyes shut briefly in acknowledgment. Blair giggled.

"Take off their belts first," Cain added. "No point wasting the gear. And give Lilith the radio so she can monitor the traffic."

He stepped into the foyer and crouched by the dead man named Wald. The mingled smells of blood and urine reached his nostrils through the mask. He barely noticed. The stink of death was as familiar to him as the fragrance of honeysuckle to a gardener.

Rolling Wald on his side, Cain removed the cop's handcuffs from a case on his belt, then found his key holder and detached it. The cuffs and the ring of keys went into Cain's side pocket.

He had an idea how to use those items. Not part of the plan, probably a mistake, but maybe . . . just maybe . . .

From the closet he retrieved his duffel, stashed there before the cops arrived. He slung the bag over his shoulder and returned to the living room.

Lilith was clipping the police radio to her belt. "Look at me," she said gaily. "I'm Officer Robinson." She leaned close to Trish, still out cold, and added, "You're under arrest."

Tyler was amused. "What's the charge?"

"Impersonating a cop," Lilith said archly, and Tyler and Blair laughed.

Even Cain had to smile. His Lilith was such a child.

"Hey, boss," Tyler said. "The Porsche is blocking

the driveway. Got to move it if we're gonna take the squad car out the rear gate."

Cain chuckled. "You've been itching to drive that hot little number since you saw it." He turned toward the dining area. "Keys to the Porsche. *Now.*"

Philip Danforth produced a key chain. Gage tossed it across the room, and Cain snagged it in a gloved fist.

"No joyriding," he warned Tyler as he passed along the keys. "We got work to do."

"You sound like my father."

I'm old enough, Cain thought, but didn't say it.

Tyler left. Blair busied himself with Wald. Cain and Lilith escorted Charles Kent away from the fireplace, to the dining area, and sat him down. He was as pale and listless as a lobotomy patient.

Cain clapped his hands, and Ally jerked as if shot. "Valuables on the table."

Silently the Kents and Danforths removed their jewelry and wristwatches. Two Rolexes, two smaller gold watches, a gold wrist bangle, diamond-studded cuff links, a gold herringbone choker, a sapphire-tipped tie clasp, sterling silver earrings, a gold brooch with a red silk flower, even Judy's silver crucifix.

Outside, the Porsche's motor turned over. Headlights rippled over the lawn.

"Wallets, too."

They complied.

"Wedding rings."

Judy started to say something, then changed her mind. "Now, on your feet."

Chairs were pushed back. The five prisoners stood, mute terror in their eyes. Cain thought of dogs waiting to be kicked.

He nodded curtly to Gage and Lilith. Their guns swung up, and Barbara moaned.

"March," Gage said.

For a moment there was no reaction. The word might have been a relic of some long-dead language, meaningless to modern ears.

"Side hall," Gage snapped. "That way."

Judy started moving obediently. Philip stood his ground. "Where are you taking us?"

Gage struck him across the face with his gun. Philip's head snapped sideways, a gash torn in his lower lip.

"Move!" Gage screamed.

Screaming was bad, Cain knew. It showed a lack of discipline, an absence of control. The kid was raw, unseasoned. All wrong for this job.

Philip offered no more resistance. He shambled after Judy, followed by Charles. Barbara and Ally, holding hands, were last to go.

"Wait." Cain grasped Ally's shoulder. "The girl stays here."

A single violent tremor shook Ally hard.

Barbara stared at Cain, her face drawn and blanched. "What for?"

"I don't answer to you, Mrs. Kent."

"Don't hurt her. Please, my God, she's a child, don't hurt her—"

"She won't be hurt. We need her help, that's all."

"Help? How can she help you? What are you going to do?"

"Get moving."

"No, please"—she reached out blindly for her

daughter—"she's only fifteen, I'm begging you, take anything in the house, anything you want—"

Gage seized Barbara by the hair and twisted her head sideways, wrenching a gasp out of her. "Shut up and march."

She was weeping as Gage shoved her toward the hall, where Lilith waited with the others.

Charles watched, looking distantly astonished, as if he hadn't known there was evil in the world.

17

Barbara took a last look at her daughter. Then the thug who'd struck Philip shoved her sharply from behind, and she stumbled into the side hallway.

The intersection with the rear hall was only a few steps away. That hall led outside to the patio. She wondered if she and the others would be taken outside.

A movie sequence unreeled in her mind. She and Charles and the Danforths lined up against the exterior wall. Spurt of silenced gunfire. Blood on the patio. Wind chimes tinkling over shattered bodies.

Past fear she was conscious of anger, cold and unforgiving. Anger at the killers, to be sure, but a different and perhaps deeper anger also, directed at her husband.

She had disliked Charles before, hated him now.

Philip, at least, had made an effort. He'd signaled with the tapping of his spoon, defied the order to march. He had guts. He had, as her father would have said, balls.

Where are *your* balls, Charles? she thought acidly.

Then the rear hall passed, and the two thugs, male and female, herded the prisoners deeper into the east wing.

On her left Ally's bedroom appeared, the room where her daughter had been held hostage when the police arrived. Through the doorway Barbara glimpsed a four-poster bed, a tidy bookcase, an Apple computer on a writing desk.

She asked herself if Ally ever would sleep in that bed again, or read those books or do homework at that desk.

Well, of course she would. The man had said he wouldn't hurt her.

And he hadn't shot that patrolwoman.

But the other officer, though—he was dead. Shot and killed in the foyer of her house, gunned down like an animal.

The hall ended at the doorway to the master suite.

How odd to enter her bedroom in the company of others, to see it through strangers' eyes. She was absurdly glad she'd made the beds.

Lace curtains billowed over the windows, the breeze carrying a perfume of roses from the front yard. The suite's opposite wall was taken up by double bifold doors that opened on a walk-in closet.

The female killer opened the doors, and her companion gestured with the gun. "In there."

"The closet?" Judy sounded more bewildered than afraid.

"Yes, damn it."

That one had a short temper and sounded young. They all seemed young, Barbara thought, except for their leader. He was about her age she guessed. Forty or forty-five.

Men of that age sometimes developed a taste for young girls. Ally looked so lovely in that white dress.

It showed a little cleavage. Was that man looking down her dress now, studying the lacy border of her bra, the hint of her white breasts?

If he forced her . . .

"In," the male thug snapped, shoving her again, and she realized she had hesitated at the threshold of the closet, wrapped in ugly thoughts.

She joined Charles and the Danforths. The closet was as large as a freight elevator, not claustrophobically crowded even with the four of them inside. Several of Charles's suits hung behind her, cellophane envelopes crinkling as they brushed her hair.

The doors banged shut. Darkness.

Bad to be here in the dark. Images came to her, images of Ally in her white dress—white, a virginal color; her daughter was still a virgin, she was quite sure of that—God, please let her be a virgin after tonight . . .

Outside, the rattle of a chain, then the click of a padlock.

Footsteps. Leaving.

The killers had gone, but the ugly images remained, and the awful thoughts, and the cold terror . . .

"He's going to hurt her," someone whispered, and with a small shock she realized it was herself. "The look in his eyes . . ."

Charles, her husband, Ally's father—he was the one who ought to have comforted her now. He didn't move.

It was Judy who took her hand in a warm, reassuring squeeze.

Alone with Ally in the dining area, Cain felt the girl's violent trembling, her helpless terror, and liked it.

Movement in the foyer. Tyler reentered the house. He knelt by Trish Robinson, rolled her over, and unbuckled her gun belt.

Ally watched the procedure with peculiar intensity. Cain tightened his grip on her shoulder.

"In the den," he said, not harshly.

They crossed the living room together. As they reached the den, Tyler slung the cop, beltless but still cuffed, over his shoulder. Blood trickled out of her hairline, striping her cheek.

He carried her through the front door. Ally watched him go.

"He won't hurt her," she whispered. "Will he?"

"You don't even know the lady. What's it to you?"

"She seemed . . . nice."

Cain smiled under his mask. "Nice people get hurt sometimes." He touched the girl's delicate chin. "How about you? You're a nice person, aren't you?"

Teardrops dewed her lashes. Her mouth worked without sound. Such a pretty mouth.

"Aren't you, Ally? Aren't you nice?"

Still smiling, he led her into the den.

18

Sergeant Ed Edinger hated coffee, all coffee, but he drank gallons of it to stay alert throughout the mid-p.m. watch. In a town with so little criminal activity that the very existence of a police department was optional, there wasn't much to engage his attention even on a Saturday night.

He supposed he ought to like it that way, but just once a high-speed chase or a hostage situation might be nice.

Just once.

The coffee nook outside his office could have used a decorator's touch. Its sole ornament was a cork bulletin board plastered with outdated memoranda, many generated by himself. The square of short-nap carpet under the folding table was a mosaic of deeply ingrained coffee stains. Ed was responsible for a few of those, as well.

He tilted the carafe and poured a steaming black arc into a souvenir mug from Palm Springs. His wife collected mugs.

Sugar and cream followed in excessive amounts. Ed would add anything to coffee, in any quantity, to make the damn stuff tolerable.

"Hey, Sarge."

Glancing up, he saw a tall, big-shouldered woman saunter up to the coffee machine, holding a Styrofoam cup. Louise Stagget, one of the two night-watch dispatchers, known universally as Lou.

Ed nodded by way of greeting. "Radio keeping you busy?" he asked, already knowing the answer. He monitored the chatter on and off throughout the night.

"Hardly. Even slower than usual." Lou drained the carafe into her cup. "Pete Wald sure seems to think so."

"What's that supposed to mean?"

"Only that he went code seven at twenty twenty-eight."

Ed found Lou's habit of using military time mildly irritating. He had to make the conversion to Pacific Daylight Time in his head, and he wasn't that good with numbers.

"Just a few minutes ago," he said, doing the math. "So what?"

"Seemed a little peculiar. You know, he'd been on duty less than a half hour. Kind of early in his watch to be taking a break."

Ed sipped his coffee and winced, his unfailing reaction. "Like you say, it's a slow night."

"He could at least cruise the shopping district or the motels by the freeway. Not everything comes in via nine-one-one."

"Well, maybe he's just not feeling so good." Ed was reluctant to criticize Pete Wald, a good friend for many years. "Bad chili or something."

"I don't think it was him."

Lou let the words hang in space as she busied herself with a filter bag, preparing to brew a new pot.

The phone in the lobby shrilled briefly, then was answered. Somewhere a police siren wailed, the sound making Ed frown in bemusement until he realized that it came from the detective squad room, where two of the guys were watching a TV cop show while filling out a burglary report.

"I think," Lou concluded after a sufficiently dramatic pause, "it was that girl."

Trish Robinson. No surprise.

Ed had suspected that Lou disliked the rookie, maybe because Robinson was twenty years younger and forty pounds lighter, or maybe just for the pure pleasure of spite.

"What about her?" he asked, taking another sip and registering another grimace.

"She's a slacker."

"A what?"

"Slacker. One of these young people nowadays who thinks the world owes 'em a living. *You* know."

"So she's young. We were too."

"But we weren't slackers. It was a different world back then. People still had a sense of responsibility. Way things are going, soon there'll be nothing *but* slackers. These damn kids'll ruin us. No values. No backbone."

"You're being too hard on her," Ed said, but he wondered. Robinson had been late for roll call. Not a good sign.

"Maybe I am." Lou shrugged. "Hey, when was the last time you got down to L.A.? Three, four years?"

"More like five. City's a hellhole. I keep my distance." He finished his coffee in a noisy slurp. "Why?"

"You ever talk to Robinson about the houses there?"

"Houses?"

"Like in Bel-Air, Beverly Hills . . ."

"Why the hell would I talk about houses?"

"Yeah, that's what I figured." Lou turned away without explanation.

Baffled, Ed watched her walk down the hall to the communications room. She shook her head once, and he caught a muttered word.

"Slacker."

Then she was gone, and Ed was left asking himself if the rookie was going to work out.

19

"Got her okay?" Blair called from the driveway.

Tyler lugged the lady cop down the flagstone path in the starlight. "Easy as taking out the garbage."

The trunk of the squad car was open, the interior light illuminating two helmet bags and some folded blankets. Blair tossed them out, and Tyler dumped the patrolwoman inside.

She groaned but didn't stir. The clasp securing her hair came loose, and a spill of blonde strands, shoulder length, fanned out in a lustrous spray.

"She's pretty, huh?" Blair said.

"Yeah." Tyler shut the trunk and heard it lock. "Soon she'll be pretty dead."

As he walked to the driver's door, he glanced through the side window. Officer Wald lay across the floor of the backseat, his right eye gone, the left staring sightlessly.

In Wald's wallet Tyler had found a photo of a red-headed wife and two high school kids posing on Stearns Wharf in Santa Barbara. Family man.

But not anymore.

He got behind the wheel and raised his ski mask, grateful to have it off. Sweat dampened his face. His ponytail was a wet mop. The camouflage paint around his eyes had run like black tears.

In the passenger seat Blair tugged off his own mask, revealing a lumpy nose and pockmarked cheeks. "Hot night, huh?"

"I grew up in Arizona," Tyler said. "Lake Havasu City. Gets to be a hundred fifteen in the summer."

"Where you gonna go once we split the haul?"

"Just south of here. Malibu. You?"

"Maybe back to San Diego. Me and Gage grew up there. Nice town."

"Lots of Mexicans."

"The Mexicans are all right. I used to do some part-time stuff with some Mexicans."

"What stuff?"

"Swiping boats. Real easy work. Just hot-wire the sucker and go."

Tyler nodded. "I helped run a chop shop out in El Centro for a while. Autos, I mean. Not a bad way to earn a living."

"The gangs are taking over the auto racket. Boats too. Not much future in it for the independent businessman."

"Well, after we get paid, the future's gonna look a lot brighter for all of us."

"You got that right," Blair said with a smile.

Though they had spent the past thirty-six hours together, this was Tyler Sinclair's longest conversation with Blair Sharkey. The kid didn't say much, and his brother Gage said even less.

Still, Tyler had seen enough of them to judge that neither measured up to Hector Avalon, the man they had replaced. Tyler had gotten to know old Hector pretty well during a week of drills conducted by Cain in the wilds of the San Jacinto Mountains. The crew had donned their black camouflage outfits, practiced with modified Glocks that fired blank rounds, and run through every possible contingency plan.

Basic training, Cain had called it. Boot camp.

Too bad the Sharkeys hadn't been part of all that. Maybe then tonight's mishap wouldn't have occurred, and the lady in the trunk wouldn't have to die.

The squad car's key had been left in the ignition. Tyler cranked it, and the engine caught. High beams snapped on. He guided the Chevy between the house and the garage, then through the backyard to the rear gate.

Had he thought of it, he would have opened the gate from inside the house; there was a switch by the rear door. Since he'd forgotten, the gate would have to be pushed by hand.

"Do it," Tyler told Blair, assuming his authority as Cain's right-hand man, a promotion he'd obtained upon Hector Avalon's demise.

The kid got out. Tyler sat in the idling Chevy, curiously at peace amid the radio's occasional low squawks. The car was a Caprice from the early '90s, a big old boat popular with cops and cab drivers.

Boat. The thought made him smile. Officer Robinson was going to wish it was a boat.

Anyway, the Caprice wasn't much of a car. Nothing like the Danforths' Porsche. Man, just sitting in that 928 GTS had been a thrill, and starting the engine . . .

Soon he would have a Porsche of his own. Not a GTS—nifty as it was, it lacked the hard-riding feel of a true sports car. The one he would buy was a brand-new 911 Carrera. Two hundred forty-seven horses and a classic design. Black exterior . . . or red; he hadn't decided.

He saw himself cruising down Pacific Coast Highway, Dr. Dre on the CD player at eardrum-bursting volume, a girl with big tits and no brains at his side.

The passenger seat creaked, but it wasn't his dream girl sliding into the Chevy, just Blair Sharkey. The gate was open.

Tyler drove through, his foot resting lightly on the gas pedal, the speedometer needle pegged at a cautious fifteen miles an hour.

"Things are going slick enough so far," Blair said.

"Would've been slicker," Tyler answered evenly, "if your baby brother hadn't gotten himself eyeballed while he was mucking around in the backyard."

"Hey, Tex, lighten up."

"I'm from Arizona, I said."

"Sorry. Just an expression. Anyway, Gage is okay."

Tyler wouldn't let it go. "How could he let the Kent woman see him?"

"I thought he was right behind me on the way to the patio. Guess he fell back. Tried to catch up by taking a shortcut past the gazebo."

"Within view of the kitchen window."

"He didn't know."

"Why didn't he?"

"We got in on this action kind of late," Blair said, getting hot.

"Sure you did. But shit, we went over it a hundred times. Cain showed you blueprints, diagrams."

"Look, he's young, all right?"

Young. Both of the Sharkey boys were young. Gage was sixteen, Blair just two years older. Tyler Sinclair, at twenty-two, felt like Methuselah by comparison.

"Yeah," Tyler said, "he's young, but he ought to be smarter. Didn't he learn anything heisting boats?"

Blair looked away. "I didn't say he was with me on those jobs. That was me and some Mexicans."

"You mean the kid's a virgin?"

"Nah, he's done some stuff. Nothing this major."

"Nobody here's done anything this major," Tyler said, stating the obvious. "What *has* he done?"

"You know, the usual. Ripping off mailboxes, busting into parked cars ... he's shoplifted some pretty nice items too."

"Sounds real small-time."

"Hey, I'll vouch for him, all right? He'll be okay. I got him into this, and I'll talk him through it. Or do you got a problem with that?"

"I don't got a problem," Tyler said coolly, "as long as he doesn't mess up again."

Blair gave no response. They finished the drive in silence.

The wide, paved path angled down a gentle grade for a quarter mile or so, past stands of live oak and bigleaf maple and dense pockets of yerba buena and fiddleneck. Night air blew in through the open windows, warm at first but cooling steadily as the lake drew near.

At the bottom of the slope, the Chevy's high beams illuminated a narrow strip of sand bordering the lake. The Kents' private dock extended out over the water, two small sport boats bobbing in moorage.

Tyler steered the squad car onto the dock and drove

to the end, boards rattling under the wheels. He shifted the gear selector into neutral, then killed the engine and lights.

Wordlessly he got out and walked to the rear of the car. The lake stretched into darkness, walled in by high wooded hillsides devoid of light.

No one lived nearby. Cain had explained in one of their many briefings that all the land around the lake once had been owned by the Ashcroft family. Barbara Kent's parents had ceded most of it to the county as a wildlife refuge and a public park, retaining ownership of the fenced estate and an easement for the path and dock.

Blair, still ticked off and not talking, joined Tyler at the back of the car. Together they put their weight against the bumper and pushed.

The dock was flat, and the sedan rolled easily at first. Then with a downward lurch the front wheels slid into space. The Chevy dipped, chassis scraping the dock.

They shoved harder, but the car's underside kept catching on gaps between the planks.

"Put some muscle into it," Tyler grunted.

Straining, they forced the Chevy forward another three feet until it was half off the dock.

It teetered briefly, balanced between the weight of the engine up front and the combined weight of Wald and Robinson in the rear.

A groan, a teeth-gritting squeal of metal on wood, and the car pitched headlong into the lake.

Water flooded through the front doors, open on both sides. The blue-and-white Caprice submerged ponderously like some immense aquatic creature returning to its element.

The rooftop light bar was last to disappear below the surface. Then the car was only a dim ghostly image retreating into the gloom.

It sank deeper than Tyler would have expected. The lake floor shelved down steeply just past the dock.

He waited. When clouds of silt rose like swirls of cream in coffee, he knew the Chevy had touched bottom.

"So long, officers," he said softly. "Have a nice day."

Leaving the dock, Tyler paused to look back at the lake's wide expanse, mirror-smooth and starlight-silvered.

He wondered if the car trunk was watertight. It was a small matter, merely the difference between suffocation and drowning for the woman inside.

"You patrol this area," he told Blair. "Any trouble, get on channel three."

"I know the drill."

"Just like your brother?" Tyler asked, and started up the path without waiting for a reply.

The night was clear and still. Stars burned holes in the black sky. Somewhere a bullfrog sang, its croaking solo sonorous as a snore.

Tyler climbed higher, toward the house. He forgot Blair and Gage Sharkey, forgot the scuttled Chevy and the unlucky lady in the trunk.

He thought about his Porsche.

Red, he decided. Definitely red.

A smile brushed his lips. He was young, and it was summer in California, and life was good.

20

In the den Cain kicked his duffel bag behind an armchair, out of his way, then released a hinged section of oak paneling to expose a wall safe with a combination lock.

"Open it," he told Ally.

The girl hugged herself, arms crossed high on her chest, as if conscious that her white dress was dangerously revealing. "Nothing's in there except, you know, stock certificates and stuff."

"Open it anyway."

"I don't know the combination."

He studied her in the spill of light from a green-shaded brass banker's lamp. Her hair was teased into ringlets of dark curls. Freckles splashed her round face. Still a child's face—but the tanned, supple legs below her hemline were the legs of a woman.

"Yes, you do," he said evenly. "I saw you open this safe last Saturday night. Only you didn't take out any stock certificates. You took out a string of pearls. They looked pretty on you."

There was something comical in the way her brown eyes widened and kept on widening in a caricature of surprise.

"You . . . saw. . . ?"

"I've watched this house on and off for weeks. With these." He showed her the binoculars. "You people never close your curtains. I guess having no neighbors makes you sort of careless."

"Oh, God . . ."

"What did you want the pearls for, anyway?"

She responded mechanically, her thoughts still focused on her shattered illusion of privacy. "Some charity thing. My mom's on the board. We had to go to the dinner." Then her eyes cleared as a question occurred to her. "How come you didn't just break in and rip us off while we were out?"

Smart girl, but he had a ready answer. "Because I needed to know the combination. And because I wanted to spend time with you, Ally."

"M-me?" A stammer broke the word in half.

"You interest me. I've watched you at other times. I went around to the woods out back, scoped you out through the fence. You don't close your bedroom curtains either."

Mingled outrage and embarrassment flushed the girl's face.

"Sometimes," Cain added, "you walk around naked, right in front of the windows. You put on a hell of a show."

Her knees shook. She reached out to grasp a table for support, and a Tiffany's catalogue, robin's-egg blue, slapped to the floor. "No . . ."

"Hey, don't blame me for peeking. Couldn't help myself. You're hot, sweetheart. That tight little ass, and those nice firm titties—"

"Stop."

"I'll bet you let your boyfriend talk about your tits. Touch 'em, too."

"I . . . I don't have a boyfriend."

"Well, you should, Ally. You really should."

She blinked back tears, catching the obvious implication.

Cain slid a gloved hand into his side pocket and fingered Wald's handcuffs.

It would be so easy. Wouldn't take long at all.

But he was playing for bigger stakes tonight. He couldn't afford to be sidetracked. Of course not. Of course.

His hand withdrew from his pocket, leaving the cuffs within.

"Open the safe."

He watched as Ally rotated the dial. The combination was 4–15–54.

"That number mean anything?" he asked.

She wouldn't look at him. "It's my mom's date of birth."

"Your mom looks younger than forty-three."

"Did you watch her get naked, too?"

"You're more my type." Cain smiled, amused by her bravado. She reminded him of the rookie cop— young and scared and trying desperately not to show it. "Now clean out whatever's inside."

"How do you know my dad doesn't keep a gun in there?"

"Maybe he does."

"Then how do you know I won't grab it and shoot you?"

"You've got better manners than that."

"Don't be so sure."

She reached in and began piling jewelry and coins and bars of bullion on a rosewood table. Cain paid less attention to the loot than to the sleek, rippling muscles of her arms. There was still some baby fat on her, but a lean, mature young woman was emerging fast.

She dug deeper. The safe seemed bottomless, a cornucopia of wealth. Cain saw stacked Krugerrands taped together, kilogram bricks of silver with Credit Suisse certificates attached, hand-crafted pendants and bracelets and earrings that must be Ashcroft family heirlooms.

"You were right." His voice was very low. "Nothing but stock certificates."

The girl bit her trembling lip.

"It's not smart to lie to me, Ally. That bitch cop lied too. Played games on the radio. Now she's dead."

The last word wrenched Ally's head sideways. "You *killed* her?"

"Bad things happen to liars."

Tears muddied her eyes. "But . . . but she was just unconscious, that's all. She was still breathing."

"Not anymore."

"You couldn't . . . ."

"I did. She's fish food." He enjoyed talking this way, like a Mafia boss in a cheap movie. "My associates put her in the lake."

"In the lake?" The girl stared at her trembling hands. "I—I go swimming there. Go swimming."

The words, soft and toneless, were spoken only to herself.

"Well, next time you take a dip"—Cain smiled

through his mask—"you can say hello to Officer Robinson. And give her my regards."

Ally resumed emptying the safe, weeping without sound, and Cain watched her, wondering why she would mourn for a woman she had never known.

21

A young girl skipping rope.

She was nine years old, in a summer dress of blue polka dots, her laughter high and thin and echoey like the keening of birds.

Marta.

The cry, so plaintive, so urgent, was Trish's own.

Marta, do you hear me?

Sweeps of the jump rope, bounce of blonde bangs. The girl was laughing, laughing. She didn't hear. She never heard.

Marta—don't!

A blur, a lens slipping out of focus, and the girl was gone, just gone.

Only her laughter persisted, mysterious and haunting—disembodied laughter in a horizonless field of white.

Are you there, Marta . . . ?

Marta, answer me!

Eyes.

Huge eyes, filling the world, staring blindly. A roach crept among a forest of stiff lashes, antennae twitching.

The eyes were bloodshot and unblinking. Marta lay

in the weeds, a discarded doll, limp and twisted, the jump rope knotted around her neck in a python's caress.

Oh, God, Marta. Trish heard suppressed sobs in her voice. *I told you not to. I told you.*

No response, no flicker of life in those staring eyes, save for the jerky progress of the roach, balanced on a glassy iris like a skater on a pond.

Trish shivered, suddenly cold, cold all over.

Wet and cold.

Wet . . .

She jerked awake.

For a disoriented moment she blinked, looking around. Vaguely she expected to see the porch light glowing through her curtains, the dark shapes of the scattered shipping cartons she still hadn't unpacked, the luminous dial of the alarm clock resting near the foam pad where she slept.

Nothing. There was nothing.

And she was not lying on the pad, and this was not her new apartment, not any place she'd ever been.

The darkness was impenetrable, absolute. Her arms were twisted awkwardly behind her. She was soaked in chilly water, pants and shirt glued to her buttocks and back.

Pants, shirt—her uniform. She'd been on duty.

A groan escaped her lips as she remembered.

The prowler call. The Kents and their dinner guests. The cartridge case on the tablecloth. Ambush. Wald dead. A stinging blow behind her right ear.

They'd knocked her out and put her here, in this lightless, freezing, watery place.

Fear squeezed her heart. Impulsively she tried to

bring her arms forward. Pain ripped her wrists as metal teeth bit down. Handcuffed—she was still handcuffed—and there was no air in here, no air, and she couldn't *breathe*.

Come on, stop it, she was hyperventilating, that's all. She had to breathe through her nose, through her nose . . .

Lips pursed, inhaling slowly, she convinced herself she wouldn't suffocate. She was all right. Yes. She could get air in her lungs and she wasn't going to die and she was all right.

The burning dampness in her eyes was a splash of tears.

What was this place? What had those bastards done with her?

She lay on her back, wrists pinned under her, knees partially bent in a semi-fetal pose. Immobility was bad, but the utter absence of light was worse.

No blindfold on her face. She was sure of that. So why was it so dark, so completely dark, without even the dim ambient light that bled into nearly any locked room?

Had they—oh, God, had they done something to her eyes? Blindness was her worst fear. That and paralysis. And now she couldn't see and she couldn't move, and the tears came faster.

She was so damn scared. Even when the gray-eyed man had held his gun on her, she hadn't been this scared. She had known what was happening, it had made some sort of sense, but this was a nightmare, a parallel universe, insanity.

A wave of shudders rippled through her body. Both

legs straightened reflexively, her shoes banging against a hard stop.

A wall.

She kicked it—again—again.

Hollow metallic thuds.

Metal wall? Some sort of bulkhead?

Her terror escalated, though she didn't know quite why. She made little mewling, grunting noises as she probed further.

Intersecting walls on either side. Maybe a yard apart.

Bigger than a coffin, but not much.

"Where am I?" she whispered, her voice hoarse and faraway.

The water pooling under her seemed colder than before. No, not colder, just more pervasive, spreading to parts of her body that had been dry only moments ago.

Spreading . . .

She stiffened. Breath held, she listened tensely. Heard a soft, continuous gurgle from behind her and below.

Water seeping in through fissures and seams.

Water that was rising steadily and would keep on rising until she was fully immersed.

Her heart pounded harder. Sightlessly she sat up, and her forehead struck a ceiling, metal also and impossibly low.

That can't-breathe sensation was toying with her again. She knew it was psychological. There was still enough air.

But for how long? Two minutes? Three?

"Let me out!" she screamed, hoping they would

hear her and show mercy. "Please let me out, *let me out!*"

The echoes of her cry clanged against the metal walls and floor and ceiling, and died unanswered.

She bit her lip to keep from screaming again. Waste of strength, of breath. Wherever she was, whatever kind of fix she was in, no one could hear her, and there was no escape.

She was trapped in this place, this room—not even a room—a sealed compartment—locker, maybe, or steamer trunk—

Trunk.

Car trunk.

The Caprice.

It rushed in on her, full comprehension, vivid and terrible.

They'd locked her in the trunk of the squad car, and dumped the car—Jesus, they'd dumped the car . . .

"In the lake," she whispered.

The words were squeezed past the strangling tightness in her throat.

They would have wanted to conceal the cruiser. The lake Wald had mentioned was an obvious place to do it. And the water trickling in, cold and powdered with fine grit—it was lake water, thick with silt from the murky bottom.

"Help me," she moaned, speaking to nobody and nothing. "Help me, please help."

But help would not come. She was alone, more alone than ever before in her life, and if she wanted to have any chance, she would have to help herself.

Yes. That was the bottom line, wasn't it?

No medals for quitters. That was what Mrs. Wilkes

used to say, Mrs. Wilkes who'd been her Girl Scout leader a million years ago.

Good words. She tested them aloud. "No medals for quitters." Again, more firmly: "No medals for quitters."

Her tortured breathing went on, as did the reckless pounding of her heart, but her thoughts calmed.

It was a locked trunk. Perhaps it could be opened. If she could find the latch . . .

To do anything she would need the use of her hands.

She groped behind her, fumbling for her gun belt, where she kept her handcuff key.

No belt. It was gone. They'd taken it from her, the sons of bitches, and she couldn't get the cuffs off, couldn't break out, and the water murmured louder, the level climbing.

Irrationally she stamped her feet on the wall, as if she could punch a hole in the car, puncture welded steel like tissue paper. The banging of hard-soled shoes on metal reverberated in the trunk, a second heartbeat, grotesquely amplified.

"No medals for quitters." The motto was her mantra. "No medals for quitters, no medals for quitters . . ."

Couldn't shed the cuffs. But did she have to?

Even manacled, she could manipulate objects with reasonable dexterity—if her hands were in front of her, not behind her back.

She worked out daily, alternating between upper body and lower body routines. Each session began and ended with stretching exercises. She was limber. She was young.

Maybe she could do it. Maybe. God, please.

She twisted sideways, head lifted to keep her mouth and nostrils above water, then arched her back and bent both legs under her.

Her hands were level with her pelvis. To succeed, she had to get them past her buttocks and behind her thighs.

It wasn't going to be easy.

Teeth clenched, she folded her legs at a still more acute angle, curving her spine to its full extension. Her knees banged the license-plate wall. Impossible to make any move in here without hitting something. It was like trying to do gymnastics in a bathtub.

Pain speared her triceps and shoulders as she forced her hands lower. She separated her wrists as far as possible, drawing the chain taut. The cuffs rode her thumb joints, friction rubbing the skin raw.

"Hell," she gasped, "this really *hurts*."

Coughing seized her. Even with her chin lifted, she'd swallowed water. The level was higher.

No medals for quitters. She had to do this. No medals for quitters. Do it or die.

With a shout of agony she dragged the handcuff chain over the twin obstructions of her buttocks. Simultaneously she snapped forward at the waist, tucking her hands under her legs.

Her hands sizzled where the steel bracelets had bitten deep. She was bleeding from the knuckles of both thumbs.

Pain and blood didn't matter. She'd done the hard part.

Now she just had to step over the chain.

Fighting to hold her head above water, she doubled up in a fetal pose. Quickly she passed her right elbow over her right knee, then pulled her right foot toward her and lifted the handcuff chain around her shoe.

Next, the left leg.

Same procedure, same result.

Abruptly her hands were in front of her. In startled wonder she raised her arms fully and touched her own face.

She'd gotten this far. At least she had a chance.

Water filled half the trunk now. The height of the compartment was only about twenty inches, leaving her less than a foot of clearance above the waterline.

She searched in the dark for the trunk latch, having no idea if it could be operated from inside. Her fingers read the grooves and contours and machine-stamped indentations on the lid as if they were inscriptions in Braille.

After several desperate seconds she found what had to be the latch, a recessed boltlike mechanism engaged by a metal claw. For the lid to open, the bolt and claw had to be separated. Her scrabbling fingers, numb with cold, slipped on the smooth metal parts, finding no purchase.

She couldn't do it. Couldn't open the lid from the inside.

But maybe she could smash the latch. With a blunt instrument.

She rolled onto her stomach. Folded back the floor mat to expose the rectangular cover of the spare-tire well. It was secured by a wing nut, the shape distinctive to her touch.

Her shaking hands, joined at the wrists, turned the nut counterclockwise till it spun free.

The air pocket was shrinking fast. Six inches, at

most, separated the waterline from the underside of the trunk lid. She had to tilt her head sideways to breathe without inhaling water.

It cost her valued seconds to wrest the cover off the tire well, then still more time to shove the unwieldy board into a corner, out of her way.

Come on, *come on.*

Beneath the spare tire her groping hands found the jack, fastened to the side of the well.

God, the water was getting really high. Four inches of clearance left.

Frantically she pried at the jack. Blocked by the tire, it refused to come loose. She couldn't get it out— damn, why couldn't anything be easy, even the simplest thing?

Wait.

Another tool, smaller and more accessible, lay beside the jack. She felt a hexagonal socket at one end.

The lug wrench.

Gripping the wrench, she guided it out of the tire well.

Two inches now. To breathe she turned on her back, her nose brushing the lid at its highest point. She swallowed a deep gulp of air, puffing up her cheeks to hold it in.

Then she submerged, hunting again for the latch.

The water was cold, the pressure like the gentle squeeze exerted on a swimmer at the bottom of a pool. Silt drifted everywhere. Her eyes closed instinctively in protection against the floating grit.

There. The latch. She'd found it.

The wrench lashed out, each impact clanking dully, the noises muted as if in a dream.

Five blows. Six.

The latch wouldn't yield, and her lungs were draining fast. Better get another breath while she could.

She arched her neck, not yet breaking the waterline, and cold metal kissed her mouth.

The air was gone, the trunk completely flooded.

Had to get the trunk open. Now, right *now*.

Savagely she pounded the latch, blows chiming in her ears, discordant music.

She wasn't going to make it. She was going to die in here, and sometime tomorrow her body would be found, stiff and frozen, the useless wrench still gripped in her two hands . . .

Something nicked her forehead—a sharp chunk of metal floating free—part of the latch, broken off.

The lid was ajar.

Done it. Thank God, she'd done it.

Out.

Wriggling, squirming, she emerged from the trunk.

Faint luminescence overhead, starlight on the surface of the lake. Nearer to her in the gloom, dark columnar shapes—the pilings of a dock or pier, rising into the light.

Needed air. God, she needed air, and the surface was still so far away.

Her pant leg snagged on a corner of the trunk lid. She kicked wildly until she pulled free. Then she was swimming clear of the car, legs bicycling as she arrowed her body upward.

Her unclipped hair coiled around her like tendrils of kelp, wrapping her face in wet strands. Through the waving net she caught a glimpse of the Caprice, abandoned and forlorn, its blue-and-white markings rendered a dull monochrome in the chancy light.

A moment later the dim ghostly shape was obscured by clouds of silt stirred up by her beating legs. She frog-kicked for the surface.

Her eyes bulged. Fire seared her chest. At any moment she would yield to instinct and take the fatal breath her body demanded.

Her lips parted . . .

And she burst through the roof of the lake, water shattering like glass, and drew air in a great shuddering whoop.

She'd made it. She was alive.

No medals for quitters. She wanted to shout the words. No medals—

Something plopped in the water a yard away, raising a splash.

She looked toward shore, and her exhilaration died.

Yards away, a dark-clad figure. Sentry on patrol. One of *them*.

It wasn't fair, it was too cruel, but she had no time to lodge her protest with the universe.

A second shot landed, closer than the first, and Trish dived back into the dark.

22

Cain was in a hurry, no time for diversions, but he'd enjoyed making the Kent girl cry.

Maybe he could have her do one more little thing for him.

"This is a nice necklace." He plucked a bauble from the table. "Same one you wore last Saturday night?"

She sniffed. "Yes."

"Put it on."

The heavy swallowing motion of her throat was good to see.

"Why?" she breathed.

"Because I said so."

"I . . . I don't . . ."

"Put it on."

With shaking hands she hooked the string of pearls around her slender neck.

"Sweet," Cain whispered, and both of them stiffened abruptly, catching the note of desire in his voice.

Quickly she took off the necklace and returned it to the pile.

Cain watched as she rummaged in the back of the safe for its last holdings. When he spoke again, his question and tone were safely neutral.

"How old are you, Ally?"

She removed a wad of travelers' checks. "Fifteen."

"Going into the ninth grade?"

"Tenth. I . . . I skipped ahead."

"Smart girl. I never made it past the ninth grade, myself. Kept getting busted—for stuff I didn't do."

This time she dared a glance in his direction, and with the glance an arched eyebrow. "Right."

And suddenly Cain knew he had to have her. It was the lifted brow that did it, and the reckless courage and adult sophistication it implied.

She was a child in some respects, a woman in others—baby fat and pert breasts, freckled nose and lipsticked mouth.

"Okay, you got me." He holstered his gun, leaving both hands free to use the handcuffs in his pocket. "Stuff I *did* do. I did all of it and lots more besides they never found out about."

"Big surprise." She started pulling leather concertina files from the safe's bottom shelf.

"Leave those. They probably *are* stock certificates."

"And if you can't steal it," she said with cold irony, "you don't want it."

"Stealing's not stealing if you don't get caught. Most times I don't. It's funny how much you can get away with, if you try. Like, say, if I touched you . . . *here.*" A gloved hand slipped under her scalloped neckline with the oily quickness of a snake and closed over the left cup of her bra. "You wouldn't tell, would you?"

No arched eyebrow this time, no sly remarks, only fear, whole and pure and beautiful to see. "Don't."

"No, you wouldn't tell." He massaged the bra cup gently. "Nobody would ever have to know. Your parents wouldn't even want to know. It would only hurt them to know."

"Don't. Please."

He rubbed harder. It was a strange kind of sexual contact, a glove against a bra, black leather against nylon lace. But he could feel the shape of her breast inside the cup, could picture it, white and firm, kneaded in his grasp.

Ally stared up at him, wide brown eyes shiny like pennies in the lamplight, freckles dusting her wet cheeks.

"You know you want it, Ally," he breathed.

"Leave me *alone!*"

She pulled away, the neckline tearing, a button popping free. Cain trapped her against a wall of bookshelves and pressed his body to hers.

Distantly he told himself that it was dangerous to go any further. This never had been part of the plan.

But hell, no harm in taking a little bonus.

The girl was ripe for deflowering. The job would take only a minute, and she would be grateful for the rest of her life.

"Please don't," she whispered over and over. "Please don't, please don't, please don't."

"Well, gosh." He used his best disappointed tone. "If that's the way you really feel . . ."

He moved back slightly. Ally had a moment to believe he was honestly releasing her—one last moment of naive innocence—and then he grabbed her arms, pinning them behind her with one hand, while with the other he reached for the hem of her dress.

"No!" She struggled, trying desperately to knee him, but unable to maneuver in such close quarters.

Cain laughed. "Hey, relax, freckle-face. I won't hurt you. I'm giving you something that feels good all over."

His hand slid between her squeezed thighs, ripped open her panties. She squirmed, arms jerking helplessly. He tugged down his sweat pants.

This would be easy. He wouldn't even need the handcuffs. He could bang her standing up, quick and dirty, her party dress hitched above her hips in a cheesecake pose.

"Here it comes, Ally." His phallus sprang erect. "Say hello to love."

She felt his hardness brush her thigh. With a scream of terror she twisted sideways, wrenching free, and her hands, quick as startled birds, flew at his eyes.

Instinctively Cain ducked, pulling away, and her clutching fingers hooked onto his ski mask.

The mask turned inside out and came loose, his face uncovered.

In the wash of light from the banker's lamp, he stared at her and she stared back, both of them frozen for some timeless moment.

Cain moved first. His arm swung up. *"Bitch."*

He smacked her.

Again.

Again.

She slumped against the shelves, her chin bearded in red, a bruise swelling the corner of her mouth.

Breathing hard, Cain got control of himself. His

erection was gone. He tucked himself in and pulled up his sweats. No loving tonight.

No loving for poor Ally—ever.

"You're in trouble now," he whispered as the girl's shoulders shook with silent sobs. "Oh, yes, pretty baby. You are in some world-class trouble now."

23

Blair Sharkey pulled a Tekna flashlight from his hip pocket and fanned its beam across the shallow waters of the lake.

He had to admit he'd thought it was a waste of time to patrol the shore. Cain wanted both the front and rear access points covered, sure, a standard precaution, but who the hell would be out here?

Well, someone was—and he knew who. That little rookie had gotten out of the trunk.

He couldn't begin to guess how she'd pulled off that stunt, but it didn't matter. As soon as she came up for air, he would wax her.

Blair was good with a gun, especially this laser-sighted Glock. Wouldn't have missed her the first two times, except he could hardly believe she was actually there. Surfacing in the starlight, she'd been a vision as unreal as a mermaid.

He wouldn't miss again.

"Come on up, Robinson," Blair whispered to the night. "Come up and die."

Trish hadn't had time for a deep breath before submerging. She couldn't stay under for long.

Pale light shifted on the water overhead, a flashlight beam restlessly skimming the surface.

She had survived one death trap only to blunder into another. Terror blended with furious, irrational indignation at a world that could toy with her so cruelly.

Roughly she pushed those distractions aside. She needed cover. Was there any place the beam couldn't touch?

The dock. Huddled alongside it, she would be screened from sight.

Staying well below the surface, she swam toward the nearest piling, her cuffed hands pawing water in a clumsy approximation of a butterfly stroke.

She didn't think he could see her. If she was wrong, she would find out when the next bullet stopped her heart.

A darting shadow.

Robinson. Swimming for the dock.

Blair lifted his gun—too late. The streak of motion had already passed behind the farthest pilings.

From the beach he had no decent angle of fire. He broke into a run, boots raising white geysers of sand.

Stealth was unnecessary. The cop was unarmed, defenseless.

For all practical purposes, she was dead already.

Mossy wood brushed Trish's hands. She gripped the piling and lifted her head to breathe, and then she heard it, felt it.

Rattle and shiver. Rapid footfalls on the planks.

He'd guessed her strategy. He was coming.

She kicked away from the piling, took refuge beneath the dock. The lake was shallower here, only six or seven feet deep. She waited, treading water, while green floating plants, some species of waterwort, swirled lazily around her.

The footsteps passed overhead, then stopped. The flashlight probed the water near the post where she had hidden moments earlier.

There was something unreal about all this. For most of her twenty-four years she'd led a monotonously ordinary life. Now here she was, handcuffed, bobbing in dark waters, while a man with a flashlight and a silenced pistol hunted her with the cold intent to kill.

He doesn't even *know* me, she thought, aware that there was no possible relevance to this fact, stupidly astonished by it nevertheless.

Blair was enjoying himself. There was an intense, almost sexual thrill in stalking human prey. It could be addictive.

He really should have radioed Cain by now. That was the drill: In case of trouble, get on channel three and report.

But Cain would send Tyler and Gage, and Blair didn't want their help. He wanted to bag Robinson himself.

It wouldn't be hard. She had to be hiding under the dock. Out of sight, but not for long.

He crossed to the ladder and descended, almost regretful the game would soon be up.

Black boots on aluminum rungs. Trish submerged. The flashlight searched for her. Even on the lake floor, her hands plowing the silty bottom, she wasn't deep enough to escape its reach.

But she didn't have to be. The thick scum of water-wort clogging the surface deflected the beam and kept her safe.

For the moment her adversary couldn't find her. But he must know she was here somewhere, and he would not stop looking until he made her dead.

To survive she had to think. Come on now, *think*.

She'd seen a pair of boats moored at the dock. If she could circle around the boats and surface behind one of them, screened from his view . . .

She moved forward along the lake floor, her lungs emptying, the need for air urgent once again.

Where was she?

Balanced on the bottom rung of the ladder, Blair peered below the dock at a green carpet of heart-shaped plants. Robinson was under there, he would bet on it, but where?

He waited another full minute, then reluctantly concluded that only a real mermaid could hold her breath this long. She must have given him the slip.

No choice now but to summon help. Together he and Tyler and Gage would flush her out of hiding.

Pocketing the flashlight, he took out his transceiver. His finger was poised over the push-to-talk button when he heard a soft splash.

It had come from behind the nearest sport boat.

Of course.

Trish couldn't help making noise when she surfaced alongside the fiberglass hull. Her craving for oxygen had reached the critical stage. Nothing mattered except air.

She gulped breath after breath, and then the boat lurched, someone hopping aboard.

Down.

Blair crossed the bow in one stride and peered over the port gunwale into the dark water.

Directly below him, a blur of silt and thrashing legs.

He fired twice. The Glock's sound suppressor was degrading with use; these shots were louder than the last.

The diver vanished under the boat. Had he nailed her? She'd been close, but he hadn't had time to aim. It was just point and shoot.

He watched hopefully for a cloud of blood.

Trish knew she'd been shot at, didn't think she'd been hit.

Still, the man knew where she was. He had the high ground. He could get her as soon as she emerged from beneath the boat.

What now, Trish? Think.

Think or die.

No blood in the water. Robinson had one of her nine lives left, it looked like.

But only one.

Blair pivoted in the bow, scanning the water on all sides. The boat was small, a Sea Rayder mini-jet, light-weight and barely bigger than a dinghy. He could cover every angle from this vantage point. She couldn't get away. She—

The boat listed with a sharp impact from below.

What the hell?

Another blow—starboard side—the boat rocking.

Trying to capsize him, the little *bitch*.

His radio dropped into the bow. He groped for a grab handle, missed it, and the boat lurched again.

Stumble. His knees banged the gunwale, momentum carrying him forward, and suddenly the world was spinning like a turntable as he was pitched headlong into the lake.

A fist of black water closed over him. For a split second he was disoriented, helpless.

But he'd grown up near water, been dunked plenty of times.

And he still had the Glock.

He whirled in a haze of his own air bubbles, scanning the dark for a target, and something flashed past his face.

A chain—handcuffs—she'd snagged him from behind, drawn the chain around his neck.

Although the surface was only inches above him, he couldn't raise his head, couldn't breathe.

The gun. Shoot her.

He raised his arm, elbow bent at an acute angle, the Glock pointing upside down over his shoulder, and risked a blind trigger pull.

Trish saw the gun come up, saw the silencer twist toward her.

She leaned hard to her left as the Glock bucked, bubbles hissing from the tube, a 9mm round blowing past her face like a torpedo.

Probably he couldn't shoot again. Probably the

water pressure would prevent the slide from cycling fully, and the gun would jam.

But she wasn't counting on it.

Knees wedged against the killer's back, she twisted her wrists, jerking the chain taut.

He fought her, thrashing savagely, a whipsawing marlin, and she hung on, her mouth squeezed shut against the urge to scream.

Her wrists were on fire, the cuffs biting deep. His larynx must have been crushed by now—God, he couldn't hold out much longer, just *couldn't*.

The gun swiveled directly at her face. He jerked the trigger. Nothing happened.

It *had* jammed, thank God.

An instant later air burst from his mouth in a silent shout, and he went limp.

The pistol dropped from his slack fingers. She pulled free, snatched it, then broke water, gasping.

Below her, the killer sank slowly into the silt, maybe unconscious, maybe dead.

Leave him there, a hard voice said in her mind.

But she couldn't. She needed the gear on his belt.

Anyway, that was the reason she gave herself as she crammed the Glock in the waistband of her pants and submerged.

She grabbed him by the neck of his nylon jacket. He was impossibly heavy, a hundred sixty pounds of inert mass.

It was a hard struggle to haul him to the surface, harder still to kick for the shore with her burden in tow.

The beach wasn't more than ten yards away, but her

vision was graying out, her heart skipping beats by the time she reached it.

Staggering, gasping, she dragged the man onto the sand and rolled him on his back.

Exhaustion dropped her to her knees. She leaned over him, staring into his face.

He was so young. A teenager. Seventeen? Not even.

With a shaking hand she felt his left carotid artery. Pulse faint but regular. Her ear to his lips, she heard no whisper of breath.

She'd been trained in CPR but had never expected to use it under circumstances like these. Part of her rebelled against the idea.

But she couldn't let him die. Though he would have killed her and laughed about it, he was a person, wasn't he? He mattered to somebody.

Pinching his nostrils, she tilted his head to face the sky. His airway should be open; still, he wouldn't breathe.

She pressed her mouth to his, blew air into his lungs. His chest lifted but didn't deflate. She fed him another breath, and this time his chest heaved as air hissed out of his mouth in a splutter of droplets.

He coughed, eyelids fluttering. Awake.

Intent on keeping him alive, she hadn't stopped to consider that he was still a threat.

She reached for the Glock, but before she could grab it, his right hand closed over the chain of her handcuffs and snapped both arms forward, holding them uselessly outstretched.

For a frozen moment he stared up at her. "You saved my life," he rasped in a voice like sandpaper.

Mutely she nodded.

He bared an evil smile. "Big mistake."

With his left hand he plucked the Glock from her waistband.

Nobody had ever taught her the proper defensive move for this situation. Instinct guided her as she ducked under the gun and thrust her upper body forward.

The crown of her head caught him hard on the chin. His jaws clacked. The Glock cast up a white puff of sand as it fell, and for the second time in five minutes, she felt him go limp.

Was he really out or just stunned? Get the gun, *get the gun.*

She scrabbled blindly for the pistol, recovered it, cycled the slide manually as she rolled on the sand, kicking clear of him in case he went for her with his knife or his fists.

When she looked up, she saw he hadn't moved. Unconscious—or faking?

Rainbows dazzled her, filling her field of vision, pulsing in sync with the ache in her head. She blinked the colors away and looked more closely at the young man in black.

Blood leaked from his mouth. His eyelids twitched. Out. Really out.

And she had the gun, and she was safe.

"Congratulations, Officer Robinson." Her sudden hoarse whisper was startling in the stillness. "You've just made your first arrest."

A laugh hiccuped out of her, and then she lowered her head and her stomach flipped and she was sick on the sand.

Death had been close, very close. She'd nearly

ended up like Wald. Nearly said goodbye to the world. Nearly.

Nausea subsided into shudders, racking her body like fever chills. Her teeth chattered, and her shoulders shook.

Trish sat on the beach and hugged herself as best she could, her chained wrists crossed over her heart.

24

"I say we break down the doors."

Philip Danforth dabbed his split lip with a mono-grammed handkerchief. A thread of light filtered through a hairline crack between the closet doors, striping his face. The reek of his sweat was acrid and close.

"That's absurd," Charles answered evenly.

"What's absurd about it? If we use our combined strength, we can blow them right off the hinges."

"Do you have any idea how much noise that would make?"

"To hell with the noise."

"Just wait a minute, Phil."

"Don't call me Phil."

"Philip. Sorry. Listen to me."

Charles was using his courtroom voice. He had found that juries were more readily persuaded by quiet self-assurance than by inflamed rhetoric. The jury in this case was a panel of two: Judy and Barbara. He would never get through to Philip, but one person alone couldn't smash open the closet.

"We can't just say to hell with the noise," Charles

went on in his reasonable way, wishing the close confines didn't require him to stand so close to Philip, nearly nose to nose. "Five armed men are out there."

"Woman." Barbara spoke as if every word were the first note of a scream. "One of them is a woman."

"All right." Charles showed no annoyance at the interruption. Never alienate the jury. "Four armed men and one armed woman. If we break out, they'll hear us and come running."

"For all we know," Philip snapped, spraying Charles with a mist of spittle, "they may have left the house by now."

"With Ally?" Barbara sat down suddenly on a wicker hamper. It creaked.

"Philip," Judy said in quiet reproach.

"Well, no." Philip softened. "Not with Ally. I just meant they could be gone."

"But they're not." Charles tapped an ear. "Listen."

From the living room came faint noises: shatter of glass or porcelain, thuds of overturned furniture.

"What are they doing?" Judy whispered.

Charles shrugged. "Wrecking the place, it sounds like."

The low groan came from Barbara.

Philip stared hard at the doors, as if willing them to open, then turned to Charles, about to embark on another line of argument. Before he could, a new sound froze him.

The quick tread of approaching footsteps.

"Maybe they've brought Ally." Barbara's whisper was as solemn as a prayer.

Rattle of a chain. Flood of light. The bifold doors opened to reveal two ski-masked figures, the gray-eyed man and his female companion, both with guns drawn.

The man spoke. "Mr. Kent, we need your help with the safe."

Charles blinked. "The safe?"

A gloved hand closed over his arm and yanked him forward.

"Where's my daughter?" Barbara screamed.

The closet doors slammed in her face.

Thrust into the brighter light and fresher air of the bedroom's glare, Charles was momentarily disoriented. He watched, dazed, as the two doorknobs were chained and padlocked.

Then the killers ushered him out of the room, down the hall.

He passed Ally's bedroom. Through the doorway he saw his daughter seated in her desk chair, wrists bound to the tubular armrest with torn bedding. Her eyes met his.

"Daddy . . ." She hadn't called him by that name in years.

The man behind him yanked the door shut. Charles whirled, an angry question riding on his lips, but it died when he looked into those cold gray eyes.

Out of the hallway. Crossing the threshold of the dining area.

Charles stopped short, staring.

He had expected some damage, but *this* . . .

The dining table had been upended and broken.

The chandelier cut loose to crash in pieces.

Every painting torn off the walls and savaged, the expensive frames splintered.

Love seat, twin sofas, matching armchairs—slashed, the leather upholstery curling in ribbons to expose gobs of foam stuffing.

In the dining area stood the man who had shot Officer Wald. His mask was off, his suntanned and stubbly face sweaty in the peculiar half-light of the one standing lamp still unbroken.

With robotic efficiency he was removing chinaware from a cabinet and smashing it on the floor. The dishes, priceless, had been in the Ashcroft family for generations.

"Good God," Charles breathed.

He turned again, intending to register a protest, and the gray-eyed man said, "In the den." To the woman: "Get back to work. This place still looks way too presentable."

Presentable, Charles thought numbly as he traversed the living room, shoes crunching glass from a ruined end table. What would it look like when they were done? The aftermath of a bomb blast?

Nearing the foyer, he noticed absently that the patrolwoman was gone.

Funny. He hadn't seen her in Ally's bedroom.

He entered the den. It was his personal retreat, a video screening room. From any of the four plush recliners facing the projection TV he could watch satellite programming or a laser disc. Or he could stack CDs in the sixty-disc player and surround him- self in music, his eyes blissfully closed.

No bliss tonight.

In the living room the vandalism continued, the noise redoubled now that the woman had joined in.

The den had not yet been trashed but soon would be. Already the safe had been violated, its contents heaped on the rosewood table near his favorite armchair.

The safe . . .

Ally must have revealed the combination. So why was he here?

He turned as the door of the den clicked shut. The gray-eyed man stood facing him across five yards of deep pile carpet under the slow revolutions of a ceiling fan. He holstered his gun, then casually stripped off his mask.

"Hello, Mr. Kent."

After all this, Charles was hardly in the mood for pleasantries. "Cain—what the *hell*?"

"Relax." Cain crossed to the bar and got out a bottle of brandy. "Have a drink . . . on the house."

"I can't go back in there with liquor on my breath."

"You can rinse out your mouth later." A loop of amber gurgled from the spout. "Take a drink. You'll need it."

"Need it? Why? What's going on? Why'd you have to get me away from the others?"

"There's been a complication." Cain handed him the snifter. "Cheers."

Charles hesitated, then decided he really did need the drink. Seeing Wald's face shot off—tasting the sprinkle of blood—

Abruptly his knees threatened to unlock. He sank into the nearest chair and tipped the snifter to his lips.

A slow burn trickled down his throat. He let his head fall back.

"Complication," he whispered.

"Yeah."

"Is it the patrolwoman?"

"She's not a problem."

"Where is she, anyway?"

"The lake."

It took a moment for the words to register. Then Charles snapped forward. "Dead?"

"Very."

"Damn it." Brandy sloshed in the pearl-shaped glass. "That was totally unnecessary."

"I decide what's necessary, Mr. Kent." Cain said it with a peculiar emphasis.

"The woman was unconscious, for God's sake. She was handcuffed and disarmed, no threat whatsoever."

"She was a cop. I hate cops."

Charles looked away, not wanting to see Cain, not wanting even to be here.

"Bad enough with just one," he breathed, "but . . . two of them." He drained the snifter. "You know what they do to cop killers?"

"One cop or two—it's death row either way." Cain smiled. "Anyway, you're the one who gave the signal."

The signal. Four words: *Take care of it.*

Out of earshot of the others, Cain had told him to say those words if somehow the patrol officers were surreptitiously alerted to what was going on. Charles had worked the signal into his conversation as the cops headed for the foyer, raising his voice to be sure Cain's thugs in the closet could hear.

So yes, he'd known the ambush would take place. But he hadn't thought either of the officers would be killed.

Had he?

He wasn't sure. He didn't know what he'd expected.

Anyway, it was too late now.

His hand shook as he offered Cain the empty glass. "More."

"That was enough."

"I've been on seltzer water all night, passing it off as vodka and soda. You're the one who wanted me to start drinking for real."

"And now I want you to stop."

The snifter made a dull thump as Charles set it down on the rosewood table.

"If it's not the patrolwoman," he whispered, "then what? You don't seem to be having any trouble trashing my house. And you got the safe open."

"Eventually. Your daughter was less than cooperative."

"You didn't hurt her?"

"Just had to raise my voice a little."

"You should have used me."

"Maybe you're right."

Charles was surprised to hear Cain say that. They had argued the point at length.

Both had agreed that every detail of the break-in had to be carried out as if Cain had no inside information. For that reason Charles had not supplied Cain with house keys or told him the alarm-system access code. Instead Cain had pirated the code with a digital decrypter, which he'd conveniently left in place to be discovered by the police.

Cain hadn't been given the combination of the safe either. For realism he would obtain it openly from some member of the Kent household, who would later include that detail in an official statement.

Charles had thought he should be selected. Cain had held out for Ally, saying that an honest witness would provide more persuasive testimony. As a lawyer, Charles knew this to be true and finally had yielded.

Barbara, of course, had never been an option. She would not be making any statements to anybody after tonight.

"If Ally did what you wanted," Charles said slowly, "what the hell's the problem? Why's she in her bedroom and not in the closet with the rest of us?"

"She hasn't been harmed."

"Barbara doesn't know that. She's practically hysterical. The agreement was that after Ally gave you the combination, you'd have her join us. Then you'd take Barbara and Judy—"

"I'm familiar with our agreement."

"So what's the delay? You can't keep us in there all night. Danforth's already talking about breaking out. The guy's a hothead, and he's had too much to drink. Your people shouldn't have pushed him around; it got him worked up. And killing that cop—"

"Forget the goddamned cops."

Suddenly Cain was leaning over the armchair. Charles stared into his eyes and saw hardness and madness there.

"We got ourselves a situation, Mr. Kent. Involving your precious daughter."

Charles coughed, a light, almost dainty sound. "What . . . what about her?"

"She saw my face."

25

Sixteen years had passed since Trish earned a Girl Scout Brownie Try-It patch by tying square knots, but there were some skills a person never forgot.

With her knife she cut a coil of nylon dock line into shorter segments. She bound her arrestee's hands and feet, trussing him like a turkey, then gagged him with the ski mask from his pants pocket.

Her hands were the only part of her that still trembled, rattling the links of the handcuff chain. The nausea and the worst of the shaking had passed quickly enough, leaving her numb and drained.

It seemed difficult to concentrate, to get her mind in gear. What was she supposed to do next? No situation remotely like this had been covered at the academy.

Well, come on, it wasn't rocket science. She had to get help. That was the logical next step. Get help.

But how?

Wald had said the Kent house was the only residence on the lake. The lightless sweep of hillsides around her seemed to confirm it.

She remembered passing trailers and mobile homes on the drive up, but the nearest ones were three or four miles away. Even to reach the road she would have to cut through the woods, impenetrable to someone who didn't know the trails, or through the Kent property, fenced and gated and patrolled.

Could she call for help somehow? Her radio had been confiscated, and the killer's was gone. Lost in the lake, presumably.

She could check out the two sport boats. There might be a portable hailer aboard.

Before looking, she emptied the young man's pockets, hopeful of finding a handcuff key.

There was none. All he had was a six-inch flashlight and a pair of lightweight, folded binoculars, remarkably compact. The flash was water resistant; she rotated the bezel switch, and a bright beam of light appeared.

She scanned his gun belt. No key holder. No cuff case.

For the moment she was stuck with the handcuffs. Grin and bear it. At least she was alive.

Pocketing the flash, she crossed the dock to the ladder and climbed into the nearest boat, the one she'd tipped from below.

It was a mini-jet, the fiberglass hull emblazoned *Sea Rayder*. The craft wasn't large, perhaps fourteen feet long, and it listed noticeably as she stepped aboard.

There was no radio installed in the cockpit console. Without an ignition key she couldn't have used a built-in unit anyway. She checked the stowage compartments but didn't find a hailer.

But in the bow she discovered the killer's walkie-talkie, dropped near a grab handle, unbroken and still dry.

Eagerly she retrieved the radio, then studied it in the starlight.

Instant disappointment. Unlike police-issue transceivers, this unit was strictly short range, capable of operating only in the simplex mode. Its signal would never get past the encircling hillsides.

Even so, she clipped the walkie-talkie to her waistband, the volume dialed low. If any transmissions were sent out over the preset frequency on channel three, she could eavesdrop.

The second boat, moored astern, was something called a Celebrity FireStar, fifteen feet long. Again, no radio gear, but she did find a waterproof package of hiking supplies: first-aid kit, compass, granola bars, matches, and a map of the lake.

In the first-aid kit, a bottle of Advil caplets. She dry-swallowed a handful. A serious headache was coming on.

Then she unfolded the laminated map and studied it in the flashlight's glow.

The map showed the Kent estate at the lake's south end, dense woods along most of the remaining perimeter. At the north shore, approximately four miles away, was a small park with a picnic area.

According to a notation on the map, the park closed at dusk and offered only minimal facilities, indicated by simple icons.

Boat launch.

Snack shop.

Rest rooms.

Pay phones.

It took a moment for the significance of the last item to register.

Phones.

If she could get there . . .

Walking would take too long; the shoreline of the many-fingered lake stretched for miles. One of the boats could make the trip in a few minutes, but each required an ignition key.

Too bad the Brownies hadn't offered a Try-It patch for hot-wiring an engine. In the movies, the procedure always looked easy, but she had not the faintest idea how to go about it in real life.

Of course, there had to be keys to these boats somewhere.

In the Kents' house, no doubt.

All she had to do was sneak inside and . . .

Inside?

Crazy. Even armed, she would be taking a suicidal risk.

She shook her head, suddenly overcome by fatigue. Nothing in her training, nothing in her life, had prepared her for what she'd been through tonight.

It was a miracle she'd survived this long. To press her luck was more than insane. It was ungrateful.

The smart thing, the sensible thing, was to melt into the woods and wait there until her unit's absence was noted and backup was sent.

But the woman with the lisp had done an awfully credible job of imitating her voice. She could fool either of the night dispatchers, Lou or Thelma, at least for a while.

How long would it take the killers to finish their work? Even now they might be preparing to leave— and before going, perhaps they would execute the hostages.

The Danforths, Mr. and Mrs. Kent . . . and Ally.

Trish thought of the girl's eyes, wide and frightened and red with tears.

Marta's eyes.

No. Wrong.

Marta was dead, and Ally was a different person entirely, and there was nothing Trish could do for her, no further action she could take.

She was wet and cold, shivering in the night breeze, hands manacled, knuckles and wrists badly abraded. Her head ached, her limbs were tender with bruises, her every muscle was sore with strain.

No medals for quitters.

Cut it out. That was ridiculous. Nobody—not even her Girl Scout leader, Mrs. Wilkes—absolutely *nobody* could blame her for quitting now.

Nobody except herself.

"Oh, hell," she murmured, disgust and self-aware amusement in her voice.

She knew what she had to do, and she would do it. Because she was a cop—a patrol officer, as she'd told the gray-eyed man with her chin lifted. She had taken an oath to protect and serve. Now it was crunch time, when those words meant something, or ought to.

Or maybe she just wanted to prove she wasn't a damn Mouseketeer.

It seemed as good a reason as any for getting herself killed.

If she was going to do this, really do it, then she needed weapons, tools, any advantage she could get. She returned to the beach. Kneeling, she inspected her captive's gear more closely.

His belt carried a sheathed knife—full-tanged, the

blade wickedly honed—and a holster for the pistol and a cartridge case for spare magazines.

She pulled the gun from her waistband. A Glock 17, made in Austria of polymer and steel, lightweight and durable.

After five shots, the sound suppressor was so badly degraded as to be useless. She unscrewed and discarded it, then removed a round from the chamber.

The bullet's distinctive crushed-in nose identified it as a Winchester Black Talon, one of the more lethal 9mm Parabellum rounds. As it entered the body, metallic barbs folded back in a six-rayed starfish shape, expanding the diameter of the wound channel.

She had read what Black Talons could do to gelatin targets that had the approximate consistency of the human torso. Her abdomen clenched, and for a moment her resolve wavered.

She thought of Wald's face, one eye staring, blood everywhere . . .

Don't.

What happened to Wald was irrelevant. She was alive and she had a job to do, so she had better get on with it.

She removed the magazine, then assumed the Weaver stance and dry-fired the Glock. The pull was light, the trigger breaking at five pounds.

She tested the high-tech sighting system. Water hadn't damaged it; the wiring was all internal, running apparently through the trigger guard into the grip, then to a battery behind the magazine well, where the Glock's butt flared.

More orange than red, the laser was the so-called daylight type, brighter than older varieties with longer wavelengths. The beam covered not less than two hundred yards.

Quickly she inspected the rest of the killer's ensemble. Black SWAT boots, heavy and padded, with steel shanks and thick rubber soles. Sweat pants and matching jacket of black nylon. Skin-tight leather gloves. A digital wristwatch, waterproof like the flashlight.

Every item was costly and carefully chosen. These people weren't amateurs. But she'd already known that.

She unhooked the man's belt and strapped it on, a difficult procedure with her hands cuffed. From the cartridge case she removed a spare magazine and heeled it into the Glock, then chambered the loose round to give herself an extra shot. The partially emptied mag went in the case alongside the one remaining spare.

She holstered the gun, then pocketed the compass. Tried to fasten the watch to her wrist, but the handcuffs rendered the small task prohibitively difficult. The watch went in a pocket also.

Granola? High in carbohydrates. She forced herself to swallow one of the bars in three gooey chews. Though her stomach remained uneasy, she needed to replace the food she'd lost.

The killer, now stripped of his gear, was still breathing, still out cold, still tied securely. She would have to leave him. She hoped he didn't choke on the gag.

Enough of this. Time was wasting.

Trish took a deep breath and decided she was ready.

Tire marks in the sand led to a wide, paved path sloping upward in a gentle grade. The house loomed above her, squares of lighted windows glowing brighter than the stars.

Such an isolated place. The end of the world, Pete Wald had called it.

As she climbed the path, a childhood memory drifted back to her—an abandoned farm, a field of weeds, an empty house with boarded windows and padlocked doors and a dry well near the back porch. Another lonely place, a place where you could cry out for help and no one would hear.

A place of death.

Trish stared up at the Kent estate and wondered if her body would be found on its grounds, blue eyes staring, a roach crawling slowly, slowly over one glazed eyeball.

After all this, she still might not survive this night. Still might end up like Marta, sprawled in the weeds.

She had turned twenty-four less than two months ago. Wald had treated her like a child. Maybe he'd been right.

But she was growing up fast.

26

Charles sat very still, absorbing the news with something like indifference, all emotional reaction on hold.

"Saw your face," he echoed blankly.

"Yes, Mr. Kent." Charles had always liked hearing his own name, but not the way Cain said it, as if a Kent were some species of flatworm. "My handsome face."

Charles felt his mouth twitch in imitation of a smile. That was a little joke Cain had just told. Not a very funny joke, but then neither of them was laughing.

Cain might have been handsome once, with his arresting gray eyes and wolfish smile, his square chin and brush-cut blond hair—until the knife had done its work. Charles had never asked about the details, but the essence of the story was written in the jagged diagonal scar that ran from Cain's right temple to the left corner of his mouth like a badly knitted seam.

And Ally had seen that face, that scar.

"How?" Charles whispered. "How did she . . . see you?"

"That doesn't matter now."

It was not like Cain to be evasive.

Charles leaned forward slowly. "What did you do to her?"

"I didn't hurt her."

"Did you . . . did you try. . . ?"

"She would have been better off," Cain said without expression, "if she'd let me."

Delayed emotion finally kicked in. A spasm of anger propelled Charles half out of his chair, hands bunched into fists.

Perhaps the fact that Cain did not move, did not flinch or frown, did not even do him the small courtesy of making some conciliatory gesture or remark—perhaps that was the reason he hesitated, then sank back down, palms flat against his thighs.

When he spoke again, his voice was toneless and dull. "She can identify you."

"Yes."

"She'll be interviewed by a police artist. There'll be a sketch . . ."

"They won't need a sketch." Cain paced, big arms swinging. Charles had seen those arms uncovered—hairy, prison-buffed, laced with popped veins. "Just a description."

He was right. The local police had modem access to data bases of known felons in several counties. A keyword search would cull the names and mug shots of all facially scarred white males of the appropriate age.

Cain would be on that list.

"They'll I.D. me in a half hour," Cain said as if tracking his thoughts. "Then they'll look into my past. And find *you*."

"Bakersfield," Charles whispered.

"You."

Two years ago Charles had read a brief write-up in the *Santa Barbara News-Press* on a brutal beating in Bakersfield, a matter of local interest only because the victim was a Santa Barbara man on a business trip.

The man had stumbled on a thief breaking into his rented Dodge in a parking garage, and had tried to be a hero. When paramedics reached him, he was nearly comatose from blood loss. His assailant most likely had left him for dead.

But he recovered, and having seen his assailant's face—his scarred face—he identified a known felon named Cain.

Even then Charles had begun to fantasize about tonight's operation. From his rap sheet Cain had sounded like precisely the sort of man he would need. And so Charles offered to relieve the overworked public defender of the case.

Barbara and Ally, passing the summer at a seaside retreat in Majorca, never knew about the week Charles spent in Bakersfield, holed up in a cheap motel where he wouldn't be recognized, breathing smog and defending Cain.

Cain was guilty, of course, but Charles had no qualms about that. Nearly all the hotshot drunk-driving movie executives and wife-beating record producers he defended were guilty too. His challenge was to persuade the jury that Cain had been wrongly identified.

The scar was the only detail the battered victim recalled. In a day and a half of cross-examination Charles got the poor bandaged son of a bitch to admit that the scar might have run from right to left or from left to right, might have ended at the assailant's mouth or continued down his chin, might have been straight or curved. The garage lighting had been poor, the encounter brief and violent, and the victim's concussion might have altered his memory.

On the stand, Cain swore he'd gone straight. He'd been in Indio that night, two hundred fifty miles southeast of Bakersfield. A disinterested witness, a girlishly lisping young lady named Lilith, confirmed his alibi.

The jury set Cain free. Justice, American style.

Charles asked nothing for his services, merely requested that Cain keep in touch. If he could mail a card to a post office box in Ventura now and then, updating the phone number where he could be reached, Charles might make it worth his while someday.

Someday had arrived. And now everything was going wrong, spiraling out of control.

The cops would look into Cain's past and learn that his attorney in the battery case had been Charles Kent. Charles could say it must be a coincidence or some sort of twisted revenge on Cain's part, but the police wouldn't buy it. Coincidences of that kind didn't happen.

Anyway, why would Cain want revenge against a man who'd obtained his acquittal? Why had Charles gone all the way to Bakersfield to take a pro bono case? Why had he stayed in an obscure motel instead of his customary lavish accommodations? Why hadn't he deducted his traveling expenses as a charitable contribution on his 1040 form?

And when investigators looked into his bank accounts, when they discovered the recent liquidation of a $100,000 certificate of deposit six months before maturity—when they learned of an account in Cain's name in Carlsbad, New Mexico, which had been credited with a matching deposit the next day—then they would have more than questions for him.

They would have handcuffs.

Two dead cops. Automatic death penalty.

It was unfair. He hadn't pulled the trigger, had never wanted them to die. Even so, he was an accomplice, and when Cain and his crew of thugs went down, Charles would go too.

"What are we going to do?" he whispered. "There's no way out."

"Sure there is." The cool authority of Cain's tone prompted Charles to lift his head. "Your daughter is the problem. If she doesn't talk, we're in the clear."

Charles didn't understand. Cain was speaking nonsense.

Of course Ally would talk. Why wouldn't she talk?

Unless . . .

It struck him like a blow. He sank deeper into the chair, overstuffed cushions swallowing him. The ceiling fan spun slowly, and the den spun with it in dizzy circles.

"My God," he croaked.

"She has to die, Mr. Kent."

It was obvious, of course. He should have seen it instantly. There was a harsh, brutal logic to the idea, a mathematical inevitability.

"No," he said in a quiet voice.

"I understand." Cain spoke almost kindly, as if he were Charles's old friend and not a hired assassin.

"It's one thing to set up your rich bitch of a wife . . . and something else to ice your own kid."

"Something else. Yes."

And it was. Killing Barbara was ugly and coarse and unpleasant, but not unthinkable. He had, in fact, contemplated the possibility for years, though he might never have acted had their marriage not deteriorated to the point where she was threatening divorce.

If she left him, she would take Ally with her—and, no less important, the Ashcroft fortune, twenty-five million dollars in real estate, securities, and assorted liquid assets, not to mention miscellaneous baubles of the sort littering the rosewood table.

He would be left with visitation rights and the earnings from his law practice, sizable earnings but trivial in comparison with what he would lose.

There was another way to end their marriage. At the wedding ceremony they had vowed, "Till death do us part."

Should Barbara die under any remotely suspicious circumstances, her husband would be the obvious suspect. But suppose one evening a gang of armed men broke into the estate and took the Kents and their dinner guests hostage. Suppose the house was trashed, the prisoners terrorized. Suppose the night of terror climaxed in Barbara's attempted rape—and when she resisted, she paid with her life.

Even in the unlikely event that the police became suspicious, they could prove nothing.

To protect Ally, Charles had wanted her out of the house for the evening. Lately, he'd argued to Barbara, their daughter had been too moody, too unpredictable. And there had been that incident at the Carltons' Christmas party, when she had yelled and made a scene.

But Barbara, in misguided loyalty to her daughter, had insisted on having her present. And now Ally had seen Cain's face, and she would have to be . . .

His mind censored the completion of that thought.

Head lolling, he stared at the floor. A black duffel bag lay alongside the chair, the flaps unzipped. Amid the confusion of gear inside, there was one recognizable object: the handle of a gun. One of those Austrian pistols Cain and his crew were toting. Glocks. This must be a spare.

A gun like that would end his daughter's life as soon as he gave the word.

Would Cain put it in her mouth? That was how he'd promised to do Barbara.

He remembered the big man talking, laughing, as they sat together in Charles's BMW, parked at the Oxnard marina after dark.

Your wife's gonna suck my pistol, Mr. Kent, he'd said with a crooked smile. *Bet I can get off just watching her. And when I come—she goes.*

Yes, Barbara could die that way. But not Ally. Not Ally.

"Not Ally," he said aloud. "Not her. It's . . . it's out of the question. I refuse to permit it."

"Permit?" Cain laughed. "I don't need your permission."

"You work for me."

"But I won't die for you. I'm going to do this. I only wanted to get things straight between us so there wouldn't be any misunderstanding later, when the rest of the money comes due."

The rest of the money. Five million dollars to be parceled out to Cain and his associates over the next five years.

"You think I'll *pay* you," Charles asked incredulously, "for murdering my daughter?"

"You'll pay." And suddenly Cain closed in fast and gripped Charles by the shoulders and shoved him hard against the headrest. "Or I'll come after you next."

The grip of his gloved hands tightened, and Charles felt the raw power of this man's fingers, fingers that could close over his throat in an instant and crush his windpipe like a paper straw.

A wild fantasy bloomed in his thoughts. Wait for Cain to release him, then snatch the Glock out of the duffel and shoot him, yes, just *shoot* the sociopathic son of a bitch.

But if he did, Cain's accomplices in the next room would kill him for it.

Anyway, he couldn't murder anybody. That is, not with his own hands. He could order it done, he could pay for it, but to do it himself . . . to do it personally . . . physically . . .

He groped for the delicate distinction that eluded him.

"You'll pay," Cain said again, a feral edge to his voice, and Charles understood that he was in the presence of a man who never made fine distinctions of conscience, a man who was more than his match in any violent contest.

That man was his contractual agent in name only.

Tonight, in every way that mattered, it was Cain who was in charge.

"Well, Mr. Kent?"

Beaten, Charles nodded, retaining just enough dignity to do it slowly. "I'll pay."

"And Ally will die."

He couldn't answer that.

"I want to hear you say it. I want us to have a verbal agreement. It's as good as a written contract in this kind of deal."

"I . . . I can't . . ."

"You can." Cain shook him roughly. "Face reality. You're not backing out now. You're in for the duration. So here's the new plan: I pop your wife *and* your kid. Two for the price of one. What do you care? You'll be dirty rich. You can buy yourself a brand-new baby girl to bounce on your goddamned knee."

The words were too cruel, there couldn't be this much malice in the world, and Charles couldn't take it anymore, couldn't endure the flood of memories the words released—his newborn daughter wailing in the doctor's hands, a caul pasted to her red face—seven years old and flying higher, still higher, on the swing that once stood out back—thirteen and delivering the valedictory address at her grammar school graduation, so proud in her cap and gown.

Replace her? A new daughter? He couldn't do it, couldn't stand it, and most of all he couldn't stand knowing that he would let it happen, because he had no choice, and because he was afraid, deathly afraid of this man Cain, and afraid of himself for unleashing Cain on his family—stupid, so *stupid*—the money didn't matter now, nothing mattered except Ally, and it was too late for her.

Shaking, Charles clutched his head in both hands and wept.

27

Crouching under the white branches of a eucalyptus tree just inside the rear gate, Trish surveyed the yard.

Getting in had been no problem. The gate had been left open, presumably so the man at the dock could reenter when called.

She doubted anyone was on patrol at the back of the house—the dock sentry would be expected to block access from the rear—but she was taking no chances. It was her modest ambition to still have a heartbeat in the morning.

The backyard was large, perhaps half an acre, but its layout was simple enough.

The paved path from the gate ran between the house's west wall and the detached garage. East of the path lay a stretch of open lawn, then a gazebo. Beside the gazebo was a garden; beyond that, a swimming pool, Jacuzzi, and cabana.

No guards were in sight. Slowly she stood.

Mounted on a post next to the eucalyptus was a security system controller. She spared a moment to examine it. If she could rearm the system with the rear gate open, the alarm would be triggered and help would come.

No good. Evidently the operator had to punch in a numeric code, similar to the personal identification number used when interfacing with automatic tellers. She didn't know the code.

Was there a panic switch? Some systems offered a single button that could be depressed to trip the alarm. Not this one, though. It might be possible to activate the panic feature by typing in some special code or symbol, but she had no idea which keys to press, and she couldn't stand here all night.

Okay, back to Plan A. She was thinking anyway. She was full of bright ideas.

Cautiously she moved forward, the Glock gripped in both hands, her arms shoulder high and horizontally extended in the pose of a tennis player at the net. Her bare forearms glistened, radial flexors standing out like taut ropes. Between her wrists the handcuff chain rattled softly.

The gazebo was her immediate destination. But reaching it would be dangerous.

She would have to cross twenty-five feet of open lawn, and although the yard was dark, she couldn't know if someone was watching from a window.

Flashback: glow of a red-orange diode, a laser beam stamping a bull's-eye on her forehead. Flashback: a bullet blowing past her face underwater.

Mustn't think about that. Mustn't think about anything.

Like those stupid ads said: Just do it.

Fast.

She darted across the treeless ground. Behind the gazebo she slid to her knees, panting.

No shots fired. At least she didn't think there had

been. Those guns were silenced, though. And she'd heard you couldn't always tell if you'd been shot.

She patted her legs, her torso, looking for holes. None.

Okay. Okay.

Her stomach rolled. That granola bar hadn't settled too well. Briefly she worried that she would be sick again.

No, ridiculous, she was fine, and every second she spent inside the Kent compound increased her odds of being seen, so come on, hurry up, get it done.

With shaking hands she put down the Glock, then unfolded the binoculars from her pocket. Warily she lifted her head over the gazebo's low wall and scoped out the house.

Lights burned in three rear windows. One pair, in the east wing, framed what looked like a bedroom.

Ally was in there. Through the binoculars Trish could see her, squirming in a chair. Tied up—and alone.

Strange that the girl had been separated from the others. Disturbing, too, as if the killers had special plans for her.

The rear entrance had been left open, the doorway a rectangle of darkness.

She focused on the remaining lighted window, closest to her. The kitchen. Barbara Kent's vantage point when she'd glimpsed a prowler by the gazebo.

Now Trish was the prowler. Peculiar thought.

The kitchen appeared empty. Only a small portion of the room was visible: the corner of a refrigerator . . . part of a cabinet . . . a wall-mounted telephone . . .

a laminated noteboard littered with partly erased messages.

Below the noteboard, keys hung on a row of pegs.

The kitchen, then, was her objective. One of those key sets would surely include keys to the boats. If she—

Behind her, a rustle of bushes.

She whirled, dropping the binoculars, grabbing the gun.

Darkness. No movement.

But she'd heard *something*.

One of them? Hiding? Drawing a bead on her?

There.

Not a bad guy, not death in a black jump suit. Only a rabbit, small and brown, frozen in profile ten feet away, observing her with one unblinking eye.

She lowered the Glock. The slight movement was enough to send the rabbit scurrying into shadows.

Catching her breath, fighting to control her racing heart, she stared after the rabbit. Such a little animal, so vulnerable, surviving only by constant watchfulness born of constant fear.

Tonight she knew the same vigilance, the same terror.

She knew how it was to be hunted.

28

Ally was afraid.

She stared at herself in the mirrored doors of her bedroom closet—dress torn, body twisted at an unnatural angle in the tubular desk chair, wrists lashed to the padded armrest with strips of bedding.

The room felt hot and stuffy. Stagnant air clogged her lungs like paste.

Having the windows open didn't help. It only reminded her of the man who'd watched her through the backyard fence on those other nights.

Watched with binoculars as she stood naked, feeling the night air on her breasts. Watched as she emerged, towelless and dripping, from the shower in the adjacent bath. Watched, perhaps, as she lay in the canopy bed and touched herself, legs twisting languorously, the sheets damp with sweat.

Cain might have seen all that.

She knew his name now, his name and his face, along with the names and faces of two associates of his. That knowledge, more than anything else, was what made her so very afraid.

They had hidden nothing from her . . . as if it no longer mattered what she saw or heard.

Cain hadn't even bothered putting on his mask again after the attack. She'd been left weeping in a corner as he stepped to the doorway of the den.

"Lilith, get in here."

The soft crackle of the police radio had preceded her entrance. Ally had found it somehow obscene to see Officer Robinson's walkie-talkie clipped to this woman's belt.

Lilith had worn no mask either. She was short and frizzy-haired, pretty except for her eyes—small, glittery eyes that liked pain.

"You heard what happened?" Cain asked.

"I heard."

"I think young Miss Kent needs to go to her room."

Lilith studied her with a stalking cat's feral gaze. "Why not take care of things right now?"

"I need to make it square with the management."

"After you do—"

"I'll do the honors." His gloved hand brushed the gun at his hip.

She pouted. "You never let me have any fun."

Ally had understood at least part of what she heard but somehow couldn't make the implication real. She had offered no resistance as Cain hustled her out of the den.

They had been entering the east wing when another man, unmasked also, appeared out of the rear hall. Lanky and sun-blasted, he could have been a movie cowboy if not for his blond ponytail and storm trooper costume. Ally recognized him as the one who'd carried Officer Robinson out of the house.

"Done?" Cain asked with a smile.

MORTAL PURSUIT

The cowboy nodded. "Done." His squinty eyes narrowed. "What've we got here?"

"Minor problem," Cain said, handing Ally over to him. "You and Lilith handle it. I'll get started trashing this place."

She had been escorted into her bedroom. From the front of the house came noises of breaking glass, as distant and unreal as the soundtrack of a movie.

Briskly Lilith unmade the bed and tore a floral-patterned sheet to ribbons. Although Ally understood that the strips would be used to tie her up, still she raised no protest. She was numb with shock and fear.

Only when the cowboy lashed her wrists behind her had she finally reacted—kicking, squirming, mewling like a hurt animal.

Lilith had subdued her with a slap that brought fresh blood to her mouth.

"Stupid little slut," she lisped. "You should've let him do it. He wasn't gonna off you. He just wanted to put in his dipstick, check the oil."

"Check the oil," the cowboy said. "I like that."

"You can look under my hood anytime, Tyler."

"Cain might revoke my license if I did."

Cain. That had been the first time Ally heard the name. Instantly she knew who was meant. The scarred man. And the cowboy was Tyler.

She had registered the names with a sick feeling of dread, while desperately searching Lilith's face for some shadow of compassion.

"The thing is," she had whispered, shamed by the tremor in her voice, "I've never . . . you know."

Lilith gave her a closer look. "You a virgin?"

163

Was there empathy in the question? "I'm fifteen," Ally said, thinking perhaps a connection had been made.

"Fifteen," Lilith echoed. "That's only two years younger than me." Her face turned hard, any illusion of tenderness instantly erased. "So what's your problem, baby? You frigid or something?"

Ally looked away, her last hope crushed. "I'm just not ready," she murmured.

Lilith mimicked her with cutting accuracy. "I'm just not ready."

Tyler produced a heartless chuckle as he knotted the binding.

"Cain had me when I was thirteen," Lilith added. "Practically busted me open, he was so frigging big. Hurt like hell." A delicious shiver racked her. "Sister, you don't know what you missed out on."

Tyler had pushed her into a chair and tied her wrists to the armrest, winding additional strips around the vertical arm support.

"What are you going to do to me?" Ally had asked desolately as the two of them departed.

Tyler had paused in the doorway, a wide grin cracking his face. "Let's just say this ain't exactly ladies' night."

Then he and Lilith had strolled down the hall, toward the sound of wreckage in the living room. Not long afterward her father had been marched past, the door pulled shut before she could do no more than call out to him.

She couldn't guess what they wanted from her dad. But their intentions toward her she understood fully.

She was to be killed. It was the only explanation for

why Tyler and Lilith hadn't worn masks, why they'd spoken so freely. To them she was dead already.

Staring at the closed door, waiting for Cain's heavy footsteps, Ally thought about her future, the future she wasn't going to have.

It had seemed so clear and tangible, more real than everyday life. Three more years, and she would be in college—someplace far away, maybe New England— far from the brooding tension and explosive outbursts of the Kent household.

Things would make sense in college. She'd been quietly certain of it. Nothing made sense here, not anymore. Her mom would be smiling one minute, in tears the next. And through her tears she would insist everything was fine, while her dad's mouth worked soundlessly and his left eyelid twitched.

The hostility between them, so chronic yet for the most part so carefully suppressed, was more unsettling than violent fights would have been. She had often wished they could just get it out in the open, *talk* to each other, instead of simmering in this hothouse of mistrust and hate.

It got to her sometimes. Like at the Carltons' Christmas party, when her folks kept needling each other with sharp, hurtful barbs, smiling sarcasm, cutting wit, until finally she couldn't take it any longer and she yelled at them to stop it, just stop it, stop it, *stop it*, and of course the party had frozen, everybody staring, her parents mortified, and the long, silent ride home—God, what a joy *that* had been. . . .

Oh, yes, it was great fun growing up rich and spoiled in the Kent household.

College, though, would be her sanctuary. She

would study anthropology, her chosen field. Hearing of her ambition, people always assumed she hoped to become the next Margaret Mead. Ally thought Mead had been a sentimental fraud. She had presented a falsely romanticized picture of the Samoans, and nobody had corrected her until a graduate student named Derek Freeman had dared to tell the story straight.

Derek Freeman was the sort of anthropologist Ally wanted to be. No lies for her, no cover-ups, no smiling through tears.

She would do field work, teach, write books, make documentary films, run a museum. Okay, realistically she might not be able to do all of that, but pieces of it were possible.

Or had been. Now nothing was possible, and her future had turned out to be only another lie.

For some reason she thought of Officer Robinson, remembering her in the moment when her eyes— amazing eyes, electric blue, their hue distinct even from across the room—had been focused on the gun in Cain's hand.

Cain hadn't shot her. He'd drowned her in the lake.

But on Ally he would use the gun. She'd seen him lightly touch the holster while saying, "I'll do the honors."

He would point the pistol at her, maybe put it in her ear or her mouth, and squeeze the trigger—perhaps one instant of unbearable pain, then nothing—and she would be as dead as Officer Robinson, as dead as her best hopes.

Damn. She wished she'd let Cain rape her. Wished

she'd shut her eyes and just let him stick it in her. Anything was better than being dead at fifteen.

Don't cry, she told herself. Not again.

But she couldn't help it. She must have cried in the delivery room, when she was spanked into this world, and she would cry now as she was ushered out.

29

Staying low, Trish crept around the gazebo, past a thicket of olive trees.

A flagstone walkway, lined on both sides by three-foot hedges of fragrant lavender, slanted diagonally toward the patio. Head down, knees bent, she followed the path, using one row of bushes for cover.

Chills crawled over her skin. Fear? Maybe just cold. She was still wet all over, her hair plastered to her forehead, her underpants groping her like clammy fingers.

On the patio now. To her right, a canvas porch swing and a scatter of redwood lawn furniture. To her left, the open door.

The tinkle of wind chimes covered the squish of her shoes as she crossed the patio to the whitewashed stucco wall.

Fast along the wall to the door frame. She took a breath, then spun inside, assuming the Weaver stance.

Nobody was there.

Into a hallway, narrow and bare. A glow from the rooms ahead guided her as she crabbed forward, her gun held close to her chest. The steel cuffs glinted faintly below the spots of dried blood on her knuckles and the bruises swelling her wrists.

From the front of the house came rare, desultory noises of destruction—shattered glass and slashed fabric. Someone was trashing the place but doing it in a strangely half-hearted way.

As the dining area and the living room came into view, she saw the extent of the wreckage in the weird patchy light of the one remaining lamp. Nearly everything breakable was in pieces.

Two of the killers, their backs to her, were methodically sweeping glazed earthenware pitchers and crystal vases from the glass-and-steel divider.

Both had taken off their masks. One was the woman, the other a blond ponytailed man.

At the intersection of the rear hall and the east wing she paused. The kitchen lay behind the wall to her right. To get inside, she would have to pass through the dining area.

A major risk. At any moment the killers might turn. But she had no choice.

Now.

Balancing speed with silence, she pivoted through the kitchen doorway and ducked behind the wall.

They hadn't seen or heard her. The carpet's thick pile had muffled her steps.

She looked toward the west end of the house. Past a laundry nook was a side door. She could exit that way.

First the keys. She holstered the Glock to free her hands. After a rapid inspection of the key rings, she chose the most complete set, cramming it deep in her pants pocket.

Got it. All right, get going, move.

She almost stepped away from the noteboard but hesitated, her gaze drawn to the phone on the wall. For a bewildered moment she had no idea why she was looking at it. Impossible to call from inside the house; the risk of being overheard was too great.

But this phone was cordless. It could be operated anywhere within range of the base unit—even in the backyard.

She might not need a boat after all.

Heart pumping, she lifted the handset and wedged it under her gun belt, hard against her hip.

In the next room a door creaked open.

She froze, motionless as the rabbit she had seen.

"I'm glad to report Mr. Kent has given his approval," said a voice she recognized too well, the voice of the man with steely gray eyes. "Isn't that right, Mr. Kent?"

Charles's voice, drained of strength: "God damn you, Cain."

Cain. Trish filed the name away.

"I take that to mean yes," Cain answered.

Laughter from the other two. Trish had no idea what that exchange had been about, and no time to contemplate it.

"You two get started on the den." Cain again, crisply authoritative. "Bag the loot and trash the place."

Dangerous to listen any longer. Time to go. Right now.

She eased away from the wall, then heard footsteps, rapid and heavy.

"This way, Mr. Kent."

The two of them—Charles and Cain—they were coming. Straight for the kitchen, it sounded like.

They would be here in five seconds. She could never get out the door fast enough. She was trapped.

Her gaze swept the kitchen. Under the sink, a cabinet. Big enough to hold her? It had to be.

On her knees. Clawing at the double doors. They swung open. Household cleansers cluttered the left side. The other side was clear

The footsteps—close. *Go.*

Pain flared in torn muscles as she squeezed in backward. Her hair brushed the garbage disposal, her shoulder bumping the trap of the sink drain.

Folded inside, she pulled both doors shut.

Darkness. Wet clothes. A cramped, airless space.

Abruptly she was back in the trunk, water rising as she groped for the latch. She suppressed a suicidal impulse to burst free.

Boots and dress shoes thumped on the kitchen tiles.

"Why are we in here?" Charles murmured in the voice of a dead man.

"Brandy on your breath. Remember?"

They stopped directly before the sink.

Too late, she remembered her wet shoes. The trail of footprints must point to the cabinet like an accusing finger.

She unholstered the Glock. The handcuff chain jingled softly. She did her best to steady her trembling arms.

Behind her head, a metal riser hooked to a valve hummed briefly with running water.

"Take this," Cain said. "Rinse out your mouth. . . . There you go. Good as new."

"Never be good as new. Never again."

"Think positive. Twenty million bucks can buy you one hell of an overhaul."

"Cain. Don't hurt her. Please."

An impatient sigh. "We already agreed—"

"I know what we agreed. But what I mean is . . . when you do it . . . don't make her suffer."

"Your darling little girl will never know what hit her."

Trish listened, her mind swirling with a rush of half-formed thoughts.

Charles Kent was part of this. Millions of dollars were involved. Barbara Kent was heiress to the Ashcroft fortune. Charles must have set her up. Hired Cain, arranged the break-in, staged the whole thing.

Now for some inexplicable reason Ally had to die. That development clearly hadn't been part of the plan, but Charles had acquiesced in it just the same.

Hollow clunk overhead—a drinking glass had been set down on the counter. The two men stepped away from the sink, and Cain grunted as if catching his balance.

"Watch it. Floor's wet."

Her shoes and her dripping uniform must have left a puddle directly in front of the sink.

Teeth clenched, she pressed the muzzle of the gun to the cabinet door. She could shoot right through it, hope for a lucky hit—

Cain again: "You spilled some of your water, Mr. Kent."

"Spill. . . ?" Charles sounded confused.

"Guess you couldn't help it. You're shaking almost as bad as that rookie cop when I said she wasn't needed anymore."

"I . . . I don't think I—"

Cain ignored the denial. "What you need is a maid." He chuckled as their footsteps receded. "Just take a look at that living room. It's a goddamned pigsty."

Gone.

Trish allowed herself to exhale.

Warily she opened the cabinet, crawled out. Her joints crackled as she stood.

She could leave now. Use the cordless phone to call 911 from the backyard.

But the response time to this location would be ten minutes even for a code three call.

Ally might not have ten minutes.

Most likely Charles was rejoining his wife and the Danforths at this moment. That was why he'd rinsed the residue of liquor from his mouth.

Once Charles was locked up, Cain would be free to do the job he'd promised.

She crept toward the kitchen doorway, heading for the east wing—and Ally's bedroom.

Of course Trish had to save Alison Kent. There was no question of that, no slightest doubt.

She might be crazy to risk it. Her lifetime allotment of luck surely had been used up by now. But . . .

No medals for quitters.

At the doorway she peered into the living room. Empty. From the den rose muffled thuds and crashes. The destruction, purely for show, continued.

Okay. Go.

Through the dining area. Into the side hallway.

At the far end—Cain and Charles Kent, their backs to her. Trish ducked back into the dining area, hugging the wall.

After a mental count of ten she dared another look. The two men were gone. Must have entered the room at the end of the hall. Through the doorway Trish saw a vanity and a mirror. Master suite, presumably.

Ally's room was closer. First door on the left, if her visualization of the house's layout was correct. She crept toward it.

Movement in the master suite.

She froze. Was it Cain?

No, only her reflection in the vanity's mirror.

But if she could see herself in the silvered glass, anyone in the master suite could see her too. Either Charles or Cain might notice at any moment. Hurry.

She reached Ally's door. Locked? Please don't let it be locked.

The knob turned freely.

Before opening the door, she lifted the Glock in her right hand.

Ally had appeared to be alone, but not every corner of the room was visible through the windows. There might be a guard.

Go in fast.

Her left hand swung the door ajar, and she pivoted through the doorway, her gaze sweeping the bedroom.

Canopy bed. Computer work station. Crowded bookcases. TV and VCR. Navajo rug tacked on the wall. Ally bound to a chair.

Nobody else.

The girl's mouth formed a round shape of surprise. Trish silenced the half-voiced cry with a wordless shake of her head.

Softly she eased the door shut and locked it.

Ally stared through a skein of disheveled hair. Her lips barely moved as she whispered, "You're *dead*."

Trish managed a smile, her first in a long time. "Not yet."

30

"My God." Barbara stared at Charles as he stumbled into the closet, shoved by the tall ski-masked man with gray eyes. "What did they do to you?"

Charles didn't answer, didn't seem to even understand. He blinked vapidly.

The doors swung shut, darkness slamming down.

"Charles?" Philip laid a gentle hand on his shoulder. "You all right?"

"Did they . . . hurt you?" Barbara whispered.

No reply.

Outside, a chain rasped, a padlock clicked, footsteps retreated.

When Barbara was sure the man had left, she switched on the flashlight she'd hidden behind her back. Charles blinked in the wavering beam.

"Philip found it on the shelf while you were gone," she said. "We put a box of earthquake supplies in here, remember?"

Still Charles was silent. She studied his face, chalky in the pale circle of light. She saw no bruises, no sign of injury, yet an awful change had come over him. His smug assurance was gone. He was a broken man, a concentration camp survivor, all hollow eyes and bloodless lips.

Then an explanation occurred to her, terrible in its plausibility.

"Is it Ally? Is she . . . ?" She couldn't finish the question, wasn't certain what horror she imagined: rape or torture or murder, or all three.

Finally Charles roused himself, a man climbing out of a deep sleep.

"No," he said in a dusty voice. "Not Ally. Ally's fine." He nodded. "She's fine. I saw her. She's fine."

"Where is she?"

"Her bedroom." Still nodding, nodding. "She's comfortable. She's fine."

"Then . . . what happened?"

"I opened the safe. That's all."

"But why do you look so . . . so . . . ?"

"I'm okay," Charles said. "Really."

Barbara exchanged a baffled glance with Judy, whose hand was absently stroking the spot between her collar bones where the crucifix had hung.

Like a patient father leading a small child, Philip ushered Charles to the wicker hamper. "Why don't you rest your feet?"

The hamper had creaked when Barbara sat on it earlier. But it registered Charles's weight not at all, as if he weren't really there, as if only his image inhabited the closet.

"That better?" Philip asked.

"Much," Charles said without visible reaction. "Much better."

The flashlight was trembling. Barbara bit her lip. "Oh, Charles."

Distantly she was surprised to hear herself speak her husband's name with a tenderness she hadn't felt in years.

31

Ally stared at Trish Robinson as she crossed the bedroom. Her attention was held by Trish's eyes, electric blue, gleaming with an intensity that was almost scary.

They were the eyes of a jungle animal, grimly determined, hypervigilant, focused exclusively on the immediate moment. Eyes that could stare death in the face.

Maybe they already had.

Then her focus shifted to Trish's hair—a wet mop—and her uniform—soaked through.

"The lake ..." Ally whispered.

"What?"

"That's where Cain said he put you."

"Temporarily."

"You got away?" The question was hushed, almost awed.

Shrug. "I'm here, aren't I?"

Trish holstered her gun and leaned over the chair, tugging at the knotted sheets. Her hands were shaking, her fingers clumsy, and Ally saw for the first time how scared she was—weak with fear but doing her best not to show it.

The fear made her more human, more real, not an apparition in a dream.

"You know martial arts?" Ally asked. "Is that how you did it?"

"They call me the dragon lady."

"No, seriously."

"Seriously—I just got lucky, okay?"

Lucky. No way. She'd been fighting. Maybe not with kung fu and tae kwan do, but it had been a battle, all right. Ally noted the abrasions on her wrists and knuckles, the cuts and bruises on her bare forearms.

But how could she have fought anybody? She was still handcuffed, her arm movements severely restricted.

Handcuffed . . .

"Hey, didn't they cuff your hands *behind* your back?"

"I moonlight as a contortionist." She gave up trying to loosen the stubborn knots and unsheathed a knife.

Cops didn't carry knives on their belts, did they? No, wait. Ally had seen Tyler remove Trish's belt before slinging her over his shoulder. The equipment she was wearing—it belonged to one of the bad guys.

Ally didn't think any of them would have given up his gear voluntarily.

"How come you know Cain's name?" Trish asked, cutting into her thoughts.

"Oh. I—uh—I know all about him." The mention of Cain made her heart speed up. "I've seen his face. He's *ugly*."

"Big surprise."

"He wants to kill me."

"What he wants and what he'll get are two different things."

Though Trish tried to say it with cool nonchalance, Ally could hear the strain stretching her voice taut, could see the tick of a muscle in her cheek that gave the lie to her smile.

The knife blade sliced neatly through the binding, and Ally was free.

She stood on wobbly legs and took a step toward the door. Suddenly her only impulse was to be out of this room, this place where she'd been certain she would die.

"Not that way." The urgent whisper came from behind her. "Help me with this."

But Trish didn't need any help. She had already unlatched one of the window screens and pushed it out of the frame by the time Ally reached her side.

She might be handcuffed and hurt and scared, maybe even as scared as Ally herself, but she sure knew how to keep her cool.

"You first," Trish said.

Ally began climbing out. "What are you, Wonder Woman or something?"

"That's me." The cuffs flashed. "Dig my Amazon bracelets."

Despite urgency and danger, Ally almost smiled.

In the hall—footsteps.

Heavy and quick.

Ally froze, halfway out the window, the blood leaving her face. She breathed one word.

"Him."

32

At the door of Ally's bedroom, Cain paused to strip off his mask.

The girl had been so eager to see his face. Now she would have the pleasure of seeing it again in the final moment of her life.

He'd told Charles his daughter wouldn't suffer. It was true. There was no time for a drawn-out encounter of the sort he preferred. He would simply enter the room, thrust the gun under Ally's chin, and make spatter-art out of her brains. A no-frills hit, slick and professional.

He wadded the mask in his back pocket, then shut his eyes and drew a slow breath, feeling the smooth expansion of his rib cage, the beat of blood in the arteries of his wrists and the veins of his neck.

This was always his way before a kill. In the stillness before violence, he liked to take a moment to sink deep into the awareness of himself, his body, the autonomic functions of his heart and lungs. Though he was not a philosophical man, he found a certain wonder in the knowledge that another human being, as alive as he was, soon would be dead by his hand. No breath, no heartbeat, no movement, no life.

Bodies in motion. Bodies at rest. That was all there was in the universe, or so he'd heard. Tonight a body in motion would be set at rest, that was all—permanently at rest. And the universe would go on, indifferent and aloof.

Ready now, he grasped the doorknob.

It wouldn't turn.

Locked.

Fear held Ally immobilized, one leg over the windowsill, the other foot planted in her bedroom.

"Shoot him," she hissed at Trish. "Through the door."

Trish shook her head. "The others will hear. Can't get them all."

The doorknob rattled.

"*Go,*" Trish breathed.

Ally's paralysis broke. Twist of her upper body, and she slipped through the window and dropped onto the flower bed bordering the house. She crushed some of her mom's geraniums and was distantly sorry about it.

Trish climbed after her, drawing the gun.

For a bewildered moment Cain stared at the door, unable to comprehend how it could be locked.

Ally was tied up, wasn't she?

Wasn't she?

Ally streaked across the yard through a tunnel of shadows. The grounds of the estate seemed enormous, bigger than three football fields. She had never imagined the yard was so large.

Trish, directly ahead, glanced back, her face pallid in the starlight, wet ribbons of hair lacing her forehead and cheeks like cracks in a marble bust.

On her right, the pool area blurred past: smear of white concrete, smell of chlorine.

The garden lay directly ahead. Trish led her into it, through high stalks of gladiolus and foxglove and pink cadmium, the plants trampled, the beautiful blooms crushed like so much wastepaper.

Ally thought it was wrong to kill the flowers—shockingly, viciously wrong that any young, healthy, blossoming thing should have to die.

Cain stepped back and delivered a powerful kick to the door, planting his boot just inside the handle. The frame splintered out, and the door flew open under his hand.

He burst inside. Scanned the room.

The desk chair—empty. Window screen—removed.

Gun in hand, he ran to the window, peered out.

In the garden, a patch of luminous white.

Ally in her party dress. A distant, moving target.

He thumbed the pressure switch on the pistol's grip.

The laser sighting system printed a two-inch circle of reddish orange light on her back.

Cain fired.

Trish glanced over her shoulder a second time and saw a silhouetted figure at the bedroom window.

Flicker of amber light.

The laser.

"Down!"

She pulled Ally to the ground behind a clump of bellflower.

The shot was nearly silent. The bullet's impact made a soft thud in the trunk of an olive tree.

Impelled by instinct, with no time for thought, Trish spun into a half crouch and lifted the Glock in two hands.

She forgot the laser sight, forgot everything except the trigger and how to use it.

She squeezed off two rounds in the direction of the window.

Cain saw the girl go down, but was she hit or had she merely taken cover?

He couldn't tell, had no chance to think about it, because out of the darkness burst two answering shots.

Bullets smacked into the exterior wall like mailed fists.

What the *hell*?

Cain threw himself clear of the window and snap-rolled into a crouch, his Glock lifted defensively.

Trish had never fired a gun without ear protection. The Glock was unsilenced, the reports shockingly loud.

"Did you get him?" Ally's suntanned shoulders, revealed by the sleeveless dress, shook with inner violence.

Trish barely heard the question over the ringing clamor in her head. "Don't think so. Come on."

She started crawling, staying low behind spikes of lupine and lady's slipper.

"Where to?" Ally whispered.

"The gate."

The splashback of the muzzle flashes had impaired her night vision. She blinked away blue afterimages as she seal-walked infantry style, elbows chewing up divots of spongy earth. The Glock was clutched tight in her right hand, the action hot.

Though the yard was dark, she felt helplessly exposed, as if she were crawling on a lighted stage before an audience of snipers.

The rear gate seemed impossibly far. A lifetime wouldn't be long enough to reach it.

She kept going, Ally beside her, the elegant white dress streaked with grass stains like muddy tracks of tears.

33

Gunshots.

Barbara stared at the closet doors, certain of what she'd heard.

Two loud cracks, distant but faintly audible, originating—she believed—somewhere outside the house.

"They're shooting," she breathed.

She turned. Her gaze swept the closet.

Philip using the flashlight to search the overhead shelves for some means of escape.

Judy still touching the space between her collar bones where the crucifix had hung.

Charles seated on the wicker hamper, blank-faced and hollow-eyed.

None of them had heard the shots or her own whispered words.

"They're *shooting*," she said again, more sharply, and as the others looked up, she thought of Ally, alone with the killers, at their mercy.

She had worried that her daughter might be molested, but the idea that she might be . . . that they could . . .

They had guns, they were ruthless, they'd killed once already, but even so, they wouldn't . . .

Ally was fifteen. A child.

They couldn't have.

God in heaven, no.

"No," she said aloud. "No." She spun toward the closet doors. "No, Ally, *Ally!*"

Her fists on the doors, drum roll of blows, the chain clanking, and Barbara raging for her daughter, refusing comfort, hysterical and knowing it and not giving a damn.

On his knees in a corner, gripping the pistol in two gloved hands, Cain tried to make sense of what had happened.

It hadn't been Ally who fired the shots. It had been someone near her—dark-clad, unseen at first glance— a lithe female figure dressed in black or . . .

Dark blue.

Police uniform.

Robinson.

Alive.

He tried to blink the thought away. It was crazy. It was laughable.

But he knew it was true.

Somehow she had jilted death. Obtained a gun. Rescued the girl.

Now she must be trying to get out of the yard. If she did, she and Ally could lose themselves in the woods.

Cain scuttled to the doorway, out of range of the window, then sprang upright and pounded down the hall.

Behind him, muffled shouts from the master suite. Barbara Kent's voice. The gunfire from the yard must have been audible even inside the locked closet, damn it.

All the prisoners would be panicking now. This was just getting better and better.

Gage's voice sputtered over the ProCom's speaker. "Heard shots, what's going on?"

Cain answered on the run. "Lilith, relieve Gage out front. Tyler, Gage—wait for me in the rear hall. *Move!*"

He cut through the kitchen, sprinted past the laundry nook, reached the side door. A control panel for the rear gate was mounted on the wall. He threw the switch.

As the gate slid shut, he returned to the kitchen, flipping switches, turning on every floodlight in the yard.

Lilith. Tyler. Gage.

All three names had sputtered over the radio clipped to Trish's belt. Though the volume was low, she'd heard the transmission clearly.

It was obvious the front gate was guarded. And the backyard would be searched—soon.

Had to get out through the rear. Not much time left. She crawled faster.

She hadn't thought she could stay afraid for so long. She'd assumed that a fear this intense would burn itself out. But apparently her body had endless reserves of adrenaline. It could feed the fire indefinitely.

The garden thinned near the gazebo, tall foliage

giving way to a carpet of vetch and Irish moss. The creeping plants provided no cover.

With a nod at Ally, Trish gave up on crawling and broke into a run, darting across a stretch of open ground as deadly as a minefield.

A succession of fragmentary thoughts crowded her mind: Black Talon cartridges—gelatin targets—wide wound channels.

She and Ally thudded to their knees behind the gazebo, miraculously intact.

"Lost my shoe," Ally gasped. "Does that matter?"

Trish struggled for breath. "Not unless you had plans to go out dancing later."

"I'll pass."

"Then take off the other one. You'll run better barefoot."

Ally removed her remaining white pump and tossed it away. There was something childlike and achingly vulnerable about her two bare feet, toes curling on the grass.

Trish looked toward the open gate. To get there, they would have to cross another, longer expanse of treeless lawn. It meant pressing their luck, but they had no choice.

"Ready for another wind sprint?" she asked.

A curt nod answered her.

Shifting into a runner's stance, Trish tensed herself for a burst of speed.

And the gate creaked, sliding shut on a railed track.

"Oh, God," Ally breathed, sinking back on her haunches. "They found the switch. They found the switch . . ."

A control switch for the gate, somewhere inside the house. That was what she must mean.

Trish felt herself trembling with a new surge of fear, an electric jolt slamming through every nerve ending in her body.

She and Ally were penned in. They could be hunted down at leisure.

Banks of lights burst ablaze. A movie moment: a prison, a night escape, sentries in watch towers, floodlights sweeping the yard.

Huddled behind the gazebo, the two of them were safe temporarily. But if they left cover, they would be caught in the glare.

From Ally, a sound like a whimper. Trish reached out awkwardly with her chained hands and touched the girl's arm.

Up close the down on her cheeks was visible, and the dusting of freckles around her eyes. Dried blood crusted a swollen lip. The scalloped neckline of her dress had been torn.

Trish wondered if Cain had raped her. The parallel to Marta was briefly too strong to be endured, and she had to look away.

"What are we going to do?" the girl murmured, hopelessness in her voice.

For a bad moment Trish had no answer. Then she remembered the cordless phone. "Call for help."

She yanked the handset free of her belt and hit the talk button. The keypad lit up, and from the receiver came the hum of a dial tone. Still within range of the base unit in the kitchen, thank God.

Ally stared in amazement. "You *are* Wonder Woman."

Trish found the strength for a smile as she touched the keypad three times. "Wonder Woman never dialed nine-one-one."

34

Wet shoes.

The thought entered Cain's mind as he stood at the kitchen window, switching on the last of the lights.

Robinson had been dumped in the lake. She would be soaked, dripping.

And the kitchen floor was wet.

Charles Kent hadn't spilled his glass, as Cain had assumed. Robinson had been in here.

The trail reached the cabinet under the sink. Kneeling, he opened the doors and beamed his flash inside.

Damp spots on the wood. Shoe prints.

She must have hidden there while Charles rinsed his mouth. Hidden right under Cain's nose.

Who *was* this woman?

A rookie. A Girl Scout. A scared kid, that's all, as fragile and untested as a newly hatched chick.

But she had an irritating habit of staying alive. A habit Cain intended to break.

He almost left the kitchen, then stopped, held by a new thought. What exactly had she been doing in here?

Every minute she'd spent in the house had been a

life-and-death gamble. She wouldn't have wasted time just looking around. Must have been in pursuit of some objective.

A knife, maybe. But hell, she had a gun.

Cain scanned the kitchen, taking in the hooded range, the refrigerator, the central island.

Dinner dishes in the sink, filmy with soap suds. Countertop TV. Family snapshots under glass. Laminated noteboard. Telephone . . .

The phone was cordless. The handset was gone.

Hell.

She could call from anywhere in the house or yard. Could be calling right now.

Cain lunged for the phone and ripped it from the wall.

One ring. Two . . .

Trish prayed for a 911 operator to answer.

The third ring was cut off, replaced by a crackling buzz.

Somehow she'd been disconnected.

She punched the talk button twice, first to terminate the transmission, then to try again.

This time the handset sounded a brief error tone and automatically shut down.

"Damn." She let the phone drop from her hand.

Ally swallowed hard. "What's wrong?"

"They're on to us." She was trying not to tremble, but the clinking of the handcuff chain gave her away. "Switched off the phone at the base."

"Jeez. I . . . I guess maybe I shouldn't ask what we do now."

"Let me think."

The problem, all too obviously, was that Cain was thinking too.

Where had she gotten the gun?

That was the question in Cain's mind as he pitched the ruined phone into the trash.

Blair, of course. He had been patrolling the lake shore. It was the only answer.

If the rookie had Blair's gun, she almost certainly would have his radio too. Might be monitoring the preset frequency.

Slowly Cain unclipped his walkie-talkie and pressed the transmit button.

"Robinson?"

Trish stiffened, hearing her name.

She looked at Ally. The girl's eyes were suddenly too big for her face.

"Hey, Robinson." Cain's voice crackled like news-paper. "You there? Or is it past your bedtime?"

After a brief inner debate she lifted her transceiver, spoke into the microphone.

"I'm here . . . Cain."

A pause. Then: "You know that much, do you?"

"I try to stay informed." She hoped he couldn't hear the tremor in her voice.

"Yeah, you're a quick-witted little Mouseketeer, I'll give you that. Donald and Mickey and ol' Uncle Walt would be real proud."

She tried a bluff. "You'd better scram. Backup's coming."

"I don't think so. That radio's short-range only, and I trashed the phone."

"Not before I got through. I was on the line just a couple seconds, but they do an instant trace on a nine-one-one call. Units are on their way right now, code three."

"Are they? Hey, Lilith, you monitoring the police traffic?"

A familiar lisping voice answered: "That's a ten-four."

"Any units dispatched to this address?"

"Negative."

Trish tried a last gambit. "They know you've got my radio. They wouldn't say anything over the air."

She waited tensely through a moment's silence, praying he would buy it.

Then a cool reply: "Nice try, Robinson. But I can always tell when you're lying."

"It's your ass," she said with forced bravado.

"No, I think it's gonna be yours. In a body bag."

Body bag. Vivid image. She could almost hear the rasp of the zipper sealing the flaps.

"You shouldn't have come back to the house," Cain added. "Why'd you do it? For the girl?"

Trish avoided Ally's gaze. "Just doing my job."

"Yeah, right. Guess I really am dealing with a hero, after all."

"I'm no hero."

A chuckle. "Modest too. You got a plan for world peace, you could be the next Miss America."

"My only plan is to put you in jail." She regretted saying it. Lame.

"I've been there," Cain said evenly. "Didn't like it. Don't intend on going back. Now let me tell you about *my* plans, blue eyes. You too, freckle-face. I know you're listening."

Ally hugged herself, a shudder blowing through her like a cold draft.

"Robinson, I'm gonna kill you quick. You'll never even know what hit you. Bang, and you're gone. That's because I respect you as an adversary"—malicious mockery soured the words—"and I never underestimate a lady with a gun. But as for Ally . . ."

Trish knew she shouldn't listen, but the man's voice held her fascinated, hypnotized. He was more than a petty criminal. He had the perverse persuasiveness born of an utter absence of doubt.

"Yeah, you, little darling," Cain breathed. "You I'm gonna do slow. I'm gonna give you some of what you didn't go for the first time. Only, I'm not putting my cock in you, no, ma'am. It'll be a knife instead, or an ice pick, something creative, and you'll scream—"

"Turn it off," Ally moaned.

Trish was wrenched out of her daze. Her fumbling hands found the power switch and depressed it.

Silence.

But the echo of Cain's words hung in the air, dark and acrid like smoke.

"He won't," Trish whispered. "He won't do . . . what he said."

"Who'll stop him?"

"I will."

"But *we can't get away* . . ."

Incipient hysteria in her voice. Trish looked at Ally—the dress riding up around her hips, her slender legs sprawled artlessly on the lawn. She was a pretty girl, would be a beautiful woman—if she made it that far.

"It's okay, Ally," she breathed, thinking hard, reviewing her options.

"No, it's not. It's not . . ." Ally sank into a fetal pose, hugging her knees. Wetness glistened in her eyes. "Oh, God. I'm sorry, Trish."

"For what?"

"For . . . being a baby." She wore an absurd smile. Her shoulders jerked feebly. "For crying. It's just . . . I'm afraid. I don't want to die."

"Me either. And we're not going to." Her mind was racing in tandem with her beating heart. "Just give me a second to figure something out."

Another second. Not much to ask for, ordinarily.

But tonight a few more seconds—a minute at most—was all the time they had.

35

"You hear me, freckle-face?" Cain frowned. "Hey, Ally? . . . Robinson?"

No response. The cop had switched off.

Well, it didn't matter. She and her little friend had heard plenty. They ought to be rattled good, not thinking straight, and that was just the way he liked it.

Still on the same frequency he said, "Lilith, you still there?"

"Of course."

"Start licking your chops, sweetheart. I'm giving the Kent girl to you. You can warm her up—and I'll finish her off."

A purr of pleasure, then a sigh. "I'd rather have Robinson."

"We don't play games with her. You in position?"

"Standing post."

"Stay alert. The rookie's armed."

"Ooh, I'm scared."

Cain had to smile at that. The only thing Lilith knew about fear was how to instill it.

Clipping the radio to his belt, he headed out of the kitchen, down the rear hall.

* * *

Eyes shut, Trish pictured the backyard's layout, looking for any kind of escape route.

The gazebo, she remembered, stood at the end of the long diagonal walkway that led to the patio. The walkway was bordered on both sides by hedges of lavender.

Earlier she had used those hedges for cover when approaching the house.

Could she do it again?

The idea seemed crazy—going *toward* the house when the killers were inside. But being crazy, it was the last thing anyone would expect.

She risked a look over the gazebo's low wall. Nobody was visible at any of the lighted rear windows. Surely the yard was under observation from some vantage point—one of the unlit windows, perhaps, or the dark hallway beyond the patio door.

But from the hall, at least, a watcher wouldn't see a person crawling low to the ground on the west side of the hedge rows.

"Okay, I've got something." She slipped onto elbows and knees again. "Follow me."

"You have a plan?" Ally whispered with desperate eagerness.

"Sort of."

Not the most reassuring answer she could have given. But a sort-of plan was the best she had to offer right now.

Tyler and Gage stood waiting for Cain at the rear doorway, nearly invisible in the darkness, their uniforms like liquid shadows.

"Where'd she get the radio?" Gage snapped as Cain approached.

The kid's face was pale, the sparse hairs of his mustache beaded with sweat. Like Lilith, he and Tyler had overheard the crosstalk. And now he was scared.

"We'll deal with that later," Cain said calmly.

"Where'd she get it?"

A screamer. Quick to panic. Way out of his depth. Blair must have been crazy to bring him along.

"From your brother." Cain showed him a sneer. "Where do you think?"

"She couldn't have. No way." Gage shook his head vigorously, starlight flashing on a gold earring below a bunched mass of oily dark curls. "That little bimbo never could take out Blair."

"That little bimbo," Cain said without inflection, "got out of a locked trunk underwater. And nearly put two bullets in me. Did you hear what I told her about not underestimating a lady with a gun? I meant it."

"Blair could handle her with his damn eyes closed."

"Maybe he had his damn eyes closed, and that's why *she* handled *him*."

"Christ . . ." A sob caught in the kid's throat.

"Hey, Gage, take it easy." That was Tyler, speaking for the first time, his tone smoothly reasonable. "Just because she got Blair's stuff doesn't mean he's dead or anything. She probably just tied him up, is all."

Cain didn't know if Tyler believed any of this, but the reassurance had its intended effect. Gage's rising panic abruptly receded.

"Think so?" he whispered. "Think my bro could be okay?"

Tyler shrugged. "Robinson's no killer. Ain't got the

stomach for it." He rapped Gage's shoulder, a gesture of manly affection. "Not like us."

"Yeah." Gage hitched in a breath, calming himself. "Yeah, not like us."

Cain smiled briefly. Nice work on Tyler's part. The problem had required a diplomatic touch, which the cowboy had neatly supplied.

"All right," he said briskly, reasserting command. "Last I saw of our two friends, they were in the garden. Assuming they continued toward the gate, they would have ended up near the gazebo."

Gage nodded. "That's where I hunkered down when Mrs. Kent turned on the light."

"I'm betting they're pinned at that spot. They can't leave without revealing themselves."

"Sitting ducks." Tyler's thin lips skinned back from his teeth in a gunslinger's bloodless smile.

"Yeah. Thing is, they know it. Cornered, Robinson will have to fight. So watch yourselves. And remember, she's the prime target. Waste her, and we can take the Kent girl alive."

Tyler gave it a thumbs-up. "No sweat."

Hugging the doorframe, Cain flipped a switch. The patio light died, but the rest of the yard remained illuminated.

He ducked low through the doorway and snap-rolled behind a redwood lounge chair.

A second later Tyler and Gage joined him. Together they crawled to the flagstone path. Bent double, Cain advanced along a row of lavender bushes bordering the walkway.

The hard part was over. Now it was time for some fun.

In his life Cain had killed two cops by his own hand. He was looking forward to number three.

36

Movement on the patio.

Trish heard a soft shuffle of nylon jump suits. Halfway along the hedge she froze, Ally behind her.

Most likely the killers would go to the gazebo, expecting their quarry to be hidden there. She didn't think they would take the path. Walled in by hedges, they would be vulnerable to ambush.

Instead they probably would do what she had done: stay low along the outside of the path, using one row of bushes for cover.

But which row? East or west? It was a coin flip. Heads, she lived; tails, she died.

She waited, breath held, supported by her elbows, the Glock clutched in both hands.

If they came this way, she could shoot one of them, perhaps. Then the others would open fire, tearing the hedge apart in a lethal fusillade.

Rustle of lavender stalks. Close.

This wasn't going to work. Abruptly she was certain of it. She'd gambled and lost.

Then she heard Cain's voice, pitched in a whisper: "Keep your heads down."

He was directly opposite her—on the other side of the path.

She'd won the coin toss. Cain and his men had chosen the parallel route. Two hedges and the flag-stone path between them were all that separated hunters from prey.

Trish remembered the use of her lungs. Swallowing fear, she started crawling again.

Cain moved forward in a crouch, leading Tyler and Gage. His footsteps were soundless, the tread of a ghost. The only noise was the tuneless clinking of the patio wind chimes, making their night music.

The gazebo's interior drew into view. Empty. Most likely Robinson and the girl were squatting at the rear.

He paused at the end of the path, hunched behind the hedge, smelling lavender and thinking.

Best move was to take Robinson by surprise. He motioned to Tyler and Gage: Stay back.

Silently Cain slipped between the hedge and the gazebo. He drew a deep breath.

Now.

He burst into the gazebo and swung his gun over the back wall, ready to shoot the rookie from above before she could react.

No one was there.

Trish wished she could be cool about this, like some TV cop. Wished she could shed the fear that was wearing her ragged.

Her stomach bubbled. A sour taste lay like some-thing furry and hot at the back of her throat. She kept puffing up her cheeks to hold in the small, nervous belches that made her eyes water.

Fear kept a person alert, Pete Wald had told her.

She was more alert now than she had ever wanted to be.

At the end of the path she paused, waiting for Ally to catch up. The patio light was off, making it easier for the two of them to wriggle behind the redwood furniture.

But to get in the door they would have to expose themselves briefly to view. Ally first, Trish second.

With luck the killers would be focusing their attention on the gazebo, their backs turned to the patio.

Yes. With luck.

Cain switched on his flash. The beam, probing the shadowed ivy at the rear of the gazebo, caught a glint of black plastic.

The handset of the cordless phone.

"They *were* here," he muttered.

Somehow they'd gotten away without being seen.

But it was impossible. Tyler and Gage had been watching the yard through the rear doorway the whole time. There was no cover their two quarries could have hidden behind. Except . . .

The same cover Cain himself had used. The hedges on the path.

He whirled, staring down the walkway, and saw a double blur of motion on the darkened patio—Ally in her white dress, Robinson right behind.

Ally disappeared into the rear hall before Cain could even lift his gun. He wouldn't have time to target the cop either.

Then she went down.

Just inside the doorway, she fell sprawling on her side.

For a split second Cain thought Tyler or Gage had taken her out with a silenced shot.

No. She'd simply lost her footing as she pivoted into the hall.

An easy kill.

The Glock beamed a thread of laser light across the yard, stamping a red-orange dot on her chest.

Trish fell on the tiled floor, wet shoes betraying her, and then she was scrabbling at the baseboard, trying to rise, her chained hands clumsy, and suddenly there was an amber glow on her uniform, close to her heart.

One chance.

She pistoned her right leg. Kicked the patio door.

The door swung shut as the bullet reached it. She heard the crunch of the jacketed hollowpoint drilling through wood. But the door was heavy, with a solid core, and though the lower panel swelled inward, the bullet didn't penetrate completely.

She twisted upright as three more bullets smacked into the door, punching new bulges in the panels and stiles.

"They just don't give up!" Ally screamed.

"Neither do we. Come on."

Trish was running again, the hallway lurching around her as her shaky knees threatened to buckle.

"I've got keys." The words came out in explosive gasps. "We'll get a car—from the garage—ram the gate."

Ally's bare feet slapped the tiles in a staccato

rhythm. "They teach you this stuff at the police academy?"

"Gate ramming? Yeah." Trish wanted to laugh, wanted to become hysterical, but she had no breath. "I came prepared."

Tyler and Gage had started shooting after Cain's bullet impacted the slammed door. They were only wasting ammo and degrading their sound suppressors.

"Hold your fire!" Cain yelled.

Gage lowered his gun and wiped a shaking arm across his face.

Tyler twirled his pistol, Wild West style. "What now, boss?"

"We keep 'em bottled up. You guard the side exit. Gage, take the rear."

Tyler broke into a run, covering ground in long, loping strides, simultaneously gangly and graceful. His black jump suit melted into the shadows between the house and the garage.

Cain was already on the radio to Lilith. "They're in the house. May try getting out through the front. Watch the door."

"You should've let me take a crack at her in the first place."

"This isn't woman's work."

"Tell that to Robinson."

"I will—right before I blow her brains out."

He terminated the transmission and quickly followed Gage to the patio.

Someone had to search the house. It was the job entailing the highest risk, so naturally he would do it. Not bravado, just basic leadership skills.

The little rookie was showing some skill of her own, he reflected. Smooth moves—using the hedge for cover, kicking the door shut. She was a street fighter, inexperienced but with the instincts and reflexes of a pro.

He'd thought his threats over the radio had rattled her. It appeared she didn't get rattled so easily.

Yeah, she was good, all right.

But as the saying went: The good die young.

37

Down the hall.

Through the dining area.

Into the kitchen.

Trish ducked low as she passed the kitchen window. Her shoes, encrusted with loose earth from the garden, were leaving even more obvious tracks than before, but there was no time to do anything about it now.

She and Ally reached the laundry nook, stopping at the side door.

"Where's the entrance to the garage?" Trish gasped, digging in her pocket for her keys.

"Right off the path."

"Okay." She gulped another breath. "Here we go again." Easing the door a few inches ajar, she peeked outside.

The guy with the ponytail. Coming this way.

Close the door, *close the door.*

She pushed it shut, engaged the lock and security chain. Probably he hadn't seen her; the laundry area was dark.

The woman named Lilith would be at the front gate by now. Cain was out back.

Nowhere to go.

There might be an unguarded window on the other side of the house. If she and Ally could slip outside, then sneak around to the garage. . .

"New plan," Trish whispered. "We try the east wing."

With Ally she retreated into the kitchen, then stopped, hearing heavy footsteps in the rear hall.

Cain.

Suicidal to cut through the living room now. Trish pulled Ally back into the laundry area.

The side door trembled, the knob jerking as it was turned from outside by the ponytailed man.

Cain's footsteps approached.

Caught between two killers.

Robinson—the mocking voice on the radio echoed in her thoughts—*I'm gonna kill you quick.*

She looked around, frantic.

Opposite the laundry nook, a door.

She opened it. Stairs led down into a dark cellar.

"There's no way out of there," Ally hissed.

The side door shuddered. The ponytailed man had attacked it with his shoulder or his boot. A crack shot through the frame.

Trish pushed Ally onto the staircase. "We don't have any choice."

Another jolt from outside, and the side door banged ajar but was stopped by the chain lock.

Ally hurried down. Trish followed, closing the cellar door, sealing the room in darkness.

Quickly she descended, gun in one hand, flashlight in the other. The intense, narrow beam played over concrete steps and cinder block walls.

The cellar was large and musty and damp. No windows. No other doors.

Just as Ally had said: no way out.

Following a trail of muddy shoe prints, Cain entered the kitchen just as the side door burst open, the security chain snapping, and Tyler pivoted through the doorway.

His Glock swung toward Cain, and for a bad moment Cain expected to get iced by friendly fire. Then Tyler's face registered recognition, and sheepishly he lowered the gun.

"Bitches locked me out," he mumbled. "I thought I was walking into a trap."

"Don't sweat it." Cain knew all of them were operating on an adrenaline high. "Just stay alert. They're somewhere close."

He studied the soiled floor, the confusion of tracks. His quarries had advanced and backtracked, their movements erratic, panicky.

Still, they'd found some sort of hiding place.

Cain opened every kitchen cabinet, looked on all sides of the central island.

Nothing.

He moved into the laundry area, thinking vaguely of the washing machine and dryer, each perhaps roomy enough for a crouching person.

Then he saw the cellar door.

Of course.

Trish swept the cellar with her flashlight's beam. "Is there a phone down here?"

"No." Ally's brown eyes, huge with fear, glinted in the dimness. "My folks just use this place for storage. Old Ashcroft heirlooms."

Trish went on exploring with her flash. The wavering funnel of light played over antique chairs wrapped in cellophane, oil portraits elaborately framed, hand-crafted dressers glazed with dust. Amid the furniture and art objects stood stacks of cardboard cartons and wooden crates, meticulously labeled and tagged.

The clutter offered no shortage of hiding places, but concealment would buy them only an extra minute or two. What they needed was a means of escape.

"How about a fuse box?" She was thinking aloud, her voice thin and strained. "We can trip the breakers, get away in the dark before they know what's happened."

Ally shook her head. "Fuse box is in the garage. Anyway, there's a backup generator. For earthquakes."

Trish kept looking. The beam of light prowled the floor. It came to rest on a wooden panel mounted in a square cement frame, near the center of the room.

"What's that?" Pointing with the flash.

"Cover for a well." Ally spoke in a robot's voice. "They built this house on the foundation of the original Ashcroft place. Well was dry, so they put a lid on it."

"We could hide in there, under the cover . . ."

"The bad guys would find us."

Trish silently conceded the point. Of course they would.

She was getting desperate, that was all. She was losing it.

"Give up, Trish." Ally's shoulders lifted in a shrug. "There's no hope."

She looked at the girl. Brambles gleamed in her unkempt hair. The white dress was a muddy rag. Her bare feet looked very small against the floor's gray expanse.

Trish thought of toe tags. She pushed the image away.

"There's always hope," she said. "Always."

Nice thought. Inspirational. Mrs. Wilkes, her long-ago Girl Scout leader, would have approved.

But the truth was, they were finished.

She must have been crazy to come back to this house, crazy to go up against Cain and his personal death squad. Even Pete Wald wouldn't have risked it, and he was a veteran cop with twenty years of field experience, while she . . . well, she was a rank amateur.

You blew it, Trish, said a small, scared voice in her mind. You screwed up after all.

Upstairs Cain's heavy footsteps rumbled closer, the footsteps of a fairy-tale giant combing his castle for intruders.

Directly outside the cellar he stopped.

The sharp intake of breath was Ally's.

Trish set down the flashlight, then aimed the Glock at the head of the staircase.

Shivering with tension, blinking sweat out of her eyes, she prepared to make a last stand.

38

Tyler followed Cain's gaze and focused on the closed door. "Cellar," he said, remembering the blueprints he'd studied.

Cain nodded. "This is the only access. They're trapped."

"Yeah. But Robinson's in a good defensive position. She can take out anybody who goes down the stairs."

"Unless we take her out first." Cain glanced at Tyler and lifted an eyebrow. "There's a way."

"How?"

"Stay here." He brushed past Tyler. "I need my duffel. Stashed it in the den."

"Hey, what's the plan, boss?"

At the kitchen doorway Cain glanced back. A smile split his face like a second scar.

"Souvenir from Yuma," he said, and he was gone.

"Why don't they come down?" Ally breathed, chewing her bruised lip, oblivious of pain.

Trish couldn't figure it out either. She tried to see the situation from Cain's point of view—the closed door, the cellar stairs . . .

It was like a drill she'd run at the academy. To barge

into the cellar was to risk being cut down in an ambush.

"They're scared I'll get the drop on them." She tested the laser sight, beaming a red dot on the door. "I've got a tactical advantage."

"You mean you can hold them off?"

She wanted to say yes, but the truth was less comforting. "Doesn't look like they're going to try a frontal assault."

"What else can they do?"

One set of footsteps departed. Cain pounded through the kitchen, into the living room.

Trish listened to him go. "They'll think of something," she said softly, somehow certain they already had.

Tyler loitered in the laundry area, staying shy of the door. Most likely it had a hollow core. Robinson could punch a bullet through it if she had a mind to.

Not a good idea to get killed now. For one thing, he didn't want to miss what was coming up.

Smiling, he remembered Yuma. It was the first time he had ever worked with Cain.

The two had met in the state prison at Lompoc, where Tyler was doing time for his role in an auto chop shop. Cain had been in for knocking over a gas station on Interstate 10, ordinarily a simple enough job, except that a state trooper had happened along at the worst possible moment.

Cain got out first. After finishing his own sentence, Tyler tracked him down in Indio. He was living in a squalid trailer, off by itself at the edge of town, amid the sun-scarred flats and humming power lines.

Lilith was there too. Though only fifteen, she'd been

Cain's girl even before his year-long stint in prison; he liked to start them young. Having seen Cain naked in the shower, Tyler sometimes wondered how the petite, slim-waisted waif could handle him.

But of course Lilith liked pain.

Cain offered Tyler work, which Tyler readily accepted. And that was how they ended up in Yuma, Arizona, long past midnight, peering through a steel chain fence at Southern Pacific Railroad's east freight yard.

A single guard desultorily performed his rounds. Cain waited for him to go inside the office and warm his hands over the radiator—it was February, cold in the desert night—then snipped through the chain link with bolt cutters, gouging a man-sized hole in the fence.

Dressed in black, Cain and Tyler and two others entered the yard and pried open the back of a freight car. After that, it was only a matter of unloading carton after carton, spiriting the boxes through the fence into a trailer hooked to Cain's van.

They had taken only as much as the trailer could hold, a mere fraction of the freight car's contents. Still, the haul had been considerable.

Marlboros. Panasonic VCRs. Nike running shoes.

And the prize catch—a crate marked DANGER: EXPLOSIVES and containing a gross of dynamite sticks.

In the underground economy there was always a seller's market for dynamite. Cain fenced it all.

Or nearly all. He had a habit of holding on to things that could prove useful.

Four of the sticks had been added to his collection.

His souvenir from Yuma.

Tyler wondered if either Trish or Ally had a birthday coming up. He hoped so.

Not that they would be getting any cake tonight— but Cain sure was going to light them one hell of a candle.

39

Had to be a way out of this. Had to be.

She could find it, she was sure she could, if she was able to fight off fear, fight off fatigue, and think.

Think.

Trish remembered the portable radio and switched it on, hoping to eavesdrop on her enemies' chatter and learn their intentions.

Channel three was silent. She scanned the other channels. Dead air.

They weren't using the radios, weren't giving her any help.

She kept the transceiver on its scanning mode and picked up the flashlight, angling the beam at the ceiling.

No ventilation ducts. No removable panels over a handy crawl space. Just bare fluorescent tubes, dark now, mounted on a sheet of poured concrete, as flat and smooth as a marble headstone.

The flash searched the floor. Concrete also, utterly featureless, unmarred even by cracks.

She was a hunted rabbit. Cornered, crouching, the dogs closing in.

"Was Cain right?"

The question startled her. She glanced at Ally. "What?"

"He said you came back to save me. Did you? Is that why you're here?"

"I . . . it's complicated."

"You should've stayed away." Weary desolation leeched the energy from Ally's voice. She sagged against an antique bureau. "Shouldn't have given up your life for me."

"Don't talk that way," Trish whispered, part of her ashamed for having had the same unworthy thought.

If she'd stayed at the lake . . . if she hadn't decided to be a hero . . .

"It's true, though." Ally spoke softly, the words almost inaudible. "You didn't have to do it, but you did. You're brave. You're the bravest person I've ever met."

"I'm not brave, Ally." She tried to smile, couldn't. "I'm so scared I can hardly stand up."

"But you're here."

Trish meditated on that. Fear wasn't cowardice, was it? A coward would have heeded those plaintive, reasonable voices in her head that had warned her to stay where she was safe.

In her whole life, twenty-four years, she had never been put in a position where bravery could be tested—until tonight.

She supposed she had passed that test.

Rabbit or not, she felt a faint uplift of pride at the thought.

Then the house shivered with someone's rapid, ponderous tread.

Cain—returning to the kitchen.

* * *

The duffel bag thumped on the counter under the white fluorescent glare. As Tyler watched, Cain rummaged inside and produced the four dynamite sticks, as well as an M–80 firecracker that would serve as a blasting cap.

"Gonna use all four?" Tyler asked, worried by the prospect.

"Got to." Cain pulled out a roll of duct tape and began taping the M–80 to one of the sticks, working deftly even with gloved hands. "These charges were manufactured for coal mining. Ammonium nitrate, relatively weak concentration. Made that way to prevent cave-ins."

"Still looks like a pretty damn big party popper to me."

"I know what I'm doing."

Tyler hoped so. He stared at the dynamite, incongruous amid the stained birch cabinets and waxed tiles, the family snapshots, the copy of *TV Guide* tented on the countertop.

Tentatively he touched one of the sticks, two feet long, four inches in diameter, paper-sealed.

Death in a brown wrapper.

He looked up at Cain, still winding tape around the detonator. In the glareless light Tyler could see the sweat gathered on the big man's face like a misting of dew, the strain tugging at the muscles of his face.

Hard night, too many unexpected complications, and there was a lot more riding on this job than a few cartons of VCRs and cigarettes.

Now all of it was at risk—because of one rookie cop who wouldn't stay dead.

Under the sleeves of Cain's nylon jacket, the massive muscles of his arms were sketchily defined, arms that could bench-press two hundred and fifty pounds, twice Trish Robinson's weight. Cain could snap that woman's neck like a damn dog biscuit.

It was crazy that she should pose any kind of threat to a man like him. Unnatural, bizarre—a field mouse challenging a hawk.

Well, Tyler mused, the mouse would be the hawk's dinner soon. The natural order of things would be restored.

"Get Gage and Lilith in here." Cain bundled the four sticks and started lashing them together with more tape. "And have Lilith grab the fire extinguisher in the foyer closet. There must be one in the kitchen too. Find it."

Tyler obeyed, first issuing the instructions over his ProCom, then searching the kitchen. By the time he found the dry-chemical extinguisher in the pantry, Gage and Lilith had entered the room.

Lilith pouted when she saw the bomb. "You said we'd get to play with the girl," she muttered sullenly.

"I'll find us another sweet young thing." Cain smiled. "One who's even younger."

Her eyes brightened. "Honest?" she lisped.

Cain pecked her cheek. "Honest."

"Boss." That was Gage, staring mesmerized at the dynamite. "You, uh, you sure this is a good idea?"

His gloved fingers twitched, and Tyler worried briefly that the kid would accidentally yank the Glock's trigger and shoot off his own foot.

Cain grunted. "Why wouldn't it be?"

"What if it sets off the fire alarm?"

"Any smoke detectors in the cellar will be vaporized before they can send a signal."

"Smoke could get up here, though."

"We'll disable the detector in the kitchen."

"There've gotta be other ones all over the house."

"That's why Tyler and Lilith are toting those extinguishers." Cain clapped Gage on the back. "Quit worrying."

Gage nodded without reply. Tyler remembered what Blair had told him. The younger Sharkey was a virgin at killing.

Well, the first time could be tough. Tyler remembered the scrawny sleepy-eyed clerk in the convenience store in Kingman—the shattering blast of the shotgun, the spray of brains, and how the space behind the cash register was abruptly empty, no person there.

His sleep had been restless for a few nights afterwards. But he'd gotten over it. Gage would too.

He shifted his attention to the bomb on the counter. The bundled dynamite was now wrapped in a plastic trash bag filled with cutlery. Cain had emptied the knife racks.

Fragmentation grenade. Nasty.

Tyler thought about what a bomb like that would do: the deafening concussive blast, and with it the shower of broken knives—red-hot spears of metal, mangled and twisted and razor-edged, impaling anything and anyone within range.

He shook his head slowly, emitting a low whistle. "Our lady friends won't be getting any older."

"You got that right." Cain finished taping the plastic bag in place, then hefted the bomb, loose knives clinking. "The two Mouseketeers are about to go for an E-ticket ride."

40

Not much longer. An attack was imminent.

Trish had heard a drawling voice on the radio summon Lilith and Gage into the kitchen. They would never leave their posts unless Cain was sure he had his quarries cornered—and was preparing to make his move.

And still there was no way out.

Probing with the flashlight, she'd checked every wall, every corner, every inch of the ceiling and floor, and found no openings. The cellar was a cage of concrete, impregnable as a pharaoh's tomb.

There was no clock in the room, but she could hear a clock ticking anyway, her life winding down to that ultimate moment when reality would be erased in a shock of pain.

Funny to breathe and know your breath soon would be stopped. Funny to hear your heart and know its beats were numbered.

This line of thought wasn't helping. She needed to focus on strategy, on ways and means, on what to *do*.

But there was nothing to do. Nothing.

No medals for quitters.

Shut up.

She was trying to think clearly, logically, but bursts of adrenalized panic kept breaking up her concentration like static interference chopping a radio signal.

Must be some tactic she could try, must be.

Had Marta been this scared?

Come on, think.

The coroner said Marta was alive and probably conscious right up to the end.

Couldn't let Ally die. *Think.*

Alive during penile penetration, alive when the jump rope tightened around her neck . . .

Trish shut her eyes, trying to push away the distracting memories, but it did no good. In the sudden darkness behind her closed eyelids, she was back at the farmhouse, on the verge of the weedy field, with the tumbledown porch to her left and, on her right, the dry well where she and Marta had cast pennies and made wishes. . . .

The well.

She opened her eyes. Beamed the flash into the middle of the room, spotlighting the well cover in its wooden frame.

"Any other wells around here?" she asked, holding her voice steady.

Ally shrugged. "One, yeah."

"Where?"

"Northwest."

"Outside the property?"

"In the woods, uh-huh. Who cares?"

"We do." Trish holstered the Glock to free her hands. "Because we're getting out that way."

Ally raised her head. "Getting out?"

"Help me get the cover off."

They tugged at the large square panel, Ally squatting by Trish's side, the flashlight resting on the floor between them, washing their faces with an eerie upward shine.

"What do you mean, getting out?" Ally whispered. Something more than tears glittered in her eyes, something like hope.

Trish spoke through clenched teeth as she struggled with the board. "There was this abandoned farm in the town where I grew up. I used to go there with . . . with a friend."

"So?"

"Behind the house was a dry well like this one. We climbed down in it once. Looked through the drainage grate." Exertion squeezed drops of sweat from her forehead. "There was a cave."

"Ground water." Ally understood. She scrabbled at the panel with the frenzied desperation of someone buried alive struggling to dig free. "It hollows out passageways. And since there's another cave near this one—"

"Passages might . . . connect." The board groaned, sliding free.

"You're right, there could be a whole cave system." Ally coughed as unsettled dust flew up from the dislodged panel. "The bedrock here is limestone, great for caves. Limestone's mostly calcium carbonate, which dissolves real easily in carbonic acid—that's just water mixed with carbon dioxide gas. The karst process, they call it."

Gasping, Trish hauled the board away from the frame. "Where'd you learn all that?"

"I'm into anthropology. Digging. You know."

Trish beamed the flash into the well. Twelve feet deep. Round walls, studded with rocks of all shapes and sizes set in troweled cement. A grate at the bottom, big enough to imply a negotiable sinkhole.

Maybe. Or maybe there was no sinkhole, no network of tunnels, no last chance.

Think positive, Trish.

Overhead, the sudden pounding of footsteps. The killers, approaching the cellar once more.

She waved Ally forward. "Down you go."

The girl descended, finding ready handholds and footholds among the larger stones. Trish tucked the flashlight under her belt, the beam angled downward, and followed.

The handcuffs made it hard for her to maneuver. She lowered herself by slow degrees.

"Take off the drain cover," she gasped to Ally, already at the bottom.

"It's stuck."

Trish glanced down at the grate, splashed by the flashlight's beam. Iron bars crosshatched in a square frame. Rusty and old, like a relic from a shipwreck.

"It's just heavy," she told the girl. "Get some leverage."

No further noise upstairs. The deadly silence of a snake poised to strike.

Cain reached up and wrenched the smoke detector out of the kitchen wall, snapping the wires. It dropped on the floor, a useless thing.

Tyler, Gage, and Lilith waited by the side exit. Cain ushered them out. Lilith was last to leave.

"Looks like you get to spread that little girl's legs after all," she said playfully.

"Do I?"

"Yeah." Giggle. "Spread 'em all over the ceiling."

She kissed him, a hot, probing kiss that shot a thrill of excitement through his groin, then hurried outside to take cover by the garage.

Alone in the hallway, Cain turned toward the cellar door.

The M–80's fuse was too long. He took a moment to trim it to a blunt, lethal stub.

Robinson and the girl would barely have time to scream.

Trish dropped to the bottom of the well. Crouching beside Ally, she hooked her fingers around the drain cover's iron grillwork.

Muscles popped in her back as she strained to lift the heavy grate. Irrelevantly she thought of blasting her lats on the rowing machine.

Ally pulled with her upper body, bending backward at the hips. Her face reddened, freckles standing out.

Together they dragged the grate clear of the opening. It clattered heavily on the well's cement floor.

Through the aperture, some sort of cavern was visible. Chalky walls. Rough floor. White encrustations of stalagmites.

Overhead, in the dark—a squeal of hinges.

The cellar door was open.

* * *

Leaning through the doorway, Cain lit the fuse and pitched the bomb like a softball in a looping underhand throw.

He had a momentary impression of red spirals traced in the dark as the bomb flew over the bannister into the center of the room.

Slam.

The door had closed.

An instant later—thump of impact, jingle of loose metal.

Keys, coins, something like that.

Whatever it was, it had landed near the well.

"Go!" Trish screamed.

Ally wriggled feet first into the hole.

Trish swung both legs over the side.

And the world exploded.

41

Cain flung himself outside, onto the paved path between the house and the garage, and a shock wave shuddered through the yard in time with a bellowing blast.

He looked back. The house's exterior wall flexed, networks of veins crisscrossing the puckered stucco. Windows cracked in the dining area, the living room. The side door was wrenched off its hinges in a cloud of greasy black smoke.

"Cain!" From somewhere far away, Tyler's yell rose above the roar. "God damn it, I *knew* you used too much!"

Wild slide through a limestone funnel, rough rock chafing her exposed skin, then another hard landing, a blade of pain knifing her ankle.

Trish hardly felt it.

Over the echoing thunderclap of the blast she heard something like hailstones pelting the well, ringing on the rocky walls and cement floor directly above her.

She dived clear of the sinkhole. Behind her, a sudden metallic clinking.

Some of the hailstones—whatever they really were—had ricocheted into the cave.

Sprawling on her stomach, she fumbled the flashlight free of her belt.

The beam found Ally huddled in a corner. Trish threw herself at the girl and covered her protectively as the limestone chamber groaned like a living thing.

Dust flew everywhere, gritty and stinging, clouds of it, coating hair and skin and clothes. Ally shook with terror.

Trish pulled her still closer, wishing she could hug the girl but unable to do so with her chained hands, and then her back sizzled with a hot wire of pain.

One of the hailstones had slashed a horizontal wound across her shoulder blades. She hissed through clenched teeth.

Other, larger debris tumbled down the sinkhole, thudding and bouncing. A fist-sized projectile smacked into the wall a few inches away.

Ally screamed.

"There, there." Trish pressed her mouth close to the girl's ear. "There, there."

Earthquake.

The thought registered distantly in Charles Kent's mind as the closet shook and Barbara and Philip and Judy cried out in distress.

Around them, a bedlam of clashing noise: rattle of bifold doors, groan of walls, squeal of floorboards, and the clothes hangers coming down in a clattering cascade.

Another hanger pole was jostled free of its mounting. An overhead shelf tipped forward, spilling shoe boxes and hats and scarves. Judy was screaming.

An hour ago Charles would have been afraid. Now he was past fear, past feelings of any kind. He was very tired. He'd never been so tired, not even after pulling all-nighters at law school, cramming for finals, shoveling knowledge into his skull with the joyless fervor of compulsion.

Back then his exhaustion had been temporary, certain to be relieved by rest, but now there could be no rest ever again.

Ally was dead.

The gunshots Barbara had heard—there could be no other explanation.

The tremors died away. Sudden silence, broken only by Judy's fitful sobs. Her husband comforted her while the beam of his flashlight traced an unsteady course around the closet, passing over heaps of fallen clothes and swirls of dust and a broken scatter of light bulbs that had been stored with other emergency supplies.

"What ... what in God's name ... what ... ?" Judy's question was a moan of fear.

"Quake," Barbara stammered, her voice raw from her earlier shouting.

Philip shook his head. "I'm not so sure. Felt more like—well, like an explosion."

"Explosion?" Barbara made a hiccuping noise. "Why would they set off an explosion? Charles already opened the safe. Didn't you, Charles?"

He heard his name and understood that some sort of answer was expected.

"Opened the safe," he echoed. "Yes."

"Then they wouldn't need to blow it open. So it must have been a quake."

Philip touched her arm. "It was. Of course it was."

Barbara stood staring blindly at the damage, her eyes wide and wild, and then she sagged, giving up.

"Or maybe not," she whispered. "Maybe you're right. First shots, now this. Oh, dear God, what's going on out there?"

All the life seeped out of her, and she dropped her head, too weary for tears.

Charles paid little attention to the exchange. He was thinking of the Weimaraner named Toto the family had put to sleep last year after the heartrending discovery of cancer. He remembered watching death creep into the dog's eyes, remembered seeing the alert stare blur into glazed emptiness.

Ally's eyes must be glassy like Toto's, her gaze unfocused and unblinking.

Hard to face that fact. Hard to make it real. But there was something worse.

He would survive.

There it was: the blunt and simple truth. He would go on. He would put all this behind him. He would spend his wife's money and after a time, rarely think of Ally at all.

Cain was a monster, but he was not the only one. Charles knew that now. He had peered deep inside himself, and at his core there was nothing. Simply nothing.

An earthquake, even the detonation of a bomb, seemed of trifling consequence when compared to that.

42

Trish didn't know how long she huddled with Ally, whether it was thirty seconds or thirty minutes, but finally the noise diminished and the debris settled.

Her ears rang. Her cheeks were wet with tears. Her whole body shook. She remembered sitting on the beach near the dock, racked by shivers and nausea. This was like that.

Come on, keep it together. No medals for quitters.

She decided she was okay. She wasn't going to faint or vomit or fall apart.

And she and Ally were alive. They'd made it. They'd escaped from the cellar, survived a bomb, for God's sake, an actual bomb.

Good job, Robinson.

The voice in her mind was Pete Wald's. She wondered if he had been grinning when he said it—that smug, patronizing grin.

She didn't think so.

Lifting her head, she looked around, beaming her flashlight through a gray sea of dust.

The ray, fanning wide, illuminated a limestone gallery opening on negotiable passages to her right and left. Winding conduits, lumpy and folded, glossy in the light, impenetrably dark elsewhere. She thought of a TV documentary she'd seen: a fiber-optic camera inserted into somebody's digestive track, snaking through intestinal corridors.

In the belly of the beast, she thought, not knowing quite where the words came from or what they meant.

She felt weirdly isolated from her environment—deafened by the blast, barely able to see in the dusty gloom, smelling and tasting only the chalk that clogged her nostrils and mouth. With her hands manacled, she was restricted even in what she could reach out and touch. She was a prisoner in some bizarre dream without the reality of physical sensation.

Except for pain. No shortage of that. Pain in her every protesting muscle—and her left ankle, injured in the fall—and her back, slashed by one of the hailstones.

Not really hailstones, of course. But what?

She aimed the flashlight lower. Littering the cavern floor were chunks of concrete and dislodged limestone, intermingled with sticks of blackened wood. Remnants of the Ashcroft heirlooms, glowing feebly, logs in a hearth.

And everywhere, strewn like seeds, were fragments of metal.

She picked up the closest one, dropped it instantly. Red hot.

It appeared to be part of a knife's serrated blade, mangled by the blast and by multiple ricochets.

Only a few had trickled into the cave through the drainage hole, but the things must have been thick as locusts in the cellar.

If she and Ally had been up there. . .

Pincushions. Dartboards.

Handcuffed, she couldn't reach behind her to examine the incision across her shoulder blades. But she hadn't lost any mobility, so apparently no major muscles had been severed.

Rest would be nice right now, a long rest after a hot shower and something cold to drink.

No such luck. Despite exhaustion, despite the pain making multiple claims on her body, she had to keep going, had to get away from here—before Cain arrived to confirm his kills.

She turned toward Ally, curled like a shrimp, floured in dust. Cuts crosshatched her legs and arms.

Gently she shook the girl alert. Ally stirred, saying something, but Trish couldn't hear it over the clangor in her head. Squatting close, she read Ally's lips.

What happened?

Trish formed one word in reply: *Bomb.*

Ally nodded, registering no reaction.

You okay? Trish mouthed.

A shaky nod. *You?*

Trish's ankle hurt worse than before, but she merely showed a tight smile, then indicated with a sideways motion of her head that it was time to go.

Awkwardly they got to their feet, Ally rubbing dust from her eyes.

Trish tested her ankle. Though tender, it supported her. The ligaments had been stretched but probably not torn. She could walk.

Digging in her pocket, she produced the compass she'd taken from the boat. The handcuffs made it impossible for her to beam the flashlight at the dial.

She handed both the compass and flash to Ally, mouthing: *Northwest.*

Ally had said the other well lay in that direction. The girl turned in a half circle, then pointed toward the right-hand passage

Trish: *You lead. I'll follow.*

Ally managed a smile. *That's a switch.*

They walked single file. Entering the passage, Trish struck her head on a low stalactite. Just what she needed. More pain. No wonder spelunkers wore helmets.

Her bad ankle and the uneven floor made every step a challenge. She had to crab along the wall to keep her balance. The limestone was rough and yellowish brown and crusted with muck that slimed her uniform in gray-green stripes. She was already so dirty that an additional layer of filth hardly mattered.

At a bend in the corridor, she glanced back, alert to the possibility of pursuit. No one was there.

Cain wouldn't give up, though. She was sure of that.

43

In the aftermath, a surreal stillness.

Tyler sat on his haunches on the grass, breathing hard, listening to the night. Somewhere in the distance a coyote bayed, the weird ululant cries like the wail of a ghost. An Arizona sound, stirring childhood memories that left him feeling briefly lost and old.

"God *damn*." That was Gage, kneeling beside him. The kid's mouth hung open, his jaw loose-hinged as a puppet's.

Flakes of stucco began dropping off the side wall onto the grass. The exterior door listed, then fell with a thump.

Clap of gloved hands. Cain's voice, brusquely businesslike: "That's all she wrote."

The four of them stood slowly. Tyler glanced at Lilith. Her lips wore a cold sheen; her eyes were dazed with pleasure. He wouldn't be surprised if she'd had herself an orgasm—a little bang to complement the big one.

The police radio at her hip squawked madly as the dispatcher named Lou reported a burst of 911 calls. People in the foothills were phoning in news of a loud noise and a sharp jolt.

"Damn," Gage muttered, addressing everyone and no one. "The cops'll be on us now."

"No, they won't." Cain shrugged. "Listen to what's coming in."

Lou was reading off the calls' points of origin. "Dodson Lane . . . Hibiscus Terrace . . . East Pinewood Drive . . ."

"That covers a ten-mile radius," Cain said with satisfaction. "It'll take our friends in blue all night to pinpoint the source, if they ever do. Now let's move."

Gage obeyed, voicing no more objections.

On the doorstep Cain paused, coughing as curls of gray smoke scarfed his face. "Better put on your masks," he said, plucking his own from his back pocket. "You'll breathe easier."

Tyler obeyed, donning his black ski mask, then followed Cain inside.

Just across the threshold, Tyler aimed the nozzle of his dry-chemical canister at the fuming remains of the cellar door, scattered on the floor like so much driftwood. Through his boots' heavy soles he could feel the heat of the floor tiles, buckled and cracked, peeling back in scorched flaps.

"Shut off the extinguisher," Lilith said abruptly.

"Hey, I'm just doing my—"

"Shut it off."

Grudgingly he silenced the hiss of aerosolized powder, then turned to Lilith. She was frozen in a pose of listening, the police radio in her hand.

"Eight-one. Four-Adam-eight-one . . . you guys still code seven? We need all available units. . . . Come in, four-Adam-eight-one . . ."

Cain swore. "Tremor probably set off every burglar

alarm in town. Cops are running out of warm bodies to answer the calls."

"What do we do?" Lilith asked.

The gray eyes in the mask's slits favored her with a cool stare. "You respond . . . Officer Robinson. I'll tell you what to say. In the meantime—Tyler, Gage, make sure the closet's secure. The prisoners will be going crazy. Try to quiet them down."

With a nod, Tyler moved off, Gage at his back.

Quickly they made their way through the kitchen, circling around the·fallen refrigerator and the strewn contents of the cabinets. Cain's black duffel lay on the floor, flaps open, gear spilling out like drool from a panting mouth.

Remarkably little smoke in here. Most of it had already exited via the side doorway, fanned by the breeze from the kitchen window.

They cut through the dining area into the hall of the east wing. It had been lit by fluorescent panels, but the tubes had shattered, and the hallway was dark.

This part of the house lay directly above the main force of the blast. Damage was extensive. Horizontal cracks ran like jagged graphs through the walls. The doorway of Ally's bedroom had collapsed, the lintel fallen, studs leaning drunkenly.

In the master suite, both bedside lamps had broken. The only illumination was a spill of light from the bathroom, where twin sconces over the sink remained intact. The furnishings had been tossed like laundry in a spin cycle, but there was a clear path to the closet.

Tyler and Gage crossed the suite. On the floor a telephone, jostled off the hook when a nightstand toppled, was shrieking like a wounded thing. Impatiently Gage ripped loose the handset and pitched it into a corner.

"Is somebody there?" Philip Danforth's voice, edgy with panic.

Tyler reached the closet, checked the hinges. "Yeah, it's okay, it's okay." He used the same tone of reassurance that had worked on Gage when the kid was losing control.

The technique was less effective this time. "What the hell happened?" Philip yelled.

"Just a minor accident."

Judy Danforth spoke up. "You mean it wasn't a quake?"

Quake. Too bad he hadn't thought of that. "No, but it sure did feel like one, huh? Some explosive charges of ours went off by mistake, is all."

"Went off by *mistake*?" Philip again. "Listen, we heard gunshots earlier. Now a bomb. What in God's name is going on?"

"Gunshots? You must've imagined that." The closet doorframe had been slightly warped, but the hinges were still intact, the padlock and chain undamaged. "Things have been real quiet here, except for this little incident."

"Where's Ally?" The feverish cry was Barbara Kent's. The closet doors thumped with hammering fists.

"Don't fret, ma'am, your daughter's fine." He glanced at Gage, now at his side. "Chopped fine," he whispered through the mask.

The kid giggled.

"Where *is* she? Bring her here, let me see her, please, *let me talk to her!*"

Tyler figured a Ouija board would be necessary for that conversation. "We'll, uh, collect her shortly."

Collect. That was rich.

Her screams and pleas continued unacknowledged as Tyler and Gage left the suite.

"Four-Adam-eight-one, come in. Eight-one . . ."

Cain listened to the crackling radio in the twilight dimness of the living room. He had moved in here with Lilith so they could escape the smoke and lift their masks.

"Ready?" he asked tensely.

She answered in Trish Robinson's voice. "That's a roger."

The mimicry was excellent. This would work.

It had to work.

Cain thumbed the transmit button and held the radio close to her face.

"Eight-one," Lilith said, reciting the words he'd taught her. "Go."

"Hey, eight-one"—Lou's raspy voice was sweetened by relief—"it sure took long enough to raise you."

Like trying to raise the dead, Cain thought.

"Sorry for the delay." Lilith spoke briskly, her lisp gone. "We were code seven. Grabbing some chow."

"Yeah, well, I kind of let that code seven slide. It's been an hour." Irritation was replacing relief. "Look, what's your location?"

"Hospers Road, west of the highway." He'd told her to say that. There was a strip of fast-food franchises out that way, a likely place for two cops to scarf down a meal.

"Okay," Lou said, "we got a ten-thirty-three at the Cracker Barrel on Johnson." A ringing alarm, just as Cain had thought. "You back in service or what?"

"Ten-four, we'll take it."

Lou signed off. "Twenty-one twenty-five."

Cain lowered the radio, and Lilith gulped a breath.

"Think she bought the story?" Her lisp had returned.

"Hell, yes."

"How long before they figure it out?"

"I'd guess at least twenty minutes before they realize the unit's disappeared. After that, a half hour or more until they think of sending a car here."

"That should be long enough. But ... but I was okay? I sounded like her?"

"You were perfect." He kissed her lightly on the mouth. "You *were* her."

A shy smile. "I can talk like Trish anytime."

"Even in bed?"

"Sure." She twirled her finger lazily against his neck. "Too bad we don't have time to do it right now."

"Sorry. Got to save myself for Mrs. Kent."

"You bastard."

But she shivered with a thrill of expectation, and he understood that she looked forward to having him inside her after he'd taken Barbara Kent—as if Barbara's death would linger on him and excite her with its residue.

He knew her mind so well. And he did love her. Though occasionally he toyed with sweet things like Ally, they were of no lasting significance. He and Lilith were soul mates. Or perhaps, he sometimes thought, it was nearer to the truth to say they had no souls.

The idea did not displease him. A soul was a conscience, and conscience was weakness. He and Lilith were predators, sleek as sharks, primitive and deadly. Her lisp and her round angelic face were the camouflage that hid her gleaming fangs.

"Come on." He clapped his hands. "We need to see the bodies."

"And then . . . Barbara Kent?"

Lilith stared up at him, a child anxious for the arrival of Santa Claus, terrified the magic sleigh would miss one special roof.

"Then Barbara," Cain promised. "She'll be joining her little girl real soon."

44

Dead end.

Ally stopped short, her flashlight beaming a pale yellow oval on a smooth limestone wall. The spot of light wavered badly, tracing lopsided spirals, because the hand that held it was palsied with stress and exhaustion and fear.

Behind her, Trish whispered, "Damn."

Her voice shook as badly as Ally's hand, no doubt for the same reasons, but at least Ally could hear her now. The ringing in her ears had subsided to a distant, monotonous chime.

"Guess we've got to double back," Ally said. "Try the other route."

The cave system was a labyrinth. Several times she'd had to decide which branch of a fork to take, relying on the compass as her guide. At the last intersection she'd guessed wrong.

She began retracing her path, leading the way with the flash. Her bare feet, scraped bloody by the unforgiving stone floors, hurt with every step.

But she couldn't complain. She had seen how badly Trish was limping. Must've sprained her left foot or ankle. If Trish could go on, so could she.

She didn't ask what they would do if the alternate route was a dead end also. Or if the flashlight's battery gave out. Or if they blundered onto a false floor—a common hazard in caves—and plunged into a lower gallery from which they could not emerge.

Lots of worries, lots of dangers, and no need to talk about any of them.

Besides, there was another question on her mind.

"So who was she?" she asked without looking back.

"Who was who?"

"Your friend. The one who used to go with you to the old farmhouse."

In the beat of silence that followed, Ally knew she had inadvertently fingered a nerve.

"Her name," Trish answered finally, "was Marta. Marta Palmer."

More silence, unbroken save by their ragged breathing and the scuffle of shoes and bare feet on the uneven floor.

Ally's flash ticked like a pendulum, lighting the narrow passageway, picking low stalactites out of the gloom. An elaborately ridged section of the gallery wall passed by, the limestone sculpted into flowing draperies, water and time conspiring to rival Michelangelo. Brown streaks of iron oxide colored the rocks, creating the surreal impression of cave paintings.

Frigid air, stirred by no breeze, wrapped her in its chill. Not too cold for her—but Trish in her wet clothes must be risking hypothermia.

Maybe it was best to keep her talking. Besides, Ally didn't like the ominous quiet of this place.

"Is she dead?" she asked. "Marta, I mean."

This time she did look back, the flashlight swinging with her gaze. She saw Trish's eyes widen in the glow.

"How . . . how'd you know?" Trish whispered.

"The way you said her name. I just had a feeling."

"You should be a psychologist."

"Anthropology's my thing." Hesitation. "I guess maybe you don't want to talk about this, huh?"

"I can talk about it. It's just that I usually don't. See, she was only nine years old. And so was I."

There was weariness in her voice, a deeper weariness than any born of injury or fatigue. This was the listlessness of old grief and remembered tears.

They arrived at the fork in the maze and started down the alternate corridor. Somewhere ahead was a soft, susurrant whisper. An aquifer, probably.

The caves were wetter here, the walls slimed with even more of the ubiquitous gray-green muck. Ally circled around a birdbath-sized pool, the murky water speckled with small darting things. Pupfish? She'd read someplace that they lived in caves.

The pool receded, but the hiss of rushing water grew louder, and the chill deepened.

"Marta was your best friend," Ally said tentatively.

"Did I make it that obvious?"

She waited for a further response, some explanation. None came.

Irrationally she was hurt that Trish wouldn't share this secret with her.

Get over it, she chided herself. It wasn't as if Trish was her sister or something. She was under no obligation to bare her soul to some inquisitive teenager she hardly knew.

The hiss resolved itself into gurgles and splashes, echoing eerily. The aquifer was close.

Her flashlight probed the dark. In the fan of light, shapeless mounds of calcite rose up like volcanic crags out of a mist. Automatically she recalled their technical names: helictites, culuphilites.

They could grow big enough to block a passageway. This latest worry teased her briefly before she pushed it aside.

Two of the dripstones had fused to form a pillar, its hourglass figure oddly aesthetic, a touch of beauty in this dismal world. Past the pillar was a dark void and a hint of freshwater spray.

Ally stepped closer to the void, the flash revealing a gap in the limestone wall. Framed in the gap, a vertical shaft. She spared a second to peer downward.

Fifty feet below coursed a subterranean stream, flowing around smooth rocks, falling away in a foaming cataract that descended out of sight. Reflected glare from her flash dappled the mossy walls in a scintillant light show.

Despite pain, despite fear, she felt her mouth smile at the spectacle. She glanced at Trish. "Really something, huh?"

Trish merely nodded, her gaze faraway.

Ally moved on, Trish following. The stream's babble diminished to a static hiss that blended with the distant clanging in her ears.

Overhead, the gallery's roof whitened with old deposits of guano. Bats had roosted here once but appeared to be long gone. She wondered if there was an egress nearby. Bats usually—

"We played together all the time."

Trish's voice was a whisper, but coming unexpectedly it seemed explosively loud in the settled stillness. Ally jumped a little.

Then she found a context for the remark. Trish and Marta. Two nine-year-old girls.

"Did you?" she asked as she caught her breath.

"Explored vacant lots, chased butterflies, got ourselves ice cream on the way home from school. Small-town stuff."

"What town?"

"Called Barnslow. Up in central California, in the mountains. Fifteen hundred people. Band concerts in the summer. A safe place, nobody was afraid—until Marta . . . until she . . ."

Trish took a breath and said it.

"She was murdered."

Ally pursed her lips. The news ought to have been shocking, but she'd grown up in the '90s, when the violent death of children was taken for granted, as much a part of everyday life as headaches and traffic jams and inconvenient weather.

"I'm sorry," she said pointlessly.

Trish didn't seem to hear. "It was a stranger who did it. They never caught him. Just someone passing through. He . . ."

Her brief pause spoke of censorship, some hurtful fact suppressed.

"He must have picked her up while she was walking home from school. She had a jump rope with her, and I . . ."

Another glitch, another edit.

"They found her in the weeds, with the jump rope around her neck."

"She was strangled," Ally said, then winced. Brilliant deduction.

"Strangled, yeah." Trish coughed. "And left in the weeds behind the farmhouse where we used to go, the farmhouse where we would sit on the porch and talk about boys and make up futures for ourselves. She was there in the weeds, sprawled in the weeds."

That phrase, *in the weeds,* seemed to hold some significance for Trish, but Ally couldn't fathom it and was afraid to pursue the issue.

"Is that why you became a cop?" she asked instead.

Trish made a noise like a chuckle. "You guessed that too? Yeah. I knew it was too late to save Marta. But there are other girls, and other strangers passing through, and . . . and bad things *do* happen—even in small towns."

Ally knew there was more to the story, but Trish didn't want to tell it. Maybe the memories were too hard to face.

New silence, deeper than before, trailed after them as they proceeded down the passage. Clutching limestone fingers snagged the ragged hem of Ally's dress. She pulled free again and again.

Abruptly she realized the snags and scrapes were becoming more numerous, the groping fingers emboldened.

The passage was narrowing. The walls were closing in.

She looked over her shoulder, caught the same awareness in Trish's eyes.

"Another dead end?" Ally whispered.

Trish didn't answer.

Swallowing fear, Ally crept forward, hunching

lower as the ceiling kissed her hair. Hardly any room to maneuver now. Ahead, a still narrower space terminating in darkness.

Desperately she probed the shadows with her flash. The pale fan of light found a small round hole at the end of the passage, looming like a hungry mouth.

"I think there's a tunnel," she breathed, her throat tight.

"Big enough for us?"

"Don't know."

On hands and knees now. Crawling to the tunnel's mouth, if that was what it was.

She played the flashlight inside. The beam illuminated a gun-barrel tube winding into the dark.

The passage was barely wider than a doggie door, but probably navigable.

"Does it go in the right direction?" Trish asked.

Ally checked the compass. "Maybe. We're heading due north now, but the tunnel looks like it bends west."

"We'll have to take it."

As if we've got a choice, Ally thought.

She eased herself horizontal and wriggled inside.

"Hope you don't have claustrophobia," she said, tasting dust from the crawlway's chalky floor.

"Speaking in public—that's my only phobia."

"Funny," Ally grunted, worming forward. "Mine too."

Or it had been, anyway. After tonight she expected to face a dazzling profusion of new fears, unhealed psychic wounds that would bleed into her dreams and make them nightmares.

Was Marta Palmer a wound in Trish's mind, her dreams? Ally thought so.

There were some things you could never escape from, it appeared. Even adulthood wouldn't rescue you. Even college wouldn't take you far enough away.

She crawled on, deeper into the dark.

45

Activating his flash, Tyler followed Gage into the cellar.

The concrete staircase, though cracked and chipped, was intact. Ragged stumps were all that was left of the bannister. The wall bristled with bundled spikes of wood splinters, sharp as porcupine quills—bits of the railing driven into the hairline fissures between the cinder blocks by the sheer force of the blast.

Below lay hell in miniature.

Flashlight beams played over a waste of rubble, the funneled light fanning through a sooty mist. Spot fires glimmered in dark corners. At the rear of the cellar, water sheeted down from a broken plumbing pipe.

Cain and Lilith combed the wreckage, shadow figures amid the smoke.

Ghosts, Tyler thought with an irrational chill. Demons.

"Hey, boss," he called, feeling a sudden need for noise in this silenced place. "Next time you kill somebody, could you make a more serious effort?"

Cain glanced up at him. His eyes glinted through slits in the ski mask. "They did go out with a bang, didn't they?"

Tyler nodded. "Wham, bam, thank you, ma'am."

Eyes burning, he reached the bottom of the stairs. Lilith's extinguisher hissed, the hose a lashing snake, as she smothered a smoldering pile of debris.

With his flash Tyler found the blast crater in the center of the room. At the deepest point, a great slab of the concrete foundation had been blown free, exposing raw bedrock like an open wound.

So much for percussion. As for fragmentation . . .

He read that story in the shrapnel glittering around him, the thousand shards of cutlery strewn on the floor and studding the wreckage.

The destruction was total. Those two charming ladies must have been killed a hundred times over.

So where were they?

Panning the cellar with his flash, he saw no splash of maroon, no body parts, not even a forlorn shoe or a scrap of the cop's uniform.

He beamed his flashlight at the crater again. Maybe the two of them had been standing right over the bomb when it blew. Maybe they'd been atomized—nothing left but dust.

Was that possible? He didn't think so.

The beam wavered, searching the floor, and found a second hole, this one at the lip of the blast crater.

But this hole hadn't been made by an explosion.

It was round, perfectly round.

"Cain."

The way Tyler said it, low and tense, made the older man turn instantly in his direction.

Cain's gaze followed the beam of Tyler's flash. He saw the hole, made a noise. A slow shuddering exhalation like a death rattle.

"Christ . . ."

Then he was crossing the room, circling the crater, peering into the smaller hole. Tyler joined him.

It was a well. A dry well, the drain uncovered, a sinkhole dropping into subterranean darkness.

"They got away." Cain stripped off his mask, heedless of smoke and dust. Fury purpled his face. "Robinson and the kid—*they got away.*"

46

Flat on her belly, working by feel in the absolute dark, Trish wriggled along a narrow tubular crawlway.

Ally was somewhere ahead, but the glow of her flashlight had vanished when the girl disappeared around a bend. Hampered by the handcuffs, Trish was finding it difficult to keep up.

By slow degrees she advanced, head hunched tortoise-like between her shoulders to avoid limestone over-hangs. The walls and ceiling were coffin-close. Despite what she'd told Ally, she felt stirrings of claustrophobia.

A shiver racked her. The caverns were chilled by the perpetual absence of sunlight and damp with perco-lating ground water, dripping like a thousand leaky faucets, coating walls and floors with filth.

She crawled onward, indifferent to the complaints of her palms and elbows, buffed raw by abrasive rock.

Never had she endured such sheer physical dis-comfort for so long. The most grueling drill at the academy, the most pitiless hike, the worst camping trip of her life had been exercises in shameless self-indulgence compared with tonight's ordeal.

She rounded another turn in the passageway, and the glare of the flash swam into view again.

"It's opening up." Ally's voice, high and shaky, echoed down the tube. "I see light."

The other well. Had to be.

And if starlight was visible, the well head must be uncovered.

Trish crawled faster.

Ahead, Ally scrambled into a grotto, then stood, beaming the flash upward. "We found it!"

"Thank God," Trish gasped.

With a last effort she emerged from the crawlway and staggered erect, coughing on stone dust. Her sore ankle throbbed, and her shirt and pants, encrusted with muck, clung skin-tight to her body.

"Guess we won't need this anymore." Ally gave back the compass. "It was a life saver, though."

Trish pocketed it. "You can thank your folks for packing supplies on their boat."

"My mom never goes out on the lake. It's my dad I've got to thank."

Her dad—the man who'd signed a death warrant on his wife and daughter.

Soon Ally would learn exactly how much she had to thank her father for. Trish felt a cold queasiness at the thought.

She turned away, studying the gallery in the flashlight's ambient glow. The walls were hung with limestone curtains, the floor scattered with elfin bones. Over the years birds and small animals must have fallen down the well and died, their skeletal remains later washed by rainwater through holes in the drainage cover into the cave.

A miniature skull caught her attention. Rabbit? Could be.

Maybe a hunted rabbit—like her.

She raised her head, peering upward at a long and treacherous sinkhole. Set in the far end of the vertical shaft, at what must be the bottom of the well, was an iron grate, a twin of the one in the cellar.

Reaching that grate posed a considerably greater challenge than climbing down the well in the cellar. There she had used the fieldstones studding the shaft as handholds and footholds. Here she would have to chimney her way up, advancing in fits and starts like an inchworm as she groped for any available crevice.

The task would be difficult under any circumstances—impossible when handcuffed.

"Think we can make it?" Ally whispered anxiously, following Trish's gaze.

Trish nodded. She knew what had to be done. "Set down the flash."

Ally propped it in a corner, the beam casting a faint flush of color, soft as candlelight, over the cryptlike chamber.

"Okay." Trish took a nervous breath and unholstered the Glock. "Now . . . now help me get these cuffs off."

Ally was mystified. "I haven't got a key."

"Yes, you do." Her face was expressionless as she handed over the gun. "This is the key."

Ally stared at the pistol, sleek and black and lethal, and she understood. A blink of her eyes, a sudden trembling of her shoulders.

"No . . ." More moan than word.

"I need my hands free in order to get out." Extending her arms, Trish braced both palms against a rock outcrop in the cave wall. "Put the muzzle against the chain."

"If I miss . . ."

"You won't."

"Oh, God. Oh, my God."

Hesitantly Ally pressed the Glock to the handcuff chain, pointing the muzzle away from Trish.

"Now touch the trigger." The girl's finger curled around it in a reluctant embrace. "Perfect. You're a natural."

"I'm scared to death."

You and me both, Trish thought.

Letting off a round at such close range risked unpredictable, perhaps lethal consequences. The bullet could be deflected in any direction, or could burst into fragments like a miniature grenade.

"It's no big deal." Trish did her best to sound confidently casual. "Just squeeze the trigger—gently, and not too fast."

"Don't know if I can."

"You've got to. Or we'll be stuck down here."

"I know, but . . . I can't. I really can't . . ."

Ally was starting to shake. That was bad. If her aim was thrown off, Trish could lose a hand.

"Come on, partner." Trish held her voice steady. "I'm counting on you."

Ally turned her head, brown eyes shining, wide and surprised. "You called me partner."

"That's what you are."

"Wonder Woman's partner." The words were spoken lightly, but she couldn't hide the tremor of pride in her voice.

"Wonder Woman didn't need a partner," Trish said. "I do. And you're it. So let's go."

Ally nodded, new firmness in the set of her mouth. "Okay. On three."

Trish waited, praying for this to work. If the gun jumped . . . if the bullet ricocheted . . .

Slowly Ally drew back the trigger, counting under her breath.

"One . . ."

Trish tensed, holding herself rigid.

"Two . . ."

The gun went off, the report thunderous in the confined space, and Trish screamed.

Pain lanced her wrists. Doubled over, she sucked air through gritted teeth. Stars flashed across her field of vision as she stared at her hands, looking for a red spurt of blood.

Somewhere close to her ear Ally was babbling in terror. "I'm sorry, it was too soon, I wasn't ready—oh, Christ, did I *shoot* you? *Talk* to me!"

God, it hurt. It hurt.

Trembling all over, Trish fought off the pain and assessed the damage.

Blood? No. Fingers? None missing. Handcuffs?

The chain was still intact.

"Damn," she breathed.

One of the welded links had been badly nicked, forming a jagged crack, but the link had not failed completely. Her hands remained manacled.

Over the ringing in her head, Trish heard herself say, "We've got to try again."

"Again?" Ally was aghast.

"Got to."

"If it didn't work the first time—"

"Second time's the charm. Come on."

Trish planted her hands on the wall once more. Her wrists, though sore, were unbroken. Already the pain was receding as her ligaments recovered from the sharp, convulsive twist.

Though she'd come through the first attempt without serious injury, she knew she was pressing her luck to risk another try.

Ally's hands hardly trembled as she pressed the muzzle against the weakened chain.

"Go for it," Trish said.

Ally nodded. No hesitation now, only a quick count—"One, two, *three*"—and a flex of her trigger finger.

Trish averted her face as dust flew up from the cavern floor in time with the deafening discharge.

The pain was bad, maybe worse than before, but at least she was ready for it. A long moment passed as she stood bent at the waist, eyes shut, enduring the sizzle of agony in her wrists, gathering the courage to look.

Then she let her gaze travel to her hands, to the steel cuffs, to the two small links joining the swivel eyelets . . .

The weakened link had given way.

The chain had been severed.

She was free.

Blinking back tears, she raised her shaking hands. Experimentally she rotated and flexed her wrists.

No broken bones, thank God. She could climb the shaft. She could go on.

"I'm okay," she gasped. "I'm okay."

"You sure?" Ally's question quavered, a breathless tremolo.

Trish nodded. Purple bruises were forming around the handcuff rings still fastened to her wrists, and blood leaked from her left forearm where a bullet fragment or a sliver of the fractured chain had bitten, but it was just a scratch.

"I'm okay," she said again. "You did great ... partner."

Ally hugged her. Trish clung to the girl with a mother's fierceness.

It was not Marta she held, but it could have been.

47

"They got away."

The echo of Cain's shout rang like an anvil on the cellar walls.

Lilith's fire extinguisher dropped from her hands. Gage made a soft, plaintive noise like the moan of a frightened child.

Cain barely noticed their reactions. His full attention was focused on the well. Rage simmered in him.

This operation had been planned for weeks. For months. Every smallest detail had been accounted for. Nothing had been left to chance. It was the opportunity of a lifetime, his passport to a better life, to a future not spent in a desert trailer or a prison cell.

And now it was jeopardized, all of it, by a rookie cop and a high school girl who didn't have the good sense to lie down and die.

"You never know." Tyler tried for a note of optimism. "They might've bought it anyhow. Shock wave could've triggered a cave-in."

"Bullshit."

"It's possible."

"No, it's not. And you know it. Those two whores are alive. God damn it, they're *alive!*"

The anger boiled over. Cain spun and seized the nearest fragment of debris, a charred and twisted thing that might have been the leg of a table.

With a bellow of fury he heaved it into the shadows, then stood panting as he struggled to get hold of his emotions.

Screaming was bad. He remembered how Gage had screamed at the hostages, inadvertently confessing his immaturity and lack of discipline.

A leader had to remain poised, assured, unflappable—even now, when every thread of his careful planning threatened to unravel, when five million dollars was dissolving like smoke before his eyes.

"You should have iced that blue-eyed bitch in the living room when you had the chance," Lilith said petulantly.

Cain nearly shot back an ugly answer, but no.

Discipline. Self-control.

"Damn straight," he replied after a brief inner struggle. "I had her three feet away, dead in my sights, and I didn't pull the trigger. Didn't want to agitate the prisoners. I fucked up."

His gaze traveled the room, meeting each face in turn. Tyler, Gage, Lilith—all with their masks off now, all watching him, surprised and impressed by his admission of failure.

"I fucked up," he repeated for emphasis. "My fault. I underestimated her. I thought she was just a scared kid. A Mouseketeer. Another bug to be squashed. But she's better than that."

Tyler set down his fire extinguisher. "So what do we do? Abort?"

"Too late to abort. The Kent girl saw my face—and

yours," he added, his glance including both Tyler and Lilith. "And her and the cop heard our names over the radio. Robinson even heard me talking to Charles Kent. She knows everything." He scanned the room and watched comprehension register on the row of faces. "We couldn't quit now if we wanted to."

"Okay." Tyler sounded unsettled. "We go after them. Search the caves. Split up—"

Cain cut him off. "Impractical. A cave system is a maze."

"Maybe they'll get lost in it," Gage said. "Just, you know, wander around till they drop."

"Nice thought." Cain smiled. "But Robinson seems to have a knack for survival. She'll find an exit. Maybe already has."

"Once they're out," Lilith asked, "where will they go?"

Cain nodded. That was the right question.

Where would they go?

48

Finally Trish let go of Ally.

"We'd better get moving," she said simply. "Somebody might've heard that shot."

Ally gave back the gun, then retrieved the flashlight and beamed it into the drainage hole.

Trish invested a moment in mental preparation for the task to come. She was no rockhound. Her knowledge of chimneying up a shaft was limited basically to stuff she'd seen on TV.

Hollywood stunt people wore safety harnesses and worked over nets. No retakes for her. Get it wrong, and she would have a long fall with a hard finish. Even if she didn't die, she would surely break a limb and be stranded in the cave.

Her heart pumped harder, a fresh spurt of adrenaline kicking in.

"No medals for quitters," she murmured.

Ally glanced at her, worried by the delay. "What?"

"Nothing." She holstered her Glock, then cupped her hands and blew into them. "Okay. Here goes. Try to hold the flash steady."

"It's easier than holding that gun."

Trish smiled at that. The smile remained fixed on

her face, her lips skinned back from her teeth in intense concentration, as she set to work.

Standing on tiptoe, she raised her arms—pops of pain in her sore shoulders—and grasped hold of a stone protrusion at the mouth of the shaft. Her skinned palms shrieked at the contact, and her tender wrists added their objections as she eased herself inside the sinkhole.

Not difficult so far. Painful, yes, but she was growing accustomed to pain.

Jamming her back against one wall, she applied counterpressure with her hands and knees, then inched higher, scrabbling for wedgeholds in the tight space. The flashlight threw her elongated shadow along the tube as she chimneyed upward.

Now she was ten feet above the floor of the grotto. Crumbs of dislodged limestone skittered down the shaft.

She levered herself higher, her body folding and unfolding, her back sliding up the wall, then her legs duckwalking at a ninety-degree angle to keep up. Probably there was something comical about this performance, but she had no breath for laughter.

Fifteen feet now. Almost there. The flashlight's beam more diffuse now, weaker with distance. Irregularities in the wall harder to see.

Work by feel, then. Come on.

She was doing it. She was nearly to the top.

Twenty feet. Her heart racketed against her ribs. Sweat glistened on her bare forearms, greasing the ugly steel bracelets decorating her wrists. She shook her head to clear stray droplets from her eyes.

With her back and her knees wedging her in place,

she looked up. The grate was within reach. Skeletal silhouettes of branches and tattered shreds of leaves darkened the grillwork—storm debris too large or sticky to fall through the cracks.

Before lifting the grate, she would need to brace herself more securely. She wiped her wet palms on her shirt and flattened them against opposite walls.

Arms rigid with isometric tension, she eased onto a football-sized bulge of rock, straddling it like a stool. Then she released her hold on the walls, letting the rock take her full weight.

She breathed hard, refilling her starved lungs. There was a dangerous grayness at the edges of her vision. She'd thought she was in good shape, but she hadn't been training for a triathlon.

Just get out of the cave, the well. The lake couldn't be far. She touched her pants pocket, felt the reassuring shape of the key ring through the fabric.

Almost over. It was almost over. She had only to do these last few simple things.

Carefully she raised her arms over her head and pushed on the grate.

Heavy. Like the one in the cellar. But at least from below she had leverage.

She pressed harder.

Heard a low, sandy crackle.

The grate must be lifting free of caked sediment.

Funny, though. She hadn't felt it move.

And the noise—odd—it almost seemed to be. . .

Beneath her.

The rock outcrop she was seated on.

Cracking at its base. Breaking away from the wall in a rush of limestone chips.

Terror stabbed her. Her hands clutched wildly at the grate.

The rock crumbled free, leaving her abruptly unsupported over a twenty-foot drop.

There was a sickening twist in the pit of her stomach, the sensation of a plummeting elevator, and she was falling—

The index and middle fingers of her right hand hooked one of the iron bars.

Suspended by two fingers, she dangled in the shaft.

"Trish!"

Ally's shout echoed hauntingly. The flashlight wavered.

She couldn't spare the strength to answer. With her left hand she groped upward. Higher. Reaching higher.

She curled a fist around another bar . . .

And the grate lurched sideways, releasing a cataract of pebbles and dust.

It was loose in its frame. Her shifting weight had tugged it partly free.

Fighting panic, she straightened her legs and probed the walls of the shaft with both feet, searching for a place to stand.

The grate moved again.

This time it jerked diagonally. The lower right corner popped out of the frame and dipped into the hole.

She screamed as the panel tilted on its side, iron rasping against stone, wet leaves and dead branches showering her in a gritty rain.

Then the grate stabilized, wedged vertically in the drain, her two hands fastened to its leading edge.

There was a stretch of time—a second or a minute—when she simply couldn't move at all. Any further attempt to find a foothold might upset the grate's precarious balance.

But she had to risk it. Her aching arms were losing their strength. Her fingers, newly slick with sweat, couldn't maintain their grip much longer.

Again her shoes brushed the limestone walls, hunting for a crevice, a shelf, anything she could brace herself against.

Chips of limestone pattered on her face and hair. The grate groaned, settling slowly into the hole as the iron edges wore away the loose, flinty rock.

Little time now. A few more seconds, and the hole would be enlarged enough to let the grate slip through.

There. Her right foot touched a slender ridge.

She planted her shoe.

The grate dropped into the shaft.

Instinctively she let go. Rush of metal past her face. Falling forward, she pistoned her arms and slammed both palms against the opposite wall, wedging her upper body horizontally in the sinkhole.

Twenty feet below, Ally jumped clear as the grate impacted the cavern floor. The flashlight threw shapeless curlicues of glare along the shaft.

"Trish?" Breathless terror spiked the cry. "You okay?"

It was hard to answer. Her mouth wasn't working right, and there was a choking tightness in her throat.

Finally she forced out words. "Just barely." She tried for a note of humor. "Got the drain cover off at least."

With her last reserves of energy she chimneyed up the remaining few feet of the shaft and struggled into the bottom of the well. She knelt, dripping beads of perspiration and trying to remember that ridiculous motto of hers, which suddenly had slipped her mind.

Still on her knees, she looked down at the pale blur of Ally's face. "Your turn."

"What do I do with the flash?"

Good question. The girl's dress had no pockets, no belt, nothing that could hold a flashlight.

"Just stand it on the floor. Aim it right up the shaft."

Ally obeyed, then stood under the sinkhole, the flash setting her dress aglow like a footlight on a stage.

"Good. Now do what I did."

"You're kidding."

Trish smiled. "Without the dramatics, I mean. When you get within reach, I'll pull you up."

Ally closed her hands around the same limestone overhang Trish had used when getting started. She struggled to boost herself into the shaft, not quite making it.

Briefly Trish feared the girl lacked the strength to execute a pull-up.

Then with a grunt of effort Ally managed the first stage of the ascent.

"You're doing fine," Trish said.

But there was a long way to go, and even now Cain might be planning his next move.

49

Cain paced the cellar, stepping over debris, thinking hard.

"Last time Robinson and the girl were on the loose, they headed straight for the rear gate. Why? What's in that direction?"

"The lake." Tyler narrowed his eyes. "There's two boats tied up at the dock."

"That doesn't make sense," Lilith said. "She was already there. She could've taken one of the boats an hour ago."

Cain had an answer for that. "Not without the ignition key." He stopped pacing. "The kitchen. That's why she went in there. The cordless phone was an afterthought. She wanted *keys.*"

Gage was unconvinced. "Hell, she could just hotwire the ignition. Blair used to do it all the time when him and them Mexicans were swiping boats."

"Not everybody's as street smart as your big brother," Lilith said with a cold smile.

Gage's eyes narrowed. "What's that supposed to mean?"

"Nothing. Except if he's such a piece of work, how come Robinson's got his gun?"

"You just shut up about Blair," Gage said in a tone meant to threaten violence but conveying a greater threat of tears.

"Both of you shut up," Cain snapped, irritated at the distraction.

Tyler got the conversation back on track. "Lilith is right. Robinson's a rookie. She's never even seen a chop shop or a stolen car. Couldn't hot-wire an electric toothbrush."

"So she comes back here, gets the keys." Cain saw it now, saw it as clearly as the room around him. "Rescuing the girl is just improvisation. What she intends to do is get away on a boat."

"And go where?" Gage asked, still belligerently skeptical for no good reason.

Cain had studied maps of this area so intensively they were now committed to memory. Other than the Kent estate, there was nothing on the lake's perimeter but woods and a picnic area, closed to the public at dusk.

He remembered visiting the picnic area on one of his exhaustive reconnoitering trips. He'd stopped by a snack shop, bought a cheeseburger, called Lilith from a kiosk outside—

"*Shit.*" The word was torn out of him like a grunt of agony. "There are phones across the lake. That's what she's after. She's still trying to get through on nine-one-one."

"How would she know about the phones?" Lilith asked.

"Maybe she's been there, like I was. Maybe her fairy godmother told her. How the hell should I know?

That's where she's going. She can make it in five minutes—once she gets to the dock."

Tyler unholstered his Glock, checked the magazine. "Unless we get there first."

"Do it," Cain said. "Take the Porsche." The two younger men were running for the cellar stairs when he added, "Wait."

They stopped, looking across a waste of rubble.

"If you need to get on the radio, don't use any of the preset frequencies. She'll be monitoring." Cain thought for a moment. The ProCom units transmitted only on the two-meter amateur bands between 140.0 and 148.0. "Set channel one to one-four-five-point-zero. That'll be our private frequency. She can't find it on the scan mode."

"Why would we need the radio?" Tyler asked as he and Gage keyed in the digits. "Ain't you coming to the party?"

"Me and Lilith will have to take a rain check. We're staying here." He threw her a glance and saw excitement flush her pale cheeks, hectic like fever. "Time to get paid."

Tyler grinned. "Mrs. Kent?"

Cain answered with a slow nod. "She's lived too long as it is."

50

Clasped hands.

Shaking with effort, Trish hauled Ally through the drainage hole, into the bottom of the well.

"Thanks, Trish." Ally coughed weakly, expelling inhaled dust. Blood measled her palms where the gritty limestone had chewed like rodent teeth. "Thanks."

The last five feet had been nearly impossible for her. More than once Trish had been sure the girl would lose her hold. She was not an athlete, and the sheer physical exertion expended in chimneying up the sinkhole had left her shivering with fatigue.

"You need to work out more," Trish said gently.

"No way." Ally hung her head, a spill of dust-glazed hair overshadowing her face. "After tonight I'm never getting out of bed again."

Trish couldn't blame her. She'd had the same thought herself.

She glanced upward at the well head, twelve feet above the drain. The feeble glow of the flashlight, abandoned in the cave, was of no use now. But the stars, bright and clear in the cloudless sky, painted the scene in a pallid wash of light.

Over the well stood a hand-cranked windlass, a

276

bucket dangling on a rope. The rope must have been wound tight on the winch once, but over time it had unspooled, the bucket pulled lower by the weight of collected rainwater.

Now the bucket hung halfway down the well. Just out of reach.

"Going to need your help again," Trish said.

Ally struggled erect.

Her bare feet were bloodied, her stylish dress as shapeless as a flour sack, her arms and shoulders scored with scratches. Brambles gleamed in disheveled hair, matted with dirt and dust.

Still she voiced no complaint. "What can I do?" she asked simply.

Wonder Woman's partner, Trish thought with a smile.

"See that bucket? I'll make like a footstool. You stand on me and pull it down."

Kneeling, Trish braced herself, hands spread. A blade of sciatica twisted through her sacroiliac as Ally stepped onto her back.

"Got it." She climbed off.

Trish tugged the line until it was taut. "Okay. We've got to shimmy up."

For once she'd found a use for her academy training. Like the other recruits, she had practiced rope climbing regularly as part of a conditioning program.

Grasping the rope with both hands, tucking it between her knees, she began to climb.

The distance was short enough, and the line seemed to be taking her weight without undue strain, but even so Trish felt a cool caress of relief when she reached the rim of the well.

Cautiously she raised her head, aware that she was an easy target for a sniper.

Nothing happened.

She climbed higher, then swung her legs over the rim and lowered herself to the ground. Pain flared in her sore ankle.

For a moment, just one moment, she surrendered herself to the warm night air fragrant with summer blossoms, the whisper of leaves, the trill of a mockingbird running through a series of whistling calls.

It was so good to be out from underground. It was like returning from the dead.

Later she would savor the feeling. Later.

Now there was work to do.

"You next," she whispered, leaning weakly on the rim.

Ally started to shimmy up, gasps of exertion echoing in the shaft. The rope twirled giddily. Starlight painted her face as a pale smear.

Trish followed the girl's slow progress, her gaze shifting intermittently to the dangerous darkness on every side.

Climbing the rope was not much of a physical challenge, but Ally's strength was nearly gone.

Come on, kiddo, Trish urged silently. You can do it.

"No medals for quitters," she called into the well.

Ally, halfway up, produced an interrogative grunt. "What?"

"No medals for quitters, I said."

"Screw you, Trish." But she climbed faster. Three quarters of the way now.

From the windlass—a sudden creak.

The knot securing the rope was coming loose.

Instinctively Trish closed both hands over the line.

But the gesture was useless. Should the knot fail, the cord would slither through her clutching fingers, branding her with rope burns. She could never hold on.

Ally was nearly to the rim.

"*Hurry,*" Trish breathed.

"Hey, like I said, screw . . ." The Ally saw how Trish gripped the rope, and she understood.

She shimmied faster, gulping air.

It would be a twelve-foot fall. Concrete floor. Broken arm, broken leg—at a minimum. Then Ally would be trapped in the well, unable to climb out or to take refuge in the caves.

Trish thought of the rabbit skull in the grotto, the scatter of assorted bones.

How many hunted animals had died here in the dark?

Ally was less than a yard from the well head.

Trish looked at the knot—unraveling still faster.

Another second, and the rope would spring free.

"*Take my hand!*"

Leaning forward, she thrust her right arm down.

Ally grasped her wrist, and the knot undid itself, the line lashing like a snake as it dropped away.

The wrenching tug of gravity nearly cost Trish her balance. With her left hand she clutched the rim of the well, digging her shoes into the dirt.

"It's okay," she gasped. "Got you."

Straining, she pushed away from the well, carrying Ally with her, and abruptly Ally's bare feet were scrabbling on the rim, finding purchase, and she was out.

"Oh, God." Ally shook all over, a rag doll in a terrier's mouth. "Oh, God, this is bad, this is bad."

"It's nearly over." Trish fought the violent trembling of her knees. "Is the lake nearby?"

Ally brought her breathing under control. "Yeah. That way."

A wide strip of pavement was visible through a gap in the trees. Trish recognized the path she'd taken when she left the dock and entered the Kents' backyard.

"Okay. Let's go."

They reached the macadam in seconds, then headed downhill, both of them hobbling.

Trish's ankle screamed with every step. She gritted her teeth against swirls of light-headedness and limped on.

Couldn't let pain stop her. Somehow she sensed with premonitory certainty that death was rapidly closing in.

51

The Porsche roared alive with a crank of the ignition key.

Gage slammed the passenger door as the car took off, accelerating from zero to sixty in five seconds.

Tyler muscled the coupe through a tight turn, then steered across the manicured lawn, past sprays of roses and stands of eucalyptus.

"Your brother told me you never killed anybody," he said over the motor's throb.

Gage swallowed. "Right."

Squeal of rubber, and the Porsche swung onto the driveway, skidding momentarily because Tyler had let off the throttle.

When he opened it up, the coupe found its footing and barreled forward, streaking between the house and garage into the rear yard.

"Not gonna freeze up on me," he said evenly, "are you, man?"

Indignant: "No way."

His high beams stabbed the back gate, already open. He had slapped the wall switch after leaving the cellar.

The gate shot past. Gone.

"Because," Tyler said, "if you are—"

"Hey." The gold earring flashed. The kid's mouth trembled, but his eyes were hard. "She might've killed Blair. Okay?"

Tyler looked at those eyes, flat and stubborn as nail heads, and for the first time he was not unhappy to have at least one of the Sharkey boys on his crew.

"Okay," he answered with a nod.

He rolled down the windows and unholstered his Glock.

At the edge of the beach Trish hesitated, pulling Ally back behind a profusion of manzanita.

"I left one of them here," she whispered. "Want to make sure he didn't get loose."

She scanned the area. A dozen yards away, a black-suited figure thrashed and squirmed like a landed fish.

He was conscious now, struggling against the nylon cord, but he hadn't freed himself. Those square knots she had tied must be pretty good. No wonder she'd earned that Try-It patch.

"No problem. Come on."

Ally's bare feet kicked up plumes of white. "You took his belt? He's got a hundred pounds on you."

"Told you I got lucky."

The yielding sand was harder to cross than the firm macadam had been. Trish puffed her cheeks, blowing hard.

When she glanced toward the killer again, she saw that he had stiffened, head lifted, staring at her.

Even in the dark, across a span of yards, she could read the hatred in his gaze. His face—flushed with exertion, distorted by the gag stuffing his mouth—was a study in still, focused fury.

Though she knew he was no threat, she felt her stomach ice over, felt the short hairs above her collar bristle in alarm.

Someone else, someone in a movie, would defuse the situation with a quip, cutting and smart. Her mind was frozen.

She looked away, conscious of the peculiar fact that nobody, to her knowledge, had ever hated her before tonight.

It was the price of being taken seriously, she supposed.

The path dipped, the lake tilting into view, and Tyler saw them.

Two darting figures. Crossing the beach. Bounding onto the dock.

His mouth stretched in a smile. "Let's party."

The Porsche rocketed down the slope.

Trish fumbled the keys out of her pocket as she and Ally reached the ladder.

"Take these."

She flipped the keys to Ally, already mounting the top rung. The girl snatched them out of the air.

For a heart-stopping instant she juggled the key ring, nearly dropping it into the black water.

Then she got a firm grip, and Trish let herself breathe again.

Ally jumped onto the nearest boat, the Sea Rayder mini-jet. Trish untied the mooring line and tossed it into the stern, then descended the ladder, drawing her gun.

Engine noise.

She looked over her shoulder.

A black coupe careening down the paved path. High beams projecting a white funnel of glare.

From the speeding car—gunfire.

Cain picked his duffel off the kitchen floor and rummaged for his roll of duct tape, the tape that would bind Judy Danforth and Barbara Kent to the headboards of the matching beds.

He had no interest in Judy, of course. But Charles Kent had insisted it would look suspicious if his wife alone was pulled from the closet.

Anyway, Judy would serve as a credible witness to the killing. She would report how the masked man had forced himself on Barbara, how he'd warned her not to fight him, and how in crazed frustration he'd finally stuck his pistol in her mouth and squeezed the trigger.

Perhaps he wouldn't even need duct tape for Barbara. Officer Wald's handcuffs were still in his pocket. He—

Wafting in through the kitchen window on a current of moisture was a string of distant pops.

Gunshots. At the lake.

Lilith heard too. Both of them turned toward the window, then looked at each other.

Cain clenched a leather fist in savage satisfaction.

"Got 'em."

Trish ducked. Sprays of splinters from the planks. Thump of a bullet drilling into a post ten inches from her head.

The coupe reached the bottom of the grade. It charged the dock.

In one continuous motion she swung off the ladder onto the Sea Rayder's fiberglass boarding step, then pivoted into the stern.

Nice move, said a voice in her mind with peculiarly objective appreciation.

At the helm Ally fumbled with the key set.

Another volley of shots ripped up the dock. The headlights brightened, the car racing closer.

Trish fired three useless shots, not even trying to aim.

Thunder.

The boat's motor. Ally had found the key. She punched the throttle.

The Sea Rayder lunged forward. Trish fell on one knee. Twist of pain in her ankle.

At the end of the dock, the coupe braked with a howl of tires. Driver and passenger leaned out. Popping corn: a crackle of reports.

The moving boat, low and fast, made a difficult target. Even so, the bullets landed dangerously near. Pockmarks peppered the foaming wake.

Kneeling in the stern, Trish was helplessly exposed. Her body went rigid, every muscle tensing in expectation of a lethal shock.

This was the worst part—to know she might be cut down when she was so close to getting away.

Then the Sea Rayder's prow lifted, the boat planing on the lake surface, and dock and shore receded, the killers out of range.

Made it.

She expelled a ragged breath, then turned toward

the helm seat on the starboard side. Ally hugged the wheel, steering like a pro, the throttle jammed fully open.

"You okay?" Trish slipped into the cockpit bench seat alongside the girl.

Shaky nod. "What'll they do now?"

Trish looked back. The coupe reversed off the dock and turned, headlights sweeping the beach like comet tails.

"I don't know. But they're not through yet."

52

The Porsche fishtailed as Tyler cranked the wheel. Lake water blurred into beach, then pavement. He gunned the engine.

"Hold on!"

The side door was open, Gage leaping out.

Tyler wanted to ask what the hell. Too late.

Gage kicked up white plumes of sand, then flopped on his knees near a dark, sprawled shape, vaguely human.

Blair, of course. Dead.

The figure moved.

"What do you know," Tyler said, genuinely surprised. The rookie really hadn't waxed the little creep after all.

Gage sliced the cord binding his brother. Blair leaned on one arm, coughing, as he unstripped a gag.

"Man, you're alive!" Gage exulted. "I *knew* you were!"

Tyler, no sentimentalist, was unmoved by this reunion. "Haul ass, both of you. We can drive around and cut 'em off!"

"You do that," Gage called back. "Me and Blair'll hot-wire the other boat and get on their tail."

Tyler was briefly astonished. The kid had an idea there.

"Right," he said, wishing he'd thought of it.

He grabbed the pull-strap handle on the passenger door and yanked it shut, then accelerated up the hill.

Distantly he was surprised to realize how much he was enjoying the feel of the fast car under his control—engine throbbing with 247 horses, oversize tires drumming, sports suspension giving him a crisp, firm ride.

Even now, in the heat of action, he appreciated the sleek, angry machine with a connoisseur's relish.

He would have a Porsche of his own. Red. Or maybe black; he still wasn't sure.

Either way, he wouldn't be denied.

"Someone's coming," Judy whispered.

Barbara heard it too: a tread of boots in the hall.

She glanced at Charles, hoping vaguely for a look of reassurance or resolve.

He was leaning forward, his gaze fixed on her with peculiar intensity, his mouth drawn taut in a blood-less line.

The thought flashed in her mind that she had seen him look this way before—when he was reaching the climax of a jury trial, closing in for the kill.

Cain moved fast down the hall of the east wing, Lilith beside him, the master suite ahead. The roll of duct tape flashed as he tossed it lazily in one hand.

At the doorway he paused, breathing in, out. Relaxing himself, preparing for the work at hand.

"All right," he said when he was calm and ready. "Here it comes. Divorce, American style."

They were donning the ski masks when their transceivers crackled. "Hey, boss. You there? Come in, boss."

"Sounds like good news." Cain smiled, unclipping his radio. "Talk to me, Tyler. Tell me they're history."

"No such luck."

Cain needed a moment to make the words real. He felt his face sag under the mask.

Tyler was still talking, his normally languid voice spiked with urgency.

"Bitches are taking a cruise. Gage and Blair—he's alive—they're trying to hot-wire the other boat. I'll cut around to the park. Open the front gate for me, will you, boss? . . . Boss?"

Lilith just stood there.

"Do it!" Cain snapped. "The switch is in the foyer."

She disappeared down the hall, and Cain stared blankly after her, wondering what else could go wrong tonight.

With Gage's knife, Blair pried off the ignition switch.

His jaw and chin ached. Hot pain seared his throat. His voice box felt crushed. Nausea bubbled in his gut, the nausea he'd fought to suppress while he lay trussed and gagged, knowing that if he puked he would choke on his own vomit.

Hatred had given him the self-control he needed. Hatred of that blonde bitch who'd outmaneuvered him. Humiliated him.

He pulled out the metal plug, exposing a cluster of

wires. No time to find a clasp to bridge the terminals. He did the job quick and dirty, jamming the knife into the switch. The steel blade conducted current across the gap, closing the circuit between battery and coil.

With a rumble the engine kicked in. A second later the stereo system snapped on, a Clarion marine CD player pumping out "Do Wah Diddy Diddy" by Manfred Mann.

Blair liked that song. He cranked the volume to the max.

Waterproof speakers shivered with the pulsing bass as the FireStar shot away from the dock.

The smoked Plexiglas windshield cut his visibility to nearly zero. He stood, peering over the frame. Spray washed his face.

The jet boat had a head start, but the gap would close quickly. Blair knew boats. The Sea Rayder was equipped with a three-cylinder, ninety-horsepower Mercury Sport Jet engine. Carrying two people, the boat had a top speed of maybe thirty-five miles an hour.

The FireStar, on the other hand, sported a V–6 Mer-Cruiser—five cylinders, more than two hundred horses.

No contest.

Ally glanced at the side mirror. "They're after us."

Pivoting in her seat, Trish saw a dark blur cresting the lake a quarter mile astern. Music pulsed above the motor's roar.

As she watched, the blur expanded, its triangular outline sliding into focus.

The second boat, of course. What was the logo she'd seen on the hull? FireStar.

The music was louder now as the boat closed in.

Gage climbed into the companion seat. "Some fun, huh?"

Blair smiled at that. His baby brother had been plenty scared going into tonight's operation, but the surge of power from the outdrive had kicked the fear out of him. He was a kid on a roller coaster.

Well, why not? Riding a fast boat to a rock beat—it was Hollywood stuff, a celluloid wet dream, and the pistol in Gage's hand only made it more hip, more '90s, a violent image for a violent time.

"You know it, bro," Blair yelled over the engine roar. "Some fun!"

53

Barbara pressed her ear to the crack between the closet doors.

"Gone." She turned to the others. "They've gone."

She felt an inexplicable lift of relief, as if there had been some personal threat, a menace directed specifically at her, in the remorseless march of boots.

"Do you think they'll be back?" That was Judy, addressing the pointless question to everyone and no one.

Unexpectedly it was Charles who answered. "They'll be back."

The words sounded curiously like a threat.

She remembered his agitation a short time earlier, the air of expectation in his body language, his intensely focused gaze. And now look at him—deflated, defeated, as if . . . as if he'd *wanted* the killers to come.

A shiver kissed the back of her neck, tickling the short hairs at the edge of her coiffure.

For a moment she wondered . . . she asked herself . . . if Charles . . . could he . . .

He seemed to feel her stare. He blinked at her.

"They'll be back," he said again. "They said they'd bring Ally, didn't they?"

Ally. So that was it. That was why he'd leaned forward in anticipation, and why he was slumped and sagging now.

"Of course, dear." Barbara smiled, dispelling whatever ridiculous notion had teased her thoughts. "Of course they did."

Cain heard the Porsche howl through the front yard as he joined Lilith in the foyer, her hand still resting numbly on the gate switch.

Together they watched the coupe vanish down Skylark Drive, taillights shrinking.

He deliberated only a moment. "We're going after him. As backup."

Lilith blinked. "But . . . Mrs. Kent?"

"She's lived forty-three years. Another half hour won't matter."

"You said the cops might start to figure it out before long. That was fifteen minutes ago."

"Schedule's tight, but we can get it done. Robinson and the girl—then Barbara. Come on. We'll take the van."

He hustled her out the door, toward the open gate. She pulled off her mask, and he saw her lower lip jutting ominously, a prelude to a tantrum.

"I wanted Mrs. Kent." She pouted, hands balled into fists. "I was all set."

"Look on the bright side. Maybe you'll nail Robinson personally."

A blink, a sudden smile, everything all right again. "Think so?"

Cain shrugged, breaking into a run. "Somebody's got to."

* * *

Trish checked the Glock's magazine.

Eleven rounds, plus one in the chamber.

In her gun belt's dump pouch were two spare mags, one fully loaded, the other partially expended by the sentry she'd subdued.

The chase boat sped closer. She made out two men aboard.

"How far to shore?" she asked Ally.

"Another couple miles. Maybe four minutes."

Trish shook her head. Four minutes was too long. The FireStar would overtake them much sooner than that.

"Keep driving," she said. "And stay low."

Blair pushed the boat to its limit, watching the tachometer register five thousand rpm.

He glanced at Gage and caught his kid brother's infectious smile.

"I'll steer," Blair shouted through a mist of spray. "You shoot."

Swinging out of her seat, Trish crawled over the stern and knelt on the port swim platform. The jet drive throbbed through the fiberglass like a straining heart.

With one hand she clutched the grab handle on her left. With the other she aimed the Glock.

She tried using the laser sight.

No good. The choppy ride made it impossible to direct the beam.

The FireStar loomed nearer, drums and guitars keep-

ing up a steady beat. She could see the passenge ·
leaning over the port side, a pistol shiny in his hand.

Steadying her gun, she fired.

Muzzle flash from the Sea Rayder.

"Bitch is shooting!" Dimly Blair perceived a kneeling figure. "In the stern. The stern!"

Gage leaned farther out, reckless with exhilaration,
and returned fire.

From the FireStar, a volley of gunshots.

Bullets slapped the water. Trish threw herself onto
the stern's fiberglass cover, sprawling flat on her belly,
legs twisted awkwardly.

Couldn't be intimidated. Had to keep the chase boat
at a distance.

Leaning on her elbows, bracing the gun in both
hands, she squeezed off another three rounds.

Blair was closing fast on the Sea Rayder, wild laughter riding on his lips, laughter born of speed and
danger and "Do Wah Diddy Diddy" pounding like a
movie soundtrack all around him.

He wished he still had his gun or, better yet, an
automatic weapon, a machine pistol or an AK–47.
Then he could be a real Hollywood hero; he could be
Schwarzenegger or Stallone, ripping bodies with bullets to the wail of a synthesizer in a hectic, garish
dance.

Jump cut: Trish Robinson's throat opening like a
second mouth.

Jump cut: Ally Kent screaming, cut down by another
spray of bullets.

Jump cut: the Sea Rayder plowing into a sandbar and igniting in a Technicolor whoosh.

Jump cut: Gage twisting backward, then dropping heavily into the companion seat, his Glock cradled loosely in his lap.

Drunk on adrenaline, Blair almost didn't realize that this last image was no film clip, no fantasy.

It was real.

Gage had been shot.

"Jesus," Blair hissed, the truth clamping hold.

The bitch cop had hit him. Gotten him bad.

The right side of his face was peeled open to red bone. His ear dangled on a flap of skin.

Blair throttled back and leaned over his brother.

"Stay with me, Gage. Stay with me."

Trish saw the chase boat drop back.

The guy riding shotgun was no longer firing at her. Reloading, maybe.

She glanced over her shoulder, past Ally. A dark land mass approached. The lake's north shore? No, not yet. Only the weedy hump of a small island.

Shore was still far away.

Too far.

Gage blinked, focusing blearily on Blair. His lips moved, but the feeble noises he produced were swallowed by Manfred Mann.

Blair looked ahead. The jet boat had widened the gap.

There was no time for him to minister to Gage—not if he still wanted Robinson.

He rammed the throttle forward and snatched the gun from his brother's hand.

Facing aft, Trish saw the FireStar surge ahead with frightening speed.

Muzzle flash. The pilot was the one shooting now.

The bullet struck the stern inches away. She averted her face from a shower of fiberglass splinters.

Close.

A second shot slammed into the underside of the boat. The pitch of the engine abruptly lowered as the Sea Rayder bucked.

Hit the motor. He must have hit the motor—

Her left leg jumped.

For a dazed instant she was baffled, wondering why it would jerk that way, like a dead frog's leg in a science experiment.

Then she felt a sudden curious numbness below her knee, numbness overtaken a heartbeat later by the worst pain she had known in her life.

It was a hot poker lancing her leg.

It was a thousand cigarettes branding her.

It was needles and electrified wires and steel claws.

Shot. Shot. *Shot.*

That one word caromed off the corners of her mind with dizzying velocity.

Her stomach twisted. She spat up something hot and wet.

Blood? Was she hemorrhaging? Had the bullet caught her higher than she realized? In the gut, the lungs?

No, it wasn't blood. Wasn't even vomit. Just saliva unspooling from her mouth in a thick, ropy strand.

The boat bounced, jarring her leg, and the pain leaped up, so strong she could hear its screaming whine in both ears, and *see* it too, a brilliant white glare that fogged her vision, erasing the night.

"We're losing speed!" Ally's shout. "I think—"

The breathless pause told Trish the girl had turned in her seat, had seen her.

"Trish—oh, God—look at you—"

"I'll be okay." Her mouth was very dry. "What's our speed?"

Ally checked the gauge. "Twenty-five. Still dropping."

Trish pushed pain away, forced herself to think.

The other bullet must have damaged the jet drive—broken an impeller blade or disabled the pump.

Whatever the specifics, the boat now had no chance of outdistancing its pursuer. And in her present condition she couldn't hope to hold off another attack.

She scanned the area. On her left lay the island she'd seen earlier, small and dark, barely more than a floating clump of reeds.

"Can you steer?" she yelled.

"Think so."

"Hook left."

Ally wrenched the wheel to port. The Sea Rayder, cornering sharply, hurled up a brilliant cascade that hung briefly in the air, Niagara's glistening veil.

The island swung around the boat, briefly eclipsing the FireStar.

"Jog north again," Trish ordered.

Ally locked the wheel to starboard, then straightened it.

With agonizing difficulty Trish pulled herself into a crouch. She holstered the Glock, fastened the strap.

"Now jump."

"*What?*"

"Jump—and swim."

Without waiting for a reply, Trish dived into the lake.

54

The sudden immersion was a heart-stopping shock. Agony sizzled through her left leg. Spirals of light-headedness wheeled around her, then receded as cold water partially numbed the wound.

Beside her, Ally plunged under the surface in a brilliant plumage of bubbles.

They broke water together.

The Sea Rayder motored away, and the FireStar, whipping into view, veered north and continued to give chase, trailing a raucous dance-club beat.

"Come on." Trish turned toward the island.

Ally swept a tangle of brown hair out of her eyes. "Can you make it?"

"Just go."

Ally obeyed, executing a strong breast stroke.

Trish swam without coordination or control. When her slapping palms churned up mud, she realized she'd reached the shallows.

On her good leg she pushed herself upright, then planted her left foot.

Her knee jellied. She collapsed with a hiss of pain.

"Oh, God." That was Ally, sloshing toward her, the

party dress pasted to her body in translucent folds. "Oh, God, oh, God."

She said it over and over, the words meaningless, infuriating somehow. Sprawled in the ooze, Trish wished the damned girl would just shut up and stop making those awful noises of horror and concern.

An elbow hooked under her armpit. Ally helped her up as Trish bit back an agonized cry.

Together they struggled forward, slogging through mud.

Gage was dying.

Blair knew it, and the knowledge ate at him like acid. As he tracked the Sea Rayder, now creeping at fifteen miles an hour, he kept tossing scared, sickened glances at his younger brother.

Even in the pale light of the instrument gauges, he could see the color draining from Gage's face as his eyes, half exposed under heavy lids, rolled up white in their sockets.

"Stay with me, bro," Blair said pointlessly, the words lost in the engine roar.

He'd finally turned off the damn CD player. The night's action didn't feel like a Hollywood movie anymore. Whatever had been fun and exhilarating was dust in his mouth.

The mini-jet's course was erratic, its speed greatly diminished. It seemed increasingly likely that his last volley of shots had hit his targets, either killing them both or at least injuring them badly enough to make operation of the boat impossible.

He could see no one at the helm or in the stern. Possibly they were slumped in their seats, leaking blood.

Like Gage.

The island met the lake in a cluster of boulders, velvety with moss. Breathing hard with strain, Ally escorted Trish through the rocks onto dry sand, then set her down behind a clump of crowfoot, speckled with pale yellow flowers half hidden among the ragged leaves.

With dulled relief Trish saw that their path was concealed by rocks and weeds. They had left no visible tracks.

She tried to remember her CPR training. Pressure points. Stop the blood flow. Right.

Weakly she ground her fist against her inner thigh, hoping to constrict the femoral artery.

"Oh, God. Oh, God . . . "

Still the same words from Ally, accompanied by grimaces and moans as she tore off Trish's left trouser leg and exposed her calf, a mound of ravaged flesh, lumpy and mangled and black with blood.

"Looks bad." Ally's voice quavered up and down the scale. "Does it hurt? Jeez, what a stupid question."

"It hurts," Trish whispered, pain nearly cheating her of breath.

"You're all bloody everywhere." The girl's fumbling fingers touched the wound. Trish stiffened, swallowing a scream. "I found a hole. No wait—I think there's another one below it. They got you twice, you were shot *twice*."

"Only once." Trish was crying now, unable to stop herself. Tears watered her world like a hard rain.

"Bullet went in and out. Forget about that. You've got to start digging. Dig a hole in the sand."

"A hole?" Terror bloomed in Ally's face. "Like . . . a grave?"

Trish managed a weak, abortive chuckle. "Hiding place, that's all. Foxhole. Right now we're too exposed."

"Got to help you first."

"No time, they'll be back any second."

"You'll bleed to death. I'll tie off the wound."

"It's all right, there's a pressure point, I've got my hand on it."

"Well, it's not working. You're still bleeding. You're bleeding worse than before."

"Look, *forget* me, I'll be fine—"

"You won't be fine, you need help—"

"There's no time."

"You can't keep bleeding like this!"

"Leave me alone and start digging, God damn it!"

"I won't. Just shut up. Shut the fuck up." Now Ally was crying too, crying soundlessly without sobs. "I won't let you die."

All the fight went out of Trish then, and she let her head fall back in defeat.

"We'll both be dead," she said in an exhausted whisper, "unless we get under cover."

Sniffles from Ally. "Then we'll be dead. I don't give a shit. I'm doing this." She tore her dress, stripping off a three-inch ribbon of fabric at the hem. "So shut up. I'm doing it." She wrapped Trish's left knee. "Just shut the fuck up, all right? All right?"

Trish nodded slowly. "All right." She almost smiled. "You've got a mouth on you, kiddo, you know that?"

"Yeah, well." Ally wiped her eyes with the back of her arm. "Guess that's what I get for hanging out with cops."

55

A padlocked gate protected the picnic-area parking lot. Tyler approached it at sixty miles an hour.

High beams gleamed on the rusted gate poles. A wall of wire mesh flew at him.

Impact.

The gate blew open, and the Porsche burst through. Heavy links of chain, snapping free, fractured the windshield. The coupe's front end sagged, mangled in the collision.

"Sorry, baby," Tyler muttered.

Killing the cop named Wald had troubled him not at all. Taking out Robinson and the girl would be a kick.

But abusing a sixty-thousand-dollar set of wheels—now, that was just unconscionable, it really was.

The Porsche skidded to a halt amid yards of white-striped asphalt. Tyler killed the lights and motor, and then he was out of the car, running hard, bloodlust roaring.

He reached the head of a trail that twisted down a shelved hillside to the lake shore. Leaning against a tree, he scoped out the lake, its mirror-smooth expanse black and glossy like wet pitch, visible over the tree-tops and the roof of the snack shop.

There. The jet boat—moving slowly, slowly, a wounded thing.

Astern, keeping a wary distance, was a second boat, the one Blair must have hot-wired.

Tyler licked his lips. Were the ladies hurt? Dead?

He checked his watch. 9:42.

By now Cain should have whacked Mrs. Kent. If the Sharkey boys could finish off their end of the job, the night's festivities would be successfully concluded.

It had better work out that way. And soon.

He'd waited long enough to be a millionaire as it was.

Ally knotted the tourniquet.

More pain, a lightning strike through her leg, and Trish groaned.

"Too tight?" Ally asked.

"No, it's okay. How's the bleeding?"

"Not so bad now."

"Elevate the wound. That should help."

Ally eased the injured leg onto a flat rock, then wiped her hands on the tattered hem of her dress, leaving red stripes.

Trish kept her hand on the pressure point near her groin. "You'll have to loosen the tourniquet in five or ten minutes. If it stays on too long ... " She didn't finish.

"What'll happen?" Ally asked fearfully.

"I could lose the leg. Below the knee."

"It could be *amputated*?"

"Don't worry about that." Trish tried to sound calm. "We'll just have to keep an eye on it, that's all."

"Maybe . . . maybe I did the wrong thing, huh? I mean, what do I know about this?"

"You did fine, Ally. You probably saved my life. I was being stupid."

"Brave."

"There may not be much difference." Trish felt her mouth slip into a smile. "*Now* will you dig the hole?"

"Hey, digging's my thing, remember?"

Trish lay on her back, listening to Ally burrow in the sand, and thought of the damage to her leg—the lean and shapely leg she'd admired in the mirror, the leg that had known a man's caress—shattered now, butchered meat.

Guns. She hated the evil things.

Amputation really was possible. From her first aid training she was aware that a tourniquet should rarely be used at all, and almost never to stanch bleeding below the elbow or knee. The limb could be lost.

Still, she hadn't lied to Ally. The blood loss had to be stopped. She couldn't afford to go into shock. Amputation was a chance she had to take.

She knew that. With cool objectivity she could calculate the risks. But there was another part of her, not cool, not objective, only a shrill scream in the back of her mind, and it was insisting that she didn't want to lose the leg, didn't want to lose the leg, please, if anybody was listening up there, she didn't want to lose the leg. . . .

With effort she tuned out that voice and tried to assess the damage.

She didn't think any bones were broken, and the blood hadn't been spurting, so apparently there was no arterial hemorrhage. The Black Talon must have passed cleanly through the fleshy part of the calf, the gastrocnemius muscle, the short trajectory allowing no time for the trademark barbs to retract fully. Probably it had entered low, exited high . . .

A shudder snaked through her as she realized how close the bullet had come to shattering her knee. An inch or two higher, and there would have been a compound fracture and a ruptured artery. The combination of crippling pain and rapid blood loss surely would have been fatal.

As it was, if the leg could be saved—and it had to be saved, please, God, she didn't want to lose the leg—then probably she could recover something close to full mobility. A limp? Maybe. Lack of sensation, diminished strength? Probably.

Her career as a police officer might have ended tonight. Well, the job was turning out to be sort of stressful anyway.

She heard herself laughing, a soft, manic sound.

"Trish?" Ally interrupted her excavation of the beach. "You . . . you okay?"

"Hanging in there, partner."

Eyes closed, she let the laughter segue to fresh tears.

Blair tracked the Sea Rayder as it continued slowing.

Ten miles an hour.

Five . . .

Finally it puttered to a stop. The boat lay on the placid water, as small and lightweight as a toy in a child's bath.

Warily he steered around the mini-jet, checking it out from all angles.

Empty.

No. Impossible. They couldn't have gotten away.

But they had.

Beside him Gage moaned. Blair looked at his brother, and pity lanced him.

The kid was rolling his head from side to side in a steady rhythm. Soft grunts escaped his lips, barely audible even with the FireStar throttled back to a low idle.

Blair knew what Gage was doing. It had been a childish habit of his brother's at the age of four or five.

At night he would sing softly in the lower bunk, rolling his head relentlessly in time with nonsense songs chanted under his breath, until slumber quieted him.

Blair, two years older, had called him a baby for doing it. But Gage *had* been a baby then, hadn't he?

And he still was. Blair Sharkey's baby brother— singing himself to his last sleep.

56

It took Cain longer than he'd expected to locate the van in the woods. He hadn't realized the clearing was so far from the road, and he kept stopping to see if he had blundered off the trail.

Finally he saw the familiar outline of the GMC Safari, its dark green finish melding with forest shadows. "There it is."

"Really got you rattled, hasn't she?"

That was Lilith. Cain turned to her. "Rattled?"

Shrug. "Never seen you like this."

"You think I'm *scared* of her?" He laced the question with incredulity. "The Girl Scout? The Mouseketeer?"

Lilith simply studied him, eyes narrowed, and abruptly he saw himself from her perspective— dripping sweat, panting raggedly, fists clenched.

"I'm not scared," Cain said.

But he wondered.

Still digging, Ally watched Trish warily.

When her laughter stopped, her breathing became more regular. Frighteningly regular, a prelude to sleep. If she slipped into unconsciousness, she might never wake.

"You found the body," Ally said, pawing sand, "didn't you?"

Trish blinked, groggy. "What?"

"Marta's body. You're the one who found it."

"How ... " She swallowed. "How could you possibly guess that?"

"You said the killer left her in the weeds. It sounded as if you'd seen her there."

"You're pretty perceptive, you know."

Ally smiled. "Growing up in a dysfunctional family kind of keeps you on your toes."

She shoveled out another heap of sand, then climbed in, squatting, and began making space for two.

The sand was dark and wet. Handling it was like kneading clay in pottery class. She sank her fingers in deep and scooped out great handfuls of ooze and flung them away.

Trish had fallen quiet once more.

"So how'd you find her?" Ally asked, disregarding courtesy.

A low groan as Trish shifted her weight. "After she disappeared, I wasn't supposed to go off by myself anywhere. But I did. I went to the farmhouse I told you about."

Ally paused in her work. "He killed her there?"

"On the porch. Keep digging."

"Right. Sorry." She resumed scooping out sand. "But you found her in the weeds."

"He dumped her out back where she wouldn't be discovered too soon."

"Were you looking for her?"

"No, I only wanted to be alone. She'd been missing for three days, and I was worried, scared, and the farm was a quiet place where I could think. I went wandering through the field . . . and then I heard this buzzing, very loud. Blowflies, big bluebottles, a whole cloud of them spinning over a spot where the weeds had been trampled."

She said nothing for a moment. Ally widened the hole and waited.

"I told myself it was a dead rabbit," Trish whispered finally. "But maybe . . . maybe I knew what it really was. Anyway, something made me look closer. The flies—I can still see them, like . . . like glitter, confetti. She was lying face up, jump rope around her neck. It's a joke, I thought; she's sticking out her tongue at me. But she never moved, and her eyes— there was a roach—it was crawling on her eye . . . "

"I'm sorry, Trish."

There was no answer, and this time Ally expected none.

Grimacing at a sudden, salty burn of tears, Blair guided the FireStar alongside the Sea Rayder. Pistol in hand, he climbed over the gunwale into the smaller boat.

Blood streaked the stern's fiberglass cover.

Robinson had lain prone in the stern as she fired aft. He'd gotten her—but there was no way of telling how badly she was hurt.

Now she and her little friend were gone. Must have dived overboard after rounding the island. It was doubtful they could swim to the far shore. Presumably they'd taken refuge on the island itself.

He boarded the FireStar, climbed behind the wheel again.

Gage was silent and still, and for a moment Blair thought his brother had drifted off to sleep.

Then he saw that it was much more than that, and much less.

"Gage." The word uninflected, a mere sound, not a name. "Hey, Gage, man."

There was no response, just as Blair had known there would be none.

He sat down heavily on the helm seat. Touched the luster of blood on his brother's neck.

The stain, though wet, was a trickle no longer. The flow of blood had stopped.

"Gage . . ."

Abruptly Blair hated the gloves he wore, the layer of black leather between his fingertips and his brother's face.

With savage impatience he stripped off the Isotoners, flung them overboard. They floated away like lily pads, shiny in the dark.

With his naked hands he caressed the familiar contours of Gage's cheek. Peeling back an eyelid, he saw a brown iris, round as a marble.

He and Gage used to flick marbles, laying bets on their skill. Blair always won, because he was the older brother, and older brothers could do anything. Older brothers were like God.

"But I'm not," he whispered. "If I was God, I'd bring you back. Give you some sense, so you wouldn't get mixed up in this shit."

He lowered his head, overcome by self-hatred and the first guilt he had ever known.

"Christ, Gage, why'd you listen to me? Why'd you want to be like *me*?"

Then his perspective shifted, guilt receding, as he saw that he was wrong.

It wasn't his fault. The rookie cop—she'd fired the fatal shot. She was the one responsible. Not him.

"Not me," Blair whispered, head lifting.

His throat hurt, a memory of the handcuff chain gouging his larynx. She'd ambushed him in the water, outmaneuvered him on shore. She'd trussed him like a broiled chicken and swiped his gear and left him with his ski mask wadded in his mouth. She might have cost him his share of five million dollars if tonight's operation didn't come off.

And she'd killed Gage.

Blair raised his head, and the noise he made, the awful noise forcing its way out of his throat, past pain, past weakness, was an animal's roar.

He slammed the throttle home, spun the wheel, and the FireStar swung south.

Toward the island . . . and vengeance.

Ally wondered if she should have pressed Trish so hard. Probably not. Still, she did seem more alert now. And—

Something sharp bit her clutching hand, wrist-deep in mire.

A shell? Not many mollusks in a freshwater lake.

Retrieving the item, she lifted it into the starlight.

"Hey, look what I found." An inch-long wedge of obsidian, opaque at the center, nearly transparent at the flaked edges. "It's an arrowhead. Chumash Indian."

Trish turned her head, focused her stare, and showed a weak but genuine smile. "Pretty cool."

Ally fingered the tiny artifact, no wider than three-eighths of an inch at its base, tapering to a cruel point. A work of craftsmanship, delicate yet deadly.

"The Chumash used to live around here," she said. "Then they sort of disappeared. Nobody knows what happened to them."

She didn't know her face was shining with excitement until she saw its glow reflected in Trish's eyes.

"You know something, kiddo?" Trish widened her smile. "You'll be a great anthropologist someday."

Ally felt herself flush with pleasure. She clutched the arrowhead tight.

"It's a rare find," she whispered. "Maybe our luck's finally starting to change."

From across the lake rose the burr of a boat engine.

57

Tyler lowered the binoculars and exhaled slowly.

The job was done. Had to be.

He had seen the mini-jet adrift, no movement visible on board. Had seen the other boat stop alongside. Had seen the pilot, probably Blair, check out the jet boat and then speed south, in the direction of the Kent estate.

The Sharkeys would hardly be leaving the area if Robinson and the Kent girl were still alive.

Slowly he unclipped his transceiver and talked on channel one. "Blair, Gage—confirm your kills."

A pause. Then Blair's voice, half obscured by engine roar.

"The only one killed is Gage, God damn it!"

Cain and Lilith heard the sizzle of radio chatter as the van swung out of the woods, onto Skylark Drive.

"She shot him," Blair went on, his voice chewed ragged by hysteria. "She shot Gage, that rookie bitch."

The transmission was fading in and out as the road twisted. Cain stopped the van and keyed the talk button on his ProCom.

"Blair. Get it under control."

"Control?" That single word was packed tight with grief and anger and contemptuous disbelief. "Screw you, Cain. I don't give a shit about control. Only thing I care about is Robinson."

"Blair—"

"I'm doing her. Swear to God, I'm taking her out!"

"Blair?" Cain said. "Blair?"

No response.

"Get down, get down!"

Ally hunkered in the pit. Trish slid after her, spirals of light-headedness swimming like moonbeams in her brain. She tried to chase them away as she huddled with the girl, listening tensely as the boat droned nearer.

When it was close, she risked a peek over the rim.

The FireStar surged toward the shallows, then veered east and flashed into profile, paralleling the shoreline.

Pilot at the helm. The seat beside him—empty? Or was there a slumped figure, one arm trailing in the water, the head lolling?

She remembered how the man in the port seat had stopped firing abruptly. She'd thought he was reloading.

No. She'd hit him. Perhaps even killed him.

"Robinson!"

The pilot. His scream thin and ragged. Did he see her? No, impossible. He was shouting in the direction of the island, that was all.

"I'm coming for you! You should've let me *drown*!"

The sentry at the dock.

Flash-card image in her mind: a reddened face, a glare of distilled hatred.

Her heart worked harder. A new rush of dizziness washed over her. She tightened her grip on the pistol.

"Big mistake, Robinson!" He was still screaming, the cries etched raw by his damaged throat. *"Big mistake!"*

The boat plowed out of sight, circling east.

"Which one is that?" Ally asked in a hush.

Trish licked her lips, so terribly dry. "The guy who loaned me the belt."

"Oh." Ally swallowed. "Sounds like he wants it back."

In the idling van, Cain repeated Blair's name, knowing it was useless.

Tyler's voice, shaken and distant: "He switched off, boss. He's at the island. Robinson and the girl must've jumped ship."

Cain started driving again, holding the radio in one hand and steering with the other. "You in the picnic area?"

"Yeah. I'll be in position if they come ashore. You send Mrs. Kent to a better place?"

"She got a phone call from the governor."

"That's real disappointing."

"Also real temporary. We'll do her when we're done backing you up."

A snort. "I don't need your help. I can handle the rookie."

Lilith grabbed her own radio. "Like you handled her when you put her in the lake?"

"Hey, fuck you—"

"She should be dead by now, okay? You had your chance. Now it's our turn."

Cain caught Lilith's gaze in the glow of the dashboard. He shook his head curtly.

Internal dissension was not what they needed now. Discipline. Stability. Teamwork.

"Keep it together," he mouthed to Lilith, too low to be heard over the air.

Lips pursed, she turned away.

"We're all getting a little hot," Cain said into his radio. "Need to cool off, take it easy, right?"

"Right." Tyler was agitated, but Cain knew he was a pro. He would swallow the insult.

"We'll be there soon. Maybe you won't need us. Maybe Blair will whack Robinson and save all of us the trouble. If not, she'll have a regular welcoming committee ready to greet her when she makes landfall."

"Hell, boss"—Tyler tried for humor—"you just want a chance to smoke the Mouseketeer yourself."

Cain had to smile. "You got that right."

58

"Where are they going?" Ally peered in the direction of the fading engine noise.

"Circling around," Trish said, the words coming with curious slowness. "I think only the pilot is a threat. The other one looked . . . hurt."

"One's enough. What did he mean, you should've let him drown?"

"I—uh—I kind of saved his life."

"Saved his life?"

"CPR. Mouth-to-mouth."

"Are you *crazy*?" Ally bit her lip. "Sorry."

"I'm sorry too. I didn't think it would work out . . . like this." Trish cleared her throat. "Can you loosen the tourniquet for me?"

"So soon?"

"I . . . I can't feel my leg anymore."

"Oh, God."

She fumbled at the knot, finally got it undone.

"Am I bleeding?" Trish asked.

Ally gently explored the area around the wound. "Not much. A lot less than before."

"Good."

"I didn't think it would stop this fast."

"It was venous blood, not arterial. That sort of wound can heal pretty quickly if you ... " Trish paused as if losing her concentration, then shook her head. "If you keep the pressure on," she finished.

Ally frowned. "What's the matter?"

"Little dizzy. Nothing to worry about."

For the first time Ally heard the flutter in her voice. "You've lost a lot of blood, Trish."

"I'm okay."

Ally hoped so. Because if Trish passed out now, they were both dead.

No further conversation for a moment. In the new quiet between them, Ally became aware of a larger stillness.

"Hear it?" she whispered.

"What?"

"Boat motor—it's gone silent."

Trish blinked, listening, then slowly nodded. "He's here."

The island was small and flat and treeless, overgrown with rushes, knee-high, chest-high, head-high, rippling in random patterns, swaying like the tresses of hula dancers in the chance rhythms of the wind.

Frogs croaked in a dismal chorus. A bird's titter mocked the night.

On hands and knees, Blair Sharkey crawled.

The leaves of rushes stroked his face like loose sheets of paper. His forearms and calves squished in deep pockets of ooze. Filth encrusted him, a second skin.

He estimated the island's size at no more than an acre. Maybe two hundred feet at its widest point. He could quarter it inch by inch, yard by yard, in no time at all.

He would find his prey.

Heart pounding.

Vision blurred.

Hands numb.

Trish had felt this way once before—after running two miles uphill at the academy on an unseasonably warm day. Her drill instructor had made her lie supine until the faintness passed.

Dehydration and fatigue had brought on the symptoms that day. Tonight she could add gunshot trauma and blood loss to the mix.

Lying prone, she'd been all right. But when she crawled into the pit, that light-headed feeling had started, subtly at first, but growing worse.

She needed to lie down again, or at least put her head between her knees. But she couldn't, not as long as she was huddled in this hole.

Okay, then. No medals for quitters. She would just have to tough it out. No medals for quitters. Stay strong, stay alert. No medals for quitters.

Her mantra helped a little. Fear helped more. The fear that kept her body supercharged with jolts of adrenaline.

Her enemy was near. She could sense it.

But she didn't know where.

Blair had already covered much of the island's eastern perimeter.

If Robinson and the Kent girl had come ashore at

the north end, and if Robinson's injury had limited her movement, then they would be close by.

Insects piped and trilled. The rushes whispered in a breath of breeze, cool and damp. Or perhaps it was Gage's ghost that moved among the reedy stems.

Blair had never thought much about such matters. He supposed anything was possible.

Stay with me, bro, he told the ghost. You don't want to miss what's coming up.

The low clicking, like distant castanets, was the chatter of Trish's teeth.

Ally studied her from inches away. Her face was pale. Sweat trickled out of her hair and beaded on her eyebrows, her lips. The gun in her hands wavered like a kite on a gusty day.

In the closeness of the pit, Trish's trembling transmitted itself to Ally's own body. Abruptly she recalled her silly fear that Trish wanted her to dig a grave. It didn't seem silly anymore.

A grave was what it was, a grave for them both. In the morning they would be found here dead—like Marta—dead and buzzing with fat blowflies.

"Hold on, Trish," Ally whispered, the words so soft she was sure they went unheard. "Please hold on."

Things were very simple sometimes. She was fifteen. She didn't want to die.

Blair's imagined contact with his brother strengthened him. He crawled faster.

He could taste it now. Could almost see Trish Robinson sprawled facedown in the dirt, her brains red and strewn. Could almost see—

Explosive noise, rapid-fire beats, the nearby rushes rustling madly.

What the *hell*?

For a wild moment he was sure he'd been discovered, sure Robinson was shooting at him, peppering the brush with bullets.

Then he understood.

Not bullets. Only a bird, nesting in the rushes, startled by his approach, bursting out of cover into the open air.

He caught a breath, then heard a new sound.

Gunshots.

Real gunshots this time.

And close.

Sudden commotion due east, and without thinking Trish swung sideways, impelled by panic and a desperate need to lash out, and she fired blindly into the night, four shots, five, click click click, the magazine empty, her ears ringing, and overhead, brushing past the stars—a flutter of wings.

"Did you get him?" Ally asked eagerly.

Shake of her head. "Bird." Her own voice was barely audible over the violent clangor in her skull. "Just a bird."

In the dark, among the rushes, Blair smiled.

The bird had drawn Robinson's fire. Purple muzzle flashes had erupted like fireworks thirty yards to the west.

He'd pinpointed her position.

He had her now.

59

Tyler counted a half dozen shots, echoing from the island.

Was it Robinson who'd fired? Or Blair? Or both?

No way to know. But if Blair was dead, Robinson could take Blair's boat and reach the picnic area in a couple of minutes.

Cain and Lilith still weren't here. To hell with them.

He didn't need any damn backup. He could take care of the cop all by himself. Was looking forward to it, in fact.

Pocketing his binoculars, he hurried down the trail into a labyrinth of trees.

The Glock was out of ammo.

Trish removed the empty mag, then fumbled a spare out of her dump pouch and tried to heel it in. Ordinarily a simple operation, but not now. Weakness and confusion cheated her of dexterity.

She gave the Glock to Ally. "Load it." Amazing how much effort was required even to speak a few words. "Just . . . just pop in the clip."

Ally did so. Trish accepted the Glock with a nod.

Dimly she knew the girl wanted reassurance, but she had none to offer.

She'd messed up. Panicked. Now the killer knew how to find her. He could approach from any direction, fire at will. Even now he might be closing in.

She tried to focus her eyes, couldn't. There were two and three of everything, and the edges of her vision were graying, and her ears still rang with the gun's reports.

Nearly blind, nearly deaf, nearly crippled, nearly unconscious . . .

Nearly dead.

Blair circled southwest, putting distance between himself and the spot where the bird had burst into flight. On elbows and knees he approached his quarry from behind.

There.

Twenty feet away. Glitter of blonde hair visible through the rushes.

Robinson. Beside her, the girl.

They were hunkered down in a shallow pit, an improvised hiding place, their backs turned.

He could nail them both, as easy as killing two baby birds in a nest.

The man knew where they were.

That thought kept beating in Ally's brain as she scanned the dark, looking everywhere at once.

He knew where they were. They had lost the element of surprise. It was an ambush no longer.

Ahead, the shore, flat and empty.

On both sides and behind—rushy thickets, five feet high, dense and opaque.

Anything could be hidden in that jungle of grasslike stalks. Anything.

"Keep your head down," Trish whispered.

"I just—"

"*Down.*"

Reluctantly Ally shrunk deeper into the hole.

Now she could see nothing but four sandy walls and, at her side, Trish—clutching the gun close to her chest, hunched forward as she searched the dark with bleary, blinking eyes.

Ally's grip on the arrowhead was painfully tight, the obsidian's sharp edges chewing into her palm.

She had thought it was a good-luck charm. She'd been wrong.

Her luck—and Trish's—finally had run out.

The girl had dropped out of sight, but Blair's prime target was still within view.

Balanced on his elbows amid the tall, concealing stalks, he steadied the Glock in both hands.

Touched the pressure switch.

The laser beam printed an amber bull's-eye on the back of Trish Robinson's head.

Memory flash.

Cain in the living room, targeting Trish's face. Pinpoint of light stamped on her forehead between her deep blue eyes.

Amber light.

Ally saw the same light now, a red-orange luster highlighting the blonde tangle at the nape of Trish's neck.

"*Look out!*"

Her cry and her lunge were simultaneous.

She pulled Trish downward, wrenching her head sideways.

Whip crack. Sand erupting in a gritty spume.

Behind them. He was *right behind them*.

No time to think, no time for calculation.

Trish thrust both hands over her head, elbows bending as she pointed the Glock upside down, the barrel grazing the rim of the pit, and she fired.

Recoil slammed into her wrists, forearms, shoulders, as she pumped the trigger again and again and again. She felt the multiple impacts vibrating through her teeth and the bones of her skull.

Her shots were blind. She ought to conserve ammunition. Ought to play it safe. But she couldn't stop her finger from flexing, couldn't stop the gun from spitting out round after round, couldn't stop even though she was screaming, or was it Ally who screamed, or both of them together?

The sudden hollow click of the trigger was shocking somehow, like the unreal stillness at the eye of a storm.

Shaking, she lowered the gun, empty now, the last round expended.

Past the chiming in her ears she heard Ally sobbing. Nothing else.

She leaned forward, head hanging, and let blood swim back into her brain. She had no idea how long she held that position, blinking at retinal flashes and hearing the ring of bells.

When her vision cleared and it seemed she would

not pass out after all, she eased herself half upright and risked a look.

The man lay in the rushes twenty feet away. She saw his hands, ungloved, pale and limp, and his gun lying nearby, and she smelled the copper-penny odor of blood.

He was dead. No doubt of it.

She had killed a man. Maybe two men. Two lives taken. Two heartbeats stopped.

Sudden tremors hurried through her. She heard a low whimpering sound, the complaint of some wounded animal, but she was the one making the noise, and she couldn't seem to stop.

On her shoulder, the light pressure of a touch. Ally's hand.

"You had to," Ally whispered. "You didn't have any choice."

Trish knew that. But the brittle logic of the argument made no headway against the reality of that ruined face . . . those bloody hollows where eyes and nose and mouth had been . . . the permanent erasure of a human being.

Slowly she laced her fingers through Ally's.

"He wasn't much older than you." Her own voice surprised her—a stranger's voice, throaty and aged "Maybe eighteen."

"He would have killed us both."

"Yes."

"So . . . so that makes it okay. Doesn't it? Doesn't it?

Trish gave no reply.

60

Cain heard the shots die away as he swung out of the van.

A distant fusillade. From the island. Had to be.

Turning in a full circle, he scanned the unlit parking lot, empty of vehicles save for the Chevy van and the battered Porsche. A plastic bag skated the asphalt, flitting from stripe to stripe like a game piece advancing on a giant board.

Tyler was nowhere in view. Tired of waiting, he must have taken up his position near the phones.

Of course, it was possible no ambush would be necessary. The last barrage of shots might have finished the job.

Cain unclipped his ProCom and activated channel one.

"Blair? You nail 'em?"

No response. He tried channel three, the original frequency.

"Blair? Come in, Blair."

The radio startled Trish when it came alive with Cain's voice. Apparently the unit was water-resistant. It had survived immersion in the lake.

"Don't answer," Ally said, fear in her eyes.

Shaking off shock and fatigue, Trish unclipped the radio. "Got to." She cleared her throat. "I have an idea."

"You read me, Blair?"

Movement at Cain's side. Lilith appeared, a dark angel materializing out of the night.

"Blair?" he inquired for the last time, already having given up hope.

Then a crackle of static and a familiar voice—the last voice he wanted to hear.

"Sorry, Cain. I'm afraid Blair can't come to the phone right now."

Robinson.

"Surprised to hear from me?" Trish asked the silent radio.

It was a challenge to hold her voice steady. She had never thought of herself as an actress, but if she could sound cool and cocky and defiantly unfazed right now, she would be eligible for an Academy Award.

After a brief pause Cain answered. "Sure am. It's after ten o'clock, Robinson. Well past your bedtime, I'd think."

"I get to stay up late on Saturdays. Ally, too. We're having kind of a slumber party out here on the island."

"Me and some friends may crash that party."

"You're not crashing anything. You know why? It's over. The good guys won."

Ally blinked at her, baffled.

"Did you, Robinson?" She could hear his controlled rage. "I must have missed that part."

"Yeah, you've been missing a lot lately. I'll fill you in. You can't get near us without a boat. Even if you could, we've got the tactical advantage. You can ask Blair about that." Another slow comber of dizziness rolled over her. She lowered her head briefly, then rallied. "This message getting through?"

A beat. "Loud and clear."

"We're dug in where you can't touch us. So you might as well pack your bags and go home. Or is there something I've overlooked?"

Cain pursed his lips, fury compressing his mouth into a bloodless line. Then he pushed the talk button.

"No, Officer. There's nothing you've overlooked."

Lilith grabbed his shoulder. "We can't let that *bitch*—"

Cain shook free of her grasp, hushed her with a frown.

He was thinking.

Robinson was right about her tactical position. If she stayed put, he would be helpless to reach her.

But he had not been quite truthful in his reply. There was one small item she'd forgotten.

Still on channel three, he keyed the transmit switch again. "Tyler, you catch that?"

"Yeah, boss."

"She's got us where she wants us. We're clearing out. No arguments." He played his hole card. "But before we leave, we're taking care of the hostages. All of them. Understood?"

A pause as Tyler processed this news. Then, warily: "Understood."

Cain clicked off. Lilith was staring at him.

"Kill the hostages," she whispered, sardonic admiration in her gaze.

Smiling, Cain nodded. "That's what I said."

"You think he means it?"

Ally was shaking all over, and Trish didn't know how to reply.

"He could," Trish whispered at last.

"But . . . *why*?"

"Out of spite. He can't hurt us directly, so he'll do it through them."

She didn't add that Cain would have a better reason for killing Charles Kent, his employer or partner or whatever he was. With the operation a failure, Charles would be only a liability, a man obviously capable of betrayal, all too likely to use his skills and influence to cut a deal with the D.A.

And if Cain was going to take the time to kill Charles, why not Barbara and the Danforths also?

Yes, it was possible. But on the other hand . . .

"It could be a trap," Trish said. "A way to lure us off the island."

Ally nodded. "What do you think the odds are?"

Trish honestly couldn't say. It was a coin toss. "Fifty-fifty, I guess."

"So what do we do?"

Trish didn't know.

Cain waited a moment, then reset his radio to channel one.

"Tyler, come in."

"I'm here, boss. Thought you might want to meet on this frequency."

"More privacy this way."

"Unless Robinson has picked up Gage's radio by now."

"If she had, she would've responded when I tried to raise Blair the first time. You still in position?"

"Sure am."

"Stay there—and stay alert."

Cain clipped the radio to his belt. Beside him, Lilith stared into the night.

"What do we do now?" she whispered.

"We wait." Cain took a slow breath, then another. In, out. In. Out. "But not for long."

61

Trish clung to Ally, using the girl as a crutch, the two of them elbowing their way through crowds of rushes toward the island's eastern shore.

The distance was short, no more than forty yards, but the strain of hopping on one leg wearied Trish almost instantly. Ally, struggling to support her, chuffed like a marathon runner in the final grueling mile.

"Even if we make it to the phones," Ally gasped, "can the police get to the house in time?"

"Don't have to." Trish had already thought of that. "Cain's probably still monitoring the police bands. Soon as he hears the units dispatched code three— he'll run."

She had no breath to add that Skylark Drive, the only route up the mountain, dead-ended just beyond the Kent estate. Cain was sure to know the risk of being trapped anywhere on that road. He would have to flee.

"But"—Ally blew hard, struggling to clear her lungs of deoxygenated air—"he could be . . . killing them . . . *right now*."

"Don't think so." Trish forced out the words through gritted teeth. "Radio transmission came in so clear,

Cain and the others must have been at the picnic area or nearby. How long will it take them to drive around the lake? Ten minutes?"

"Maybe fifteen. Road's all curvy. Can't go . . . too fast."

"So we might have time."

"It'll be close," Ally breathed.

Trish couldn't argue.

Though she winced with every step, the pain was welcome. It meant the feeling in her lower leg had come back. Maybe the leg hadn't been starved of blood long enough to suffer permanent damage. Maybe she wouldn't have to wear a prosthetic below her left knee for the rest of her life.

Or maybe she was headed straight into a trap, and the rest of her life would prove too short to matter.

She and Ally had reached the decision together, with no discussion, only a meeting of eyes. Trish had seen the stark terror in the girl's face, the awful fear for her parents, the desperate plea—and in her own mind she had heard the damnably persistent Mrs. Wilkes saying, *No medals for quitters.*

Trish meant to have a few words with that woman when this was all over.

Beside her, Ally moaned.

"You okay?" Trish asked.

"Just thinking. I . . . did a stupid thing at this cock-tail party . . . last Christmas."

"And?"

"Never told my mom and dad . . . I was sorry. That's all."

They went on, Ally staring blankly ahead, Trish thinking of Mr. Charles Kent.

His daughter wanted to apologize to *him*. The ugly irony of it was amusing somehow, or would have been if she could have obtained the appropriately distanced perspective.

Saving Charles hadn't been a factor in Trish's decision. She would risk nothing for that man.

But Barbara Kent and Philip and Judy Danforth . . . they were innocent. They were worth the risk.

Worth dying for? She couldn't say, almost didn't care. Her own survival seemed somehow trivial, a mere luxury unworthy of serious consideration with so many other lives at stake.

She wondered if this was some sort of depersonalized reaction to shock or if it was what people called courage—or if there was any difference.

The soil grew spongier. Wet sand sucked at her shoes and Ally's bare feet like a succession of hungry mouths. Rushes yielded to sedges, then to bristling ranks of cattails waist-deep in water.

The FireStar floated close to shore. In his haste the killer named Blair had simply abandoned the boat in a shallow cove, trusting to a semicircle of mossy boulders to prevent it from drifting far.

The port seat was still occupied by the slumped masculine figure Trish had seen earlier. His left arm trailed limply, and his chin rested on his chest.

Dead like his partner.

Probably.

But she wasn't making any assumptions.

"Quiet now," she whispered.

Screened from the boat by cattails, she and Ally waded in together, algae swirling around them in lacy ribbons of green.

Where the cattails thinned, Trish halted. "Okay. Let me go."

Ally released her hold. Trish submerged up to her neck. A water bug as large as her thumb skittered away, its carapace shiny in the starlight.

Crammed under her belt was Blair's Glock. She withdrew the gun and held it above the water as she slipped forward.

Waterlilies papered the shallows, prolific as weeds. She maneuvered among them, the agony in her leg partially relieved by the water's soothing buoyancy.

She reached the FireStar's stern. Hugging the hull, she circled around to starboard.

A breath of courage, and she grasped the gunwale with her left hand and hoisted herself up, aiming the Glock with her right.

"Freeze."

Caution was unnecessary. She knew it as soon as she saw him at close range.

A bullet—one of *her* bullets—had opened his neck and the side of his face, exposing a red waste of bone. Blood soaked his jump suit and lacquered the molded seat.

Most of his face was intact. His mouth hung open. His eyes gazed unblinking at his lap.

At least he wasn't looking at her. She didn't think she could stand it if he'd been looking at her.

If anything, he was younger than his companion. Sixteen? She had been a high school sophomore at sixteen. Staying out late on a Friday night had been the limit of her daring.

Finally she turned toward shore and found her voice. "It's safe."

Ally swam to the boat, climbed aboard, and helped Trish get settled on the bench seat at the rear of the cockpit.

"Try not to look at him," Trish said.

Ally shrugged, nonchalant. "He doesn't scare me. It's the ones who are still alive that I'm worried about."

Spoken like a battle-hardened warrior. Well, wasn't she?

Even so, Trish noticed that the girl did her best to avert her face as she slipped behind the wheel.

"Hey," Ally said, "how do we start this thing?"

"No key?"

She shook her head. "He hot-wired it, I guess."

"Can you figure out what he did?"

"You mean you don't *know*? I thought cops knew all this stuff."

Not rookie cops, Trish thought. "Give me a few years."

Ally hunched close to the control console. "There's a knife on the floor. It looks like . . . oh, I get it."

She inserted the blade in the switch, and the engine started.

"Just have to complete the circuit, see?" Ally shrugged. "Easy."

Trish shook her head. It *was* easy, absurdly easy. She could have done it herself, had she only known how. She need never have risked a return to the house.

"They should have taught you this stuff in cop

school," Ally said as she guided the boat out of the cove.

Trish felt her mouth slide into a weary smile. "Tonight I'm learning a lot of things they didn't teach at school."

62

"They're leaving the island." Lilith breathed the words above the drone of a distant motor.

Cain nodded slowly, tasting the woody sweetness of the night air. "Now let's just hope they're coming our way."

He stood with Lilith at the trailhead adjacent to the parking lot, the best point from which to view the lake. His binoculars, trained on the dark hump of the island, caught a shimmer of movement near the eastern shore.

The boat. It flashed in a spill of starlight as the prow swung north—toward the picnic area.

"Our two Mouseketeers are taking the cheese," he said with satisfaction, and Lilith shivered.

He tracked the boat until it vanished behind the treetops. Then he pocketed the binoculars.

"Move out."

"Wait." Lilith dialed the volume higher on the police radio.

The same throaty voice, the woman named Lou: "Eight-one, you still en route to that ten-thirty-three? Eight-one? Four-Adam-eight-one?"

"It's taken the unit too long to respond." Cain frowned. "Dispatcher's getting worried."

"Should I answer?"

He shook his head. "Even these local yokels may not fall for the same trick twice. And I don't want them figuring out the last transmission was faked. We told them the car was on Hospers Road. That's where we want them to be looking. Now, let's go."

The dirt trail twisted down the hillside, past stands of black oak growing tall and thick-boled in the rich, dry soil.

Cain moved with unaccustomed lightness, his steps muffled though there was as yet no need for stealth. Lilith was a shadow at his side, supple and silent, the contours of her costume flowing like tendrils of ink.

Somewhere near the phones Tyler already was lying in wait. There was a good chance he would get Robinson.

If he didn't, Lilith would—or Cain himself.

This was it.

Endgame.

From the stowage compartment under the bench seat Trish took out the first-aid kit she'd found earlier.

She dry-swallowed a handful of Advil caplets, then examined the remaining items in the waterproof case.

Antibiotic cream.

Band-Aids of various sizes.

Moistened towelettes.

Sterile pads, both nonstick and adhesive.

Rolled gauze.

Digital thermometer, tweezers, mineral oil, and a five-yard spool of rayon tape.

With towelettes and sterile pads she blotted up blood from the ugly gashes in her leg, fighting new waves of vertigo as the damaged nerves screamed.

Next, antibiotic. She used it all.

Then two more sterile pads, the adhesive kind, pressed to the wounds.

Quickly she wrapped her calf in gauze. As she secured the dressing with tape, the boat neared shore.

To her right lay a long stretch of beach. To her left, willows edged the water.

"Go toward the trees," she told Ally. "And sit lower."

Approaching the wooded area was a calculated risk. She and Ally would be less exposed there—but their enemies, if any were present, would be better camouflaged.

As the boat drew near shore, Trish leaned forward and rummaged in the dead man's dump pouch, extracting a single magazine. She inserted it in her own Glock, then holstered the weapon.

The other gun was almost fully loaded: fifteen rounds, plus one in the chamber. Blair must have put in a fresh mag before coming ashore.

Willows eclipsed the stars. A tangle of floating deadwood, branches torn loose in storms and washed into the shallows, scraped the FireStar's starboard side. Ally eased back on the throttle as the prow nuzzled a bank of crumbly earth.

"Kill the motor," Trish said.

Ally removed the knife from the ignition switch, opening the circuit, and the engine died.

Silence.

No one had shot at them. Nothing had stirred in the shadows beyond the trees.

"Okay. This is for you." Trish gave the second Glock to Ally. "Remember how to use it?"

Ally drew a shallow breath. "I remember."

"Tell me where to find the phones."

"They're outside the snack shop in the picnic area. Northeast, maybe five hundred feet. I can take you right to them."

Trish met her gaze. "I'm going alone."

"What?" Hurt and bafflement welled in Ally's eyes. "You . . . you can't even *walk*."

Leaning over the side, Trish plucked one of the branches from the water. The limb of a ponderosa pine, five feet long, stripped of needles, black as coal.

"I can lean on this."

"You can lean on *me*. We're *partners*."

"And we've each got a job to do. You keep the boat ready for a quick getaway."

"It's *my* folks who're in trouble. If just one of us goes, it should be me."

"You're not a cop," Trish snapped, then gentled her voice. "Look, there's no time for this, all right?"

Ally turned in her seat, as stiff and mute as the corpse by her side.

Trish wanted to say more, but a new argument would only waste more seconds, and seconds might cost lives.

Unassisted, she pulled herself upright and struggled over the transom onto the steep bank directly alongside the FireStar.

Her shoes sank into damp earth. She planted the branch. Though her leg seethed, it did not fold.

Propping the crutch under her left armpit, she advanced, moving with an alacrity that surprised her.

"Wait."

Ally's voice. Trish turned as the girl scrambled off the boat. Something gleamed in her open palm.

The arrowhead.

She had no pockets. Must have been holding it the whole time. Clutching it in her fist, a talisman.

"For luck," Ally said.

Trish accepted the coin-sized wedge of obsidian, glassy and hard, and slipped it into her pocket.

Though she wanted to say some words of thanks, her voice seemed to have left her.

Instead she simply nodded, a deep nod that left her hair hanging across her face for a long moment, then turned and limped quickly away, deeper into the woods.

The boat had fallen silent by the time Cain and Lilith reached the edge of the beach. Crouching behind a clump of sunflowers, Cain unfolded his binoculars and swept the scene.

Barbecue pits scored the sandy strip in a ragged line.

A volleyball net rippled between two poles.

An upturned lifeguard platform reclined on the beach as if stargazing.

Across a sparkle of placid water lay the dark hump of the island and, farther away, the dim glow of the

Kent estate, tiny squares of windows burning pinholes in the black hillside.

No movement anywhere. No boat in the shallows. No footprints in the sand.

Cain lowered the binoculars and glanced at Lilith, squatting beside him.

"Must've come ashore in the woods," he breathed. "You look there. I'll check out the picnic area. And stay off the air. They may have gotten hold of Gage's radio by now."

"Where do we meet?"

"Back at the parking lot." She was starting to move away when Cain added: "If the Kent girl's unarmed— take her alive."

Lilith frowned. "Isn't it getting a little late for fun and games?"

"It won't take any extra time. There are two beds in the master bedroom. I can do Ally and her mom side by side." He smiled. "Double the fun."

"You're the boss. How about Robinson?"

His smile vanished. "Kill her on sight."

Lilith's only reply was to release the safety catch on her Glock.

They separated. Cain prowled north, retracing his route along the dirt pathway.

He looked back once in the direction of the trees and saw Lilith dissolve into grainy darkness, a shadow merging with other shadows, smoke fading in air.

A sudden inexplicable sense of misgiving almost prompted him to call her back.

Ridiculous.

His Lilith might behave like a child at times, but she

was fully capable of fending for herself. She was as helpless as a tigress.

Of course, Cain reflected as he moved on, Officer Robinson had proved herself a tigress too.

63

Harried by light-headedness, Trish reached a dirt trail at the edge of the woods.

On the far side lay a eucalyptus grove, scattered with long wooden tables, lacquered and gleaming in the starlight. Beyond the tables wavered the suggestion of a building, white and small.

The snack shop? If so, the phones waited there.

And maybe an ambush.

Wet with sweat, leaning on her crutch, she unholstered the Glock. Holding the gun felt good. Its weight and solidity were as reassuring as a handshake.

But she knew whatever comfort the gun provided was increasingly illusory. She couldn't steady her hand, couldn't aim, couldn't hope to hit anything except by luck—and she had already pressed her luck to the breaking point tonight.

A high, tuneless buzz filled the space between her ears. Pure will held her upright.

No medals for . . .

Oh, to hell with it.

Swallowing fear, she hobbled into the grove. Behind the nearest eucalyptus, she sank to the ground.

The crutch would only slow her down now. She left the pine branch propped against the tree, where she could retrieve it later.

If there was a later.

Barefoot, the Glock gripped in two hands, Ally crept through the woods.

She had waited only long enough to fasten the FireStar's mooring line to a willow tree before heading away from shore. Trish had been moving fast, but Ally thought she could catch up.

No way Trish was going into danger alone. Suppose she felt faint again. Suppose she collapsed and couldn't get up.

She needed help, and that was that, and if she didn't like it, well, too damn bad.

The darkness was thick and heavy on all sides, a blanket of night. Though there was no trail to follow, Ally was fairly sure she knew the way. Another twenty yards or so, and she—

Pain punched like a hot needle through the sole of her right foot. Bramble, twig, something sharp.

She hissed a curse, then dropped instantly into a defensive crouch, aware that her voice must have carried in the stillness.

"Ally?"

The whisper reached her from a nest of shrubs and shadows fifty feet away.

Seal-walking on her belly, Trish advanced to the next eucalyptus and the next, until the trees thinned.

Then she wriggled alongside a garbage can—*Don't*

Trash Our Park, it warned—and from there to an adjacent picnic table. She took cover under the built-in bench, her breath coming in explosive gasps.

On her elbows she struggled to the end of the table, then peered out from under the bench.

The building was now less than ten feet from her. A plywood hut, white-painted, the awning emblazoned *Bobby's Snack Shack*.

A *Closed* sign was wedged in a window near the door. At the corner of the shop stood twin kiosks.

Pay phones.

Between herself and the phones—no more tables, no trash cans, no trees, only a bare span of lawn.

Her heart racketed in her ears. She crawled forward, aware of her terrible vulnerability.

On the margin of her sight, a blur of motion.

Gun?

No. A bat, a little brown bat, flitting among the eucalyptus branches.

Bats just like that one had fluttered over the field near the old farmhouse while she and Marta sat together on the porch in the summer twilight.

The memory was vivid, achingly real.

She kept going. Reached the front wall of the shop. Crouched against it, strips of peeled paint flapping in her hair.

Motionless against a white background, she could have been a target on a shooting range.

Her enemies never would have a better chance than this.

Eyes wide, head pounding, she waited for the fatal shot.

64

Ally's heart sped up. She licked her lips and peered into the night. "Trish?"

"Yeah. It's me." A dark, slender shape, unmistakably female, took substance among the tangled foliage. "You okay?"

"I'm fine, just hurt my foot, you're not mad, are you?" Ally knew she was babbling. "I'm sorry, I know I was supposed to stay by the boat, but I couldn't let you go by yourself, I just *couldn't*."

"It's all right."

She blinked, catching her breath. "Is it?"

"Get over here."

Relief lifted her. Quickly she moved forward, limping a little on her bloodied foot.

Trish was just ahead, a kneeling figure in silhouette, wearing a gun belt, a pistol in her hand.

"I'm glad you're not ticked off or anything," Ally whispered. "I really thought you'd kill me."

Very close now, and in the shadows Trish was rising, her gun lifting as she stood.

Stood—without the crutch.

This wasn't Trish, *wasn't Trish*.

Ally threw herself to the ground behind a leafy scrim of manzanita, and a cork popped.

After an endless moment Trish relaxed, breath sighing out of her, and lowered the Glock.

Her gamble had paid off. Cain and his accomplices really had cleared out.

Clinging to the wall, she pulled herself upright, then crabbed to the corner of the shop and faced the first kiosk.

She lifted the handset, blinking back tears of relief.

It would be so good finally to ask for help. So good no longer to carry this weight of responsibility for so many lives.

Her trembling finger stabbed the keypad three times.

Nine-one-one.

She put the phone to her ear.

No ringing.

No dial tone.

Silence.

She stared at the phone. The thought occurred to her that she needed money, had to feed a quarter into the slot, and she didn't have a quarter—

Stop.

A 911 call didn't require payment. She knew that. She was just getting hysterical.

She touched the digits again.

The silence continued.

Out of order. Must be.

Well, there was a second phone. Maybe that one would work.

Please, God, please let it work.

She tried replacing the handset, but her shaking hand released it too soon, and it fell.

The handset thumped on the grass, trailing a severed cord.

Sabotaged.

Her gaze shifted to the other kiosk. A cut cord dangled from that handset also.

They *were* here.

Or had been. Could have left by now. But she didn't think so.

Creak of hinges.

The shop door.

She started to turn, and powerful arms seized her from behind, crushing her stomach, driving breath from her lungs.

A gloved hand chopped her wrist. The Glock fell.

She was disarmed, helpless.

Finished.

65

In a tree trunk inches from Ally's head, a thump of impact. Splintered bark sprayed her hair.

For a bewildered moment she could make no sense of what was happening, and then she remembered Lilith in the living room, impersonating Trish, the mimicry eerily persuasive.

Another pop, and the manzanita rustled, the bullet kicking up dirt near her face.

She lurched sideways, then flung out her arms and launched into a furious crawl, struggling through a dense ground cover of buckbrush and dogwood and blueblossom.

A third bullet chased her, missing by a half yard.

Hot breath on Trish's cheek. A moplike fall of hair brushing her neck.

Ponytail. The man with the ponytail. On the radio Cain had called him Tyler.

He scrabbled at her belt buckle. Undid it. The belt dropped away.

Then he was hauling her through the doorway into a cramped, airless room musty with the lingering odor of grease.

A counter ran along the left wall. He slammed her against it, and she doubled over, gasping. His pelvis dug into the small of her back. Leather fingers pinned her wrists at her side.

Close to her ear, a western drawl: "Where is she?"

For a moment, stunned and winded, Trish honestly did not understand the question.

"Who?" she croaked. "Where's who?"

He took her imcomprehension as defiance. With a pelvic thrust he rammed her spine, driving her forward, the counter's sharp edge biting into her abdomen.

"The brat," he snarled. "Where is she?"

Past pain, past fear, she understood that this was why he hadn't shot her through the door or window. This was why he'd taken her alive.

For Ally. He wanted her to give up Ally.

She wouldn't, of course. Not ever.

"Safe," Trish hissed. "That's where she is. She's *safe*."

Ally crawled through weeds and wildflowers, driven only by the mindless urge to flee, get away, put distance between herself and her pursuer, and then rationality reasserted control.

She had to think. Think like Trish. What would Trish do?

Take cover. Shoot back. Even if her aim was wild, she could buy time.

She scrambled behind a black oak, clambering over a pile of thick and twisted roots fisted tightly in the earth. Rough bark chafed her shoulder blades through the ragged dress. Crouching low, she raised the pistol—

But there was no pistol.

She stared at her empty hands.

"Alison," a lisping voice cooed from the shadows, "you lost your gun . . . "

66

"You'll tell me, Trish," the man named Tyler breathed. "You'll tell me exactly where to find your traveling companion."

She wished she had never admitted her nickname in the presence of Cain and his thugs. She hated hearing it from this man's mouth.

Through gritted teeth she whispered, "No chance."

"Oh, yes. You'll tell."

The way he said it wasn't good. He sounded much too sure of himself.

He released his hold on her wrists. Reached across the counter to a stainless steel sink. Plugged the drain, then ran cold water from the tap in a foaming gush.

She listened to the hiss of water, her mind frozen.

"Now listen, Trish." His voice was a hiss also. "Our schedule's getting kind of hairy. We may not have time to hunt down some high school whore and still get paid. And we *will* get paid. I got a red Porsche, showroom new, just waiting for me."

The sink was half full now.

"So here's the thing. I'm gonna kill you, okay? We both already know that. But it can be easy, or it can be hard. Easy way is with a bullet. Hard way—well, it's like this."

In one motion he thrust her forward and plunged her head into the sink.

For a wild moment Ally imagined Lilith as some sort of evil spirit, not human at all, a supernatural presence able to snatch a gun away.

No. Quit it.

The real answer was much more obvious. Harassed by bullets, confused by fear, she had simply dropped the pistol when she started to crawl.

And Lilith, tracking her, had picked it up.

Wonder Woman's partner, she thought in a scalding wave of self-reproach. Sure.

Breath streamed from Trish's mouth in agitated bubbles. As if from a distance she sensed the pops and jerks of her own shoulders as she struggled to break free of his grasp.

It was the car trunk again. Cold water rising until the air pocket was gone. Ache in her lungs, terrible need to draw a breath, mounting helplessness and terror—

He yanked her head back, his fingers knotted in her hair. She gulped air, water running like tears down her face.

"You like that, Trish? *You like that?*"

A spasm of dry retching was the only answer she could give.

He jostled her into silence. "Didn't think you would. So talk to me." He leaned close, his whisper caressing her right ear. "Talk and I'll go easy on you, I promise I will."

She shook all over. Couldn't face another submersion, couldn't stand the thought of the inevitable moment when she inhaled water and felt her lungs ice over.

In the woods, a light snapped on.

Ally hugged the tree as white glare diffused through the misty air on both sides of her. The beam of Lilith's flash, probing the night.

Facing an unarmed adversary, Lilith could afford to reveal her position. And Ally, sheltered only by the tree, couldn't move without being instantly seen.

Don't come this way, she prayed. Go in another direction. Please, please don't find me.

"Alison . . ."

The girlish singsong raised a skitter of gooseflesh on Ally's bare arms.

The cone of light swayed, exploring the foliage on either side of the oak but never straying far enough to give her a chance at escape.

Crackle of sticks. Boots treading closer. The glare brightened, droplets of mist sparkling in a funnel of white.

Too late she saw a torn fragment of her dress snagged on the bark, fluttering in the breeze, marking her position like a flag.

An elfin titter, and she knew Lilith had seen it too.

"I think you're behind that tree, Alison . . ."

She choked back a moan.

* * *

"Be smart, Trish," Tyler breathed fiercely. "Tell me where she is."

Had to say something, or he would dunk her again.

Her answer came without conscious preparation. "The island. I came alone. Left her . . . on the island."

"That's a lie."

"No, really—"

"You wouldn't take the boat and strand her there. If you got caught, she'd be a sitting duck."

"I . . . I didn't think of that."

"You think of everything," he said, and pushed her under.

Loose hairs waved around her face. Air dribbled from her pursed lips. A high, tuneless buzz filled the space between her ears. Somewhere someone was screaming, and someone else was saying, *It's all right*, and neither voice was hers.

Out.

He jerked her head up, and she was coughing, then gasping, then coughing again, real tears mixing now with the water on her face.

"I don't like liars," Tyler snarled. "You got that?"

No hope of talking her way out of this. She had to take action, fight back. Somehow.

"Now, Trish"—his voice ominously gentle again—"I'll ask you real nicely just once more."

Her forearms were still wedged between his body and her own, but he wasn't holding them anymore. She had some limited mobility.

"Where's your sidekick at?"

She groped blindly behind her, looking for a weapon,

a diversion, anything to save her from going back down into the wet and the dark.

"Last chance." His breath stirred the fine down on her cheek. "Talk to me, and talk straight—or next time, sweetheart, you ain't coming up for air."

67

Nowhere to hide.

Blindly, pointlessly, Ally tried pressing closer to the tree, willing her body in some magical way to become one with the bundled roots and the branching canopy of leaves.

Then the ambient glow coalesced into a single focused orb, and she lifted her head, looking past the flashlight at the pale crescent of a smile.

"Now look what we have here." Lilith released a low, velvety purr. "The virgin princess."

"Talk!" Tyler screamed. "Last chance."

Trish probed the unknown space at her back, and her hand touched leather.

His belt.

Sheathed to the left side—his combat knife.

"Okay," she gasped. "I'll tell." Bending her wrist, she closed her fingers over the knife's handle. "You . . . you'd find her anyway."

"That's right, Trish. Finally you're getting smart."

Lilith took a step forward, and Ally saw the gun in her right hand, its muzzle staring down at her.

"Cain told me to take you alive if I could. But I don't know. I've never shot anybody before." A giggle, light and airy. "Guess I'm sort of a virgin too."

The gun steadied, the laser diode beaming a red-orange line at Ally's chest.

"I think," Lilith said, "it's time for me to lose my innocence."

Careful, careful.

Draw the knife without sound, without pressure.

"I sent her—"

The knife sliding, whisper quiet.

"—up the hill—"

Her grip precarious, elbow bending as her hand lifted, threatening to give her away.

"—to wait by the road."

"Why there?"

"For an ambulance . . . once I called for help."

The blade nearly free.

"Makes sense," he whispered. "Thanks, Trish. By the way—I'm the one who locked you in that trunk."

He shoved her forward, submerging her again, and she lost her grip on the knife.

"Cain won't like it," Ally whispered, her throat dry.

Lilith shrugged. "He won't know."

"He knew when Trish lied—on the radio."

Hesitation.

Ally pressed her small advantage. "Doesn't he know you better than Trish? Won't he be . . . disappointed in you?"

Wait now. Nothing further she could say. Her life was Lilith's toy.

The laser winked out.

"You're a smart girl, Alison." The childish voice was flat, empty of affection. "I'll bet you get good grades."

Ally lifted her chin, feeling an absurd access of pride. "Straight A's."

"Well,"—Lilith smiled—"you'll be starting a whole new education soon."

Trish was drowning, drowning for real this time, drowning as the gloved hands held her under with savage tenacity, and her last hope was the knife, the knife, *she had to get the knife.*

She flailed behind her, pawing empty space, unable to close her fists over anything solid.

Her lungs were emptying fast. Little time left.

He'd tried to drown her in the lake, the bastard, and now he was going to finish the job in six inches of water, and she couldn't break free.

There.

She touched the handle, wrapped her fingers around it, and with her final strength she jerked the knife out of its sheath and twisted it sideways and drove the blade blindly to her right.

Momentary resistance, then a sickening surrender as the point punched through clothes and skin.

Tyler howled. Weakened by pain, he released her.

She left the knife inside him. Whipped her head out of the sink. Pivoted, gasping, in a spray of droplets. Lunged for the holster at his hip.

He had the same thought, but not in time. When he

scrabbled at the holster, it was already empty, the Glock in her shaking grasp.

Her wounded leg threatened to buckle. Awkwardly she reached out with her left hand, grasping the counter for support, then backed toward the doorway. Through a net of dripping hair she watched him, ready to shoot but not wanting to.

Tyler sagged. A red glaze coated his jump suit below the haft of the embedded knife. Sweat popped out of the pores on his forehead and cheeks. His eyes were feverish and bright.

"You stuck me," he grunted, and she could almost taste the dryness of his mouth, the same dryness she had known after being shot. "Hurt me bad."

Grimacing, he tugged at the knife buried in his side until the blade slid free like a red tongue.

When he looked up again, his mouth formed a smile. "Now it's your turn to be hurting."

The threat seemed pitiful, a crippled dog's feeble bark.

"I don't think so," she breathed, and took another backward step.

Cold.

Metal lips kissed the nape of her neck.

Behind her, a whisper: "But I do."

Cain's voice.

And Cain's gun, the muzzle chilly on her skin.

He had entered through the doorway while her back was turned.

"Drop the gun," Cain ordered.

Her hand opened. She watched the Glock fall, feeling nothing, her emotions on hold.

"I tried to make her say where the girl is." Tyler

gasped out the words like a last testament. "She told me a story. I don't know if it's true."

Cain was unconcerned. "Lilith will handle the girl."

Trish shut her eyes.

Lilith. The one with the cold, flat eyes that gleamed with malice.

Ally would have no chance against her.

It was over, then. Over for both of them.

A cough from Tyler. "So do it. Waste her."

Trish waited, thinking emptily that she had started the night with Cain's gun to her head, and now here she was, two hours and a lifetime later, in this mean little shop amid the racks of Lay's potato chips and the napkin dispensers and the stale smell of grease, and nothing had changed.

"Turn around, Trish." Cain said it almost gently, as if addressing a child.

She hesitated.

"Come on now. Don't be shy." He was breathing slowly, deeply, like a man in a trance. "I just want one last look at those big blue eyes."

Tyler tried a chuckle but managed only another dry cough.

She turned slowly, transferring her grip on the counter from her left hand to her right, ashamed somehow of her lameness. She hated having them see her like this, beaten in so many ways.

A broad chest swung into view. A shiny Glock, unsilenced, in a gloved hand. Past the gun, the grainy smear of a face.

She raised her head, meeting Cain's eyes, those smoke-gray eyes that had studied her through holes in a ski mask last time.

No mask now. She saw his face.
God—his *face*.
Her lips parted. She whispered one word.
"You."

68

"I've got it."

Barbara turned toward the rear corner of the closet, where Philip Danforth knelt amid the fallen wardrobes and the dislodged shelves, shining the flashlight at the wall.

"Got what?" she asked.

His answer made her heart speed up: "A way out."

She was crouching at his side an instant later.

"I've been checking the walls for damage." Excitement trembled in his voice. "The explosion shook this place pretty hard. Look here."

Her gaze followed the pointing flash. One of the heavy oak panels, four feet wide and eight feet high, had been wrenched partly free of the studs.

"We can pull the panel away," Barbara whispered, "and crawl through."

"Can we really?" That was Judy. "Thank God. Thank God."

From his perch on the wicker hamper, where he seemed permanently enthroned, Charles spoke up. "In case you've forgotten, there's another wall on the opposite side."

Philip glanced at Barbara. "Is it oak?"

She had to think for a moment, imagining the layout of the bedroom suite. "No. It's the linen closet in the master bath. Drywall, not oak. Half-inch drywall."

A shrug from Philip. "We can punch right through that."

"They'll hear us," Charles said.

"I'm not talking about busting down the damn doors." Philip was losing his patience. "This won't make nearly as much noise."

"They might hear us anyway. Even if they don't, suppose they happen to come back while you're crawling through—"

"Then they'll shoot me." Philip's face was sweaty in the flashlight's glow, the cut on his lip an ugly vertical line. "I'll risk it."

"They may shoot all of us. Will you risk *that*?"

"I will," Barbara snapped, fed up with her husband's weakness, his unaccountable passivity.

Judy touched the bare spot at her throat where her fingers sought a crucifix. "Me too."

"Now wait a minute—"

"You're outvoted, Charles." Philip spoke briskly, a man in a hurry. "Three to one." He turned to Barbara. "We need a tool to pry the panel loose. Crowbar, claw hammer, something like that."

"Damn it." Charles made one last effort. "You're all getting hysterical. You need to calm down and think—"

Judy whirled on him. "Oh, shut your fucking mouth."

There was a moment of politely shocked silence, and even Judy seemed to blush. But no one apologized.

Barbara broke the stillness. To Philip: "How about this?"

She handed him a heavy wooden hanger salvaged from the heap of clothes. Philip wedged one corner of the triangular frame into the crack between the panel and the stud.

"Could work," he grunted, applying pressure.

As Barbara watched tensely, the panel shuddered outward a fraction of an inch, the long screws groaning.

"It's coming," she whispered, exultation singing in the words.

Judy managed a tremulous half-smile.

And Charles ... he simply watched, rigid on the hamper, his facial muscles oddly slack, his eyes empty—as if he were witnessing the death of hope.

69

"Come on, boss," Tyler growled, "do her."

Cain didn't bother to answer. His gaze remained fixed on Trish Robinson.

"You know me," he said softly.

It was not a question. He had heard her astonished whisper, had seen the recognition in her eyes.

Slowly she nodded. "I know you."

"How?"

"Marta Palmer."

The name was meaningless to him. He waited.

"She was nine years old. You picked her up as she was walking home from school." Her voice was low and steady, the voice of a judge pronouncing sentence. "You made her take you to a secluded place, an abandoned farmhouse she knew about. And when you got there, you raped her, and you killed her, and you left her in the field with a jump rope tied around her neck."

The jump rope was what did it. He remembered that detail. The rest was largely lost in a haze of distance, but the jump rope stood out in his mind with photographic clarity. He could see the braided red-and-white cord, the rubber handles. Could see his wrists twisting as he jerked the line taut. Could see the girl's eyes swelling, her lips skinned back in a leering rictus.

Marta Palmer. Yes. He remembered.

But . . .

"How could you know?"

He seized Trish by the shoulders, whirled her away from the counter, slammed her against the opposite wall.

"That was fifteen years ago." He leaned close, his mouth inches from hers. "How the hell could you *know*?"

She did not blink, did not stammer.

"Because," she said simply, "I was there."

A beat of silence.

Cain flicked his gaze away from her, directing it down a deep well of memory, then refocused on her face.

"There were two of them," he breathed. "Two little girls."

"Yes."

"Walking home together."

"Yes."

"You were the other one."

"Yes."

He saw it in his mind: a blurred kinescope of that September day. Two schoolgirls on a tree-shaded road. Wavering spots of sunlight dappled their hair, blonde hair, shiny and soft.

He'd had other girls, girls no older than these—but never two at once. The challenge prompted him to stop his red convertible alongside the pair, under a maple tree's spreading bouquet of golden leaves.

One girl was tall for her age and flirtatious, eager to show off an imagined sophistication. She was an easy mark.

Her friend was different. Quiet. Wary. Cain remembered a thin, thoughtful face and perceptive eyes.

Blue eyes. Trish Robinson's eyes.

"You tried to coax us both into the car," Trish whispered, providing commentary for the filmstrip unspooling in his thoughts. "Too hot to walk, you said. Hop in. You'd take us up the road."

His usual M.O. at the time. He'd been unscarred then. Presentable. Tanned and windburned after days on the open road.

"You put a cassette into the tape player. Said we could listen to some tunes."

The taller girl had accepted his offer, mischievously aware that she was breaking her parents' rules, smug in her rebellion.

"Marta went along," Trish breathed. "I didn't."

Cain nodded slowly. "You told her not to go."

"Yes. I told her." She shut her eyes against the memory. "But she went anyway. And . . . and I . . . "

"You ran. And bought yourself fifteen years." He smiled. "I hope you made the most of them."

"For Christ's sake, boss." Tyler sagged against the counter. "What the hell are you waiting for? Make her dead."

"Haven't you been listening?" Cain asked evenly. "Officer Robinson is a voice from my past."

"She's a damn bug you can't squish, that's what she is. Now's the time"—he coughed, grimacing, his hand pressed to the stab wound—"to stomp her once and for all."

Cain nodded. Objectively he knew Tyler was right. He had Robinson where he wanted her. Just pull the trigger, and she would be dead, no threat ever again.

But . . .

As a child she had been meant for him.

And when he looked into her face, he saw her not as a woman of twenty-four, exhausted and injured, wearing the ragged remnants of a police uniform, but as a nine-year-old girl in shorts and a T-shirt, toting a bookbag, her hair brilliant in an aureole of sun.

The clarity of the image, its visceral, almost tactile reality, was what decided the issue in his mind.

Cain holstered his Glock, then spun Trish around, mashing her face against the wall, and yanked her arms behind her back.

She still wore the handcuffs, but the chain had snapped.

"Shot 'em off, huh?" He chuckled. "Too bad. Those bracelets looked real good on you. Luckily I got a brand-new pair."

He dug in his pocket. Produced the cuffs taken from Wald's belt. Snapped them over her wrists.

"Boss," Tyler mumbled, "we really don't have time for this."

Cain was unfazed. "Of course we don't. Not now. But later . . . "

He turned Trish to face him. Cupping her chin, he tilted her head at an angle.

"Later you'll cry like Marta did. You'll call for your mommy too. And after you've cried and screamed for a good long while, I'll put a rope around your neck and I'll finish you just the way I would've done it on that farmhouse porch."

He wanted her to flinch from the words, but she merely stared at him, those blue eyes seeing too much.

"Move," he snapped, and pushed her roughly toward the door.

She staggered, her left knee buckling. He caught her from behind. For the first time he noted the bandage on her leg.

"What's this, Trish? Bullet?" His tongue clucked in mock sympathy. "Somebody poke a hole in you?"

She nodded in answer, pain squeezing her mouth in a bloodless line.

"Well, my friend's hurt just as bad." He tossed a glance at Tyler, stooping awkwardly to retrieve his Glock. "Maybe worse. And he's still ambulatory. Now *march*."

She took another step, nearly fell again. Cain held her up by the collar.

Through gritted teeth she gasped, "I can't."

"Then I've got to carry you. But if I do, I'll make sure you're not faking it." He slid his gun barrel slowly under her nose, letting her smell the lubricant. "You know what it means to be kneecapped, Trish?"

A slow swallow rippled down her throat. She looked down at the Glock, then at his face, and he read the anguish and the fury in her eyes.

"March," he said again, and let go.

With what must have been a concentrated effort of will, she stayed erect.

Her leg was shaking as she advanced another step, but this time she did not totter, did not fall. Head lowered, sweat shining on her face, she hobbled across the threshold, not looking back.

She had guts. Cain conceded that much as he followed her out the door. The little rookie would have made one hell of a cop.

If she had lived.

70

"Eight-one. Go."

"Hey, eight-one, it sure took long enough to raise you."

"Sorry for the delay. We were code seven. Grabbing some chow."

Ed Edinger paced the small equipment room adjacent to the dispatchers' office. Radio transmissions were recorded here, on antique reel-to-reel machines.

Normally the long-playing reels were changed only at the end of each shift, but tonight one reel had been replaced ahead of schedule.

The original reel now played on another machine.

"Yeah, well, I kind of let that code seven slide." Lou's voice rasped over cheap speakers, sounding even more scratchy than usual. "It's been an hour. Look, what's your location?"

"Hospers Road, west of the highway."

That was Robinson, of course. Funny thing, though. There was an unusual quality to her speech pattern, a formality that seemed somehow artificial.

"Okay," Lou was saying, "we got a ten-thirty-three at the Cracker Barrel on Johnson. You back in service or what?"

"Ten-four, we'll take it."

"Twenty-one twenty-five."

Ed glanced at his watch. The time was 10:16. Forty-one minutes had passed since the unit had been dispatched.

The tape continued playing, other units on the air. He didn't listen. He was thinking.

The whole exchange troubled him. It was highly uncharacteristic of Pete Wald to have gone code seven at all, let alone so early in his shift. And to stay out of service for an hour, then be tardy in responding when called . . .

Grabbing some chow, Robinson had said. On Hospers Road.

Nothing over that way except some fast-food hamburger joints. Pete avoided those places on his doctor's orders. Cholesterol.

And Robinson's voice . . . Ed couldn't shake the feeling that there was something wrong, indefinably *wrong*, about her voice.

He stopped pacing. "Find the previous transmission," he told the clerk operating the tape machine. "About an hour earlier."

The clerk checked Lou's log, then rewound the tape while Ed waited, massaging his forehead with a weary hand.

What a night.

First some sort of sonic boom or explosion or minor earthquake had rocked the foothills, precipitating a deluge of frantic calls and tripping every motion-sensitive burglar alarm in town.

He had telephoned Cal Tech in Pasadena, but the

seismology lab had been unable to explain the event or pinpoint its source. A mystery, and a major hassle.

And now 4–Adam–8–1 was missing. Wald and Robinson had never responded to the 10–33 on Johnson Way. Efforts to raise them had proved futile so far.

When the tape counter was in approximately the right place, the clerk backed and filled, nitrous-oxide voices squealing over the speakers, until he located the start of the exchange.

"We're clear of the detail," Robinson was saying. "No sign of a prowler."

Lou: "Guess Pete was right. You didn't need backup."

"Ten-four."

"Hey, is that the Kent place?"

"Ten-four."

"Thought I recognized the address. I saw it on a house tour once. Nice digs."

"Yeah, it's nice. A lot like some places I've seen in L.A."

"L.A.?"

"You know. Bel-Air, Beverly Hills. Ed and I were just talking about that. About how things are in L.A."

What the hell?

"Play that part again," Ed said.

The clerk rotated a dial to the left, backing up the tape.

"—lot like some places I've seen in L.A."

"L.A.?"

"You know. Bel-Air, Beverly Hills. Ed and I were just talking about that. About how things are in L.A."

"Again," he told the clerk.

Squeal of tape through the pinch rollers.

"—seen in L.A."

"L.A.?"

"You know. Bel-Air, Beverly Hills. Ed and I were just talking about that. About how things are in L.A."

How things are in L.A.

Things are in L.A.

In L.A.

"Christ," he whispered, remembering.

Roll call. She'd been late. He'd read her the riot act.

Now, down in L.A. it's a different story. L.A.'s got two thousand homicides a year. That's where all the crazies are.

His usual spiel. The only words pertaining to Los Angeles he'd ever spoken in her presence.

Homicides. Crazies.

A clue.

The poor scared kid had tried delivering a clue.

Ed left the bewildered clerk and barged through the connecting doorway into the dispatchers' room. Lou's cubicle was nearer.

She opened her mouth to ask a question. He cut her off.

"The Kent estate—what's the address?"

"Twenty-five hundred Skylark."

"Send all available units, code two high." He caught his breath. "We got ourselves a ten-ninety-nine."

Lou's eyes were wider than he'd ever seen them. Ten-ninety-nine was the code for an emergency—an officer down.

She visibly collected herself. "Right. Code two high, you said?" Normally an officer-needs-help call would justify going code three, sirens screaming.

Wald nodded. "Right. Could be a dicey situation.

We don't want to announce . . . hold on." Whoever had Robinson's radio would be monitoring the police bands. "On second thought, I'll give the order. Have everybody meet me on tac three."

A tactical frequency, operating in the simplex mode. Its limited range would enable him to contact the patrol units without being overheard by anyone at the Kent house.

Sheriff's department too—better call the substation on his cell phone—might need SWAT—and an ambulance . . .

"Ed!" Lou's shout stopped him halfway to the door. "What's this all about?"

"I think we misjudged Robinson." He fumbled for the keys to his squad car. "Looks like she's not a slacker after all."

71

It took all of Trish's strength to limp along the dirt path in the cold starlight.

Cain was directly behind her, Tyler farther back. She'd cut him pretty badly. The wound might prove fatal if untreated.

Of course her own situation was looking fairly terminal as well.

She didn't want to think about Ally. Lilith must have found her by now. Killed her, perhaps—or captured her alive.

Trish wasn't sure which prospect was worse.

"I almost didn't do her," Cain said abruptly.

Momentarily confused, Trish thought he meant Ally, then realized it was Marta he was thinking of.

"Why not?" she gasped without turning.

"Because of you. I knew you could describe me to the police. Did you?"

She covered another yard, suffered another spear of agony through her leg. "Yes."

"And?"

"Nothing." Each word, like each step, was an effort. "No computerized searches back then. And . . . " She sucked air, blew hard. "And I didn't get the license plate."

A grunt of humor. "Not real observant for a cop."

"Wasn't a cop. I was . . . nine years old."

They marched higher up the trail. Black oaks formed an irregular colonnade on either side, silhouetted trunks standing out like bands of India ink against the faintly glowing mist.

"I should've taken you when I took her." Cain again, remorselessly worrying the open wound of their shared past. "Should've grabbed you and pulled you into the car."

"Why didn't you?"

"You never got quite close enough. You were just out of reach. One more step, and I would've had you. Then I wouldn't have had to worry about the police."

"If you were so worried, why'd you go through with it at all?"

"Some things you just don't pass up."

Although she couldn't see him, she knew a cruel and hungry leer had spread across his face.

"Your little friend was so cute, so cuddly." He made a lip-smacking sound that sickened her. "I like 'em young, you know. The younger, the better. Marta was real good, Trish. A man would pay serious money for a taste of what she had."

The ache in her leg was worse, but it couldn't compete with the sudden furious throbbing of her skull.

She saw it again: Marta in the weeds, a roach crawling on her unblinking eye. Heard her own voice keening: *I told you. Marta, I told you . . .*

"You didn't just *want* her," she whispered. "You *needed* her. You had to have her."

"Just like I gotta have you, blue eyes."

"It's a compulsion with you—killing young girls."

"Sort of a bad habit I've never been able to shake."

"How many have there been?"

"Believe it or not, I've lost count. Maybe . . . couple dozen."

Couple dozen. She shut her eyes.

It was only a number, but behind it lay suffering impossible to calculate. The agony of victims, the grief of parents, the hurt of friends.

And all because of this one man, roaming the back roads, passing uninvited from town to town, stringing his daisy chain of corpses through a line of weedy fields.

"Did one of them give you that scar?" she hissed, hoping the answer was yes.

"My little beauty mark? No, that's a souvenir from prison."

"At least you can't pick up schoolgirls anymore." Anger made her harsh. "Not with that face."

He merely laughed. "There are other girls. Runaways. Underage hookers. They're not too particular about their escorts."

"So you still do it?"

"Every now and then. Got this trailer, real isolated, soundproofed." Chuckle. "You'll be seeing it soon."

I'll bet, she thought, acid trickling in her belly.

"There was one girl," he went on, "cadging quarters at an interstate rest stop. All of thirteen years old. I took her back to my place for the usual treatment. But this girl, well, she *liked* pain. She got off on it. So I let her live."

"Lilith," Trish breathed.

"You catch on quick, Officer. Maybe you'll make detective someday."

The path grew steeper. Her wounded leg wobbled. She knew what would happen if she fell. Cain would sling her over his shoulder like a sack of garbage . . . but first he would blow out both her knees with Black Talon rounds.

Or maybe he would decide carrying her wasn't worth the trouble, and simply end her life with a bullet to the brain.

That way would be better—quicker—than what she had in store at that trailer of his.

No medals for quitters. She kept going.

"You know, it's funny." Cain's words, low and thoughtful. "Back then you tried to talk Marta out of going with me. Tonight you nearly shot down this whole operation. Every time we get together, you mess with my plans. You're like a bad penny, Robinson. You just keep turning up."

"You're the bad penny," she whispered, jaws clenched.

"Maybe so." A pleasant laugh. "But you're the one who's being taken out of circulation."

She crested the rise and found herself at a parking lot, empty save for a dark van and the Porsche she'd seen in the Kents' driveway earlier.

Lilith stood near the Porsche. For a frightened moment Trish didn't see Ally.

Was she dead?

Then her wavering gaze fastened on a white dress, a pale face—Ally, alive, seated on the passenger side of the Porsche.

"Go." Cain gave her a shove, and she stumbled forward.

Lilith, fists on hips, drilled a cold stare into Cain. "Why didn't you ice her?"

"Turns out she's an old friend." Cain's voice was merry. "We've got a lot of catching up to do."

Trish hobbled alongside the Porsche. Through the open window Ally gazed up at her. She was buckled into her seat, hands bound with what looked like a cut-off segment of the shoulder harness. Despair shadowed her face.

Meeting her eyes, Trish mouthed three words: *There's always hope.*

The same words she'd said in the cellar. She wondered if Ally would remember.

She did. A faint smile flickered on the girl's lips.

Then the car was behind her, Cain steering her to the van. Automatically she tried to identify the make and model. Either a Chevy Astro or a GMC Safari. Three or four years old. Black or dark green. California tags.

Couldn't read the plate, but she supposed it didn't matter.

Cain slid open the door panel on the passenger side. A dome light winked on, illuminating a cloth-upholstered bench seat.

"In," he ordered.

She paused, unsure she could manage the upward step into the rear compartment, and unwilling to leave the open air, the smell of woods, the lake breeze, all the things she might never know again.

"Do it, Trish," Cain said softly. "This is one ride you're not turning down."

72

With a groan of protest, the four-by-eight panel finally came free, opening an exit in the closet wall.

"Did it," Philip gasped, blinking perspiration away.

Only the drywall remained, the last barrier. Barbara, guiding the work by flashlight, pulled off her left pump and handed it to Philip. "Use this."

The two-inch heel made a serviceable tool. Crouching low, Philip attacked the bottom portion of the drywall.

Each tap was loud. Charles might have been right, Barbara reflected nervously. The noise could draw the killers.

It took Philip less than a minute to break open an irregular hole two feet wide, bracketed by wooden studs.

"Okay," he said without bravado, "I'm going through."

Charles stood up. "Just you? Alone?"

There was something odd about the way he said it, as if he felt threatened by the prospect.

Philip shook his head. "We've got to stick together."

"Right." Charles nodded, manic intensity gleaming

in his eyes. "We stick together. Nobody goes any-where alone."

Barbara wondered if her husband was having a breakdown.

Philip crawled into the linen closet, then pushed on the door. It groaned—the explosion must have warped the frame—but yielded to his pressure.

When it was fully open he scrambled out. A whisper: "Coast is clear."

Barbara looked at Judy, who took the flash and waved her on. "You next."

On hands and knees Barbara squeezed through the hole, splinters and bent screws clutching at her dress and hair. Her head bumped against the linen closet's bottom shelf. Philip helped her to her feet, then knelt to assist his wife.

Blinking, Barbara looked around at the master bath. The medicine cabinets, unlatched, had spilled their contents on the marble countertop and in the porcelain basin and across the tile floor. Above the sink, twin sconces still glowed, the bulbs unbroken, but the mirror had shattered, as had the skylight over the Roman tub.

Her mind barely registered the damage. The important thing was that the killers had not come. And in the darkened bedroom just beyond the doorway, there ought to be a telephone.

Stick together, Philip had said. But Judy was taking forever to struggle through the gap. Charles would follow. Philip was preoccupied with helping. Another minute would pass before all four of them were out.

She couldn't wait that long.

Kicking off her other pump, she moved to the doorway and cast a sidelong glance down the hall.

Dark. Silent. She didn't think anyone was there.

A breath of courage, and she left the bathroom. Barefoot, she crossed the suite, staying close to the spill of light from the bathroom, avoiding broken glass and fallen plaster.

Quickly around the nearest bed. A frightened pause: Was that a footstep in the hall?

No, nothing. Get to the phone. Hurry.

Normally it rested on the nightstand next to her favorite lamp, the one with the seashell shade. Now lamp and phone were a spray of ceramic shards and a tangle of wires on the floor.

She stooped, groping in the shadows for the handset, but it had been ripped from the base and discarded somewhere, and she couldn't find it.

When she stood, she saw Judy and the two men gathered in the bathroom doorway. She held up the useless base unit in explanation.

"Where are your other phones?" Philip whispered as Barbara rejoined the group.

He could have asked Charles, of course. But judging by the glazed vacancy of his stare, Barbara doubted her husband would have answered.

"Ally's room," she said. "Just down the hall."

Philip hesitated. "You don't happen to keep a gun around?"

"Sorry."

"Maybe we won't need it. Place is pretty quiet. They may have left."

Charles flinched at the words. Barbara wondered why.

Single file they crept down the lightless hall to the first door on the right.

Ally's room—but the doorway had collapsed. The gap between the warped frame and the door, wedged ajar by debris, was too narrow to permit entry.

Barbara peered inside, her gaze roving over a shadowed waste of toppled bookcases and fallen curtains and broken glass, hunting fearfully for some sign of her daughter.

If Ally was in there, she was hidden in the wreckage. And making no sound. No sound at all.

Trembling, she turned away and caught Philip's interrogative glance. With effort she focused on the immediate problem.

A telephone. Where?

"Kitchen," she said, her voice hushed. "Or we could go out the back door, circle around to the garage, use the car phone."

Philip thought for a moment, his eyes cutting toward the far end of the hallway with the eerie regularity of a metronome.

"Safer to stay inside," he decided. "Doesn't sound like they're in the house, but they may be patrolling the yard."

"Why would they?" Judy asked.

Philip shrugged. "Why would they do any of this?"

Charles looked away.

Quickly to the end of the hall, Philip in the lead. He pivoted into the dining area, then motioned for the others to follow.

Into the kitchen, the only part of the house still brightly lit. Barbara blinked in astonishment at the scorched ruins of the cellar doorway, then reached for the cordless phone.

But there was no phone—no handset, no base unit, only the bracket sagging from the wall on loosened screws.

Damn.

"Our other phone's in the den," she said, answering Philip's unspoken question. "Across from the foyer."

She was moving toward the kitchen doorway when she noticed Charles, half hidden behind the central island, stooping low.

He felt her stare and straightened instantly, a hand on his lapel. "Some of their equipment," he whispered.

Barbara glanced over the island and saw a black duffel bag, its contents strewn across the floor.

"Thought there might be something useful—a cell phone or a radio." Charles frowned. "No luck."

"How about a gun?" Philip asked.

"No luck, I said."

"Well"—Philip shrugged—"it was worth a look."

They left the kitchen, Philip still the leader, Barbara second in line.

Distantly she was glad Charles had searched the bag, even though he'd found nothing of value. At least he was trying.

Really, it was the first positive thing her husband had done all night.

73

Cain beckoned to Lilith and Tyler, then followed Trish inside the van. Roughly he pushed her into the bench seat. She huddled there, panting, while he stared down thoughtfully at the dirty mop of her hair.

Even handcuffed, she couldn't be trusted. She'd already demonstrated considerable talent as an escape artist. Getting out of a locked trunk underwater was a stunt worthy of Houdini.

But Houdini himself couldn't shed a pair of cuffs if his hands were in plain sight.

Cain surveyed the rear compartment. Bolted to the doorframe was a padded grab bar. He tested the mounting. Secure.

Groping in his pocket, he produced the key set taken from Officer Wald's belt. From the slight widening of Trish's eyes, he could see she recognized the item.

"Every time a bell rings," Cain whispered, "an angel earns his wings." He jingled the keys. "Sounds like your partner's flying right now."

She didn't answer.

The van rocked on its springs as Lilith hopped into the rear compartment.

"Got to uncuff the Mouseketeer for a second," Cain said. "If she moves . . . if she even breathes too hard . . . grease her."

Lilith unholstered her Glock, the silencer already discarded, and pressed the muzzle against Trish's cheek.

Bending low, Cain reached behind the cop and jerked her wrists sideways. With Wald's handcuff key he unlocked the left cuff. Trish offered no resistance as he pulled her right arm forward and up, bringing her wrist alongside the grab bar.

The open handcuff dangled on its short chain. Deftly he threaded it under the bar, then raised her left arm and snapped the cuff over her wrist again.

She was manacled to the doorframe, her hands at eye level.

Perfect.

"You wanted me, boss?" Tyler, peering in through the side doorway.

Cain studied him. The younger man looked pale, his eyes glazed. "Feel okay to drive?" he asked dubiously.

"How far?"

"Back to the Kent place. So we can finish things."

Nod. "I can make it."

The statement seemed an expression of optimism more than fact, but Cain was prepared to accept it. He didn't want Lilith at the wheel. He wanted her in the rear compartment, standing guard. Her cool, feral gaze never missed a thing.

"I'll take the Porsche," he said briskly. "Tyler drives the van. Lilith, you stay back here with the Girl Scout." He smiled at Trish. "You *were* a Girl Scout, weren't you?"

She looked away. "No."

Cain merely laughed, amused by the transparency and pointlessness of the lie. He tossed Wald's keys to Lilith, then climbed out and shut the side panel with an echoing slam.

Quickly across the parking lot, his boots slapping asphalt in a clockwork rhythm. The Porsche was unlocked. He slipped behind the wheel.

Ally glanced at him, and he favored her with a cold smile.

"I just knew we'd be together again, freckle-face."

She lowered her head, a shudder dancing lightly over her thin shoulders.

The keys were in the ignition. Cain guided the Porsche forward. Headlights flared in the rearview mirror as the van lumbered in pursuit.

Out the gate, onto the winding road. He opened the throttle, enjoying the engine's power. Behind him, the van struggled to keep up.

On a short straightaway, he studied the girl's profile in the glow of the dashboard. Wetness gleamed in the corner of her eye.

"Scared, Ally?"

"No."

"You ought to be. I got some real special plans for you."

The Porsche rounded a curve, hugging the rutted road. The van's headlights dimmed as Tyler fell farther behind.

Cain thought about what would come next. With duct tape he would bind Ally and Barbara to the two beds in the master suite. Then snuff them both, quick and nasty—the girl first, followed by her mother.

The rearview mirror was dark now, the van lost to sight. He was alone with Ally, the two of them as closely confined as travelers in a space capsule, and as far removed from the rest of the world.

He thought of Marta. She had been his passenger too.

"What about Trish?" Ally asked above the engine's hypnotic drone. "What'll happen to her?"

It was touching how she fretted about her hero even in the last minutes of her life.

"Trish gets to hang around for a little while. Another ten, twelve hours maybe." Cain pictured the things he and Lilith would do in the trailer. "If she lasts that long."

"She'll find a way out," Ally whispered.

"Not this time."

"You always underestimate her."

Despite himself, Cain nodded. The same thought had pestered him.

Then he saw Trish Robinson as she was now: disarmed, handcuffed, guarded, a prisoner with a gun to her head.

His last fears faded.

"The rookie's good," he said mildly. "I'll give you that." He smiled again, a private smile. "But she's finished now."

74

Crossing the living room was perilous. The broad bay window, curtains open, afforded a clear view to anybody who might be stationed outside.

Barbara kept her head down, staying close to Philip as he navigated a course through a surreal archipelago of overturned and mutilated furniture. A single lamp remained standing, a brass torchier, stoic as a lighthouse in a storm.

The destruction here was not the work of an explosion. It was deliberate vandalism, senseless and grotesque. Barbara knew she would feel something later about the loss of her precious heirlooms and valued antiques, but Ally was her sole concern now.

Had the bastards killed her? Kidnapped her? Or was she lying injured somewhere, unable to call for help?

Philip reached the den, washed in the glow of a ceiling light. He looked cautiously inside, then entered, Barbara right behind.

The first thing she noticed was the wall safe, open and empty. Some remote part of her mind calculated the losses, covered by insurance but irreplaceable in personal terms.

Her gaze widened, taking in the rest of the room, Charles's private retreat, his refuge. She died a little to think how he must feel to see his big-screen television smashed, his elaborate sound system cannibalized, his leather armchairs gutted like stockyard animals.

But when she glanced at him, she saw nothing in his face—no hurt, no anger, only a curious resolve, the look of a decision reached.

No time to wonder about that. The important thing was the phone on the desk, the phone that must have been sabotaged like the others.

But no.

The phone was in place, seemingly undamaged. The mayhem had been interrupted before that corner of the room had been touched.

Barbara reached the desk in two strides. She lifted the handset, put it to her ear, heard the hum of a dial tone, the most welcome sound she could ever hope to hear, other than Ally's laughter.

"It works." Her words hushed and solemn like a prayer.

For a moment she just stood there, marveling at the reality of a lifeline to the larger world.

"Nine-one-one," Judy said gently.

Of course. Stupid of her to freeze up like that.

She tapped one digit, and from across the room a harsh voice ordered, "*Stop.*"

Her husband's voice.

Baffled, she glanced up, and the glance hardened into a stare.

Charles stood just inside the doorway, his blazer unbuttoned, a black pistol in his trembling hand.

With a sickening switch of perspective, she saw what was really going on.

Saw why Charles had tried to talk her out of reporting the prowler in the backyard.

Saw why he had behaved so inexplicably ever since.

The violence of this night was not random. It was a plot, carefully planned, professionally executed, and its ultimate target could only be herself.

"Let go of the phone," Charles said evenly.

Judy and Philip stood frozen, stares fixed on the gun that had appeared so unexpectedly in Charles's hand, like a palmed card in a magic trick.

Barbara knew her husband well enough to see through his pose of cool assurance. The gun shook, just slightly but enough, and his left eyelid twitched.

Would he shoot her? Did he have the nerve?

Before tonight she wouldn't have thought so. But if he'd hired assassins, staged this ugly show, then he was capable of anything.

She released the handset. It thumped on the desk.

"Now come over here."

"Charles." Philip sounded less angry than disappointed. "What's this all about?"

"Marital problems." He chuckled. "A little domestic discord in the Kent household."

Barbara reached him. Up close she saw the mustache of sweat fringing her husband's smile.

"Stand with them," he said.

She eased alongside the Danforths. "I'm sorry," she whispered to them. Obscurely she felt responsible for all this.

"Quiet," Charles snapped.

She ignored the order. "Where's Ally?"

"I said, be quiet."

"Where is she? What did they do to her?"

"Shut up!"

"Is she . . . alive?"

In the beat of silence that followed, she heard his answer.

"God damn you, Charles."

"We had no choice," he said as Judy began to pray softly and Philip's hands tightened into fists. "She saw Cain's face—the man I hired. She had to die." The gun lifted. "And so do you."

Judy moaned.

"You're going to kill us yourself?" Barbara breathed, unable to quite make it real. "All three of us?"

"Have to. My friends appear to have left early." He licked his lips. "So here's the new story. Philip broke out of the closet, but we were caught trying to call for help. I'm the only one who got away."

"How lucky for you," Philip said with cool contempt.

"Yes, well"—a faltering smile—"I've always been quick on my feet."

Barbara stared at him, full comprehension finally settling in. "You're serious about this."

"Yes . . . dear."

She lifted her chin, and in that moment she knew she was her father's girl, an Ashcroft, facing death with aristocratic poise.

"Then," she whispered, "start with me."

Charles aimed the shaking gun.

Headlights.

They splashed across the curtained windows as a powerful engine hummed up the drive. Barbara recognized it: the Danforths' Porsche.

Charles blinked, registering the car's arrival, and the gun lowered fractionally.

"On second thought," he said, "I'll let Cain handle it." He giggled, a manic, mirthless sound. "That's what I'm paying him for."

75

The van rumbled down the dark road, punished by ruts and potholes.

Lilith, one knee on the bench seat, one foot on the floor, trained her Glock and her gaze on Trish. With each rough jostle she smiled.

"Something funny?" Trish asked, arms swaying as the handcuff chain slid back and forth along the grab bar.

"It's just that my finger's pretty tight on the trigger. We get bounced hard enough, the gun might go off by accident." She put a mocking emphasis on the last word.

"Cain wants me alive," Trish said evenly.

Lilith showed a sweet smile. "But I don't."

Trish was silent. She didn't want to engage Lilith in conversation. She wanted the girl to be distracted, to look the other way.

Until now her focused stare had been as unwavering as a cobra's.

The Kent house wasn't far. Cain must be there by now. The van was slower, and Tyler had been driving poorly, the knife wound taking its toll, but he would pull through the gate before long.

Still, there was a chance.

Between them, Cain and Lilith had made two mistakes.

Cain hadn't buckled her in.

And Lilith hadn't pocketed Wald's keys.

The key ring dangled from her left hand, loosely held, glinting in the dome light's glow.

"Cut yourself shaving, Robinson?"

Lilith was looking at her left calf, the bandages dark with blood.

"Flesh wound," Trish said mildly.

"Painful."

"Not much." A lie.

"Really?"

Flash of motion, Lilith propelling her boot into the injured leg, shock wave of agony, Trish biting her lip to stifle a scream.

Lilith smiled. "How about now?"

Trish didn't answer. She needed her full concentration to suppress the waves of dizziness swarming over her.

When her vision cleared, she saw Lilith still watching her, the cool, attentive eyes refusing even to blink.

The keys flashed, tantalizing.

Look away, you sadistic little *bitch*.

"You don't cry so easily," Lilith lisped, "do you, Robinson?"

"Guess not."

Up front, Tyler slumped lower in his seat, the van cutting its speed.

"I hate crybabies." Lilith's stare was appraising now, a connoisseur's scrutiny. "They never last. The other kind, the ones like you, can take much more punishment." A thoughtful grin. "We can keep you going a long time."

The van drifted to the right.

Tyler's head—nodding.

Trish slowly wrapped both hands around the grab bar. "A minute ago you wanted to shoot me."

"I'm starting to think Cain had the right idea."

"Are you?"

Get ready . . .

"You're just too good to waste." Lilith's tongue prowled her lips. "I want to hear you scream, Robinson. I want—"

Crunch of gravel.

The van swerving off the road.

"Tyler?" Lilith spun toward the front. "Hey, wake up, asshole!"

Hands locked on the grab bar, Trish hoisted herself off the seat.

Lilith shook Tyler alert.

Trish drew back her knees, lower legs extended, feet together.

The van lurched to the left as Tyler cranked the wheel.

Lilith turned.

Now.

Trish pistoned her right leg, slamming a brutal kick into the girl's face.

Lilith's nose crunched like a snail. She twisted, fell writhing on the floor, spitting up blood, the gun still in her hand but the keys flying free.

The van skidded back onto the road.

Trish snagged the key ring between her shoes. Flipped it upward, snatched it out of the air.

Tyler released the wheel, clutching at his sidearm holster.

The handcuff key was the smallest one on the ring. Trish inserted it in the left cuff and turned.

Tyler's gun was out.

The handcuff popped open.

Tyler pivoted in his seat.

Trish ducked, and the handcuff chain snaked through the gap between the grab bar and the ceiling, the empty cuff coming with it.

Gunshot.

The rear window puckered, Tyler's bullet missing as she dived to the floor, spread-eagle on Lilith, the Glock whipping toward her, and Trish seized the girl's wrist and held the gun away, grappling with her in a tangle of limbs.

"Shoot her!" Lilith screamed the words. "Tyler, she's on top of me, shoot her, *shoot her*!"

Tyler's gun angled down, pointing blindly, and Trish threw her body to the left, the world cartwheeling, she and Lilith trading places.

Lilith's eyes widened as she understood who was on top now. She opened her mouth in the beginning of a scream—

And Tyler fired into the rear compartment, two shots, three, bullets ripping through Lilith's shoulder and abdomen and neck, Trish wincing as the deflected rounds burst out of Lilith's body in new trajectories, drilling into the bench seat and the wall, and then Tyler was shouting, "Did I get her? Lilith?"

Blood foamed from the girl's mouth. She sagged, dead weight, the Glock still clutched in her hand, muzzle pressed to the back of the driver's seat.

"Did I get her?"

"You got her," Trish whispered, and she curled the forefinger of her left hand over Lilith's trigger finger and squeezed.

The gun blew a scorched hole in the seat. Tyler wailed, a wounded animal, and his gun discharged, thunder rolling through the van, and Trish fired again, again, again, the driver's seat bucking, the van skidding, her finger flexing convulsively, emptying the gun, until somewhere a horn blared, an idiot noise, monotonous and pointless.

She abandoned the Glock in Lilith's frozen grip. Pushed the girl aside, struggled upright, thrust her head into the front compartment, and there was Tyler, dead, slumped over the wheel, his back blooming red roses, his forehead sounding the horn as the van weaved, driverless, at reckless speed.

The road veered to the left. Directly ahead, a dense stand of pines.

The van would meet those trees at sixty miles an hour less than three seconds from now.

76

Cain hustled Ally out of the Porsche. She struggled fiercely, her bound hands thrashing. He hardly noticed.

His thoughts were on the final stage of the night's operation, so long delayed.

Mr. Kent would not like hearing his daughter raped and murdered just outside the closet doors. He'd told Cain to do her quickly, painlessly. But after all the trouble she had caused, she wasn't going to leave the world without a scream or two.

Anyway—Cain smiled—it would do Charles good to eavesdrop on the girl's death. The experience would put him in the appropriately grief-stricken frame of mind. He would cry real tears in the presence of the police.

Up the flagstone steps with Ally. Into the foyer.

Cain paused to retrieve his roll of duct tape.

"For you, sweetcakes," he said, twirling the spool.

He was feeling fine. The plan had worked, actually *worked*. In spite of every imaginable setback, he would complete his assignment and earn his pay.

Five million dollars ... split three ways now, not five.

He stepped out of the foyer, then froze, Ally stiff at his side, both of them staring at the doorway of the den.

Charles Kent stood there, gun in hand, standing guard over his wife and the Danforths.

There was a moment when mother and daughter locked gazes, a moment electric with a shared thrill of anguish, and then Ally sagged in Cain's arms, resistance sighing out of her.

Charles ignored the girl. His frightened stare was focused on Cain.

"They got free, found a phone." The words spilled out in a panicky jumble, his voice an octave too high. "I had to stop them."

Cain pushed Ally effortlessly into a slashed armchair.

"Very resourceful, Mr. Kent." He spoke in a monotone, aware that everything had ended for him, his hopes and plans, his grand dreams—all of it ashes now. "Where did you get the gun?"

"From your duffel bag. In the kitchen."

Cain nodded slowly. "From my duffel bag . . ."

"I checked the clip. It's loaded."

"Yes. Yes, it is."

He was very calm. He breathed in, out.

In. Out.

The little ritual he always performed before a kill.

77

Trish lunged for the steering wheel.

Out of reach.

The wall of pines rushed closer. The horn blared.

She stretched between the bucket seats. Her groping hand closed over the wheel and wrenched it hard to the left.

Scream of tires.

The van skidding.

Trees blurring past the windshield.

Rattle of branches, shatter of glass. Forked fingers thrust through a side window, then whipped away.

The van careened into the middle of the road, still speeding at sixty, slammed by every rut and pothole, the shocks creaking like old mattress springs.

She had to get Tyler's boot off the accelerator.

Grunting with strain, she squeezed into the front compartment. Her wounded leg pulsed with angry flare-ups of pain. The bandage might have come loose; she thought she was bleeding again.

The driver's seat bucked and wobbled, the frame shattered. Roughly she jostled it, the open handcuff dangling from the locked cuff on her right wrist, a bauble on a charm bracelet, coruscating in the dashboard's light.

With a gasp of effort she shoved the broken seat all the way back, then crowded next to Tyler and pried him from the wheel, silencing the horn.

Even in death, he wouldn't let up on the gas. The speedometer crawled toward seventy.

She kicked his right leg until his boot lifted off the pedal.

The road curved again. She knew this spot. Intersection with Skylark Drive.

Kneeling on the edge of the driver's seat, grappling with the wheel, she steered through a shrieking turn.

The van barreled north on Skylark. Toward the Kent estate.

She tried to find the brake, and then Tyler inclined sideways, his head in her chest, the blood-matted ponytail bristling on her chin like a wet paintbrush.

Get him out of the seat, *out of the seat.*

Reaching across the body, she threw open the door. Snatched the Glock from his slack fingers, jammed it in her waistband, pushed him away, and another sharp curve flashed out of nowhere.

She grabbed the wheel, swinging the van to the right.

Inertia tugged Tyler through the doorway. As he was sliding out, she remembered his ammo pouch. She fumbled at it, hoping to grab a spare magazine—too late.

Tyler fell, bouncing and flopping on the road, then rolled away in a confusion of limbs.

She twisted upright and saw the double yellow line whip into another switchback coil.

Spin of the wheel, the van slewing, a cloud of gravel pelting the chassis, and then the road straightened and she pumped the brake pedal.

The speedometer dipped to fifty. She kept it there. Still a reckless speed, but she couldn't afford caution, not now.

Momentarily she took her hand off the wheel to check Tyler's Glock.

Empty.

Lilith's ammo pouch might contain a spare mag, but there wasn't time to stop the van and climb into the back.

No medals for quitters.

She would go in unarmed.

78

Charles coughed, an incongruously delicate sound. "We'll . . . we'll have to do them all."

"Of course." With his gun Cain motioned to the prisoners. "On the couch."

Wordlessly Philip and Judy sat at one end of the sofa, facing Ally. Torn cushions deflated under them like punctured tires. Barbara seated herself at the opposite end, shoulders back, lips pursed.

A woman sitting for a portrait. She made a telling contrast with her husband—restless, anxious, sweating, a false smile glued to his face.

Cain stepped back, preparing for the bloody but necessary work at hand.

"Are you going to . . . " Charles swallowed. "I mean . . . right here?"

Cain nodded. "Right here."

Philip drew his wife close. Barbara stiffened, waiting.

"They'll know it was you."

The small, tremulous voice was Ally's. She stared directly at her father.

Charles flicked a glance in her direction, then

looked hastily aware. "They won't know anything. I'll say I escaped. I'm the sole survivor."

"They won't believe you."

He nearly delivered some sharp retort. Cain cut him off.

"She's right, Mr. Kent."

Charles took a moment to register the words. "What?"

"It's too convenient this way." Cain tried not to think of the money, the five million, his better future. "With other witnesses to verify your story, you would have been in the clear. Without them, you'll be the obvious suspect."

"Nobody can prove—"

"They won't have to *prove*. They'll interrogate you. They'll make you crack."

"I can handle them. I'm a lawyer, God damn it!"

"You're weak."

The two words, uttered so softly, absorbed Charles's tirade like a pillow absorbing a fist.

"You'll fold. You'll talk. You'll implicate me."

"Why . . . why would I?"

"To cut a deal. You're a lawyer, like you said. You know all the angles."

"This is *crazy*."

"It's what you'll do. It's what men like you always do. I'm just the hired hand, the trained ape. You'll sell me out without a second thought . . . if you can."

Comprehension flashed on Charles Kent's face.

His gun came up fast.

He fired at Cain.

A trio of shots at a distance of ten feet, reports echoing in the room. Judy screamed.

And Cain laughed.

Brian Harper

* * *

Directly ahead, the Kent estate, gate open. Trish slowed to forty, gripping the wheel in preparation for a tight turn.

The driver's door banged fitfully against the frame. She'd never closed it.

Forget the door. Get ready.

Now.

She veered to the right, and the van hooked sharply, leaning on two wheels, and the wrought-iron gatepost slammed into the open door and sheared it from its hinges in a shower of sparks.

Then the gate was behind her, the house rushing up. Through the bay window the living room was visible.

Posed in the glow of a single lamp, a waxworks tableau: the Kents, the Danforths—and Cain.

Trish floored the gas.

Cain's laughter rose over the distant rumble of the van pulling into the yard. There was a metallic bang—Tyler might have hit the gate—but he didn't turn and look. His full attention was focused on Charles, poor Charles, bewildered and shaking and about to die.

"Should have checked the clip more closely, Mr. Kent. The gun in my duffel—it's one we used in our training exercises. Specially modified . . . to fire blanks."

"Blanks," Charles whispered.

"Handloaded 'em myself. Black powder in extra-length cases." Cain raised his Glock. "*My* gun has live ammo."

Squeeze of the trigger, a loud percussive jolt, and

414

Charles stiffened, staring down at his lapel, where a dark red trickle ran like spilled grape juice.

"See the difference?" Cain asked.

Charles didn't answer, didn't move, just stood there, still holding the gun in a white-knuckled grip.

Cain pivoted toward Ally. His Glock brushed her cheek. Her eyes were round and unblinking above the gleam of the barrel.

"Your turn, freckle-face."

Barbara screamed. Cain tightened his finger on the trigger—

And the bay window blew apart in a shower of shards.

He looked up.

Glare.

Headlights like a dragon's eyes. The van bursting through the front wall.

And he knew.

Robinson.

79

Trish steered through a dazzle of flying glass, aiming the van at Cain and Charles Kent, the only standing figures in the room.

Cain leaped sideways out of her path. Barbara rolled with Ally behind the armchair. Philip pulled his wife to cover.

Only Charles remained motionless, stiff and dazed, showing no reaction even as the van bore down.

Thump of contact, and he was hurled onto the hood, head and shoulders bursting through the windshield. Trish averted her face, crumbs of safety glass dusting her hair.

Gun in his hand. She saw the twitch of a finger, was sure he was going to shoot.

Then he sagged over the dashboard, eyes glazed, face slack, and she understood why he hadn't tried to flee.

He'd been shot. He was dying . . . or already dead.

The gun dropped in her lap. A Glock. One of Cain's. She prayed it was loaded as she snatched it up and flung the van into a shrieking turn.

The prisoners were hidden behind the furniture. Cain alone was on his feet.

Leaning out the open doorway, steadying the gun against a whirl of motion, Trish squeezed off five rounds.

Cain returned fire. Bullets strafed the van. The rear windows puckered and fell away in a rain of gummed shards.

The room's only lamp disappeared under her tires, and the bulb winked out. Darkness now except for the swirl of her headlights and the dashboard's glow.

Ahead, something white and flat expanded in the windshield frame—a wall—the dining area wall—

She spun the wheel hard to the left, floored the brake pedal.

The van howled, skidding on the carpet, swinging sideways, and the wall came up fast.

Impact.

Both headlights went dark, the dashboard gauges too, darkness everywhere, and the world was up-ended, the van rolling over, a kicked can.

Trish clung to the steering wheel with one hand, clutching the gun with the other. The horn was blaring and someone was screaming, a high-pitched scream curiously like her own, and then the roof pancaked as the van landed upside-down, and there was silence.

She was caught in a cage of folded metal, the busted driver's seat pinning her to the dash.

From across the room, more gunfire, punishing the van's side panel. Cain, blasting the wreckage, trying to kill her while she was trapped inside.

She pushed free of the seat. Scrambled toward the driver's doorway. Out.

As she threw herself to the floor, Cain targeted the

front passenger window and ripped up the interior in a wild fusillade.

The van was wedged in the entrance to the side hall. She crawled to the rear, panting, dripping sweat, her heart beating so hard she could see it, actually see it, in pulsing retinal scintillations across her field of vision.

Wetness.

A pool of spreading liquid on the floor.

Gasoline from the van's ruptured fuel tank. Fumes rising, the smell acrid in her nostrils.

And Cain was still shooting, his bullets glancing off metal, hurling up sparks. *Sparks—*

She flung herself into the hall of the east wing, and with a heart-stopping *whoosh*, the envelope of fumes flashed into white heat, engulfing the van in flame.

Backward glance. Heat scorched her eyebrows. The hallway blazed, walls and ceiling veined with fire, brushstrokes of flame painting magical frescoes on the cracked plaster. Somewhere a smoke detector shrilled.

Exposed in the hall, lit by the fireglow, she was utterly vulnerable if Cain could get past the burning wreck.

And he would. She knew he would. He wouldn't stop until he was certain she was dead.

Her leg flared with new agony as she retreated farther down the hall, away from flame and smoke, in search of cover.

Ally's bedroom appeared on her left, but the doorframe had collapsed, wedging the door nearly shut, and she couldn't force it open or squeeze through the crack.

Keep going, then. Hurry.

Ahead, the master suite. Gulping breath, she stumbled across the threshold and hugged the wall.

A bar of light fanned from the bathroom directly to her right. In the dim glow, the loose handcuff swinging pendulously, she checked the Glock's magazine.

Eight rounds.

She wouldn't miss this time.

Trembling, she peered into the hall just as a silhouetted figure materialized out of the mist.

Bellow of rage: *"Robinson!"*

"You want me?" she whispered. "You *got* me."

She whipped out from behind the doorframe, and suddenly she was a cadet in the academy again, taking target practice on the range.

Aim for the kill zone.

Now.

She pumped out four shots rapid-fire.

And Cain didn't go down, *he didn't go down.*

He was shooting back, bullets blowing through the doorframe and the thin drywall, and Trish ducked into the bathroom, stunned, unable to guess how she had failed to hit him when she'd had him dead in her sights.

Footsteps pounded in the hall.

She looked around. No windows. No exits.

This was where she had to make a stand.

Quick check of the magazine again. Four rounds left, plus one in the chamber.

But . . .

The cartridge cases . . . God, the cases . . .

The crimped ends held no bullets, only cardboard wads.

Blanks.

That was why Cain hadn't been hit, why her shots had proved so maddeningly ineffective.

It was a damn prop gun, a Hollywood fake, loaded with *blanks*.

Cain's footsteps drummed closer. Nearly here.

Defenseless, she couldn't fight him. Had to hide. Hide and hope.

The door to the linen closet hung ajar. She glanced inside, discovered a gap in the wall below the bottom shelf.

No time for questions. Go.

On hands and knees she wriggled through the hole into a larger space, dark and smelling of fabric softener and shoe polish.

Closet. Big one. The walk-in kind.

Noise in the bathroom. Cain, looking for her.

She pulled herself upright, stumbled into double doors. Locked from the outside.

From next door, a shout of triumph. *"I . . . found . . . you!"*

She still held tight to the gun, the useless gun, but not useless if only she could find live ammo for it, even a single round.

Crackle of wood, clatter of falling objects. A shelf in the linen closet had been torn loose.

Didn't even need a full cartridge. A blank round had both primer and powder. All she needed . . .

The faint light from the bathroom was snuffed out. He'd wedged the shelf into the gap, sealing her in.

All she needed was a bullet.

The floorboards trembled. Cain was leaving the bathroom.

A bullet—nothing special, an inch of lead, a missile, a projectile—

Cain circled around to the locked doors.

A projectile.

She groped in her pants pocket.

"Figured it out yet, Robinson?" His footsteps stopped outside the closet. "You're shooting blanks!"

Her hand closed over the arrowhead.

"Want a live cartridge?" Rattle of a key. "I'll give you one!"

With shaking fingers she tamped the arrowhead into the barrel of the pistol.

"Hey, what the hell, Robinson!" Rasp of a chain. "We're old friends . . ."

The arrowhead slid down the barrel, lodged in place.

"I'll give you the *whole damn clip!*"

The doors burst wide, Cain stepping in.

Trish pivoted toward him.

He saw. Turned.

She ducked under his Glock.

Rammed her gun against his temple.

Pumped the trigger once.

The pistol bucked in her hand, the discharge loud and close, the powder in the blank round igniting . . .

And in a rush of expanding gas the arrowhead was propelled out the barrel and through Cain's forehead and into his brain.

His head jerked back, a cry stillborn in his throat.

Unmoving, Trish stared at him as slowly his head

lowered, his gaze fixed on her, the cold gray eyes registering shock and hatred and disbelief.

From the scorched hole in his forehead oozed a thread of blood.

He swayed. The Glock slipped out of his hand.

She looked into his eyes a moment longer, mesmerized, and then he fell slowly backward, ponderously, a toppled oak, and thudded on the floor.

Still she didn't look away. She gazed down, her hands holding fast to the empty gun, her teeth chattering, shoulders jumping.

She was certain he would rise again. He couldn't be dead, not really. He was evil, pure evil.

Nothing could kill him. Nothing could stop him. And no one could beat him, ever.

But she had.

The truth of it finally clamped down.

Over. It was over. The long night . . . over.

She stared down at the man with the scarred face and the bloody crater in his temple. The man who had taken Marta away—Marta and other girls.

Now there he was, a limp, bloodied thing supine at her feet, his gray gaze clouded, gloved hands harmless at last.

"Did it," she whispered between aching gasps. "No medals for . . . I did it . . . no medals . . . I *did* it."

Lights flickered in the lace curtains of the bedroom windows. Christmas lights, she thought vaguely— blue and red, twinkling, pretty.

Was it Christmas? Christmas in August.

She found the idea funny, but she couldn't seem to laugh.

Clinging to a bureau, she circled the body,

then lurched past the master bath into the bedroom doorway.

Heat flushed her face. Smoke clogged the far end of the hall, glittering with a dance of embers. She wondered about Ally. Had to check on Ally . . .

She took a shambling step forward, and a gruff masculine voice ordered, *"Freeze!"*

The command came out of nowhere. She blinked, uncomprehending.

"Drop your weapon, *drop your weapon*!"

Then she saw him—a uniformed figure halfway down the hall, his gun aimed at her.

A cop. And the red-and-blue lights . . . patrol cars. Of course.

She released the Glock, then just stood there, knees shaking, as the man warily advanced, his features taking form out of the gloom.

Hairless head. Steel-rimmed glasses. Sergeant Edinger.

He recognized her in the same moment. "Robinson . . . ?"

Languid ripples trembled through her. The hall rotated slowly, a world on its axis, as Edinger approached at a run.

Her eyesight was doubling. With effort she focused on his face. She had something to tell him, something important.

"They're not," she whispered. "They're not . . . "

"Take it easy, Robinson."

"They're not *all* . . . in L.A."

There. She'd said it. She hoped he understood. And remembered.

A hum filled her head, growing in volume, and with

the hum rose a sea of white spangles, brilliant and clean.

She dropped away into the hum and the white. If an arm reached out to break her fall, she didn't know it.

80

Her eyes opened, and she was on a gurney being trundled out the front door of the Kent house, into the night air.

Hoses ran from the oxygen mask on her face and the I.V. drip in her arm. "Watch it," someone said as she was carried down the flagstone steps. "Don't tangle the lines."

You're a mess, Trish, she thought blearily. First week on the job, and already you're burned out.

Lightbars pulsed around her—four patrol cars, two ambulances. Parked alongside the smashed front wall, a fire truck.

Barbara Kent, coughing weakly into a mask of her own, was lifted into the first ambulance on a stretcher. Philip and Judy Danforth, shell-shocked and sooty, were already seated on a bench in the rear.

But where was Ally? Trish craned her neck, didn't see the girl.

"Relax, Officer." One of the medics. "You'll be okay."

"Ally," she murmured through the mask, but no one heard, and perhaps she hadn't said it at all.

A stretch of blankness, a missing beat. She was

jostled alert as the medics latched the gurney into the back of the second ambulance.

Blood pressure cuff on her arm. "Start her on dopamine."

Quick hands rummaged in a cabinet near her head. Among the boxes of gear she made out a peculiar rolled-up thing like a tarp.

Body bag. That's what it was.

Cain's voice drifted back, promising to put her in a bag like that.

She shivered. One of the medics spread a blanket over her legs, leaving only the left calf uncovered. He was cutting away the bandages.

"Looks like gunshot trauma. Why aren't we rolling?"

"Got another passenger. Here she comes."

A stretcher came through the rear doorway and slid onto the bench across from Trish.

Sideways glance, and there she was—Ally, masked and I.V.'d, eyelids fluttering like moth wings as she slipped in and out of consciousness.

"Hey, partner," Trish whispered.

The girl rolled her head, brown eyes widening.

"Trish." Ally caught her breath, and for the first time Trish saw the stripes of tears glistening on her sooty face. "When the van blew up, I thought . . . I thought you were . . . "

She didn't finish, and didn't need to.

"Came close," Trish said. "By the way, thanks for the good-luck charm. It really worked."

Smile. "You can keep it."

"I—uh—sort of gave it away. To a mutual friend."

The doors banged shut, a siren cried, rattle and bump as the ambulance cut across the Kents' front lawn.

Scissors snipped through the remnants of Trish's uniform and Ally's party dress. The medics reported pulse rates and respirations and blood pressure readings, and up front a radio crackled with a dispatcher's voice, but all of that seemed far away.

"My dad was part of it," Ally whispered. "He was . . . with Cain."

Trish reached across the narrow space between them and clasped the small pale hand. "I know."

They lay quietly, holding hands. One of the medics said something about Demerol. That was a painkiller, wasn't it?

It would be good to have no pain. And a bath. Trish wondered if they would let her have a bath, even if only a sponge bath. She was so dirty, so tired, and every part of her was a separate, throbbing ache.

On the radio the driver was reporting to the hospital. "Fifteen percent dehydration . . . one gunshot trauma, one smoke inhalation . . . It's a war zone back there. She must've bandaged the wound herself, like my old corpsman in 'Nam. . . . A rookie too, can you believe that? She'll have some story to tell . . . ETA in ten minutes."

His cool monotone lulled her half asleep. Or maybe it was the Demerol they'd mentioned.

Whatever the reason, she was fading, fading, when Ally said, "Trish . . . "

She blinked alert. "Yes?"

"You won't leave me, will you? I mean, once we're out of the hospital . . . "

Trish gave her hand a gentle squeeze. "What makes you think I'd split up a winning team?"

"Well, you know, Wonder Woman usually flies solo."

"Nice try, kiddo." She shut her eyes, pain receding. "But it's not that easy to get rid of me."

From Ally, a low giggle. "Yeah. I noticed."

Trish smiled, and Ally went on laughing softly, a bright girlish sound, Marta's laughter from long ago, as the ambulance carried them away.

FEAR IS ONLY THE BEGINNING